COLOR OF DARKNESS/MALCOLM

Books by James Purdy

James Purdy

Color of
Darkness

Malcolm

Introduction by
Tony Tanner

1974
Doubleday & Company, Inc., Garden City, New York

Acknowledgment is made to New Directions Publishing Corporation
for permission to reprint COLOR OF DARKNESS
and to Farrar, Straus & Giroux, Inc.
for permission to reprint MALCOLM

ISBN: 0-385-09559-7
Library of Congress Catalog Card Number: 74–4650
Printed in the United States of America

Introduction

A man is sitting in his house with his son and his house-keeper. His wife has left him but his memory of her has faded. In fact he suddenly realizes he cannot remember the color of her eyes. This realization is followed by the more disturbing one that he cannot recall the color of the eyes of his son or indeed his housekeeper. This is all part of an accelerating emotional amnesia which he is experiencing. The eyes are pre-eminently the organ of attention and recognition, not necessarily, as Sartre would have it, turning people into objects, but, properly employed, turning what would otherwise be merely passing objects into people. The man is losing the essential human ability to recognize and attend. He is an important man and as a result is seldom at home. "You're gone all the time," his son says, and indeed even when present he is an absent father. Only his work has meaning, "but its meaning to everything else was tenuous." As a result we see a family situation which is not a family, a trinity in which all the relationships have gone wrong and nothing holds together. The real mother is long gone, and the housekeeper has become a paid surrogate; the father is a vacancy with a funny look on his face—"Like you didn't know anything," says his son; and it is the little boy who is, of course, the victim, playing with paper birds and sleeping with his toy crocodiles, temporary consolations for his un-parented condition. One night the man takes off his wedding ring as though finally realizing that what it is supposed to symbolize has so utterly drained away that it is now entirely meaningless. Next day the little boy is found chewing something which he refuses to give up until the father forces him to spit it on the floor. It is the ring. Suddenly the boy kicks the father in the groin and runs upstairs, calling down an obscene word. It is an instinctive gesture against the point of generation, a violent protest against being born but not being loved, a hopeless cry of rage and pain for the true parents he never had and for the ring which brought no new unities but only new separations. The little boy's eyes are as "blue as the sea" but in this world of fading communications and non-reciprocations too many of the eyes are really the "color of darkness" as they start to brim with nothingness. Thus in the first story in his first collection James Purdy with an originality, sureness of touch, economy, and gift for the sudden suggestive episode, which have only increased as his work has developed, defined one area of human experience which he has since gone on to explore in a variety of brilliant ways. It is strange indeed to think that Purdy has at times been regarded as a peripheral writer, dealing with the twilit margins of minority experience, when it is clear that one of his abiding concerns is nothing less than the question of what has gone wrong, in every sense, with the modern family. Given that the family is the basic unit in our society, and that society itself is a family in a wider sense, it is hard to imagine a more important or central topic. Purdy can tell us quite as much as R. D. Laing about the "politics of the family" and in addition he conveys to us what might be called the poetics of the family, terribly deranged as that poetry has often become.

Most of the stories in this first collection address themselves to some aspect or another of a family situation. Where "Color of Darkness" concentrates on the effect of the absent-present father, "Why Can't They Tell You Why?" shows us the terrifying destructive mother, a ruthless presence or force annihilating the life it brought into the world. In this story the child is mentally ill and his one comfort is a box of photographs of his father—it is all he knows of him. When his mother takes him down to the basement to force him to throw the beloved photographs into the furnace, we realize how literally infernal conditions may evolve in ordinary family life. The last picture of the child, crouched over the box of photographs, hissing at his mother like a dying animal, spewing out "the heart of his grief," is unforgettable. It is as though one was present at some ultimate nightmare of the family situation gone wrong, some secret archetypal terror nascent in the mother-son relationship. "Eventide" offers a sensitive and acute portrait of a possessive mother, whose "blind mother love" prevents her from accepting the fact that her son has left home to make a life on his own. She would have preferred to have him in his grave "perfect in death"—so terrible, and so real can mother love be. Other stories deal with marriages, bringing us back to all the strangeness and mystery of that union which we take now, perhaps, too lightly. "Don't Call Me by My Right Name" is a sympathetic account of a woman who feels she just cannot accept her married name. It is not her, and yet there is no one else for her to be. You could call the story a miniature study of an identity crisis, but to generalize is to miss its peculiar poignancy. At one point she says to her husband, "I wonder how I will get out of here, Frank." "Out of where, dear?" he asks. "Out of where I seem to have got into." It is a question in various forms asked by many of Purdy's bewildered figures, and just where we seem to have got into —all of us—is another matter his fiction explores.

"Man and Wife" focuses on one of those moments in which fissures appear in apparently ordinary situations and a frightening, almost palpable unreality starts to seep into the room just as, on other occasions, Purdy gives us the feeling of darkness pre-empting light and repossessing the house of the living dead. The husband says frankly, "I have no character, Maud," "I feel as though everything was beginning to go away from me." It is a trance-like conversation in which the pain felt and the words spoken have drifted far apart. Meanwhile the refrigerator clatters more and more loudly. It is as though utterance has passed to objects —in a world where people don't really talk, things do. The moving story "Sound of Talking" gives us an even more painful conversation between a man who is a paraplegic and his wife, who knows that both her speaking and her silence irritate him because he is in constant pain. She talks on, in a semi-automatic blur of fact and fantasy. In her trapped distractibility she indulges the idea that she would like to buy a raven, but when the husband surprisingly offers her the money to do so she suddenly realizes that she doesn't want it; in fact "she knew she wanted nothing." The experience of living on after all volition has died is one which many of Purdy's characters endure, and one of Purdy's achievements is to have given us a sort of topography of emotionlessness by which we may be helped to explore our own feeling and unfeeling selves. The husband in this story is an actual paraplegic, but many of Purdy's characters are paralyzed in some way or another, mentally, emotionally, spiritually. If we don't live in a society of people literally dead from the waist down, we can appreciate the metaphor and recognize how imperfectly most of us walk through the world. This is why, I think, Purdy shows us so many figures going through life in a state of emotional somnambulism, encountering a vacancy which, to some extent, they have secreted into the environment. To be sure, there are plenty of things in this world—such as the cosmetics, movies, and strawberry sodas which sustain the drab existence of the two ladies in "A Good Woman"—but too often they are synthetic substitutes, displacing a lost reality, replacing forgotten feelings. The emptiness spreads and spreads.

Since so many of Purdy's stories center on what we might call conversation without communication—"sound of talking" is characteristically exact—it is worth making an observation about his depiction of the relationship of his characters to language. It is immediately noticeable that many of his characters speak awkwardly, uncertainly, often in clichés, or in clusters of words which seem not to belong to them. And that is literally true. The language does not belong to them: they belong to the language. More than once a person is described as speaking "as though to get the quotation right" or "as though quoting somebody"—the comparison recurs in *Malcolm* and throughout Purdy's work. What is a quotation? It may be an enriching contact between two contexts, a way of giving added relevance to a moment by introducing into it an echo from some previous experience and thus diminishing its contingency. Or it can be an inert phrase displaced from its proper context in a lame attempt to apprehend, or bestow texture on, a present moment felt to be lacking in definition and quality. That is to say, quoting can be an attempt to "textualize" a moment by recourse to other texts. The result can be a tessellation of incongruities, not adding a sense of continuity to an occasion but bringing out the latent feeling of discontinuity (this is an effect we find in Chekhov, a relevant name in this connection as I will later suggest). Now it is obviously one thing to know what and why you are quoting—as, say, Milton with the Bible, or Joyce with practically everyone—and quite another to, as it were, automatically recycle stale linquistic fragments which seem to hover in the air you breathe. Many people effectively live their lives quoting in this way, consciously or more often unconsciously drifting through the linguistic detritus of forgotten modes and outdated discourses. In *Malcolm*, Malcolm says something and then wonders "where he had ever heard what he had just said." Of the hapless wife in "Sound of Talking" it is said that "a whole whirlwind of words waited for her." This again is very central to the world as Purdy re-creates it in his fiction. Of course it is true that man is always born into a language: the words are waiting for him, and it is possible to see man as a vehicle through which language utters itself and explores all its possibilities. But given a certain degree of consciousness man can use language; recognizing the degree to which he is its necessary servant, he can to an increasing extent master it. In Purdy's characters that consciousness is too often sadly lacking. More than that, the words that wait for them tend to be in a state of deterioration, an incoherent assortment of odds and ends. What Purdy is proposing is the radical difficulty of authentic utterance in the contemporary world. What we often have instead is an unsemantic buzz. Sound of talking.[1]

In the story "Color of Darkness" the father says to his son, "Soon you will be all grown up." The boy makes two replies. "I don't think so," and "How long does it take?" The instinctive foreboding and the unanswerable question point to Purdy's ongoing preoccupation with the whole mystery of "growing up," or to be more precise, with various ways of not growing up and the endless number of factors and forces in the world which seem to prevent the process or pervert it. When R. D. Laing started to work with the families of mentally unstable children who had been labeled schizophrenics, he realized that it was a mistake to assume that an individual had a stable basic identity within the family, and that you could isolate him or her from the context of relations in which he or she was having to "grow up" and treat the illness in separation from this context. "People have identities. But they may also change quite remarkably as they become different others-to-others. It is arbitrary to regard any one of these transformations or *alter*ations as basic, and the others as variations. Not only may the one person behave differently in his different alterations, but he may experience himself in different ways. He is liable to remember different things, express different attitudes, even quite discordant ones, imagine and fantasize in different ways." So Laing set out to try to see "what sort of world the family had fleshed out for itself, both as a whole and differentially for each of its members." At the end of the book (*Sanity,*

---

[1] A note on the so-called obscenities which people sometimes employ in Purdy's work—such as "motherfucker," "son of a bitch," "motherless bastard," and so on: it should be appreciated that since what Freud called the incomparable genius of the language has evolved and retained these phrases as dread terms of abuse, clearly they lead deep down to an awareness of the most taboo acts, particularly connected with the mother, which is still alive in us today. Purdy deploys these phrases with real care—see particularly the last words of "63 : Dream Palace"—and he does this, I believe, to make us hear again the frightening literal meaning they contain, and how intimately connected this meaning often is with something wrong in family relationships.

Madness, and the Family) he concludes by describing the
plight of a girl who cannot understand herself in relation
to herself, her family, men in general. Her apparent mental
illness was, Laing suggests, the result of a desperate attempt
to demystify a totally mystifying situation; she was "struggling to make sense of a senseless situation—senseless at any
rate from her position within it." Purdy's fiction does not
need the corroborative support of Laing's work, but it is
worth pointing out that in his own unique way Purdy has
been making comparable discoveries about the relationship of the child to the family in his explorations of the endless difficulties involved in "growing up."

Where many of his short stories show actual families in
disarray or going damagingly wrong, in his first novella and
first novel Purdy started from the point at which the youth
has lost his actual family and become both a literal and
metaphysical orphan. In this passive predicament of being
abandoned unfamilied to the world, the question for the
boy becomes what substitute "families" or nexus of relationships the world will offer him or seek to impose on him.
What happens now to the obligatory, mystifying ordeal of
growing up? Thus in "63 : Dream Palace" Fenton Riddleway
and his brother Claire have been precipitated out of their
rural West Virginia home into the generic modern city—
Chicago crossed with Dante's Inferno—after their mother
died. Fenton finds his way to the park in the middle of the
city in which men wander aimlessly all night, and his first
words are—"How do you get out?" But as the story reveals,
you can no more get out than go back. Exits are as impossible as retreats. You can only go deeper in. Or die. Fenton
and Claire are waiting in a house on "63 Street," waiting,
like many figures in modern literature, for essential aid
which will never come. Fenton's instinct tells him that it's
"a not-right-kind of place at all . . . a not-right house," and
the phrase aptly covers the world so many of Purdy's abandoned figures feel they are in.

The man who befriends him and in a sense initiates him
into the world is a failed writer, Parkhearst Cratty, and

among his first reactions to this oddly appealing youth is a sense that there is something excessive about him: "everything about him was too large for him, the speech, the terrible clothes . . . the possible gun, the outlandish accent." The relating of accent, language, clothes, and weapon is worth noting. They are all things that in different ways are "imprinted" (to use a key word from the story) on the unformed child by society; the accents, the words, the clothes, the guns are all equally waiting. It is Fenton's un-at-easeness in them—words as well as clothes—which marks him as somehow a stranger in this world, a stray spirit from another unrecoverable place. His progress through the world into which he has fallen—if progress is the right word—can be related to the different buildings he enters, starting from the rotting house on a vacant lot which is his base in the city. Although these vary from an ALL NIGHT THEATER to the mansion of the imperious mother figure, Grainger, to the apartment of a decadent actor, in a way they all seem similar to Fenton: which is right, because they are all part of the architecture of addiction, perversion, and fantasy which makes up the world he finds himself in. The modern city is indeed a Dream Palace. But what a dream! Fenton's house is on an endless street which contains an endless number of taverns so that he can drink in a different one each day. The endless variety of potations, toxic, potent, and addictive, which society pours into the young vessel can be added to the clothes it dresses him up in, the words it puts in his mouth, the rooms of experience into which it thrusts him, and, perhaps, the violence it puts into his hands, as indicating what a perverted process the whole business of growing up has become in the modern world. Claire refuses this world altogether (he wants to move on to a "real house") but Fenton is half desirous of an initiation, a new life. His recurring dream reveals the ambiguity of it all for him: in this dream "wonderful things seem like they're going to happen, getting married to a rich woman and living in a mansion and dressing up like a swell and all that, but at the same time it's all scary spooky and goddamned rot-

ten . . ." It is a moving moment when Fenton—half innocent, half murderous, loving his sick brother and hating him
for it, dallying with the corruption he despises—experiences
a nausea of the spirit and says he is sick "where your soul's
supposed to be," and adds, "If there was a God . . . none of
this would happen." The direct allusion to the supreme
absent Father is a risk, but in the context it works.

Fenton's own tormentedly ambivalent reaction to all
around him explains, I think, the particular atmosphere of
the book which Purdy has evoked. For instance, when Fenton listens to Parkhearst talking to a man he feels that "Both
of these men said things as though nothing was really important except the gestures and the words with which they
said them." It is as though, thinks Fenton, life for them is
like a too long and overacted movie. In this world substance
is ignored in favor of surface, and life itself treated as a syn-
thesized flow of images. Where is true Being in all this? How
can you grow up in a film? At another point Parkhearst looks
at Fenton and Grainger and thinks they seem "more real
and less real than anybody living he had ever known." This
suggests an extreme ontological uncertainty. It also suggests a dream, since nothing is less real and more real than
the vivid, frightening, and inexplicable figures and episodes
that beset the mind during what Baudelaire referred to as
"that sinister adventure called sleep." Fenton is struggling
through a dream. Only it happens to be the dream of life. It
is a struggle which brings him to a vacant attic, burying
the brother he loved and killed. It is worth noting that the
attic contains, besides an empty box and an old wedding
veil, four pictures—a girl in her wedding dress, a young man
in hunting costume, Christ among thieves, and a poem concerning mother love. The juxtaposition of images evoking
female sexuality, male aggression, spirituality beset by secu-
larity, and the fathomless mystery of mother love reminds
us once again that Purdy is concerned with the marriage
which goes wrong, the energy which goes astray, doomed
endeavors of the spirit, and that engendering and devouring
love which in some way must touch us all, whether by being

withheld or by being overbestowed. And the veil in the empty box is perhaps an appropriate piece of attic litter in a society which has given itself over to vestments and vacancies.

One further point should be made about the technique of this novella, for in it Purdy introduced for the first time the writer, or would-be writer, the narrator figure, thus enabling him to explore the ambiguities in the relationship of the writer to his "material" (many other writers have done this, of course, but for every writer it is a separate exploration of his own sense of the implications of the narrating activity). The novella starts with the failed writer Parkhearst talking to the greatwoman Grainger about Fenton. The phrases "real identity," "vague as a dream," "more real to you than anybody" occur almost immediately, indicating that the boy provoked central questions about identity and reality for this pair who, in different ways, both tried to possess him— she with her late husband's clothes, he with his words. The would-be appropriators are now left with their own emptiness in a darkening house and in an attempt to put something into that emptiness Parkhearst once again tries to tell the story of Fenton Riddleway. It is intimated that in the telling, Parkhearst's voice gradually seems to recede from his listener, fainting away "into indistinguishable sounds." Sounds of talking. It is as though, in trying to possess Fenton, in text or texture, they were losing him and continue to lose him, in the process losing some contact with reality or Being. As Parkhearst admits, he cannot write about Fenton "because I never found out who he was." In treating the boy as "material" (he uses the word ashamedly), the writer has lost access to his immateriality—the inner reality of the boy's being, or what Henry James called the fourth dimension without a sense of which you are only dealing with surfaces and mass. Fenton instinctively reacts against Parkhearst's subtle exploitation of him. "Are you trying to make us a show," he asks; "You're not trying to *use* us, are you?" The sad truth is that he is; as though he has lost any other way of establishing contact with people and reality. When Fenton finally kills his brother, who is "more real" to him than anything else he has found in this world, it could be an indirect indictment of a society which has, on a larger scale, murdered reality, as once MacBeth murdered sleep. It is appropriate that after the deed Fenton doesn't know whether he is now awake or has never been awake. For once a person has lost his grasp of what truly constitutes reality and authentic Being, the world does indeed become phantasmagoric and nothing is but what is not.

There is another kind of writing in the story—Fenton's note papers. When Claire asks him if Parkhearst writes for the same reason as he does, Fenton replies, "No, I only put things down there to clear up in me what we're going to do next." The distinction suggested is between a writing which exploits others and a writing which liberates the self; the difference perhaps is between trying to get hold of something through definition and trying to get rid of something through clarification. There are all kinds of narrators in Purdy's work; they may vary from the people who try to "novelize" the life of Cabot Wright (*Cabot Wright Begins*), to Jeremy desperately trying to put together a "version" of an extraordinary piece of family history (*Jeremy's Version*), to the paid "memoirist" Albert Peggs, who yearns to escape from the not-right language which is imprisoning his mind ("More than anything else . . . the money, the humiliation, the hate of this great house where I was paid memoirist, it was the language spoken which was now becoming mine that made me go out of my head"—*I Am Elijah Thrush*). The point is that through these various figures Purdy makes us aware of both the compulsions and the ambiguities inherent in the narrating process, constantly reminding us that the subject will forever elude the story. Just so the termination of the narrative about Fenton Riddleway coincides with his vanishing.

Purdy's first novel, *Malcolm*, again traces out a not growing up in a not-right world. The narrator this time is Purdy himself and the unique stylistic atmosphere of the book deliberately defies definition, partly because it is evoking a world in which stability of definitions has been lost and all differentiations are fading. There are echoes and traces of myth, fairy tale, and allegory; looked at in one light the book seems to be almost a religious-metaphysical parable, in another it offers itself as a grotesque satire, in yet another we seem to see the outlines of the familiar initiation theme but oddly refracted as if taking place in the subaqueous realms of a dream. To select one reading of the book and isolate that for concentration would be misleading, for this sense that all the genres seem to be running together—rites turning into riots, metaphysics yielding to absurdity—is part of the world of the book in which all is adrift and the center cannot hold, nor can the circumference, nor can anything in between. To be sure, there is a central theme and a firm narrative line. Malcolm is the young orphaned boy, abandoned by a father who may never have existed, who suddenly finds himself in the world, with no connections or directions. He is the beautiful blank on whom different people try to write different things, the latency who seems available for expediting everybody else's fantasies. As he moves through the world he is both wanted and rejected, taken hold of and handed on. His inheritance consists largely of a range of beautiful clothes, the significance of which in connection with the theme of establishing, or donning, a social identity is quite clear by now. Once again, Malcolm's progress takes him through a number of different buildings, though this time the progress is quite clearly a regress since the first building he visits belongs to an undertaker, while he spends his last days in the house of a nymphomaniac teen-age pop star. When he dies and is buried it is even disputed whether there was in fact a corpse, so the whole notion of initiation is weirdly reversed to give a feeling of increasing desubstantiation. This accelerating regression into non-being is paralleled by references to different drinks which are pressed on Malcolm. In his own hotel room, that antechamber in which Malcolm waits in between worlds, it is noticeable that he drinks iced water. As he moves through the different habitations of the world that colorless liquid gives way to such drinks as chocolate, wine, whiskey, and so on, just as his own pure blankness is unavoidably stained by experience. The paradox is, of course, that the more he imbibes or generally takes in from his surroundings, the less real he seems to become. In this inverted world apparent nourishment actually empties the recipient. Another of Malcolm's habits in his hotel room is important. He listens to sea shells which his father had given him. It is as though part of him is on a quest, not for destinations, but for origins, and there is a sense that way back behind his more or less mythical father Malcolm can discern his true origin in the undifferentiated oceanic flow.

From his stationary expectant position on the beach in front of the hotel, Malcolm is, as it were, propelled into the world by the astrologer Mr. Cox, who regards himself as "*the* city," even "civilization." He is the would-be director of other people's lives, the choreographer of their movements, the patterner of their relationship—though, as he discovers, events are beyond the control of his science, and though he can manipulate what he considers to be the right people into the right situations, "nothing happens." The limits on his powers of plotting and predicting are an important aspect of the world of the book in which life, people, and events no longer conform to any conceivable classification of any imaginable zodiac. There is no longer any concordance between existence and signs—in the fullest sense of that word; hence the completely illogical world which Purdy evokes. However, if there limits to Mr. Cox's powers, in his role of spirit of the city he acts as Malcolm's midwife, as it were, delivering him to materiality, ushering him into a world of "things." Perhaps the most notable aspect of this procedure, as he conducts it, is the fact that he gives Malcolm not "people" but "addresses." This of course points to the various houses Malcolm will enter, way stations of his long short life. But the word can refer to dress, and also to speeches and "bearing in conversation" (Oxford English Dictionary). The word thus nicely brings together clothes, abodes, and modes of talk, which in varying combinations do indeed make up the world to which Mr. Cox invites Malcolm to "give yourself up." As Malcolm makes his way through this world, all three aspects of "address" seem to partake of the same unreality. He finds himself in a world of shawls, veils, curtains, and screens; the changing architecture turns out to be a series of bizarrely confused articulations of emptiness; the talk—of which more later— is a mêlée of clichés. As the domineering female Madame Girard pronounces, "Texture is all . . . substance nothing." By the same token in this world addresses are everything, people nothing. While still on the bench Malcolm says to Mr. Cox, "I suppose if somebody would tell me what to do, I would do it." It is an accurate account of what awaits him, for he moves off into a world of arbitrary imperatives and supposititious realities in which he will be variously "addressed," in every sense of the word, but where he will find no authentic relationships (even though perverted surrogate forms of the father, mother, and wife temporarily present themselves) and hence, since the two are intimately connected, no authentic identity.

Instead of genuine people, relationships, communications, what do we find? Here is where Purdy achieves some of his most original effects. For if there is nothing inside people controlling expression, gesture, and speech according to genuine emotional promptings, then all these are liable to become totally arbitrary, unpredictable, and discontinuous—and this is what he shows happening. Expressions change with lightning speed for no reason whatever; intense interest can turn into utter boredom, friendliness to suspicion, enthusiasm to indifference. This complete lack of syntax in the language of the face can reach a nihilistic state. For example: "She wore a look of extreme suspicion, together with mechanical expectation and boredom." The all but impossible combination of epithets produces a self-contradictory surface which effectively cancels itself semantically. That surface is both the sentence in the book and the face in the story. When it comes to gesture and behavior, logic and motive seem to have vanished and what is left is an unsupervised pantomime of fragments of manners, so that ridiculously misplaced stylized politeness will suddenly give way to outrageous rudeness. Similarly, when it comes to talking, characters seem to have no control over the volume of their voice, more often than not liable to give speeches at people in loud voices, having lost the pitch of true intimacy. Much is shouted, but little is said. "Suddenly" is a common word—people suddenly stand up, sit down, start to speak, stop speaking, and so on. Action and speech alike are eruptive and evaporative. Where people cannot properly talk to other people, they are likely instead to order them around, for we know how power plays tend to take over in the absence of love. From his first encounter with Mr. Cox (who is said to "command people to be their worst") Malcolm is often "commanded" and continually hears commanding voices around him. It is in an appropriate pun that we learn that his funeral was a completely private affair dominated entirely by the ambiguous mother figure, Madame Girard—"and, so to speak, a command performance."

All this may be related to a heightening of what we could call the Chekhovian effect. Chekhov often shows us a group of people, lapsing from full humanity, talking but seldom listening, walking around in their own solipsistic buzz. They give the impression of not knowing what they are going to say next—discontinuity is part of their very mode of being. An example of the sort of effect I mean may be seen at the start of Act II of *The Cherry Orchard* when the governess Charlotta muses aloud about the fact that she has no proper identity, does not know who her parents were, nor how old she is. Needless to say, nobody listens. In the middle of this monologue on what may be regarded as fairly serious matters, she takes out a cucumber and begins to eat it. Similarly in *Malcolm* during what seems to be an impassioned oration on the matter of love, Madame Girard picks up a brioche, chews it, and breaks off to mention "by the way, that brioche was stale," and at the end of what is one of the most serious speeches she gives she suddenly murmurs in a low voice,

"Who has stolen my parasol?"—"like an old actress breaking off at rehearsal." There is no continuity of attention, no congruity between gesture and speech, no consonance of body and mind. Problems of identity and love are indeed matters of life and death, yet they suddenly seem to have the same importance, or unimportance, as cucumbers, brioches, and umbrellas. Needless to say, such reductive equivalencies may be at once absurd and pathetic. We get a glimpse of figures who would be more fully human if only they could remember how to be.

Malcolm's reaction to this world of random commands and empty speeches is constantly to fall asleep, as if there is nothing real to hold his attention. Once again, his uneasy relationship to the language around him is of paramount importance. We learn early on that he has "very little *command* of the language, and could seldom do more than copy down some of the things which his new friends said" (my italics). He often gropes around for a word—as to Girard Girard, "I don't know what it is, sir . . . Maybe to address you so sounds . . . *insubordinate*, I believe they say." He tries to quote and copy and adjust his speech according to the people he is with, but he always gives the impression of being astray in an alien tongue. Not surprisingly he has never read a complete book. He says, "I only know what people tell me," and he is the continual recipient, not so much of information but of "sounds of talking." Like Fenton he tries to write down some of the things that happen to him, and near the end when he is dying of "acute alcoholism and sexual hyperaesthesia" (the excessive intake of a toxic liquid and the debilitating emission of a vital one—the deadly opiates of a totally material world), he records the conversations he has had and finds it easier to write them in French! He is simply not at home in the available language any more than he is at home in the given world. Indeed in a certain way he is not at home in his body, in which he seems to exist as an expectant but bemused guest (not for nothing does the novel start in a hotel, not a home). This comes out in little things, for instance in odd noises which he makes and which seem to surprise him as much as the people he is with; at one point a violent hiccup suddenly comes from him, at another "Malcolm made a sound, which resembled a coo, and which he had never heard come from himself before, so that he sat up straight, startled." Coos, hiccups (in Fenton Riddleway's case it was farts), these, like words, are strange bodily noises, and Malcolm seems to have equally imperfect control over all of them. His relation to existence seems so tenuous that it is hardly surprising that at his funeral there should be a "ceremony," a "casket," and a "special plot" (which put together could also describe the book) but no body.

The atmosphere throughout these strange proceedings is one of decline (just as in "63 : Dream Palace" it feels "so late out everywhere"), nowhere more clearly registered than in the following beautiful paragraph: "Everywhere in the house, no matter at what hour, one felt that it was afternoon, late afternoon breaking into twilight, with a coolness, too, like perpetual autumn, an autumn that will not pass into winter owing to some damage perhaps to the machinery of the cosmos. It will go on being autumn, go on being cool, but slowly, slowly everything will begin to fall piece by piece, the walls will slip down ever so little, the strange pictures will warp, the mythological animals will move their eyes slightly for the last time as they fade into indistinction, the strings of the bass will loosen and fall, the piano keys wrinkle and disappear into the wood of the instrument, and the beautiful alto sax shrivel into foil." Purdy's vision is certainly autumnal rather than vernal, though to limit a writer of such extended and nuanced awareness to any one season would be a mistake. He is as much a poet of bewildered youth as he is an elegiast of emotionally depleted age, as aware of the problems of the state of contemporary language as he is of the sad and often ruinous dislocations in the modern family. And he takes us to a place where, at one time or another, we all have to go. In "63 : Dream Palace" at one point Parkhearst looks at Claire watching his brother and realizes that "it was plain that between him and nothing there was only Fenton." After reading Purdy's work it becomes that much more difficult to dodge or postpone that question which is crucial for all of us—what do *we* have between ourselves and nothing? A part of the answer can be—writing of the order of James Purdy's. For that we can only be grateful.

Tony Tanner

Color of Darkness

FOR

DAME EDITH SITWELL

IN

ENGLAND

AND

JULES ARVID

AND

OSBORN ANDREAS

IN

AMERICA

Contents

Sometimes he thought about his wife, but a thing had begun of late, usually after the boy went to bed, a thing which *should* have been terrifying but which was not: he could not remember now what she had looked like. The specific thing he could not remember was the color of her eyes. It was one of the most obsessive things in his thought. It was also a thing he could not quite speak of with anybody. There were people in the town who would have remembered, of course, what color her eyes were, but gradually he began to forget the general structure of her face also. All he seemed to remember was her voice, her warm hearty comforting voice.

Then there was the boy, Baxter, of course. What did he know and what did he not know. Sometimes Baxter seemed to know everything. As he hung on the edge of the chair looking at his father, examining him closely (the boy never seemed to be able to get close enough to his father), the father felt that Baxter might know everything.

"Bax," the father would say at such a moment, and stare into his own son's eyes. The son looked exactly like the father. There was no trace in the boy's face of anything of his mother.

"Soon you will be all grown up," the father said one night, without ever knowing why he had said this, saying it without his having even thought about it.

"I don't think so," the boy replied.

"Why don't you think so," the father wondered, as surprised by the boy's answer as he had been by his own question.

The boy thought over his own remark also.

"How long does it take?" the boy asked.

"Oh a long time yet," the father said.

"Will I stay with you, Daddy," the boy wondered.

The father nodded. "You can stay with me always," the father said.

The boy said *Oh* and began running around the room. He fell over one of his engines and began to cry.

Mrs. Zilke came into the room and said something comforting to the boy.

The father got up and went over to pick up the son. Then sitting down, he put the boy in his lap, and flushed from the exertion, he said to Mrs. Zilke: "You know, I am old!"

Mrs. Zilke laughed. "If you're old, I'm dead," she said. "You must keep your youth," she said almost harshly to the father, after a pause.

He looked up at her, and the boy suddenly moved in his father's arms, looking questioningly at his father. He kissed his father on his face.

"He's young yet," the boy said to Mrs. Zilke.

"Why, of course. He's a young man," she said. "They don't come no younger for fathers."

The father laughed and the boy got up to go with Mrs. Zilke to his bed.

The father thought about Mrs. Zilke's remark and he listened as he heard her reading to the boy from a story-book. He found the story she read quite dry, and he wondered if the boy found anything in it at all.

It was odd, he knew, that he could not remember the color of his wife's eyes. He knew, of course, that he must remember them, and that he was perhaps unconsciously trying to forget. Then he began to think that he could not remember the color of his son's eyes, and he had just looked at them!

"What does he know?" he said to Mrs. Zilke when she came downstairs and sat down for a moment with the newspaper. She lit a cigarette and blew out some smoke before she replied to him. By then he was looking out the window as though he had forgotten her presence and his question.

"He knows everything," Mrs. Zilke said.

The father came to himself now and looked at her gently.

"They all do now, don't they," the father said, meaning children.

"It seems so," the woman said. "Yes," she said, thinking. "They know everything."

"Everybody seems forty years old to me," the father said. "Even children maybe. Except they are complete mysteries to me. I don't know what to say to any of them. I don't know what they know, I guess."

"Oh, I understand that. I raised eight kids and I was always thinking the same thing."

"Well, that relieves me," he told Mrs. Zilke.

She smiled, but in her smile he thought he saw some thought reserved, as though she had not told everything.

"Of course we never know any other human being, do we?" he told Mrs. Zilke, hesitating as though to get the quotation right.

She nodded, enjoying her cigarette.

"Your son is lonely," she said suddenly.

The father did not look at her now.

"I mean by that," she went on, "it's too bad he's an only child."

"Doesn't he have other children over here, though. I thought—"

"Oh, it's not the same," Mrs. Zilke said. "Having in other youngsters like he does on Saturday and all. It's not enough."

"Of course I am gone a good deal."

"You're gone all the time," she said.

"That part can't be helped, of course. You see," he laughed, "I'm a success."

Mrs. Zilke did not return his laughter, he noticed, and he had noticed this before in plain strong old working women of her kind. He admired Mrs. Zilke tremendously. He was glad she had not laughed with him.

"No one should have just the one child," she told him.

"You know," he said, confidentially, "when you have just your work, as I do, people get away from you."

He looked at the bottle of brandy on the bookshelf.

"Would you have a pony of brandy with me, Mrs. Zilke."

She began to say no because she really didn't like it, but there was such a pleading look on his young face, she nodded rather regally, and he got up and poured two shots.

"Thank you for drinking with me," he said suddenly, as though to brush away something that had come between his words and his memory.

"Quite a bouquet," she said, whiffing first.

"You are really very intelligent," he told Mrs. Zilke.

"Because I know the bouquet," she said coldly.

"Oh, that and a lot of other things."

"Well, I don't know anything," Mrs. Zilke said.

"You know everything," he remarked. "All I have is my work."

"That's a lot. They need you," she said.

He sat down now, but he did not touch the brandy, and Mrs. Zilke having smelled the bouquet put her tiny glass down too.

They both sat there for a moment in silence as though they were perhaps at communion.

"I can't remember the color of my wife's eyes," he said, and he looked sick.

Mrs. Zilke sat there as though considering whether this had importance, or whether she might go on to the next topic of their talk.

"And tonight, would you believe it, I couldn't remember the color of his!"

"They're blue as the sea," Mrs. Zilke said rather gruffly, but with a kind of heavy sad tone also in her voice.

"But what does it matter about those little things," she said. "You're an important man!"

He laughed very loud at this, and Mrs. Zilke suddenly laughed too. A cord of tension had been snapped that had existed between them earlier.

The father lifted his glass and said the usual words and Mrs. Zilke took her glass with a slight bored look and sipped.

"I can taste the grapes in that all right," she said.

"Well, it's the grapes of course I buy it for," he replied in the tone of voice he might have used in a men's bar.

"You shouldn't care what color their eyes are or were," Mrs. Zilke said.

"Well, it's my memory about people," he told her. "I don't know people."

"I know you don't," she said. "But you have other things!"

"No, I don't. Not really. I could remember people if I wanted to."

"If you wanted to," Mrs. Zilke said.

"Well, why can't I remember my wife's eyes," he brought the whole thing out. "Can you remember," he wanted to know, "the color of eyes of all those in your family."

"All forty-two of them," she laughed.

"Well, your husband and your sons and daughters."

"Oh, I expect I can," she was rather evasive.

"But you do, Mrs. Zilke, you know you do!"

"All right, but I'm just a woman about the house. You're out in the world. Why should you know the color of people's eyes! Good grief, yes!"

She put her glass down, and picked up some socks she had been darning before she had put the boy to bed.

"I'm going to work while we talk," she said with a firmness that seemed to mean she would be talking less now and that she would probably not drink the brandy.

Then suddenly closing his own eyes tight he realized that he did not know the color of Mrs. Zilke's eyes. But suddenly he could not be afraid anymore. He didn't care, and he was sure that Mrs. Zilke would not care if he knew or not. She would tell him not to care. And he remembered her, which was, he was sure, more important. He remembered her kindness to him and his son, and how important they both were to him.

"How old *are* you?" Baxter asked him when he was sitting in his big chair with his drink.

"Twenty-eight, I think," the father said vaguely.

"Is that old enough to be dead?" the son wondered.

"Yes and no," the father replied.

"Am I old enough to be dead?"

"I don't think so," the father replied slowly, and his mind was on something else.

"Why aren't we all dead then?" the son said, sailing a tiny paper airplane he had made. Then he picked up a bird he had made out of brown paper and sailed this through the air. It hit a philodendron plant and stuck there in it, as though it were a conscious addition.

"You always think about something else, don't you?" the boy said, and he went up and stared at his father.

"You have blue eyes," the father said. "Blue as the sea."

The son suddenly kissed his father, and the father looked at him for a long time.

"Don't look funny like that," the boy said, embarrassed.

"Like what?" the father said, and lowered his gaze.

The son moved awkwardly, grinding his tiny shoes into the carpet.

"Like you didn't know anything," the boy said, and he ran out into the kitchen to be with Mrs. Zilke.

After Mrs. Zilke went to bed, which was nearly four hours after the boy had gone, the father was accustomed to sit on downstairs thinking about the problems in his work, but when he was at home like this he often thought about *her*, his wife of long ago. She had run off (this was almost the only term he used for her departure) so long ago and his marriage to her had been so brief that it was almost as though Baxter were a gift somebody had awarded him, and that as the gift increased in value and liability, his own relation to it was more and more ambiguous and obscure. Somehow Mrs. Zilke seemed more real to him than almost anybody else. He could not remember the color of her eyes either, of course, but she was quite real. She was his "mother," he supposed. And the boy was an infant "brother" he did not know too well, and who asked hard questions, and his "wife," who had run off, was just any girl he had gone out with. He could not remember her now at all.

He envied in a way Mrs. Zilke's command over everything. She understood, it seemed, everything she dealt with, and she remembered and could identify all the things which came into her view and under her jurisdiction. The world for her, he was sure, was round, firm, and perfectly illuminated.

For him only his work (and he remembered she had called him a man of importance) had any real meaning, but its meaning to everything else was tenuous.

As he went upstairs that night he looked into his son's room. He was surprised to see that the boy was sleeping with an enormous toy crocodile. The sight of the toy rather shocked him. For a moment he hesitated whether or not to remove the toy and then deciding not to disturb him, he went to his room, took off all his clothes, and stood naked, breathing in front of the opened window. Then he went quickly to bed.

"It's his favorite doll," Mrs. Zilke said at breakfast. "He wouldn't part with it for the world." She referred to the toy crocodile.

"I would think it would give him nightmares," the father said.

"He don't have nightmares," Mrs. Zilke said, buttering the toast. "There you are, sir!" and she brought him his breakfast.

The father ate silently for a while.

"I was shocked to see that crocodile in his bed," he told Mrs. Zilke again.

"Well, that's something in you, is all," she said.

"I expect. But why couldn't it have been a teddy bear or a girl doll."

"He has those too. It just happened to be crocodile night last night," Mrs. Zilke said, restless now in the kitchen.

"All right," the father said, and he opened the newspaper and began to read about Egypt.

"Your boy needs a dog," Mrs. Zilke said without warning, coming in and sitting down at the table with him. Her hands still showed the traces of soap suds.

"What kind?" the father said.

"You're not opposed to it, then?" Mrs. Zilke replied.

"Why would I oppose a dog." He continued to look at the newspaper.

"He's got to have something," Mrs. Zilke told him.

"Of course," the father said, swallowing some coffee. Then, having swallowed, he stared at her.

"You mean he doesn't have anything?"

"As long as a parent is living, any parent, a child has something. No, I didn't mean *that*," she said without any real apology, and he expected, of course, none.

"I'd rather have him sleeping with a dog now than that crocodile."

"Oh, that," Mrs. Zilke said, impatient.

Then: "All right, then," he said.

He kept nodding after she had gone out of the room. He sat there looking at his old wedding ring which he still wore. Suddenly he took the ring off his finger for the first time since he had had it put on there by the priest. He had left it on all these years simply because, well, he wanted men to think he was married, he supposed. Everybody was married, and he had to be married somehow, anyhow, he knew.

But he left the wedding ring lying on the table, and he went into the front room.

"Sir," Mrs. Zilke called after him.

"Just leave the ring there," he said, thinking she had found it.

But on her face he saw something else. "You'll have to take the boy to buy the dog, you know. I can't walk on hard pavements any more, remember."

"That will be fine, Mrs. Zilke," he said, somehow relieved at what she said.

The dog they bought at the shop was a small mongrel with a pitifully long tail, and—the father looked very close:

brown eyes. Almost the first thing he did was to make a puddle near the father's desk. The father insisted on cleaning it up, and Baxter watched, while Mrs. Zilke muttered to herself in the kitchen. She came in finally and poured something white on the spot.

The dog watched them too from its corner, but it did not seem to want to come out to them.

"You must make up to your new little friend," the father said.

Baxter stared but did not do anything.

"Go to him," the father said, and the son went over into the corner and looked at the pup.

The father sat down at his desk and began to go through his papers.

"Did you have a dog?" Baxter asked his father.

The father thought there at the desk. He did not answer for a long time.

"Yes," the father finally said.

"What color was it," the son asked, and the father stirred in his chair.

"That was so long ago," he said almost as though quoting himself.

"Was it gray then?" the boy wanted to know.

The father nodded.

"A gray dog," the son said, and he began to play with his new pet. The dog lifted its wet paw and bit the boy mildly, and the boy cried a little.

"That's just in fun," the father said absentmindedly.

Baxter ran out into the kitchen, crying a little, and the small dog sat in the corner.

"Don't be afraid of the little fellow now," Mrs. Zilke said. "Go right back and make up to him again."

Baxter and Mrs. Zilke came out of the kitchen and went up to the dog.

"You'll have to name him too," Mrs. Zilke said.

"Will I have to name him, Daddy?" the boy said.

The father nodded.

After supper all three sat in the front room. Baxter nodded a little. The father sat in the easy chair smoking his pipe, the pony of brandy near him. They had gathered here to decide what name to choose for the dog, but nobody had any ideas, it seemed, and the father, hidden from them in a halo of expensive pipe smoke, seemed as far away as if he had gone to the capital again.

Baxter nodded some more and Mrs. Zilke said, "Why, it still isn't bedtime and the little man is asleep!"

From below in the basement where they had put the pup they could all hear the animal's crying, but they pretended not to notice.

Finally, Mrs. Zilke said, "When he is housebroken you can sleep with him, Baxter."

Baxter opened his eyes and looked at her. "What is that?" he said.

"When he learns to take care of himself, not make puddles, you can have him in bed with you."

"I don't want to," the boy said.

Mrs. Zilke looked stoically at the father.

"Why don't you want to, sweetheart," she said, but her words showed no emotion.

"I don't want anything," the boy said.

Mrs. Zilke looked at the father again, but he was even more lost to them.

"What's that hanging loose in your mouth." Mrs. Zilke suddenly sprang to attention, adjusting her spectacles, and looking at the boy's mouth.

"This." The boy pointed to his lips, and blushed slightly. "Gum," he said.

"Oh," Mrs. Zilke said.

The clock struck eight.

"I guess it *is* your bedtime," Mrs. Zilke said.

She watched the boy.

"Do you want to go to bed, Baxter," she said, abstractedly.

The boy nodded.

"Say goodnight to daddy and kiss him," she told him perfunctorily.

The boy got up and went over to his father, but stopped in front of the rings of smoke.

"Goodnight," the boy lisped.

"What's that in his mouth," the father addressed his remark to Mrs. Zilke and his head came out of the clouds of smoke.

Mrs. Zilke got up painfully now and putting on her other glasses looked at the boy.

"What are you sucking?" Mrs. Zilke said, and both of them now stared at him.

Baxter looked at them as though they had put net about him. From his long indifference to these two people a sudden new feeling came slowly into his dazed, slowly moving mind. He moved back a step, as though he wanted to incite them.

"Baxter, sweetheart," the old woman said, and both she and the father stared at him as though they had found out perhaps who he was.

"What do you have in your mouth, son," the father said, and the word *son* sounded queer in the air, moving toward the boy with the heaviness and suggestion of nausea that the dog puddle had given him earlier in the afternoon.

"What is it, son," the father said, and Mrs. Zilke watched him, her new understanding of the boy written on her old red face.

"I'm chewing gum," the boy told them.

"No, you're not now, Baxter. Why don't you tell us," Mrs. Zilke whined.

Baxter went over into the corner where the dog had been.

"That dog is bad, isn't he," Baxter giggled, and then he suddenly laughed loudly when he thought what the dog had done.

Meanwhile Mrs. Zilke and the father were whispering in the cloud of tobacco smoke.

Baxter sat down on the floor talking to himself, and playing with a broken piece of Tinker Toy. From his mouth still came sounds of something vaguely metallic.

Then Mrs. Zilke came up stealthily, a kind of sadness and kindness both in her face, like that of a trained nurse.

"You can't go to sleep with that in your mouth, sweetheart."

"It's gum," the boy said.

Mrs. Zilke's bad legs would not let her kneel down beside the boy on the floor as she wished to do. She wanted to have a close talk with him, as she did sitting by his bed in the nursery, but instead now, standing over him, so far away, her short heavy breathing sounding obnoxiously in the room, she said only, "You've never lied to me before, Baxter."

"Oh yes I have," Baxter said. "Anyhow this is gum," and he made the sounds again in his mouth.

"I'll have to tell your father," she said, as though *he* were already away in Washington.

"It's gum," the boy said in a bored voice.

"It's metal, I think," she said looking worriedly at the boy.

"It's just gum." The boy hummed now and played with the Tinker Toy.

"You'll have to speak to him," Mrs. Zilke said.

The father squatted down with the son, and the boy vaguely realized this was the first time the father had ever made the motion of playing with him. He stared at his father, but did not listen to what he was talking about.

"If I put my finger in your mouth will you give it to me?" the father said.

"No," the boy replied.

"You wouldn't want to swallow the thing in your mouth," the father said.

"Why not," the boy wondered.

"It would hurt you," the father told him.

"You would have to go to the hospital," Mrs. Zilke said.

"I don't care where I go," the boy said. "It's a toy I have in my mouth."

"What sort of toy," the father wondered, and he and Mrs.

Zilke suddenly became absorbed in the curiosity of what Baxter had there.

"A golden toy," the boy laughed, but his eyes looked glassy and strange.

"Please," the father said, and he put his finger gently on the boy's lips.

"Don't touch me!" the son called out suddenly. "I hate you!"

The father drew back softly as though now he would return to his work and his papers, and it was Mrs. Zilke who cried out instead: "Shame!"

"I do hate him," the boy said. "He's never here anyhow."

"Baxter," the father said.

"Give your father what's in your mouth or you will swallow it and something terrible will happen to you."

"I want it right where it is," the boy said, and he threw the Tinker Toy at Mrs. Zilke.

"Look here now, Baxter," the father said, but still sleepily and with no expression.

"Shut your goddamn face," the boy spat out at his father.

The father suddenly seized the boy's chin and jaw and forced him to spit out what he had.

His wedding ring fell on the carpet there, and they all stared at it a second.

Without warning the son kicked the father vigorously in the groin and escaped, running up the stairs.

Baxter stopped deliberately from the safety of the upper staircase and pronounced the obscene word for his father as though this was what he had been keeping for him for a long time.

Mrs. Zilke let out a low cry.

The father writhing in pain from the place where the boy had kicked him, managed to say with great effort: "Tell me where he learned a word like that."

Mrs. Zilke went over to where the ring lay now near the Tinker Toy.

"I don't know what's happening to people," she said, putting the ring on the table.

Then, a weary concern in her voice, she said, "Sir, are you hurt?"

The tears fell from the father's eyes for having been hit in such a delicate place, and he could not say anything more for a moment.

"Can I do anything for you, sir?" Mrs. Zilke said.

"I don't think right now, thank you," he said. "Thank you." He grunted with the exquisite pain.

"I've put your ring up here for safekeeping," she informed him.

The father nodded from the floor where he twisted in his pain.

You May Safely Gaze

"Do we always have to begin on Milo at these Wednesday lunches," Philip said to Guy. Carrying their trays, they had already picked out their table in the cafeteria, and Philip, at least, was about to sit down.

"Do I *always* begin on Milo?" Guy wondered, surprised.

"You're the one who knows him, remember," Philip said.

"Of course, Milo is one of the serious problems in our office, and it's only a little natural, I suppose, to mention problems even at one of our Wednesday lunches."

"Oh, forget it," Philip said. Seated, he watched half-amused as Guy still stood over the table with his tray raised like a busboy who will soon now move away with it to the back room.

"I don't dislike Milo," Guy began. "It's not that at all."

Philip began to say something but then hesitated, and looked up at the cafeteria clock that showed ten minutes past twelve. He knew, somehow, that it was going to be Milo all over again for lunch.

"It's his attitude not just toward his work, but life," Guy said, and this time he sat down.

"His life," Philip said, taking swift bites of his chicken à la king.

Guy nodded. "You see now he spares himself the real work in the office due to this physical culture philosophy. He won't even let himself get mad anymore or argue with me because that interferes with the development of his muscles and his mental tranquillity, which is so important for muscular development. His whole life now he says is to be strong and calm."

"A muscle ascetic," Philip laughed without amusement.

"But working with him is not so funny," Guy said, and Philip was taken aback to see his friend go suddenly very pale. Guy had not even bothered to take his dishes off his tray but allowed everything to sit there in front of him as though the lunch were an offering he had no intention of tasting.

"Milo hardly seems anybody you and I could know, if you ask me," Guy pronounced, as though the final decision had at last been made.

"You forget one of us *doesn't*," Philip emphasized again, and he waved his fork as though they had finally finished now with Milo, and could go on to the real Wednesday lunch.

But Guy began again, as though the talk for the lunch had been arranged after all, despite Philip's forgetfulness, around Milo.

"I don't think he is even studying law anymore at night, as he was supposed to do."

"Don't tell me that," Philip said, involuntarily affecting concern and half-resigning himself now to the possibility of a completely wasted hour.

"Oh, of course," Guy softened his statement, "I guess he goes to the law library every night and reads a little. Every waking hour is, after all, not for his muscles, but every real thought, you can bet your bottom dollar, *is*."

"I see," Philip said, beginning on his pineapple snow.

"It's the only thing on his mind, I tell you," Guy began again.

"It's interesting if that's the only thing on his mind, then," Philip replied. "I mean," he continued, when he saw the black look he got from Guy, "—to know somebody who is obsessed . . ."

"What do you mean by that?" Guy wondered critically, as though only he could tell what it was that Milo might be.

"You said he wanted to devote himself to just this one thing." Philip wearily tried to define what he had meant.

"I tried to talk to Milo once about it," Guy said, now deadly serious, and as though, with all preliminaries past, the real part of his speech had begun. Philip noticed that his friend had still not even picked up his knife or fork, and his food must be getting stone cold by now. "'Why do you want to look any stronger,' I said to Milo. He just stared at me, and I said, 'Have you ever taken a good look in the mirror the way you are now,' and he just smiled his sour smile again at me. 'Have you ever looked, Milo?' I said, and even I had to laugh when I repeated my own question, and he kind of laughed then too . . . Well, for God's sake, he knows after all that nobody but a few freaks are going to look like he looks, or will look, if he keeps this up. You see he works on a new part of his body every month. One month he will be working on his pectorals, the next his calf muscles, then he will go in for a period on his latissimus dorsi."

Philip stopped chewing a moment as though seeing these different muscle groups slowly developing there before him. Finally, he managed to say, "Well at least he's interested in something, which is more than . . ."

"Yes, he's interested in *it*, of course," Guy interrupted, "—what he calls being the sculptor of his own body, and you can find him almost any noon in the gym straining away while the other men in our office do as they please with their lunch hour."

"You mean they eat their lunch then." Philip tried humor.

"That's right," Guy hurried on. "But he and this Austrian friend of his who also works in my office, they go over to this gym run by a cripple named Vic somebody, and strain their guts out, lifting barbells and throwing their arms up and around on benches with dumbbells in their fists, and come back an hour later to their work looking as though they had been in a rock mixer. They actually stink of gym, and several of the stenographers have complained saying they always know when it's exercise day all right. But nothing stops those boys, and they just take all the gaff with as much good humor as two such egomaniacs can have."

"Why egomaniacs, for God's sake," Philip wondered, putting his fork down with a bang.

"Well, Philip," Guy pleaded now. "To think of their own bodies like that. These are not young boys, you know. They must be twenty-five or so, along in there, and you would think they would begin to think of other people, other people's bodies, at least." Guy laughed as though to correct his own severity before Philip. "But no," he went on. "They have to be Adonises."

"And their work suffers?" Philip wondered vaguely, as though, if the topic had to be continued, they might now examine it from this aspect.

"The kind of work young men like them do—it don't matter, you know, if you're good or not, nobody knows if you're really good. They do their work and get it out on time, and you know their big boss is still that old gal of seventy who is partial to young men. She sometimes goes right up to Milo, who will be sitting at his desk relaxed as a jellyfish, doing nothing, and she says, 'Roll up your sleeves, why don't you, and take off your necktie on a warm day like this,' and it will be thirty degrees outside and cool even in the office. And Milo will smile like a four-year-old at her because he loves admiration more than anything in the world, and he rolls up his sleeves and then all this bulge of muscle comes out, and the old girl looks like she'd seen glory, she's that gone on having a thug like that around."

"But you sound positively bilious over it," Philip laughed.

"Philip, look," Guy said with his heavy masculine patience, "doesn't it sound wrong to you, now seriously?"

"What in hell do you mean by wrong, though?"

"Don't be that way. You know goddamn well what I mean."

"Well, then, no, I can't say it is. Milo or whatever his name."

"You know it's Milo," Guy said positively disgusted.

"Well, he is, I suppose, more typical than you might think from the time, say, when you were young. Maybe there weren't such fellows around then."

"Oh there were, of course."

"Well, now there are more, and Milo is no exception."

"But he looks at himself all the time, and he has got himself tattooed recently and there in front of the one mirror in the office, it's not the girls who stand there, no, it's Milo and this Austrian boy. They're always washing their hands or combing their hair, or just looking at themselves right out, not sneaky-like the way most men do, but like some goddamn chorus girls. And oh, I forgot, this Austrian fellow got tattooed too because Milo kept after him, and then he was sorry. It seems the Austrian's physical culture instructor gave him hell and said he had spoiled the appearance of his deltoids by having the tattoo work done."

"Don't tell me," Philip said.

Guy stared as he heard Philip's laugh, but then continued: "They talked about the tattoo all morning, in front of all the stenogs, and whether this Austrian had spoiled the appearance of his deltoid muscles or not."

"Well, it *is* funny, of course, but I couldn't get worked up about it the way you are."

"They're a symbol of the new America and I don't like it."

"You're terribly worked up."

"Men on their way to being thirty, what used to be considered middle age, developing their bodies and special muscles and talking about their parts in front of women."

"But they're married men, aren't they?"

"Oh sure," Guy dismissed this. "Married and with kids."

"What more do you want then. Some men are nuts about their bowling scores and talk about that all the time in front of everybody."

"I see you approve of them."

"I didn't say that. But I think you're overreacting, to use the phrase . . ."

"You don't have to work with them," Guy went on. "You don't have to watch them in front of the one and only office mirror."

"Look, I've known a lot of women who griped me because they were always preening themselves, goddamn narcissists too. I don't care for narcissists of either sex."

"Talk about Narciss-uses," said Guy. "The worst was last summer when I went with Mae to the beach, and there *they* were, both of them, right in front of us on the sand."

Philip stiffened slightly at the prospect of more.

"Milo and the Austrian," Guy shook his head. "And as it was Saturday afternoon there didn't seem to be a damn place free on the beach and Mae wanted to be right up where these Adonises or Narciss-uses, or whatever you call them, were. I said, 'We don't want to camp here, Mae,' and she got suddenly furious. I couldn't tell her how those birds affected me, and they hardly even spoke to me either, come to think about it. Milo spit something out the side of his mouth when he saw me, as though to say *that for you.*"

"That was goddamn awful for you," Philip nodded.

"Wait till you hear what happened, for crying out loud. I shouldn't tell this during my lunch hour because it still riles me."

"Don't get riled then. Forget them."

"I have to tell you," Guy said. "I've never told anybody before, and you're the only man I know will listen to a thing like this. . . . You know," he went on then, as though this point were now understood at last between them, "Mae started staring at them right away. 'Who on earth are they?' she said, and I couldn't tell whether she was outraged or pleased, maybe she was a bit of both because she just fixed her gaze on them like paralyzed. 'Aren't you going to put on your sun tan lotion and your glasses?' I said to her, and she turned on me as though I had hit her. 'Why don't you let a woman relax when I never get out of the house but twice in one year,' she told me. I just lay back then on the sand and tried to forget they were there and that she was there and that even I was there."

Philip began to light up his cigarette, and Guy said, "Are you all done eating already?" and he looked at his own plate of veal cutlet and peas which was nearly untouched. "My God, you are a fast eater. Why, do you realize how fast you

eat," he told Philip, and Philip said he guessed he half-
realized it. He said at night he ate slower.

"In the bosom of your family," Guy laughed.

Philip looked at the cafeteria clock and stirred unceremoniously.

"But I wanted to finish telling you about these boys."

"Is there *more?*" Philip pretended surprise.

"Couldn't you tell the way I told it there was," Guy said,
an indeterminate emotion in his voice.

"I hope nothing happened to Mae," Philip offered weakly.

"Nothing ever happens to Mae," Guy dismissed this impatiently. "No, it was them, of course. Milo and the Austrian
began putting on a real show, you know, for everybody, and
as it was Saturday afternoon, as I said, nearly everybody
from every office in the world was there, and they were all
watching Milo and the Austrian. So, first they just did the
standard routine, warm-ups, you know, etc., but from the
first every eye on the beach was on them, they seemed to
have the old presence, even the life guards were staring at
them as though nobody would ever dare drown while they
were carrying on, so first of all then they did handstands
and though they did them good, not good enough for that
many people to be watching. After all somebody is always
doing handstands on the beach, you know. I think it was
their hair attracted people, they have very odd hair, they
look like brothers that way. Their hair is way too thick, and
of course too long for men of our generation. . . ."

"Well, how old do you think I am?" Philip laughed.

"All right, of *my* generation, then," Guy corrected with
surliness. He went on, however, immediately: "I think the
reason everybody watched was their hair, which is a peculiar
kind of chestnut color, natural and all that, but maybe due
to the sun and all their exercising had taken on a funny
shade, and then their muscles were so enormous in that
light, bulging and shining with oil and matching somehow
their hair that I think that was really what kept people
looking and not what they did. They didn't look quite real,
even though in a way they are the style.

"I kept staring, and Mae said, 'I thought you wasn't going to watch,' and I could see she was completely held captive by their performance as was, I guess, everybody by then on the goddamn beach.

"'I can't help looking at freaks,' I told Mae, and she gave me one of her snorts and just kept looking kind of bitter and satisfied at seeing something like that. She's a great woman for sights like that, she goes to all the stock shows, and almost every nice Sunday she takes the kids to the zoo. . . ."

"Well, what finally did come off?" Philip said, pushing back his chair.

"The thing that happened, nobody in his right mind would ever believe, and probably lots of men and boys who saw it happen never went home and told their families."

"It should have been carried in the papers then," Philip said coolly and he drank all of his as yet untouched glass of water.

"I don't know what word I would use to describe it," Guy said. "Mae has never mentioned it to this day, though she said a little about it on the streetcar on the way home that afternoon, but just a little, like she would have referred to a woman having fainted and been rushed to the hospital, something on that order."

"Well, for Pete's sake now, what did happen?" Philip's ill humor broke forth for a moment, and he bent his head away from Guy's look.

"As I said," Guy continued quietly, "they did all those more fancy exercises then after their warm ups, like leaping on one another's necks, jumping hard on each other's abdomens to show what iron men they were, and some rough stuff but which they made look fancy, like they threw one another to the sand as though it was a cross between a wrestling match and an apache dance, and then they began to do some things looked like they were out of the ballet, with lots of things like jumping in air and splits, you know. You know what kind of trunks that kind of Narciss-uses wear, well these were tighter than usual, the kind to make a bullfighter's pants look baggy and oversize, and as though they had planned it, while doing one of their big movements, their trunks both split clear in two, at the same time, with a sound, I swear, you could have heard all over that beach.

"Instead of feeling at least some kind of self-consciousness, if not shame, they both busted out laughing and hugged one another as though they'd made a touchdown, and they might as well both been naked by now, they just stood there and looked down at themselves from time to time like they were alone in the shower, and laughed and laughed, and an old woman next to them just laughed and laughed too, and all Mae did was look once and then away with a funny half-smile on her mouth, she didn't show any more concern over it than the next one. Here was a whole beach of mostly women, just laughing their heads off because two men no longer young, were, well, exposing themselves in front of everybody, for that's all it was."

Philip stared at his empty water glass.

"I started to say something to Mae, and she nearly cut my head off, saying something like *why don't you mind your own goddamn business* in a tone unusually mean even for her. *Don't look damn you if you don't like it* was what my own wife said to me.

Suddenly Philip had relaxed in his chair as though the water he had drunk had contained a narcotic. He made no effort now to show his eagerness to leave, to hurry, or to comment on what was being said, and he sat there staring in the direction of, but not at, Guy.

"But the worst part came then," Guy said, and then looking critically and uneasily at Philip, he turned round to look at the cafeteria clock, but it showed only five minutes to one, and their lunch hour was not precisely over.

"This old woman," he continued, swallowing hard, "who had been sitting there next to them got out a sewing kit she had, and do you know what?"

"I suppose she sewed them shut," Philip said sleepily and still staring at nothing.

"That's exactly correct," Guy said, a kind of irritated disappointment in his voice. "This old woman who looked at least eighty went right up to them the way they were and she must have been a real seamstress, and before the whole crowd with them two grown men laughing their heads off she sewed up their tights like some old witch in a story, and Mae sat there as cool as if we was playing bridge in the church basement, and never said boo, and when I began to really let off steam, she said *Will you keep your big old ugly mouth shut or am I going to have to hit you over the mouth with my beach clogs.* That's how they had affected my own wife."

"So," Guy said, after a pause in which Philip contributed nothing, "this country has certainly changed since I grew up in it. I said that to Mae and that was the final thing I had to say on the subject, and those two grown men went right on lying there on the sand, every so often slapping one another on their muscles, and combing their hair with oil, and laughing all the time, though I think even they did have sense enough not to get up and split their trunks again or even they must have known they would have been arrested by the beach patrol."

"Sure," Philip said vacantly.

"So that's the story of Milo and the Austrian," Guy said.

"It's typical," Philip said, like a somnambulist.

"Are you sore at me or something," Guy said, picking up his and Philip's checks.

"Let me pay my own, for Christ's sake," Philip said.

"Listen, you *are* sore at me, I believe," Guy said.

"I have a rotten headache is all," Philip replied, and he picked up his own check.

"I hope I didn't bring it on by talking my head off."

"No," Philip replied. "I had it since morning."

Don't Call Me by My Right Name

Her new name was Mrs. Klein. There was something in the meaning that irritated her. She liked everything about her husband except his name and that had never pleased her. She had fallen in love with him before she found out what his name was. Once she knew he was Klein, her disappointment had been strong. Names do make a great difference, and after six months of marriage she found herself still not liking her name. She began using more and more her maiden name. Then she always called herself on her letters Lois McBane. Her husband seldom saw the mail arrive so perhaps he did not know, and had he known she went by her old name he might not have cared enough to feel any particular hurt.

Lois Klein, she often thought as she lay next to her husband in bed. It is not the name of a woman like myself. It does not reflect my character.

One evening at a party when there had been more drinking for her than usual, she said offhand to him in the midst of some revelry: "I would like you to change your name."

He did not understand. He thought that it was a remark she was making in drink which did not refer to anything concrete, just as once she had said to him, "I want you to begin by taking your head off regularly." The remark had meant nothing, and he let it pass.

"Frank," she said, "you must change your name, do you hear? I cannot go on being Mrs. Klein."

Several people heard what it was she said, and they laughed loudly so that Lois and Frank would hear them appreciating the remark.

"If you were all called Mrs. Klein," she said turning to the men who were laughing, "you would not like to be Mrs. Klein either."

Being all men, they laughed harder.

"Well, you married him, didn't you," a man said, "and we guess you will have to keep his name."

"If he changed his name," another of the men said, "what name would you have him change it to?"

Frank put his hand on her glass, as though to tell her they must go home, but she seized the glass with his hand on it and drank quickly out of it.

"I hadn't thought what name I did want," she said, puzzled.

"Well, you aren't going to change your name," Frank said. "The gentlemen know that."

"The gentlemen do?" she asked him. "Well, I don't know what name I would like it changed to," she admitted to the men.

"You don't look much like Mrs. Klein," one of the men said and began to laugh again.

"You're not friends!" she called back at them.

"What are we, then?" they asked.

"Why don't I look like Mrs. Klein?" she wanted to know.

"Don't you ever look in the mirror?" one of the men replied.

"We ought to go, Lois," her husband said.

She sat there as though she had heard the last of the many possible truths she could hear about herself.

"I wonder how I will get out of here, Frank," she said.

"Out of where, dear?" he wondered. He was suddenly sad enough himself to be dead, but he managed to say something to her at this point.

"Out of where I seem to have got into," she told him.

The men had moved off now and were laughing among themselves. Frank and Lois did not notice this laughter.

"I'm not going to change my name," he said, as though to himself. Then turning to her: "I know it's supposed to be wrong to tell people when they're drunk the insane whim they're having is insane, but I am telling you now and I may tell the whole room of men."

"I have to have my name changed, Frank," she said. "You know I can't stand to be tortured. It is too painful and I am not young anymore. I am getting old and fat."

"No wife of mine would ever be old or fat," he said.

"I just cannot be Mrs. Klein and face the world."

"Anytime you want me to pull out is all right," he said. "Do you want me to pull out?"

"What are you saying?" she wanted to know. "What did you say about pulling out?"

"I don't want any more talk about your changing your name or I intend to pull up stakes."

"I don't know what you're talking about. You know you can't leave me. What would I do, Frank, at my age?"

"I told you no wife of mine is old."

"I couldn't find anybody now, Frank, if you went."

"Then quit talking about changing our name."

"*Our* name? I don't know what you mean by *our* name."

He took her drink out of her hand and when she coaxed and whined he struck her not too gently over the mouth.

"What was the meaning of that?" she wanted to know.

"Are you coming home, Mrs. Klein?" he said, and he hit her again. Her lip was cut against her teeth so that you could see it beginning to bleed.

"Frank, you're abusing me," she said, white and wide-eyed now, and as though tasting the blood slightly with the gin and soda mix.

"Mrs. Klein," he said idiotically.

It was one of those fake dead long parties where nobody actually knows anybody and where people could be pushed out of windows without anybody's being sure until the morrow.

"I'm not going home as Mrs. Klein," she said.

He hit her again.

"Frank, you have no right to hit me just because I hate your name."

"If you hate my name what do you feel then for me? Are you going to act like my wife or not."

"I don't want to have babies, Frank. I will not go through that at my age. Categorically not."

He hit her again so that she fell on the floor, but this did not seem to surprise either her or him because they both continued the conversation.

"I can't make up my mind what to do," she said, weeping a little. "I know of course what the safe thing is to do."

"Either you come out of here with me as Mrs. Klein, or I go to a hotel room alone. Here's the key to the house," he said, and he threw it on the floor at her.

Several of the men at the party had begun to notice what was really going on now. They thought that it was married clowning at first and they began to gather around in a circle, but what they saw had something empty and stiff about it that did not interest and yet kept one somehow watching. For one thing, Mrs. Klein's dress had come up and exposed her legs, which were not beautiful.

"I can't decide if I can go on with his name," she explained from the floor position to the men.

"Well, it's a little late, isn't it, Mrs. Klein," one of the men said in a sleepy voice.

"It's never too late, I don't suppose, is it?" she inquired. "Oh, I can't believe it is even though I feel old."

"Well, you're not young," the same man ventured. "You're too old to be lying there."

"My husband can't see my point of view," she explained. "And that is why he can't understand why his name doesn't fit me. I was unmarried too long, I suppose, to suddenly surrender my own name. I have always been known professionally and socially under my own name and it is hard to change now, I can tell you. I don't think I can go home with him unless he lets me change my name."

"I will give you just two minutes," Mr. Klein said.

"For what? Only two minutes for what?" she cried.

"To make up your mind what name you are going out of here with."

"I know, men," she said, "what the sensible decision is, and tomorrow, of course, when I'm sober I will wish I had taken it."

Turning to Frank Klein, she said simply, "You will have to go your way without me."

He looked hurriedly around as though looking for an exit to leave by, and then he looked back to her on the floor as though he could not come to a decision.

"Come to your senses," Frank Klein said unemphatically.

"There were hundreds of Kleins in the telephone directory," she went on, "but when people used to come to my name they recognized at once that I was the only woman going under my own special name."

"For Jesus Christ's sake, Lois," he said, turning a peculiar green color.

"I can't go with you as Mrs. Klein," she said.

"Well, let me help you up," he said.

She managed to let him help her up.

"I'm not going home with you, but I will send you in a cab," he informed her.

"Are you leaving me?" she wanted to know.

He did not know what to say. He felt anything he said might destroy his mind. He stood there with an insane emptiness on his eyes and lips.

Everyone had moved off from them. There was a silence from the photograph and from the TV set which had both been going at the same time. The party was over and people were calling down to cabs from all the windows.

"Why won't you come home with me?" she said in a whisper.

Suddenly he hurried out the door without waiting for her.

"Frank!" she called after him, and a few of the men from the earlier group came over and joked with her.

"He went out just like a boy, without any sense of responsibility," she said to them without any expression in her voice.

She hurried on out too, not waiting to put her coat on straight.

She stood outside in the fall cold and shivered. Some children went by dressed in Hallowe'en costumes.

"Is she dressed as anybody?" one of the children said pointlessly.

"Frank!" she began calling. "I don't know what is happening really," she said to herself.

Suddenly he came up to her from behind a hedge next to where she was standing.

"I couldn't quite bring myself to go off," he said.

She thought for a minute of hitting him with her purse which she had remembered to bring, but she did nothing now but watch him.

"Will you change your name?" she said.

"We will live together the way we have been," he said not looking at her.

"We can't be married, Frank, with that name between us."

Suddenly he hit her and knocked her down to the pavement.

She lay there for a minute before anything was said.

"Are you conscious?" he said crouching down beside her. "Tell me if you are suffering," he wanted to know.

"You have hurt something in my head, I think," she said, getting up slightly on one elbow.

"You have nearly driven me out of my mind," he said, and he was making funny sounds in his mouth. "You don't know what it means to have one's name held up to ridicule like this. You are such a cruel person, Lois."

"We will both change our names, if you like," she said.

"Why do you torture me?" he said. "Why is it you can't control your power to torture?"

"Then we won't think about it, we will go home," she said, in a cold comforting voice. "Only I think I am going to be sick," she warned.

"We will go home," he said in a stupid voice.

"I will let you call me Mrs. Klein this one evening, then

tomorrow we will have a good talk." At the same moment she fell back on the walk.

Some young men from the delicatessen who had been doing inventory came by and asked if there was anything they could do.

"My wife fell on the walk," he said. "I thought she was all right. She was talking to me just a moment ago."

"Was it your wife, did you say?" the younger man leaned down to look at her.

"Mrs. Klein," Frank replied.

"You are Mr. Klein, then?"

"I don't understand," the older of the two young men said. "You don't look somehow like her husband."

"We have been married six months."

"I think you ought to call a doctor," the younger man said. "She is bleeding at the mouth."

"I hit her at a party," Frank said.

"What did you say your name was?" the older man asked.

"Mr. Klein. She is Mrs. Klein," Frank told them.

The two men from the delicatessen exchanged looks.

"Did you push her?" the one man asked.

"Yes," Frank said. "I hit her. She didn't want to be Mrs. Klein."

"You're drunk," the one man ventured an opinion.

Lois suddenly came to. "Frank, you will have to take me home," she said. "There is something wrong with my head. My God," she began to scream, "I am in awful pain."

Frank helped her up again.

"Is this your husband?" the one man asked.

She nodded.

"What is your name?" he wanted to know.

"It's none of your business," she said.

"Are you Mrs. Klein?" he asked.

"No," Lois replied, "I don't happen to be Mrs. Klein."

"Come on, J. D., we can't get mixed up in this," the younger man said. "Whatever the hell their names are."

"Well, I'm not Mrs. Klein, whoever you are," she said.

Immediately then she struck Frank with the purse and he fell back in surprise against the building wall.

"Call me a cab, you cheap son of a bitch," she said. "Can't you see I'm bleeding?"

Eventide

Mahala had waited as long as she thought she could; after all, Plumy had left that morning and now here it was going on four o'clock. It was hardly fair if she was loitering, but she knew that certainly Plumy would never loiter on a day like this when Mahala wanted so to hear. It was in a way the biggest day of her whole life, bigger than any day she had ever lived through as a girl or young woman. It was the day that decided whether her son would come back to live with her or not.

And just think, a whole month had rolled past since he left home. Two months ago if anyone would have said that Teeboy would leave home, she would have stopped dead in her tracks, it would have been such a terrible thing even to say, and now here she was, talking over the telephone about how Teeboy had gone.

"My Teeboy is gone," that is what Mahala said for a long time after the departure. These words announced to her mind what had happened, and just as an announcement they gave some mild comfort, like a pain-killer with a fatal disease.

"My Teeboy," she would say, like the mother of a dead son, like the mother of a son who had died in battle, because it hurt as much to have a son missing in peacetime as to have lost him through war.

The room seemed dark even with the summer sunshine outside, and close, although the window was open. There was a darkness all over the city. The fire department had been coming and going all afternoon. There were so many fires in the neighborhood—that is what she was saying to

Cora on the telephone, too many fires: the fire chief had just whizzed past again. No, she said to Cora, she didn't know if it was in the white section of town or theirs, she couldn't tell, but oh it was so hot to have a fire.

Talking about the fires seemed to help Mahala more than anything. She called several other old friends and talked about the fires and she mentioned that Teeboy had not come home. The old friends did not say much about Teeboy's not having returned, because, well, what was there to say about a boy who had been practicing to leave home for so long. Everyone had known it but her blind mother love.

"What do you suppose can be keeping my sister Plumy?" Mahala said to herself as she walked up and down the hall and looked out from behind the screen in the window. "She would have to fail me on the most important errand in the world."

Then she thought about how much Plumy hated to go into white neighborhoods, and how the day had been hot and she thought of the fires and how perhaps Plumy had fallen under a fire truck and been crushed. She thought of all the possible disasters and was not happy, and always in the background there was the fresh emotion of having lost Teeboy.

"People don't know," she said, "that I can't live without Teeboy."

She would go in the clothes closet and look at his dirty clothes just as he had left them; she would kiss them and press them to her face, smelling them; the odors were especially dear to her. She held his rayon trousers to her bosom and walked up and down the small parlor. She had not prayed; she was waiting for Plumy to come home first, then maybe they would have prayer.

"I hope I ain't done anything I'll be sorry for," she said.

It was then, though, when she felt the worst, that she heard the steps on the front porch. Yes, those were Plumy's steps, she was coming with the news. But whatever the news was, she suddenly felt, she could not accept it.

As she came up the steps, Plumy did not look at Mahala

with any particular kind of meaning on her face. She walked
unsteadily, as if the heat had been too much for her.

"Come on in now, Plumy, and I will get you something
cool to drink."

Inside, Plumy watched Mahala as if afraid she was going
to ask her to begin at once with the story, but Mahala only
waited, not saying anything, sensing the seriousness of
Plumy's knowledge and knowing that this knowledge could
be revealed only when Plumy was ready.

While Mahala waited patiently there in the kitchen,
Plumy arranged herself in the easy chair, and when she was
once settled, she took up the straw fan which lay on the
floor.

"Well, I seen him!" Plumy brought the words out.

This beginning quieted the old mother a little. She closed
her mouth and folded her hands, moving now to the middle
of the parlor, with an intentness on her face as if she was
listening to something high up in the sky, like a plane which
is to drop something, perhaps harmless and silver, to the
ground.

"I seen him!" Plumy repeated, as if to herself. "And I seen
all the white people!" she finished, anger coming into her
voice.

"Oh, Plumy," Mahala whined. Then suddenly she made a
gesture for her sister to be quiet because she thought she
heard the fire department going again, and then when there
was no sound, she waited for her to go on, but Plumy did
not say anything. In the slow afternoon there was nothing,
only a silence a city sometimes has within itself.

Plumy was too faint from the heat to go on at once; her
head suddenly shook violently and she slumped in the chair.

"Plumy Jackson!" Mahala said, going over to her. "You
didn't *walk* here from the white district! You didn't walk
them forty-seven blocks in all this August heat!"

Plumy did not answer immediately. Her hand caressed
the worn upholstery of the chair.

"You know how nervous white folks make me," she said
at last.

Mahala made a gesture of disgust. "Lord, to think you walked it in this hot sun. Oh, I don't know why God wants to upset me like this. As if I didn't have enough to make me wild already, without havin' you come home in this condition."

Mahala watched her sister's face for a moment with the same figuring expression of the man who comes to read the water meter. She saw everything she really wanted to know on Plumy's face: all her questions were answered for her there, yet she pretended she didn't know the verdict; she brought the one question out:

"You did see Teeboy, honey?" she said, her voice changed from her tears. She waited a few seconds, and then as Plumy did not answer but only sank deeper into the chair, she continued: "What word did he send?"

"It's the way I told you before," Plumy replied crossly. "Teeboy ain't coming back. I thought you knowed from the way I looked at you that he ain't coming back."

Mahala wept quietly into a small handkerchief.

"Your pain is realer to me sometimes than my own," Plumy said, watching her cry. "That's why I hate to say to you he won't never come back, but it's true as death he won't."

"When you say that to me I got a feeling inside myself like everything had been busted and taken; I got the feeling like I don't have nothing left inside of me."

"Don't I know that feeling!" Plumy said, almost angrily, resting the straw fan on the arm of the chair, and then suddenly fanning herself violently so that the strokes sounded like those of a small angry whip. "Didn't I lose George Watson of sleeping sickness and all 'cause doctor wouldn't come?"

Plumy knew that Mahala had never shown any interest in the death of her own George Watson and that it was an unwelcome subject, especially tonight, when Teeboy's never coming back had become final, yet she could not help mentioning George Watson just the same. In Mahala's eyes there really had never been any son named George Watson;

there was only a son named Teeboy and Mahala was the only mother.

"It ain't like there bein' no way out to your troubles: it's the way out that kills you," Mahala said. "If it was good-bye for always like when someone dies, I think I could stand it better. But this kind of parting ain't like the Lord's way!"

Plumy continued fanning herself, just letting Mahala run on.

"So he ain't never coming back!" Mahala began beating her hands together as if she were hearing music for a dance.

Plumy looked away as the sound of the rats downstairs caught her attention; there seemed to be more than usual tonight and she wondered why they were running so much, for it was so hot everywhere.

Her attention strayed back to Mahala standing directly in front of her now, talking about her suffering: "You go through all the suffering and the heartache," she said, "and then they go away. The only time children is nice is when they're babies and you know they can't get away from you. You got them then and your love is all they crave. They don't know who you are exactly, they just know you are the one to give them your love, and they ask you for it until you're worn out giving it."

Mahala's speech set Plumy to thinking of how she had been young and how she had had George Watson, and how he had died of sleeping sickness when he was four.

"My only son died of sleeping sickness," Plumy said aloud, but not really addressing Mahala. "I never had another. My husband said it was funny. He was not a religious man, but he thought it was queer."

"Would you like a cooling drink?" Mahala said absently.

Plumy shook her head and there was a silence of a few minutes in which the full weight of the heat of evening took possession of the small room.

"I can't get used to the idea of him *never* comin' back!" Mahala began again. "I ain't never been able to understand that word *never* anyhow. And now it's like to drive me wild."

There was another long silence, and then, Mahala suddenly rousing herself from drowsiness and the heat of the evening, began eagerly: "How did he look, Plumy? Tell me how he looked, and what he was doing. Just describe."

"He wasn't doin' nothin'!" Plumy said flatly. "He looked kind of older, though, like he had been thinking about new things."

"Don't keep me waiting," Mahala whined. "I been waitin' all day for the news, don't keep me no more, when I tell you I could suicide over it all. I ain't never been through such a hell day. Don't you keep me waitin'."

"Now hush," Plumy said. "Don't go frettin' like this. Your heart won't take a big grief like this if you go fret so."

"It's *so* unkind of you not to tell," she muffled her lips in her handkerchief.

Plumy said: "I told you I talked to him, but I didn't tell you where. It was in a drinking place called the Music Box. He called to me from inside. The minute I looked at him I knew there was something wrong. There was something wrong with his hair."

"With his hair!" Mahala cried.

"Then I noticed he had had it all made straight! That's right," she said looking away from Mahala's eyes. "He had had his hair straightened. 'Why ain't you got in touch with your mother,' I said. 'If you only knowed how she was carryin' on.'

"Then he told me how he had got a tenor sax and how he was playing it in the band at the Music Box and that he had begun a new life, and it was all on account of his having the tenor sax and being a musician. He said the players didn't have time to have homes. He said they were playing all the time, they never went home, and that was why he hadn't been."

Plumy stopped. She saw the tenor sax only in her imagination because he had not shown it to her, she saw it curved and golden and heard it playing far-off melodies. But the real reason she stopped was not on account of the tenor sax but because of the memory of the white woman who had come out just then. The white woman had come out and put her arm around Teeboy. It had made her get creepy all over. It was the first time that Plumy had realized that Teeboy's skin was nearly as light as the white people's.

Both Teeboy and the woman had stood there looking at Plumy, and Plumy had not known how to move away from them. The sun beat down on her in the street but she could not move. She saw the streetcars going by with all the white people pushing one another around and she looked around on the scorched pavements and everyone was white, with Teeboy looking just as white as the rest of them, looking just as white as if he had come out of Mahala's body white, and as if Mahala had been a white woman and not her sister, and as if Mahala's mother and hers had not been black.

Then slowly she had begun walking away from Teeboy and the Music Box, almost without knowing she was going herself, walking right on through the streets without knowing what was happening, through the big August heat, without an umbrella or a hat to keep off the sun; she could see no place to stop, and people could see the circles of sweat that were forming all over her dress. She was afraid to stop and she was afraid to go on walking. She felt she would fall down eventually in the afternoon sun and it would be like the time George Watson had died of sleeping sickness, nobody would help her to an easy place.

Would George Watson know her now? That is what she was thinking as she walked through the heat of that afternoon. Would he know her—because when she had been his mother she had been young and her skin, she was sure, had been lighter; and now she was older looking than she remembered her own mother ever being, and her skin was very black.

It was Mahala's outcries which brought her back to the parlor, now full of the evening twilight.

"Why can't God call me home?" Mahala was asking. "Why can't He call me to His Throne of Grace?"

Then Mahala got up and wandered off into her own part of the house. One could hear her in her room there, faintly kissing Teeboy's soiled clothes and speaking quietly to herself.

"Until you told me about his having his hair straightened, I thought maybe he would be back," Mahala was saying from the room. "But when you told me that, I knew. He won't never be back."

Plumy could hear Mahala kissing the clothes after she had said this.

"He was so dear to her," Plumy said aloud. It was necessary to speak aloud at that moment because of the terrible feeling of evening in the room. Was it the smell of the four o'clocks, which must have just opened to give out their perfume, or was it the evening itself which made her uneasy? She felt not alone, she felt someone else had come, uninvited and from far away.

Plumy had never noticed before what a strong odor the four o'clocks had, and then she saw the light in the room, growing larger, a light she had not recognized before, and then she turned and saw *him*, George Watson Jackson, standing there before her, large as life. Plumy wanted to call out, she wanted to say *No* in a great voice, she wanted to brush the sight before her all away, which was strange because she was always wanting to see her baby and here he was, although seventeen years had passed since she had laid him away.

She looked at him with unbelieving eyes because really he was the same, the same except she did notice that little boys' suits had changed fashion since his day, and how that everything about him was slightly different from the little children of the neighborhood now.

"Baby!" she said, but the word didn't come out from her mouth, it was only a great winged thought that could not be made into sound. "George Watson, honey!" she said still in her silence.

He stood there, his eyes like they had been before. Their beauty stabbed at her heart like a great knife; the hair looked so like she had just pressed the wet comb to it and perhaps put a little pomade on the sides; and the small face was clean and sad. Yet her arms somehow did not ache to hold him like her heart told her they should. Something too far away and too strong was between her and him; she only saw him as she had always seen resurrection pictures, hidden from us as in a wonderful mist that will not let us see our love complete.

There was this mist between her and George Jackson, like the dew that will be on the four o'clocks when you pick one of them off the plant.

It was her baby come home, and at such an hour.

Then as she came slowly to herself, she began to raise herself slightly, stretching her arms and trying to get the words to come out to him:

"George Watson, baby!"

This time the words did come out, with a terrible loudness, and as they did so the light began to go from the place where he was standing: the last thing she saw of him was his bright forehead and hair, then there was nothing at all, not even the smell of flowers.

Plumy let out a great cry and fell back in the chair. Mahala heard her and came out of her room to look at her.

"What you got?" Mahala said.

"I seen *him!* I seen *him!* Big as life!"

"Who?" Mahala said.

"George Watson, just like I laid him away seventeen years ago!"

Mahala did not know what to say. She wiped her eyes dry, for she had quit crying.

"You was exposed too long in the sun," Mahala said vaguely.

As she looked at her sister she felt for the first time the love that Plumy had borne all these years for a small son Mahala had never seen, George Watson. For the first time she dimly recognized Plumy as a mother, and she had suddenly a feeling of intimacy for her that she had never had before.

She walked over to the chair where Plumy was and laid her hand on her. Somehow the idea of George Watson's being dead so long and yet still being a baby a mother could love had a kind of perfect quality that she liked. She thought then, quietly and without shame, how nice it would be if Teeboy could also be perfect in death, so that he would belong to her in the same perfect way as George Watson belonged to Plumy. There was comfort in tending the grave of a dead son, whether he was killed in war or peace, and it was so difficult to tend the memory of a son who just went away and never came back. Yet somehow she knew as she looked at Plumy, somehow she would go on with the memory of Teeboy Jordan even though he still lived in the world.

As she stood there considering the lives of the two sons Teeboy Jordan and George Watson Jackson, the evening which had for some time been moving slowly into the house entered now as if in one great wave, bringing the small parlor into the heavy summer night until you would have believed daylight would never enter there again, the night was so black and secure.

Why Can't They Tell You Why?

Paul knew nearly nothing of his father until he found the box of photographs on the backstairs. From then on he looked at them all day and every evening, and when his mother Ethel talked to Edith Gainesworth on the telephone. He had looked amazed at his father in his different ages and stations of life, first as a boy his age, then as a young man, and finally before his death in his army uniform.

Ethel had always referred to him as *your father*, and now the photographs made him look much different from what this had suggested in Paul's mind.

Ethel never talked with Paul about why he was home sick from school and she pretended at first she did not know he had found the photographs. But she told everything she thought and felt about him to Edith Gainesworth over the telephone, and Paul heard all of the conversations from the backstairs where he sat with the photographs, which he had moved from the old shoe boxes where he had found them to two big clean empty candy boxes.

"Wouldn't you know a sick kid like him would take up with photographs," Ethel said to Edith Gainesworth. "Instead of toys or balls, old photos. And my God, I've hardly mentioned a thing to him about his father."

Edith Gainesworth, who studied psychology at an adult center downtown, often advised Ethel about Paul, but she did not say anything tonight about the photographs.

"All mothers should have pensions," Ethel continued. "If it isn't a terrible feeling being on your feet all day before the public and then having a sick kid under your feet when you're off at night. My evenings are worse than my days."

These telephone conversations always excited Paul because they were the only times he heard himself and the
photographs discussed. When the telephone bell would ring
he would run to the backstairs and begin looking at the
photographs and then as the conversation progressed he
often ran into the front room where Ethel was talking, sometimes carrying one of the photographs with him and making
sounds like a bird or an airplane.

Two months had gone by like this, with his having attended school hardly at all and his whole life seemingly
spent in listening to Ethel talk to Edith Gainesworth and
examining the photographs in the candy boxes.

Then in the middle of the night Ethel missed him. She
rose feeling a pressure in her scalp and neck. She walked
over to his cot and noticed the Indian blanket had been
taken away. She called Paul and walked over to the window and looked out. She walked around the upstairs, calling him.

"God, there is always something to bother you," she said.
"Where are you, Paul?" she repeated in a mad sleepy voice.
She went on down into the kitchen, though it did not seem
possible he would be there, he never ate anything.

Then she said *Of course*, remembering how many times
he went to the backstairs with those photographs.

"Now what are you doing in here, Paul?" Ethel said, and
there was a sweet but threatening sound to her voice that
awoke the boy from where he had been sleeping, spread
out protectively over the boxes of photographs, his Indian
blanket over his back and shoulder.

Paul crouched almost greedily over the boxes when he
saw this ugly pale woman in the man's bathrobe looking at
him. There was a faint smell from her like that of an un-
covered cistern when she put on the robe.

"Just here, Ethel," he answered her question after a
while.

"What do you mean, *just here*, Paul?" she said going up
closer to him.

She took hold of his hair and jerked him by it gently as

though this was a kind of caress she sometimes gave him.
This gentle jerking motion made him tremble in short successive starts under her hand, until she let go.

He watched how she kept looking at the boxes of photographs under his guard.

"You sleep here to be near them?" she said.

"I don't know why, Ethel," Paul said, blowing out air from
his mouth as though trying to make something disappear
before him.

"You don't know, Paul," she said, her sweet fake awful
voice and the stale awful smell of the bathrobe stifling as
she drew nearer.

"Don't, don't!" Paul cried.

"Don't what?" Ethel answered, pulling him toward her
by seizing on his pajama tops.

"Don't do anything to me, Ethel, my eye hurts."

"Your eye hurts," she said with unbelief.

"I'm sick to my stomach."

Then bending over suddenly, in a second she had gathered up the two boxes of photographs in her bathrobed
arms.

"Ethel!" he cried out in the strongest, clearest voice she
had ever heard come from him. "Ethel, those are my candy
boxes!"

She looked down at him as though she was seeing him
for the first time, noting with surprise how thin and puny he
was, and how disgusting was one small mole that hung from
his starved-looking throat. She could not see how this was
her son.

"These boxes of pictures are what makes you sick."

"No, no, Mama Ethel," Paul cried.

"What did I tell you about calling me Mama," she said,
going over to him and putting her hand on his forehead.

"I called you Mama Ethel, not Mama," he said.

"I suppose you think I'm a thousand years old." She raised
her hand as though she was not sure what she wished to do
with it.

"I think I know what to do with these," she said with a pretended calm.

"No, Ethel," Paul said, "give them here back. They are my boxes."

"Tell me why you slept out here on this backstairs where you know you'll make yourself even sicker. I want you to tell me and tell me right away."

"I can't, Ethel, I can't," Paul said.

"Then I'm going to burn the pictures," she replied.

He crawled hurrying over to where she stood and put his arms around her legs.

"Ethel, please don't take them, Ethel. Pretty please."

"Don't touch me," she said to him. Her nerves were so bad she felt that if he touched her again she would start as though a mouse had gotten under her clothes.

"You stand up straight and tell me like a little man why you're here," she said, but she kept her eyes half closed and turned from him.

He moved his lips to answer but then he did not really understand what she meant by *little man*. That phrase worried him whenever he heard it.

"What do you do with the pictures all the time, all day when I'm gone, and now tonight? I never heard of anything like it." Then she moved away from him, so that his hands fell from her legs where he had been grasping her, but she continued to stand near his hands as though puzzled what to do next.

"I look is all, Ethel," he began to explain.

"Don't bawl when you talk," she commanded, looking now at him in the face.

Then: "I want the truth!" she roared.

He sobbed and whined there, thinking over what it was she could want him to tell her, but everything now had begun to go away from his attention, and he had not really ever understood what had been expected of him here, and now everything was too hard to be borne.

"Do you hear me, Paul?" she said between her teeth, very close to him now and staring at him in such an angry way he closed his eyes. "If you don't answer me, do you know what I'm going to do?"

"Punish?" Paul said in his tiniest child voice.

"No, I'm not going to punish this time," Ethel said.

"You're not!" he cried, a new fear and surprise coming now into his tired eyes, and then staring at her eyes, he began to cry with panicky terror, for it seemed to him then that in the whole world there were just the two of them, him and Ethel.

"You remember where they sent Aunt Grace," Ethel said with terrible knowledge.

His crying redoubled in fury, some of his spit flying out onto the cold calcimine of the walls. He kept turning the while to look at the close confines of the staircase as though to find some place where he could see things outside.

"Do you remember where they sent her?" Ethel said in a quiet patient voice like a woman who has endured every unreasonable, disrespectful action from a child whom she still can patiently love.

"Yes, yes, Ethel," Paul cried hysterically.

"Tell Ethel where they sent Aunt Grace," she said with the same patience and kind restraint.

"I didn't know they sent little boys there," Paul said.

"You're more than a little boy now," Ethel replied. "You're old enough. . . . And if you don't tell Ethel why you look at the photographs all the time, we'll have to send you to the mental hospital with the bars."

"I don't know why I look at them, dear Ethel," he said now in a very feeble but wildly tense voice, and he began petting the fur on her houseslippers.

"I think you do, Paul," she said quietly, but he could hear her gentle, patient tone disappearing and he half raised his hands as though to protect him from anything this woman might now do.

"But I don't know why I look at them," he repeated, screaming, and he threw his arms suddenly around her legs.

She moved back, but still smiling her patient, knowing, forgiving smile.

"All right for you, Paul." When she said that *all right for you* it always meant the end of any understanding or reasoning with her.

"Where are we going?" he cried, as she ushered him through the door, into the kitchen.

"We're going to the basement, of course," she replied.

They had never gone there together before, and the terror of what might happen to him now gave him a kind of quiet that enabled him to walk steady down the long irregular steps.

"You carry the boxes of pictures, Paul," she said, "since you like them so much."

"No, no," Paul cried.

"Carry them," she commanded, giving them to him.

He held them before him and when they reached the floor of the basement, she opened the furnace and, tightening the cord of her bathrobe, she said coldly, her white face lighted up by the fire, "Throw the pictures into the furnace door, Paul."

He stared at her as though all the nightmares had come true, the complete and final fear of what may happen in living had unfolded itself at last.

"They're Daddy!" he said in a voice neither of them recognized.

"You had your choice," she said coolly. "You prefer a dead man to your own mother. Either you throw his pictures in the fire, for they're what makes you sick, or you will go where they sent Aunt Grace."

He began running around the room now, much like a small bird which has escaped from a pet shop into the confusion of a city street, and making odd little sounds that she did not recognize could come from his own lungs.

"I'm not going to stand for your clowning," she called out, but as though to an empty room.

As he ran round and round the small room with the boxes of photographs pressed against him, some of the pictures fell upon the floor and these he stopped and tried to recapture, at the same time holding the boxes tight against him, and making, as he picked them up, frothing cries of impotence and acute grief.

Ethel herself stared at him, incredulous. He not only could not be recognized as her son, he no longer looked like a child, but in his small unmended night shirt like some crippled and dying animal running hopelessly from its pain.

"Give me those pictures!" she shouted, and she seized a few which he held in his fingers, and threw them quickly into the fire.

Then turning back, she moved to take the candy boxes from him.

But the final sight of him made her stop. He had crouched on the floor, and, bending his stomach over the boxes, hissed at her, so that she stopped short, not seeing any way to get at him, seeing no way to bring him back, while from his mouth black thick strings of something slipped out, as though he had spewed out the heart of his grief.

Man and Wife

"How could it happen to you in good times if you didn't do nothing wrong?" Peaches Maud said.

"Peaches, I am trying to tell you," Lafe replied. "None of the men in the plant ever liked me." Then as though quoting somebody: "I am frankly difficult."

"Difficult? You are the easiest-to-get-along-with man in the whole country."

"I am not manly," he said suddenly in a scared voice, as though giving an order over a telephone.

"Not manly?" Peaches Maud said and surprise made her head move back slightly as though the rush of his words was a wind in her face.

"What has manly got to do with you being fired?" She began walking around the small apartment, smoking one of the gold-tipped cigarettes he bought for her in the Italian district.

"The foreman said the men never liked me on account of my character," Lafe went on, as though reporting facts he could scarcely remember about a person nearly unknown to him.

"Oh, Jesus," Maud said, the cigarette hanging in her mouth and a thin stream of smoke coming up into her half-closed eyes. "Well, thank God we live where nobody knows us. That is the only thing comes to mind to be grateful for. And for the rest, I don't know what in hell you are really talking about, and my ears won't let me catch what you seem to be telling."

"I have done nothing wrong, Peaches Maud."

"Did you ever do anything right?" She turned to him with hatred.

"I have no character, Maud," he spoke slowly, as though still quoting from somebody.

It was true, Maud thought, puffing vigorously on the Italian cigarette: he had none at all. He had never found a character to have. He was always about to do something or start something, but not having a character to start or do it with left him always on the road to preparation.

"What did the men care whether you had a character or not?" Maud wanted to know.

For nearly a year now she had worn corsets, but this afternoon she had none, and, it being daylight, Lafe could see with finality how fat she was and what unsurpassed large breasts stuck out from her creased flesh. He was amazed to think that he had been responsible so long for such a big woman. Seeing her tremendous breasts, he felt still more exhausted and unready for his future.

"They told me in the army, Peaches, I should have been a painter."

"Who is this *they?*" she inquired with shamed indignation.

"The men in the mental department."

Lafe felt it essential at this moment to go over and kiss Maud on the throat. He tasted the talcum powder she had dusted herself with against the heat, and it was not unwelcome in his situation. Underneath the talcum he could taste Maud's sweat.

"All right, now." Maud came down a little to him, wiping his mouth free of the talcum powder. "What kind of a painter did these mental men refer to?"

"They didn't mean somebody who paints chairs and houses," Lafe said, looking away so that she would not think he was criticizing her area of knowledge.

"I mean why did they think you was meant for a painter?" Maud said.

"They never tell you those things," he replied. "The tests test you and the mental men come and report the findings."

"Well, Jesus, what kind of work will you go into if it ain't factory work?"

Lafe extricated a large blue handkerchief dotted with

white stars and held this before him as though he were waiting for a signal to cover his face with it.

"Haven't you always done factory work?" Peaches Maud
summarized their common knowledge in her threatening
voice.

"Always, always," he replied in agony.

"Just when you read how the whole country is in for a
big future, you come home like this to me," she said, suddenly triumphant. "Well, I can tell you, I'm not going back
to that paint factory, Lafe. I will do anything but go back
and eat humble pie to Mrs. Goreweather."

"I don't see how you could go back." He stared at her
flesh.

"What meaning do you put in those words?" she thundered. Then when he stared at her uncomprehending: "You
seem to lack something a husband ought to have for his
wife."

"That's what everything seems to be about now," he said.
"It's what I lack everywhere."

"Stop that down-at-the-mouth talk," she commanded
evenly.

"All the way home on the streetcar I sat like a bedbug."
He ignored her.

"Lafe, what have I told you?" She tried to attract his attention now back to herself.

"I have always lacked something and that lack was in my
father and mother before me. My father had drink and my
mother was easily recognized as. . . ."

She pulled his arm loosely toward her: "Don't bring that
up in all this trouble. She was anyhow a mother. . . . Of
course, we could never afford for me to be a mother. . . ."

"Maybe I should go back and tell the men all the things
I lack they still don't know about."

"You say things that are queer, all right," Maud said in a
quieter voice, and then with her old sarcasm: "I can kind of
see how you got on the men's nerves if you talked to them
like you talk at home."

"You're beginning to see, you say, Peaches?" Lafe said,

almost as though he were now the judge himself, and then he began to laugh.

"I wish you would never laugh that way," Maud corrected him. "I hate that laugh. It sounds like some kid looking through a bathroom window. Jesus, Lafe, you ought to grow up."

He continued to laugh for a few moments, giving her the chance to see he had already changed a little for her. It was his laughing that made her pace up and down the room, despite the heat of July, and listen with growing nervousness to the refrigerator make its clattering din.

"I can see what maybe the men meant," she said in her quiet triumph-tone of voice, and at the same time putting rage into her eyes as they stared at the refrigerator.

"Christ, I hated every goddamn man."

"You can't afford to hate nobody! You can't go around hating men like that when you earn your bread with them."

"You hated Mrs. Goreweather."

"Look how unfair! You know Mrs. Goreweather had insanity in her family, and she pounced on me as a persecution target. You never even hinted there was any Mrs. Goreweather character at the factor."

"I was *her!*"

"Lafe, for Jesus' sake, in all this heat and noise, let's not have any of this mental talk, or I will put on my clothes and go out and get on the streetcar."

"I'm telling you what it was. The company psychiatrist told me I was the Mrs. Goreweather of my factory."

"How could he know of her?"

"I told him."

"No," she said stopping dead in the room. "You didn't go and tell him about her!" She picked up a large palm straw fan from the table and fanned with angry movements the large patches of sweat and talcum powder on her immense meaty body. As Lafe watched her move the fan, he thought how much money had gone to keep her in food these seven peculiar years.

"I am not a normal man, Peaches Maud," he said without

conviction or meaning. He went over to her and touched her shoulder.

"I'll bet that psychiatrist isn't even married," Maud said, becoming more gentle but suddenly more worried.

"He wasn't old," Lafe said, the vague expression coming over his face again. "He might be younger than me."

"If only that damn refrigerator would shut up," she complained, not knowing now where to turn her words.

She went over to the bed and sat down, and began fanning the air in his direction, as though to calm him or drive away any words he might now say.

"You have no idea how that refrigerator nags me sometimes when you can be gone and away at work. I feel like I just got to go out when I hear it act so."

"Maud," he said, and he stopped her arm from fanning him. "I have never once ceased to care for you in all this time and trouble."

"Well, I should hope," she said, suddenly silly, and fanning her own body now more directly.

"You will always attract me no matter what I am."

"Jesus, Lafe!" And she beat with the fan against the bedpost so that it shook a little.

Then they both noticed that the refrigerator was off.

"Did I jar it still?" she wondered.

But the moment she spoke it began again, louder and more menacing.

"I am not a man to make you happy." Lafe touched her shoulder again.

"I thought I told you I couldn't stand that mental talk. I have never liked having you say you felt like a bug or any other running of yourself down. Just because you lost your job don't think you can sit around here with me in this heat and talk mental talk now."

"Maud, I feel I should go away and think over what it is I have done to myself. I feel as though everything was beginning to go away from me."

"What in Jesus' name would you go away on?" she ex-

claimed, and she threw the fan in the direction of the refrigerator.

"I realize now how much of me there is that is not right,"
he said, as though he had finally succeeded in bringing this
fact to his own attention.

"Jesus! Jesus!" she cried. "How much longer do I, an old
married woman, have to listen to this?"

"Peaches Maud!" he said, standing up and looking down
at her squatting bulk on the bed. "There's no point me post-
poning telling you. Why I am without a job should be no
sort of mystery for you, for you are after all the woman I
married. . . . Have you been satisfied with me?"

"Satisfied?" she said, becoming quiet again, and her hand
rising as though still in possession of the fan. "Lafe, listen a
moment." Peaches spoke quickly, holding her finger to her
face, as though admiring a strain of music. "Did you ever
hear it go so loud before? I swear it's going to explode on
us. Can they explode, do you suppose?"

He stood there, his face and body empty of meaning, not
looking where she pointed to the refrigerator.

Maud broke a piece of chewing gum in two and, without
offering him the other piece, began to unfold the tin foil
and then to chew the gum industriously but with a large
frown between her eyes as though she could expect no
pleasure from what she had put into her mouth.

"You never let me show you nothing but the outside," he
said, his face going white and his eyes more vacant.

"Well, that's all anybody human wants to hear," she
shouted, but she felt a terrible excitement inside, and her
mouth went so dry she could hardly chew the gum.

"Peaches Maud, you have to listen to what I am trying to
tell you." He touched her jaws as though to stop her chewing. "First of all you must answer my first question. Have
you been satisfied with me?"

Peaches Maud felt welling up within her for the first time
in seven years a terrible tempest of tears. She could not explain why or from where these tears were coming. She felt

also, without warning, cold and she got up and put on her kimono.

"Don't tell me no more now." She faced him, drawing the kimono sash tight about her.

The refrigerator clattered on in short unrhythmic claps as though to annihilate all other sound.

"Answer my question, Peaches." He took her hand up from the folds of the kimono.

"I bought this for you in Chinatown." He made an effort to raise his voice.

"I don't want to hear no memory talks, Lafe, for the love of Christ!" And she looked down at him suddenly as though she had gone up above him on a platform.

"Maud," he coaxed, putting a new and funny hopeful tone into his voice, "I can forget all that mental talk like you say. I did before anyhow. The men in the army tried to make me feel things too, with their tests, and here I went and married you."

"Stop it now," she began to make crying sounds. "I can't bear to hear no more of that talk, I tell you. Put it off for later. I don't feel up to hearing, I tell you."

"We both quick change and make up our minds, don't we?" he said, briefly happy. He kissed her on the face.

"Don't kiss me when I feel like I do," she said peevishly.

Then without any warning, shouting as though something had stung her: "What did the company psychiatrist tell you?"

"You got to answer my first question first," Lafe said, a kind of mechanical strength coming to him.

"I can't answer until I hear what he told you," she said.

"Peaches," he pleaded with her.

"I mean what I said now." She began to sob a little.

"No, don't tell me after all, Lafe." Her face was open now and had a new empty weak quality he had never seen on it before. I feel if it's what I am fearing I'd split open like a stone."

"How could it be that bad?" he seemed to ask himself this question.

"I can tell it is because you keep making it depend on me being satisfied. I know more than you think I know."

Then she began to scream at him again as though to stop any tears that might have force enough to fall.

"What did you do at that factory that wasn't human? Oh, I thank Jesus we don't live in the same neighborhood with them men that work with you. This apartment may be hell with nothing but foreigners around us and that busted refrigerator and no ventilation but heat from the roof, but thank Jesus nobody don't know us."

"You won't answer me, then?" he said, still as calm and empty in his movements as before.

"You're not a woman," she told him, "and you can't understand the first question can't be answered till I know what you done."

"I asked the psychiatrist if it was a crime."

"Well, what did he tell you?" Peaches Maud raised her voice as though she saw ahead some faint indication of escape.

"He said it depended. It was what the men thought where you had to work."

"Well, what in the name of Christ did the men think?"

"They thought it was a crime."

"Was it a boy you were stuck on?" Peaches Maud said, making her voice both empty and quiet, and at the same time all the tears came onto her face as though sprayed there by a tiny machine, in one second.

"Did the psychiatrist call you up, Peaches?" he said, and he took hold of the bedpost and stared away from her.

Then, when she did not answer, he went over to her: "Did he, Peaches?" He took her by the hands and waited for her to answer.

"You leave loose of me, Lafe Krause. Do you hear? Leave loose of my hands."

"Peaches," he called in a voice that seemed to come from under the floor.

"Don't call me that old love name," she wept. "I'm an old fat woman tied down to a . . ."

She waited before she said the word, listening as though for any sound that might perhaps rescue them there both together.

"Did he call you up?" Lafe kept on, but his voice carried now no real demand, and came as though at a still greater distance from under where they stood.

Listening sharply, Maud felt it was true: the refrigerator had stopped again, and the silence was high and heavy as the sky outside.

"*Did he call you, Maud, did he?*"

"No," she answered, finally, still feeling he had to be addressed at some depth under where she was standing. "It was your mother. She told me before we got married. I said I would take a chance."

"The old bitch told you," he reflected in his exhausted voice.

"Considering the way the son turned out, the mother can hardly be blamed," Maud said, but her voice was equally drained of meaning.

"Peaches," he said, but as if not addressing the word to her at all, and going rapidly over to the refrigerator and opening up the door.

"The little light is out that was on here," he said dully.

"There ain't no point in fussing with it now," she remarked.

"Maybe I could fix it," he said.

"I doubt that. I doubt you could, Lafe Krause. I don't think I would want you to fix it anyhow, even if you could. . . ."

"Don't you want me to do nothing for you then anymore?" He turned with a slight movement toward her, his eyes falling on her breasts.

"I can't stand the pressure, I can't," she shouted back at him. "Why did you have to go and do it?"

"I didn't do nothing," he explained, as though trying to remember what had been said and what had not. "That's why it's so odd. They just felt I looked like I was going to, and they fired me."

"Jesus, I don't understand," she said, but without any tears on her face now. "Why did this have to happen to me when I can't bear to hear about anything that ain't human."

But her husband was not listening to her words or noticing whether she had tears or not. He was looking only at what was she, this fat, slightly middle-aged woman. She looked as though she had come to her permanent age, and he knew then that though he was but twenty-eight, he might as well be sixty, and the something awful and permanent that comes to everybody had come at last to him. Everything had come to an end, whether because he had looked at boys, or whether because the men had suddenly decided that yes, there was something odd in his character.

"Peaches," he said, and as he paused in his speech, the name he had always called her seemed to move over into the silence and vacancy of the broken refrigerator. "I will always stand by you anyhow, Peaches Maud."

You Reach for Your Hat

People saw her every night on the main street. She went out just as it was getting dark, when the street lights would pop on, one by one, and the first bats would fly out round Mrs. Bilderbach's. That was Jennie. Now what was she up to? everyone would ask, and we all knew, in company and out. Jennie Esmond was off for her evening walk and to renew old acquaintances. Now don't go into details, the housewives would say over the telephone. Ain't life dreary enough without knowing? They all knew anyhow as in a movie they had seen five times and where the sad part makes them cry just as much the last showing as the first.

They couldn't say too much, though. Didn't she have the gold star in the window, meaning Lafe was dead in the service of his country? They couldn't say too much, and, after all, what did Jennie do when she went out? There wasn't any proof she went the whole hog. She only went to the Mecca, which had been a saloon in old World War days and where no ladies went. And, after all, she simply drank a few beers and joked with the boys. Yes, and well, once they told that she played the piano there, but it was some sort of old-fashioned number and everybody clapped politely after she stopped.

She bought all her clothes at a store run by a young Syrian. Nobody liked him or his merchandise, but he did sell cheap and he had the kind of things that went with her hair, that dead-straw color people in town called angel hair. She bought all her dresses there that last fall and summer, and they said the bargain she got them for no one would ever believe.

Then a scandalous thing. She took the gold star out of the window. What could it mean? Nobody had ever dreamed of such a thing. You would have thought anyone on such shaky ground would have left it up forever. And she took it down six months after the sad news. It must mean marriage. The little foreign man. But the janitor said nobody ever called on her except Mamie Jordan and little Blake Higgins.

She went right on with her evening promenades, window-shopping the little there was to window-shop, nodding to folks in parked cars and to old married friends going in and out of the drug store. It wasn't right for a woman like Jennie to be always walking up and down the main street night after night and acting, really acting, as if she had no home to go to. She took on in her way as bad as the loafers had in front of the court house before the mayor ordered the benches carried away so they couldn't sit down. Once somebody saw her in the section around the brewery and we wondered. Of course, everyone supposed the government paid her for Lafe's death; so it wasn't as if she was destitute.

Nobody ever heard her mention Lafe, but Mamie Jordan said she had a picture of him in civilian clothes in her bedroom. He wasn't even smiling. Mamie said Jennie had had such trouble getting him to go to Mr. Hart's photography studio. It was right before his induction, and Jennie had harped on it so long that Lafe finally went, but he was so mad all the time they were taking him he never smiled once; they had to finish him just looking. Mamie said Jennie never showed any interest in the picture and even had toilet articles in front of it. No crepe on it or anything.

Mamie didn't understand it at all. Right after he was reported missing in action she went down to offer her sympathy and Jennie was sitting there eating chocolates. She had come to have a good cry with her and there she was cool as a cucumber. You'd never have known a thing had happened. It made Mamie feel so bad, because she had always liked Lafe even if he never would set the world on fire, and she had burst out crying, and then after a little while Jennie cried too and they sat there together all evening weeping and hugging each other.

But even then Jennie didn't say anything about Lafe's going really meaning anything to her. It was as though he had been gone for twenty years. An old hurt. Mamie got to thinking about it and going a little deeper into such a mystery. It came back to her that Lafe had always gone to the Mecca tavern and left Jennie at home, and now here she was out there every night of her life.

Mamie thought these things over on her way to the movie that night. No one had ever mentioned Jennie's case lately to her, and, truth to tell, people were beginning to forget who Lafe was. People don't remember anymore. When she was a girl they had remembered a dead man a little longer, but today men came and went too fast; somebody went somewhere every week, and how could you keep fresh in your memory such a big list of departed ones?

She sighed. She had hoped she would run into Jennie on her way to the movie. She walked around the court house and past the newspaper office and she went out of her way to go by the drygoods store in hopes she would see her, but not a sign. It was double feature night; so she knew she would never get out in time to see Jennie after the show.

But the movie excited her more than ever, and she came out feeling too nervous to go home. She walked down the main street straight north, and before she knew it she was in front of the Mecca. Some laboring men were out front and she felt absolutely humiliated. She didn't know what on earth had come over her. She looked in the window and as she did so she half expected the men to make some underhanded move or say something low-down, but they hardly looked at her. She put her hands to the glass, pressing her nose flat and peering in so that she could see clear to the back of the room.

She saw Jennie all right, alone, at one of the last tables. Almost before she knew what she was doing, she was walking through the front door. She felt herself blushing the most terrible red ever, going into a saloon where there were no tables for ladies and before dozens of coarse laboring men, who were probably laughing at her.

Jennie looked up at her, but she didn't seem surprised. "Sit down, Mamie." She acted just as cool as if they were at her apartment.

"I walked past," Mamie explained, still standing. "I couldn't help noticing you from outside."

"Sweet of you to come in," Jennie went on. Something in the dogged, weary quality of her voice gave Mamie her chance. She brought it right out: "Jennie, is it because you miss him so that you're . . . here?"

The old friend looked up quickly. "Dear Mame," she said, laughing, "that's the first time I've heard you mention him in I don't know how long."

Jennie simply kept on looking about as if she might perhaps find an explanation for not only why she was here but for the why of anything.

"I wish you would let me help you," Mamie continued. "I don't suppose you would come home with me. I suppose it's still early for you. I know my 'Lish always said time passed so fast with beer."

Jennie kept gazing at this frowsy old widow who was in turn gazing at her even more intently. She looked like her dead mother the way she stared.

"I understand," Mamie repeated. She was always saying something like that, but Jennie didn't weigh her friend's words very carefully. She wasn't quite sure just who Mamie was or what her friendship stood for, but she somehow accepted them both tonight and brought them close to her.

"You may as well drink. May as well be sheared for a sheep as a lamb."

"I believe I will," Mamie said, a kind of belligerence coming into her faded voice.

"Charley," Jennie called, "give Mamie some bottle beer." The "girls" sat there laughing over it all.

The smile began to fade from Jennie's mouth. She looked at her old friend again as if trying to keep fresh in her mind that she was really sitting there, that she had come espe-

cially. Mamie had that waiting look on her face that old
women always have.

The younger woman pulled the tiny creased photograph
from her purse. Mamie took it avidly. Yes, it was coming, she
knew. At last Jennie was going to pour herself out to her.
She would know everything. At last nothing would be held
back. In her excitement at the thought of the revelation to
come, she took several swallows of beer. "Tell me," she kept
saying. "You can tell old Mamie."

"He wasn't such a bad looker," Jennie said.

The friend leaned forward eagerly. "Lafe?" she said.
"Why, Lafe was handsome, honey. Didn't you know that?
He was." And she held the picture farther forward and shook
her head sorrowfully but admiringly.

"If he had shaved off that little mustache, he would
have been better looking. I was always after him to shave it
off, but somehow he wouldn't. Well, you know, his mouth
was crooked. . . ."

"Oh, don't say those things," Mamie scolded. "Not about
the dead." But she immediately slapped her hand against
her own mouth, closing out the last word. Oh, she hadn't
meant to bring that word out! We don't use that word about
loved ones.

Jennie laughed a little, the laugh an older woman might
have used in correcting a small girl.

"I always wondered if it hurt him much when he died,"
she said. "He never was a real lively one, but he had a kind of
hard, enduring quality in him that must have been hard to
put out. He must have died slow and hard and knowing to
the end."

Mamie didn't know exactly where to take up the thread
from there. She hadn't planned for this drift in the conversation. She wanted to have a sweet memory talk and she
would have liked to reach for Jennie's hand to comfort her,
but she couldn't do it now the talk had taken this drift. She
took another long swallow of beer. It was nasty, but it
calmed one a little.

"I look at his picture every night before I climb in bed,"

Jennie went on. "I don't know why I do. I never loved him, you know."

"Now, Jennie, dear," she began, but her protest was scarcely heard in the big room. She had meant to come forward boldly with the "You did love him, dear," but something gray and awful entered the world for her. At that moment she didn't quite believe even in the kind of love which she had seen depicted that very night in the movies and which, she knew, was the only kind that filled the bill.

"You never loved him!" Mamie repeated the words and they echoed dully. It was a statement which did not bear repeating; she realized that as soon as it was out of her mouth.

But Jennie went right on. "No, I never did love Lafe Esmond."

"Closing time!" Charley called out.

Mamie looked around apprehensively.

"That don't apply to us," Jennie explained. "Charley lets me stay many a night until four."

It was that call of closing time that took her back to her days at the cigar factory when fellows would wait in their cars for her after work. She got to thinking of Scott Jeffreys in his new Studebaker.

She looked down at her hands to see if they were still as lovely as he had said. She couldn't tell in the dim light, and besides, well, yes, why not say it, who cared about her hands now? Who cared about any part of her now?

"My hands were lovely once," Jennie said aloud. "My mother told me they were nearly every night and it was true. Nearly every night she would come into my bedroom and say, 'Those lovely white hands should never have to work. My little girl was meant for better things.'"

Mamie swallowed the last of the bottle and nodded her head for Jennie to go on.

"But do you think Lafe ever looked at my hands? He never looked at anybody's hands. He wasn't actually interested in woman's charm. No man really is. It only suggests the other to them, the thing they want out of us and always get. They only start off by complimenting us on our figures. Lafe wasn't interested in anything I had. And I did have a lot once. My mother knew I was beautiful."

She stopped. This was all so different from anything Mamie had come for. Yes, she had come for such a different story.

"Lafe married me because he was lonesome. That's all. If it hadn't been me it would have been some other fool. Men want a place to put up. They get the roam taken out of them and they want to light. I never loved him or anything he did to me. I only pretended when we were together.

"I was never really fond of any man from the first."

Mamie pressed her finger tightly on the glass as if begging a silent power in some way to stop her.

"I was in love with a boy in the eighth grade and that was the only time. What they call puppy love. Douglas Fleetwood was only a child. I always thought of forests and shepherds when I heard his name. He had beautiful chestnut hair. He left his shirt open winter and summer and he had brown eyes like a calf's. I never hardly spoke to him all the time I went to school. He was crippled, too, poor thing, and I could have caught up with him any day on the way home, he went so slow, but I was content to just lag behind him and watch him. I can still see his crutches moving under his arms."

Mamie was beginning to weep a little, a kind of weeping that will come from disappointment and confusion, the slow heavy controlled weeping women will give when they see their ideals go down.

"He died," Jennie said.

"When Miss Matthias announced it in home economics class that awful January day, I threw up my arms and made a kind of whistling sound, and she must have thought I was sick because she said 'Jennie, you may be excused.'

"Then there were those nice boys at the cigar factory, like I told you, but it never got to be the real thing, and then Lafe came on the scene."

Here Jennie stopped suddenly and laughed rather loudly.

Charley, who was at the other end of the room, took this for some friendly comment on the lateness of the hour and waved and laughed in return.

Mamie was stealthily helping herself to some beer from Jennie's bottle.

"Drink it, Mame," she said. "I bought it for you, you old toper." Mamie wiped a tear away from her left eye.

"As I said, I was tired of the cigar factory and there was Lafe every Friday at the Green Mill dance hall. We got married after the big Thanksgiving ball."

"Why, I think I remember that," Mamie brightened. "Didn't I know you then?"

But Jennie's only answer was to pour her friend another glass.

"He went to the foundry every morning after I had got up to cook his breakfast. He wouldn't go to the restaurants like other men. I always had such an ugly kimono to get breakfast in. I was a fright. He could at least have given me a good-looking wrapper to do that morning work in. Then there I was in the house from 4:30 in the A.M. till night waiting for him to come back. I thought I'd die. I was so worn out waiting for him I couldn't be civil when he come in. I was always frying chops when he come."

She took a big drink of beer.

"Everything smelled of chops in that house. He had to have them."

Charley began again calling closing time. He said everybody had to clear the place.

"It ain't four o'clock, is it?" Mamie inquired.

"No, not yet. I don't know what come over Charley tonight. He seems to want to get rid of us early. It's only one-thirty. I suppose some good-lookin' woman is waiting for him."

Yes, the Mecca was closing. Jennie thought, then, of the places she had read about in the Sunday papers, places where pleasure joints never closed, always open night and day, where you could sit right through one evening into another, drinking and forgetting, or remembering. She heard there were places like that in New Orleans where they had this life, but mixed up with colored people and foreigners. Not classy at all and nothing a girl would want to keep in her book of memories.

And here she was all alone, unless, of course, you could count Mamie.

"I was attractive once," she went on doggedly. "Men turned around every time I went to Cincinnati."

Mamie, however, was no longer listening attentively. The story had somehow got beyond her as certain movies of a sophisticated slant sometimes did with her. She was not sure at this stage what Jennie's beauty or her lack of it had to do with her life, and her life was not at all clear to her. It seemed to her in her fumy state that Jennie had had to cook entirely too many chops for her husband and that she had needed a wrapper, but beyond that she could recall only the blasphemies against love.

"My mother would have never dreamed I would come to this lonely period. My mother always said that a good-looking woman is never lonely. 'Jennie,' she used to say, 'keep your good looks if you don't do another thing.'"

The craven inattention, however, of Mamie Jordan demanded notice. Jennie considered her case for a moment. Yes, there could be no doubt about it. Mamie was hopelessly, unbelievably drunk. And she was far from sober herself.

"Mamie Jordan," she said severely, "are you going to be all right?"

The old friend looked up. Was it the accusation of drink or the tone of cruelty in the voice that made her suddenly burst into tears? She did not know, but she sat there now weeping, loudly and disconsolately.

"Don't keep it up any more, Jennie," she said. "You've said such awful things tonight, honey. Don't do it anymore. Leave me my little mental comforts."

Jennie stared uncomprehendingly. The sobs of the old woman vaguely filled the great empty hall of the drinking men.

It was the crying, she knew, of an old woman who wanted something that was fine, something that didn't exist. It was the crying for the idea of love like in songs and books, the love that wasn't there. She wanted to comfort her. She wanted to take her in her arms and tell her everything would be all right. But she couldn't think of anything really convincing to say on that score. She looked around anxiously as if to find the answer written on a wall, but all her eyes finally came to rest on was a puddle of spilled beer with Lafe Esmond's picture swimming in the middle.

No, you can't really feel sorry for yourself when you see yourself in another, and Jennie had had what Mamie was having now too many times, the sorrow with drink as the sick day dawned.

But the peculiar sadness evinced by Mamie's tears would not go away. The sore spot deep in the folds of the flesh refused to be deadened this time, and it was this physical pang which brought her back to Lafe. She saw him as if for a few illumined seconds almost as though she had never seen him before, as though he were existing for her for the first time. She didn't see exactly how the dead could know or Lafe could be in any other world looking down on her, and yet she felt just then that some understanding had been made at last between them.

But it was soon over, the feeling of his existing at all. Lafe wasn't coming back and nobody else was coming back to her either. If she had loved him she would have had some kind of happiness in looking at his photograph and crying like Mamie wanted her to. There would be consolation in that. Or even if they had brought him home to her so she would be able to visit the grave and go through the show and motions of grief. But what was him was already scattered so far and wide they could never go fetch any part of it back.

Clasping Mamie by the arm, then, and unfolding the handkerchief to give to her, she had the feeling that she had been to see a movie all over again and that for the second time she had wept right in the same place. There isn't anything to say about such private sorrow. You just wait till the lights go on and then reach for your hat.

A Good Woman

Maud did not find life in Martinsville very interesting, it is true, but it was Mamie who was always telling her that there were brighter spots elsewhere. She did not believe Mamie and said so.

Mamie had lived in St. Louis when her husband was an official at the head of a pipeline company there. Then he had lost his job and Mamie had come to Martinsville to live. She regretted everything and especially her marriage, but then she had gradually resigned herself to being a small town woman.

Mamie was so different from Maud. "Maud, you are happy," she would say. "You are the small town type, I guess. You don't seem to be craving the things I crave. I want something and you don't."

"What is it you want?" Maud asked.

The two women were sitting in Hannah's drug store having a strawberry soda. Mamie was reminded, she said, of some old-fashioned beer parties she and her husband had been invited to in Milwaukee when they were younger.

Mamie did not know what it was she wanted. She felt something catch at her heart strings on these cool June days and she would purposely remind herself that summer would soon be over. She always felt the passing of summer most keenly before it had actually begun. Fall affected her in a strange way and she would almost weep when she saw the falling maple leaves or the blackbirds gathering in flocks in deserted baseball parks.

"Maud, I am not young," Mamie would say, thinking of how bald and whitish and grubby her husband was getting.

Maud put down her ice-cream spoon, the straw hanging half out of the dish, and looked at her. Maud was every bit three years younger than Mamie, but when her best friend talked the way she did, Maud would take out her purse mirror and stare wonderingly through the flecks of powder on the glass. Maud had never been beautiful and she was getting stout. More and more she was spending a great deal of money on cosmetics that Mr. Hannah's young clerk told her were imported from a French town on the sea coast.

"If I could only leave off the sweets," Maud said, finishing her soda.

"Maud, are you happy?" Mamie sighed. But Maud did not answer. She had never particularly thought about happiness; it was Mamie who was always reminding her of that word. Maud had always lived in Martinsville and had never thought much about what made people happy or unhappy. When her mother died, she had felt lonely because they had always been companions. For they were not so much like mother and daughter as like two young women past their first youth who knew what life was. They had spent together many a happy afternoon saying and doing foolish young things, in the summer walking in the parks and fairgrounds and in the winter making preserves and roasting fowl for Thanksgiving and Christmas parties. She always remembered her mother with pleasure instead of grief. But now she had Mamie for a friend and she was married to Obie.

Her marriage to Obie had been her greatest experience, but she did not think about it much any more. Sometimes she almost wished Obie would go away so that she could remember more clearly the first time she had met him when he was an orchestra leader in a little traveling jazz band that made one-night stands near the airport in Martinsville. Obie had been so good looking in those days, and he was still pretty much the same Obie, of course, but he was not Obie the bandleader anymore. But once he had quit playing in orchestras and had become a traveling salesman, Maud's real romance had ended and she could only look out her window on to the muddy Ohio River and dream away an afternoon.

Obie and Mamie had talks about Maud sometimes. "We spend too much," Obie would say to her. He said he lived on practically nothing on the road. They both agreed she was not very practical. And she spent too much on cosmetics and movies. Mamie did not say so much about the movies because she knew she was the cause there of Maud's spending more than her income allowed, but then it was not Mamie surely who advised her the night of the carnival to buy that imported ostrich plume fan with the ruby jewels in the center and a good many other things of the same kind. And how could Maud give up the pleasure of the movies, or the ice cream or perfumes she got at Mr. Hannah's drug store? And what would Mr. Hannah do for star customers, for that was what Mamie said she and Maud were. They were actually out of all Martinsville his star customers, though they never purchased anything in his pharmacal department.

"Maud," Mamie said, "what do we get out of life anyway?"

Maud was not pleased with Mamie's taking this turn in the conversation. She did not like to get serious in the drug store as it spoiled her enjoyment of the ice cream and she had to think up an answer quickly on account of Mamie's impatience or Mamie would not be pleased and would think she was slow-witted, and she was sure Mamie thought she was slow-witted anyhow.

When Maud left Mamie that day she began to think it over. She walked slowly down the street, going north away from Mr. Hannah's drug store.

Mr. Hannah was standing by his green-trimmed display window, watching her as she walked to her yellow frame house over the river.

"What do we get out of life anyway?" Mamie's words kept humming about in her mind but she was so tired from the exhaustion of the warm dusty day that she did not let herself think too much about it. She did not see why Mamie had to keep thinking of such unpleasant things. It depressed her a little, too, and she did not like the feeling of depression. She did not want to think of sad things or whether life was worth living. She knew that Mamie always enjoyed the sad movies with unhappy endings, but she could never bear them at all. Life is too full of that sort of thing, she always told Mamie, and Mamie would say, pouting and giving her a disappointed look, "Maud, you are like all small town housewives. You don't know what I am feeling. You don't feel things down in you the way I feel them."

As she sauntered along she saw Bruce Hauser in front of his bicycle shop. Bruce was a youngish man always covered with oil and grease from repairing motorcycles and machines. When he smiled at Maud she could see that even his smile was stained with oil and car paint and she found herself admiring his white teeth.

She heard some school boys and girls laughing and riding over the bridge on their bicycles and she knew that school was out for the summer and that was why they were riding around like they were. It had not been so very long since she had gone to school, she thought, and for the second time that day she remembered her mother and the warm afternoons when she would come home from school and throw her books down on the sofa and take down her red hair, and her mother and she would eat a ripe fruit together, or sometimes they would make gooseberry preserves or marmalade. It was all very near and very distant.

The next day she felt a little easier at finding Mamie in a better humor and they went to a movie at the Bijou. It was a comedy this afternoon and Maud laughed quite a lot. On the way home Mamie complained that the movie had done nothing to her, had left her, she said, like an icicle, and she felt like asking for her money back.

When they sat down in Hannah's drug store, they began reading the BILL OF FARE WITH SPECIALTIES—for though they had sat in the same booth for nearly five years and knew all the dishes and drinks, they still went on reading the menu as if they did not know exactly what might be served. Suddenly Mamie said, "Are you getting along all right with Obie, Maud?"

Maud raised her too heavily penciled eyebrows and thought over Mamie's question, but instead of letting her answer, Mamie went on talking about the movie, and when they were leaving the drug store, Maud told Mr. Hannah to charge her soda.

"Why don't you let me pay for yours?" Mamie said, pulling her dress which had stuck to her skin from the sticky heat of the day.

Maud knew that Mamie would never pay for her soda even if she happened to be flat broke and hungry. She knew Mamie was tight, but she liked her anyway. Maud owed quite a bill at Mr. Hannah's and nearly all of it was for strawberry sodas. If Obie had known it, Maud would have been in trouble all right, but she always managed to keep Obie from knowing.

"I know," Mamie said on the way home, "I know, honey, that you and Obie don't hit it off right any more."

Maud wondered how Mamie knew that, but what could she say to deny it? She said, "Obie has to work out of town too much to be the family man I would like him to be."

When Maud got home that night she found that Obie had arrived. He was a little cross because she had not prepared dinner for him.

"I was not sure you was coming," Maud said.

She prepared his favorite dinner of fried pork chops and French fried potatoes with a beet and lettuce salad and some coffee with canned milk and homemade preserves and cake.

"Where was you all day?" Obie asked at the table, and Maud told him she usually went to a movie with Mamie Sucher and afterwards she went to the drug store and got a soda.

"You ought to cut down on the sweets," Obie said, and Maud remembered having caught a reflection of herself that day in the hall mirror, and she knew she was a long way from having the same figure she had had as a girl. For a moment she felt almost depressed as Mamie said she was all the time.

While Maud was doing the dishes, Obie told her that he had some good news for her, but she knew from the first it was not really good news. Obie told her that he had quit his traveling job and was going to sell life insurance now. He said he was getting too old to be on the road all the time. He wanted to have a little home life for a change, and it wasn't right for Maud to be alone so much.

Maud did not know what to say to him. The tears were falling over her hands into the dishwater, for she knew Obie would never make as much money selling life insurance as he had made on the road as a traveling salesman, and she knew there wouldn't be any more money for her for a long while. And all of a sudden she thought of the time when she had first begun getting stout and the high school boys has quit asking her for dances at the Rainbow Gardens and didn't notice her anymore.

The next time Maud saw Mamie was a week later, and Mamie was curious to know everything and asked how Obie was getting along these days.

"He quit his sales work," Maud said, and she felt the tears beginning to come, but she held them back by breathing deeper.

"I'm not a bit surprised," Mamie said. "I saw it coming all the time."

They walked over to the movie, and it was a very sad one. It was about a woman who had led, as Maud could see, not a very virtuous life. She had talked with three or four such women in her lifetime. The woman in the picture gave up the man she was in love with and went away to a bigger town. Mamie enjoyed it very much.

On the way home Mamie wanted Maud to come and have a soda.

"A strawberry soda?" Maud said, putting on some more lipstick and looking in at the green display windows with their headache ads and pictures of cornplasters. "I can't afford it."

"What do you mean, you can't afford it?" Mamie said.

"Obie has to make good at his insurance first," Maud told her.

"Come on in and I will buy you one," Mamie said in a hard firm voice, and though Maud knew Mamie did not want to spend money on her, she couldn't bear to go home to an empty house without first having some refreshment, so she went in with her.

As soon as they had finished having their sodas, Mr. Hannah came over to Maud and said he would like to have a few words in private with her.

"I am paying for this," Mamie said as if she suspected trouble of some sort.

Maud made a motion with her hand and started to walk with Mr. Hannah toward the pharmacy room.

"Do you want me to wait outside?" Mamie said, but she got no reply.

An old woman with white gloves was sitting in a booth looking at Maud and Mr. Hannah. Maud knew her story and kept looking at her. She was to have married a young business man from Baltimore, but the day before the wedding the young man had died in a railroad accident. Ever since then, the old woman had not taken off her white wedding gloves.

"Well, Maud," said Mr. Hannah, his gray old eyes narrowing under his spectacles, "I've been meaning to talk over with you the little matter of your bill and have been wondering whether or not . . ."

Maud could feel the red coming up over her face. She knew the old woman with the white gloves was hearing all of it. Maud feared perhaps she had put on too much rouge, for Mr. Hannah was giving her peculiar looks.

"How much is the bill?" she managed to say.

Mr. Hannah looked over his books, but he did not need to look to know how much Maud owed.

"Thirty-five dollars," he said.

Maud moved slightly backwards. "Thirty-five?" she repeated without believing, and she looked over on the books where her account was listed in black purplish ink. "Surely," Maud said, "that must be a mistake."

"Well, you have been having sodas on credit for more than six months," Mr. Hannah said, grinning a little.

"Not surely thirty-five dollars' worth," Maud told him, working the clasp on her purse, "because," she said, "I can't pay it, Obie isn't making full salary and I can't give it to you now at all."

"No hurry to collect yet," Mr. Hannah said and there was a little warmth coming into his voice. "Ain't no hurry for that," he said.

Suddenly Maud could not control her tears. They were falling through her fingers into a small handkerchief embroidered with a blue bird and a rose bush.

"No, Maud," Mr. Hannah said, "I will be real easy on you. Maybe you would like to talk it all over in the pharmacy room," he said taking her arm, and before she knew her own mind he had led her into the back room.

"Don't in any case," Maud begged him, sobbing a little, "don't in any case, Mr. Hannah, tell my husband about this bill."

"No need at all, no need at all," he said, turning on the light in the pharmacy room. Mr. Hannah was staring at her. Maud was not beautiful, really. Her powder-spotted mirror told her that, and she had a receding chin and large pores. But Mr. Hannah was looking. She remembered now how he had led a singing class at the First Presbyterian Church and he had directed some girls to sing "America the Beautiful" in such a revised improper way that the elders had asked him to leave the church, and he had, and soon after that his wife had divorced him.

As Mamie Sucher was not there to prompt her, Maud did not know what more to say to him. She stood there looking at the bill. She knew it could not be thirty-five dollars. She knew she was being cheated and yet she could not tell him to his face he was lying. It was the only drug store in town where she could get sodas on credit. All the other stores made you pay on leaving or before you drank your soda.

Maud stood there paralyzed, looking at the bill, and her face felt hot and sticky.

Then Mr. Hannah said something that pleased her. She did not know why it pleased her so much. "Maud, you beautiful girl, you," he said.

He was holding her hand, the hand with her mother's ruby ring. "Why don't you ever come into the pharmacy room," he said. "Why do you have to wait for an invitation, good friends like us?" And he clasped her hand so tightly that the ring pressed against her index finger, painfully. She had never been in the pharmacy room before but she did not like the whiffs of drugs and the smell of old cartons of patent medicines that came from there. "Maud, you beauty," he said.

Maud knew that she should say something cold and polite to Mr. Hannah, but suddenly she could not. She smiled and as she smiled the rouge cracked a little on her lips. Mr. Hannah was saying, "Maud, you know you don't have to stand on form with an old friend of the family like me. You know, Maud, I knowed you when you was only a small girl. I knowed your mother well, too."

She laughed again and then she listened to the flies on the screen, the flies that were collecting there and would be let in.

She tried to take the bill from his hand. "I will give it to my husband," she said.

"He will be very mad," Mr. Hannah warned her.

"Yes," Maud breathed hard. It wasn't possible for a man like Obie to believe that she could come into this drug store of Mr. Hannah's and buy only strawberry sodas and make that large a bill, and she knew Obie would never believe her if she told him.

"Well, give me the bill, Mr. Hannah," she said, but Mr. Hannah was still muttering about how dangerous such little things were to the happiness of young married people. Maud thought right then of a time when her mother had gone walking with her and Maud had a new pink parasol and all of a sudden a dirty alley cur had jumped on her as if to spoil her new parasol, not purposely but only in play, and she had said, "Oh, hell," and to hear her swear for the first time had given her mother a good laugh. And now she said so that Mr. Hannah could scarcely hear, "Oh, hell," and he laughed suddenly and put his arm around her.

She had thought everything like that was over for her and here was Mr. Hannah hugging her and calling her "beauty."

She knew it was not proper for her to be in this position with an old man like Mr. Hannah, but he wasn't doing anything really bad and he was so old anyhow, so she let him hug her and kiss her a few times and then she pushed him away.

"I ain't in no hurry to collect, you know that, Maud," Mr. Hannah said, and he had lost his breath and was standing there before her, his old faded eyes watering.

"Of course, my husband ought to see this bill," Maud said, but she just couldn't make the words have any force to sound like she meant it.

"You just go home and forget about it for a while, why don't you, Maud," he said.

She kept pushing a black imitation cameo bracelet back and forth on her arm. "You know how my husband would feel against it," she said.

Then Mr. Hannah did something that was even more surprising. He suddenly tore up the bill right in front of her.

Maud let out a little cry and then Mr. Hannah moved closer to her and Maud said, "No, Mr. Hannah, no, you let me make this right with you because Obie will soon be getting a check." She became actually frightened then with him in the dark, stale-smelling pharmacy room. "Some day," she said, "some day I will make this right," and she hurried out away from Mr. Hannah and she walked quickly, almost unconsciously, to the screen door where the flies were collecting before a summer thunder shower.

"I will make this right," she said, and the old druggist followed her and shouted after her, "You don't need to tell him, Maud."

"Don't call me Maud," she gasped.

She stopped and looked at him standing there. She laughed. The screen door slammed behind her and she was in the street.

It was getting a little late and Mamie was gone and the street was almost empty. She felt so excited that she would have liked to talk to Mamie and tell her what had happened to her, but she was too excited to talk to anyone and she hurried straight toward her house near the river.

Just as she got to the bridge she saw Bruce Hauser. She said, "Good evening, Bruce, how are you?" She could not say any more, she was that excited, and without waiting a minute to talk to Bruce, she took out her key and unlocked the door. As she was about to go up the stairs, she caught a reflection of herself in the hall mirror. She stared into it. Maud felt so much pleasure seeing herself so young, that she repeated Mr. Hannah's words again, "Maud, you beauty, you beauty." She was as pretty and carefree this June day as she had been that time when she and her mother had walked with the new pink parasol—long before she had met Obie—and they had joked together, not like mother and daughter, but like two good girl chums away at school.

Fred Parker had not seen Mr. Graitop since college days and yet he recognized him at once. Mr. Graitop's face had not changed in twenty years, his doll-small mouth was still the same size, his hair was as immaculately groomed as a department store dummy. Mr. Graitop had always in fact resembled a department store dummy, his face wax-like, his eyes innocent and vacant, the doll-like mouth bloodless and expressionless, the body loose and yet heavy as though the passions and anguish of man had never coursed through it.

Fred on the other hand felt old and used, and he was almost unwilling to make himself known to Mr. Graitop. The fact that he remembered him as Mr. Graitop instead of by his first name was also significant. One did not really believe that Mr. Graitop had a first name, though he did and it was Ezra. Fred had remembered him all these years as Mister. And now here he was like a statue in a museum, looking very young still and at the same time ancient, as though he had never been new.

"Mr. Graitop!" Fred cried in the lobby of the hotel. The hotel was said to be one of the world's largest, perhaps the largest, and Fred felt somehow the significance of his meeting the great man here where they were both so dwarfed by physical immensity, their voices lost in the vastness of the lobby whose roof seemed to lose itself in space indefinitely.

Mr. Graitop's face broke into a faint but actual smile and his eyes shone as though a candle had been lighted behind his brain.

"You are *him*," Fred said with relief. He was afraid that perhaps there was another man in the world who looked like Graitop.

"Yes, you are not deceived in me," Mr. Graitop said, pale and serious.

Fred was going to say *twenty years*, but he decided this was not necessary. He was not sure that Graitop would know it was twenty years, for he had always denied facts of any kind, changing a fact immediately into a spiritual symbol. For instance, in the old days if Fred had said, "It has been twenty minutes," Graitop would have said, "Well, *some* time has passed, of course." He would have denied the twenty because they were figures.

"You are just the same, Mr. Graitop," Fred said, and almost at once he wished he had not called to him, that he had hurried out of the world's largest hotel without ever knowing whether this was the real Graitop or only his twenty-year younger double.

As they were at the entrance of the Magnolia Bar, Fred ventured to ask him if he would have a drink, although it was only ten o'clock in the morning.

Mr. Graitop hesitated. Perhaps because he did remember it was twenty years, however, he nodded a quiet assent, but his face had again emphasized the bloodless doll expression, and one felt the presence of his small rat-terrier teeth pressed against the dead mouth.

"Mr. Graitop, this is unbelievable. Really not credible."

Mr. Graitop made odd little noises in his mouth and nose like a small boy who is being praised and admonished by the teacher at the same time.

Fred Parker already felt drunk from the excitement of having made such a terrible mistake as to renew acquaintance with a man who had been great as a youth and was now such a very great man he was known in the movement as the great man.

"What is your drink now, Mr. Graitop?" Fred spoke as though on a telephone across the continent . . . . "After twenty years," he explained, awkwardly laughing.

Mr. Graitop winced, and Fred felt that he did so because he did not like to be called by his last name even though he would not have liked to be called by his first, and perhaps also he did not like the twenty years referred to.

As Graitop did not answer immediately but continued to make the small-boy sounds in his nose and throat, Fred asked in a loud voice, "Bourbon and water, perhaps?"

"Bourbon and water," Mr. Graitop repeated wearily, but at the same time with a somewhat relieved note to his voice as though he had recognized his duty and now with great fatigue was about to perform it.

"I can't tell you how odd this is," Fred said nervously emphatic when they had been served.

"Yes, you said that before," Mr. Graitop said and his face was as immobile as cloth.

"But it is, you know. I think it's odd that I recognized you."

"You do?" Mr. Graitop sipped the drink as though he felt some chemical change already taking place in his mouth and facial muscles and perhaps fearful his changeless expression would move.

Then there was silence and strangely enough Mr. Graitop broke it by saying, "Your name is Fred, isn't it."

"Yes," Fred replied, paralyzed with emotion, and with his drink untouched. He suddenly noticed that Graitop had finished his.

"Graitop, won't you have another?" Fred asked, no invitation in his voice.

Graitop stared at him as though he had not understood actually that he had already finished one.

"Don't you drink, sir?" Fred said, surprised at once to hear his own question.

"No," Graitop replied.

"Another bourbon and water," Fred told the bartender.

"You know," Fred began, "this reminds me of one semester when we were roommates and we neither of us went to the football game. We could hear the crowd roaring from our room. It sounded like some kind of mammoth animal that was being punished. It was too hot for football and you tried to convert me to atheism."

Mr. Graitop did not say anything. Everybody had heard of his great success in introducing "new Religion" to America so that when many people thought of "new Religion" they thought immediately of Graitop.

It was a surprise to Fred to remember that Graitop had been a practicing atheist in the college quadrangles, for he remembered it only this instant.

"You were one, you know," Fred said almost viciously.

"We are always moving toward the one path," Graitop said dreamily, drinking his second drink.

Although Fred was a hard drinker, he had swiftly lost all his appetite for it, and he knew that it was not the early hour. Very often at this hour, setting out as a salesman, he was completely oiled.

"Is it the new religion that keeps you looking so kind of embalmed and youthful," Fred said, as though he had had his usual five brandies.

"Fred," Mr. Graitop said on his third drink, with mechanical composure, "it is the only conceivable path."

"I liked you better as an infidel," Fred said. "You looked more human then, too, and older. I suppose you go to all the football games now that you're a famous man."

"I suppose I see a good many," Graitop said.

"Fred," Mr. Graitop said, closing his eyes softly, and as he did so he looked remarkably older, "why can't you come with us this time?"

Fred did not know what to say because he did not exactly understand the question.

"There is no real reason to refuse. You are a living embodiment of what we all are without *the* prop."

"I'm not following you now," Fred replied.

"You are, but you won't let yourself," Graitop said, opening his eyes and finishing his third drink. He tapped the glass as though it had been an offering for Fred.

Fred signaled for another drink for Graitop just as in the past he would have for himself. His own first drink remained untouched, which he could not understand, except he felt nauseated. He realized also that he hated the great man and had always hated him.

"Well, what am I?" Fred said as he watched Graitop start on his fourth drink.

"The embodiment of the crooked stick that would be made straight," the great man replied.

"You really do go for that, don't you. That is," Fred continued, "you have made that talk part of your life."

"There is no talk involved," Mr. Graitop said. "No talk, Fred."

I wonder why the old bastard is drinking so much, Fred nearly spoke aloud. Then: "Graitop, nobody has ever understood what makes you tick."

"That is unimportant," his friend replied. "It, too, is talk."

"Nobody ever even really liked you, though I don't suppose anybody ever liked St. Paul either."

"Of course, Fred, you are really with us in spirit," Graitop said as though he had not heard the last statement.

Fred looked at his drink which seemed cavernous as a well.

"Graitop," he said stonily, "you discovered Jesus late. Later than me. I'd had all that when I was twelve . . . ."

"You're part of the new movement and your denying it here to me only confirms it," Mr. Graitop informed him.

"I don't want to be part of it," Fred began and he tasted some of his drink, but Graitop immediately interrupted.

"It isn't important that you don't want to be part: you are part and there is nothing you can do about it. You're with us."

"I couldn't be with you," Fred began, feeling coming up within him a fierce anger, and he hardly knew at what it was directed, for it seemed to be larger than just his dislike, suspicion, and dread of Graitop.

Then Mr. Graitop must have realized what only the bartender had sensed from the beginning, that he was not only drunk but going to be sick. Fred had not noticed it at all, for he felt that he had suddenly been seized and forced to relive the impotence and stupidity of his adolescence.

With the bartender's help, he assisted Mr. Graitop out of the bar. In the elevator, Graitop grew loud and belligerent and shouted several times: "It's the only path, the only way."

"What is your room number?" Fred said hollow-voiced as they got out of the elevator.

"You are really part of our group," Graitop replied.

Fred took the key out of Graitop's pocket and nodded to the woman at the desk who stared at them.

"You are completely oiled," Fred informed Graitop when the latter had lain down on the bed. "And yet it doesn't convince me any more than your preaching."

"I wonder if I had appointments," Graitop said weakly. "I was to speak to some of our people . . . ."

"I wonder which of us feels more terrible," Fred replied. "This meeting after twenty years [and he shouted the number] has been poison to both of us. We hate one another and everything we stand for. At least I hate you. You are probably too big a fraud to admit hate. I'm saying this cold sober, too, although I guess just the inside of a bar oils me up."

"You are a living embodiment of sin and sorrow and yet you are dear to us," Graitop said, looking at the ceiling.

"What the hell are you the living embodiment of, what?" Fred said and he began loosening his friend's clothing. Before he knew it, he had completely undressed Mr. Graitop as mechanically as he undressed himself when drunk. As his friend lay there, a man of at least forty, Fred was amazed to see that he looked like a boy of sixteen. Almost nothing had touched him in the world. So amazed and objective was Fred's surprise that he took the bed lamp and held it to his face and body to see if he was not deceived and this forty-year-old man was not actually a palimpsest of slightly hidden decay and senility. But the light revealed nothing but what his eye had first seen—a youth untouched by life and disappointment.

He looked so much like God or something mythological that before he knew what he was doing Fred Parker had kissed him dutifully on the forehead.

"Why did you do that?" Mr. Graitop said, touching the place with his finger, and his voice was almost human.

Fred Parker sat down in a large easy chair and loosened his necktie. He did not answer the question because he had not heard it. He felt intoxicated and seriously unwell.

"How in hell do you live, Graitop?" he said almost too softly to be heard. "Are you married and do you have kids?"

"Yes, yes," Graitop replied, and he began to drivel now from his mouth.

Fred got up and wiped off his lips, and put the covers over him.

"A missionary," Fred Parker said. "But of what?"

"Don't be a fool," Graitop said sleepily. Suddenly he was asleep.

Fred Parker watched him again angrily from the chair.

"Who in hell are you, Graitop?" he shouted from the chair. "Why in hell did I run into you. Why in hell did I speak to you . . . . Why don't you look and act like other men?"

Fred called room service for ice, whiskey, and water. He began immediately the serious drinking he should not have been without all morning.

"When the bastard is conscious, I will ask him who he is and what he means to do."

"It's all right, Fred," Mr. Graitop said from time to time from the bed. "You are really with us, and it's all all right."

"I wish you wouldn't use that goddamn language, Graitop," he said. "You don't have the personality for a missionary. Too young and dead looking. Too vague."

From the bed there came sounds like a small boy sleeping.

Sound of Talking

In the morning Mrs. Farebrother would put her husband in the wheelchair and talk to him while she made breakfast. As breakfast time came to an end he would sink his thumb into the black cherry preserves or sometimes he would take out an old Roman coin he had picked up from the war in Italy and hold that tight. In the summertime it helped to watch the swallows flying around when the pain was intense in his legs, or to listen to a plane going quite far off, and then hear all sound stop. There was a relief from the sound then that made you almost think your own pain had quit.

This morning began when Mrs. Farebrother thought of her trip to the city the day before, how she stared at the two young men on the train, for they reminded her of two brothers she had known in high school, and of course her visit to the bird store.

As her husband's pain grew more acute, which happened every morning after breakfast, she would talk faster, which she knew irritated him more, but she felt that it distracted him more from his pain than anything else. Her voice was a different kind of pain to him, and that was diversion. For a while he held on to an iron bar when he had suffered, then he had pressed the Roman coin, and now he dabbed in the cherry preserves like a child.

"You know what I would like?" Mrs. Farebrother said. "I almost bought one yesterday in the bird store."

She moved his wheelchair closer to the window before telling him. "A raven."

"Well," he grunted, not letting his pain or anger speak this early. He hated birds, even the swallows which he watched from the kitchen were not silent enough for him.

"Ever since I was a little girl those birds have fascinated me. I never realized until the other day that I wanted one. I was walking down the intersection and I heard the birds' voices being broadcast from that huge seed store, all kinds of birds broadcasting to that busy street. I thought a bird might be a kind of amusement to us."

Here Mrs. Farebrother stopped talking as she moved him again, her eyes trying to avoid looking at his legs. Many times she did not know where to look, she knew he did not like her to look at him at all, but she had to look somewhere, and their kitchen was small and what one saw of the outdoors was limited.

"Do you need your pill," she said with too great a swiftness.

"I don't want it," he answered.

"I have plenty of nice ice water this morning," she said, which was a lie. She didn't know why she lied to him all the time. Her anguish and indecision put the lies into her mouth like the priest giving her the wafer on Sunday.

"Tell me about the bird store," he said, and she knew he must be in unusual pain and she felt she had brought it on him by telling about her outing. Yet if she had made him begin to suffer, she must finish what had started him on it, she could not let him sit in his wheelchair and not hear more.

"I went up two flights to where they keep the birds," she began, trying to keep her eyes away from his body and not to watch how his throat distended, with the arteries pounding like an athlete's, his upper body looking more muscular and powerful each day under the punishment that came from lower down. But his suffering was too terrible and too familiar for her to scrutinize, and in fact she hardly ever looked at him carefully: all her glances were sideways, furtive; she had found the word in the cross-word puzzles one evening *clandestine;* it was a word which she had never said to anybody and it described her and haunted her like a face you can't quite remember the name for which keeps popping up in your mind. When they lay together in bed she touched him in a clandestine way also as though she might

damage him; she felt his injuries were somehow more sensitive to her touch than they were to the hand of the doctor.
She slept very poorly, but the doctor insisted that she sleep
with him. As she lay in the bed with him, she thought of only
two things, one that he could not approach her and the other
when would he die.

Thinking like this, she had forgotten she was telling a
story about the bird store. It was his contemptuous stare that
brought her back to her own talking: "It was a menagerie of
birds," she said, and stopped again.

"Go on," he said as though impatient for what could not
possibly interest him.

"Vergil," she said looking at his face. "Verge."

She did not want to tell the story about the raven because
she knew how infuriating it was to him to hear about pets of
any kind. He hated all pets, he had killed their cat by throwing it out from the wheelchair against a tree. And all day
long he sat and killed flies with a swiftness that had great
fury in it.

"The men up there were so polite and attentive," she said,
hardly stopping to remember whether they were or not, and
thinking again of the young men on the bus. "I was surprised because in cities you know how people are, brusque,
never expecting to see you again. I hadn't gone up there to
see anything more than a few old yellow canaries when what
on earth do you suppose I saw but this raven. I have never
seen anything like it in my life, and even the man in the shop
saw how surprised and interested I was in the bird. What
on earth is that? I said, and just then it talked back to me.
It said, *George is dead, George is dead.*"

"George is *what?*" Vergil cried at her, and for a moment
she looked at him straight in the face. He looked as though
the pain had left him, there was so much surprise in his
expression.

"George is dead," she said and suddenly by the stillness of
the room she felt the weight of the words which she had not
realized until then. Sometimes, as now, when the pain left
his face all her desire came back for him, while at night when

she lay next to him nothing drew her to him at all; his dead weight seeming scarcely human. She thought briefly again about the hospital for paraplegics the doctor had told her about, in California, but she could never have mentioned even *paraplegic* to Vergil, let alone the place.

"What was the guy in the bird shop like?" he said, as though to help her to her next speech.

"Oh, an old guy sixty or seventy," Mrs. Farebrother lied. "He said he had clipped the bird's tongue himself. He started to describe how he did it, but I couldn't bear to hear him. Anything that involves cutting or surgery," she tried to stop but as though she had to, she added, "Even a bird . . . ."

"For Christ's sake," Vergil said.

"I have never seen such purple in wings," Mrs. Farebrother went on, as though a needle had skipped a passage on the record and she was far ahead in her speech. "The only other time I ever saw such a color was in the hair of a young Roumanian fellow I went to high school with. When the light was just right, his hair had that purple sheen. Why, in fact, they called him the raven; isn't that odd, I had forgotten . . . ."

"Let's not start your when-I-was-young talk."

She thought that when he grunted out words like this or when he merely grunted in pain he sounded like somebody going to the toilet, and even though it was tragic she sometimes almost laughed in his face at such moments. Then again when sometimes he was suffering the most so that his hair would be damp with sweat, she felt a desire to hit him across the face, and these unexplained feelings frightened her a great deal.

But today she did not want him to suffer, and that is why she did not like to tell about the raven; she knew it was hurting him somehow—why she did not know, it was nothing, it bored her as she told it, and yet he insisted on hearing everything. She knew that if he kept insisting on more details she would invent some; often that happened. He would keep asking about the things that went on outside and she would invent little facts to amuse him. Yet these "facts" did not seem to please him, and life described outside, whether true or false, tortured him.

"Oh, Verge, I wished for you," she said, knowing immediately what she had said was the wrong thing to say; yet everything was somehow wrong to say to him.

"Then I said to the man in charge, doesn't the raven ever say anything but George is . . . ." She stopped, choking with laughter; she had a laugh which Vergil had once told her sounded fake, but which somehow she could not find in her to change even for him.

"Then the man gave me a little speech about ravens," Mrs. Farebrother said.

"Well?" he said impatiently. His insistence on details had made her tired and gradually she was forgetting what things had happened and what things had not, what things and words could be said to him, what not. Everything in the end bore the warning FORBIDDEN.

"He said you have to teach the birds yourself. He said they have made no effort to teach them to talk." Mrs. Farebrother stopped trying to remember what the man had said, and what he had looked like.

"Well, he must have taught the bird to say *George is dead,*" Vergil observed, watching her closely.

"Yes, I suppose he did teach him that," she agreed, laughing shrilly.

"Had there been somebody there named George?" he said, curious.

"I'm sure I don't know," she said abstractedly. She began dusting an old picture-frame made of shells. "I imagine the bird just heard someone say that somewhere, maybe in the place where they got it from."

"Where did they get it from?" he wondered.

"I'm sure nobody knows," she replied, and she began to hum.

"*George is dead,*" he repeated. "I don't believe it said that."

"Why, Verge," she replied, her dust rag suddenly catching in the ruined shells of the frame. Tired as her mind was and many as the lies were she had told, to the best of her knowledge the bird had said that. She had not even thought it too odd until she had repeated it.

"Maybe the old man's name was George," Mrs. Farebrother said, not very convincing. A whole whirlwind of words waited for her again: "I asked him the price then, and do you know how much he wanted for that old bird, well not old, perhaps, I guess it was young for a raven, they live forever . . . . Fifty dollars!" she sighed. "Fifty dollars without the cage!"

He watched her closely and then to her surprise he drew a wallet out from his dressing gown. She had not known he kept a wallet there, and though his hands shook terribly, he insisted on opening it himself. He took out five ten-dollar bills, which oddly enough was all that was in it, and handed them to her.

"Why, Verge, that isn't necessary, dear," she said, and she put her hands to her hair in a ridiculous gesture.

"Don't talk with that crying voice, for Christ's sake," he said. "You sound like my old woman."

"Darling," she tried to control her tears, "I don't need any pet like that around the house. Besides, it would make you nervous."

"Do you want him or don't you," he said furiously, pushing up his chest and throat to get the words out.

She stopped in front of the wheelchair, trying to think what she *did* want: nearly everything had become irrelevant or even too obscure to bear thinking about. She fingered the five ten-dollar bills, trying to find an answer to please both of them. Then suddenly she knew she wanted nothing. She did not believe anybody could give her anything. One thing or another or nothing were all the same.

"Don't you want your raven," he continued in his firm strong male voice, the voice he always used after an attack had passed so that he seemed to resemble somebody she had known in another place and time.

"I don't really want it, Vergil," Mrs. Farebrother said quietly, handing him the bills.

He must have noticed the absence of self-pity or any attempt to act a part, which in the past had been her stock-in-trade. There was nothing but the emptiness of the truth on her face: she wanted nothing.

"I'll tell you what, Verge," she began again with her laugh and the lies beginning at the same time, as she watched him put the money back in his wallet. Her voice had become soothing and low, the voice she used on children she sometimes stopped on the street to engage in conversation. "I'm afraid of that bird, Vergil," she confessed, as though the secret were out. "It's so large and its beak and claws rather frightened me. Even that old man was cautious with it."

"Yet you had all this stuff about ravens and Roumanians and high school," he accused her.

"Oh, high school," she said, and her mouth filled with saliva, as though it was only her mouth now, which, lying to him continually, had the seat of her emotions.

"It might cheer things up for you if something talked for you around here," he said.

She looked at him to determine the meaning of his words, but she could find no expression in them or in him.

"It would be trouble," she said. "Birds are dirty."

"But if *you* want him, Verge," and in her voice and eyes there was the supplication for hope, as if she had said, If somebody would tell her a thing to hope for maybe she would want something again, have desire again.

"No," he replied, turning the wheel of the chair swiftly, "I don't want a raven for myself if you are that cool about getting it."

He looked down at the wallet, and then his gaze fell swiftly to the legs that lay on the wheelchair's footrest. She had mentioned high school as the place where life had stopped for her; he remembered further back even than Italy, back to the first time he had ever gone to the barbershop, his small legs had then hung down helplessly too while he got his first haircut; but they had hung *alive*.

"Of course you could teach the bird to talk," she said, using her fake laugh.

"Yes, I enjoy hearing talk so much," and he laughed now almost like her.

She turned to look at him. She wanted to scream or push him roughly, she wanted to tell him to just *want* something, anything for just one moment so that she could want something for that one moment too. She wanted him to want something so that she could want something, but she knew he would never want at all again. There would be suffering, the suffering that would make him swell in the chair until he looked like a god in ecstasy, but it would all be just a man practicing for death, and the suffering illusion. And why should a man practicing for death take time out to teach a bird to talk?

"There doesn't seem to be any ice after all," Mrs. Farebrother said, pretending to look in the icebox. It was time for his medicine, and she had quit looking at anything, and their long day together had begun.

Cutting Edge

Mrs. Zeller opposed her son's beard. She was in her house in Florida when she saw him wearing it for the first time. It was as though her mind had come to a full stop. This large full-bearded man entered the room and she remembered always later how ugly he had looked and how frightened she felt seeing him in the house; then the realization it was someone she knew, and finally the terror of recognition.

He had kissed her, which he didn't often do, and she recognized in this his attempt to make her discomfort the more painful. He held the beard to her face for a long time, then he released her as though she had suddenly disgusted him.

"Why did you do it?" she asked. She was, he saw, almost broken by the recognition.

"I didn't dare tell you and come."

"That's of course true," Mrs. Zeller said. "It would have been worse. You'll have to shave it off, of course. Nobody must see you. Your father of course didn't have the courage to warn me, but I knew something was wrong the minute he entered the house ahead of you. I suppose he's upstairs laughing now. But it's not a laughing matter."

Mrs. Zeller's anger turned against her absent husband as though all error began and ended with him. "I suppose he likes it." Her dislike of Mr. Zeller struck her son as staggeringly great at that moment.

He looked at his mother and was surprised to see how young she was. She did not look much older than he did. Perhaps she looked younger now that he had his beard.

"I had no idea a son of mine would do such a thing," she said. "But why a beard, for heaven's sake," she cried, as though he had chosen something permanent and irreparable which would destroy all that they were.

"Is it because you are an artist? No, don't answer me," she commanded. "I can't stand to hear any explanation from you. . . ."

"I have always wanted to wear a beard," her son said. "I remember wanting one as a child."

"I don't remember that at all," Mrs. Zeller said.

"I remember it quite well. I was in the summer house near that old broken-down wall and I told Ellen Whitelaw I wanted to have a beard when I grew up."

"Ellen Whitelaw, that big fat stupid thing. I haven't thought of her in years."

Mrs. Zeller was almost as much agitated by the memory of Ellen Whitelaw as by her son's beard.

"You didn't like Ellen Whitelaw," her son told her, trying to remember how they had acted when they were together.

"She was a common and inefficient servant," Mrs. Zeller said, more quietly now, masking her feelings from her son.

"I suppose *he* liked her," the son pretended surprise, the cool cynical tone coming into his voice.

"Oh, your father," Mrs. Zeller said.

"Did he then?" the son asked.

"Didn't he like all of them?" she asked. The beard had changed this much already between them, she talked to him now about his father's character, while the old man stayed up in the bedroom fearing a scene.

"Didn't he always," she repeated, as though appealing to this new hirsute man.

"So," the son said, accepting what he already knew.

"Ellen Whitelaw, for God's sake," Mrs. Zeller said. The name of the servant girl brought back many other faces and rooms which she did not know were in her memory. These faces and rooms served to make the bearded man who stared at her less and less the boy she remembered in the days of Ellen Whitelaw.

"You must shave it off," Mrs. Zeller said.

"What makes you think I would do that?" the boy wondered.

"You heard me. Do you want to drive me out of my mind?"

"But I'm not going to. Or rather it's not going to."

"I will appeal to him, though a lot of good it will do," Mrs. Zeller said. "He ought to do something once in twenty years at least."

"You mean," the son said laughing, "he hasn't done anything in that long."

"Nothing I can really remember," Mrs. Zeller told him.

"It will be interesting to hear you appeal to him," the boy said. "I haven't heard you do that in such a long time."

"I don't think you ever heard me."

"I did, though," he told her. "It was in the days of Ellen Whitelaw again, in fact."

"In *those* days," Mrs. Zeller wondered. "I don't see how that could be."

"Well, it was. I can remember that much."

"You couldn't have been more than four years old. How could you remember then?"

"I heard you say to him, *You have to ask her to go.*"

Mrs. Zeller did not say anything. She really could not remember the words, but she supposed that the scene was true and that he actually remembered.

"Please shave off that terrible beard. If you only knew how awful it looks on you. You can't see anything else but it."

"Everyone in New York thought it was particularly fine."

"Particularly fine," she paused over his phrase as though its meaning eluded her.

"It's nauseating," she was firm again in her judgment.

"I'm not going to do away with it," he said, just as firm.

She did not recognize his firmness, but she saw everything changing a little, including perhaps the old man upstairs.

"Are you going to 'appeal' to him?" The son laughed again when he saw she could say no more.

"Don't mock me," the mother said. "I will speak to your

father." She pretended decorum. "You can't go anywhere with us, you know."

He looked unmoved.

"I don't want any of my friends to see you. You'll have to stay in the house or go to your own places. You can't go out with us to our places and see our friends. I hope none of the neighbors see you. If they ask who you are, I won't tell them."

"I'll tell them then."

They were not angry, they talked it out like that, while the old man was upstairs.

"Do you suppose he is drinking or asleep?" she said finally.

"I thought he looked good in it, Fern," Mr. Zeller said.

"What about it makes him look good?" she said.

"It fills out his face," Mr. Zeller said, looking at the wall-paper and surprised he had never noticed what a pattern it had before; it showed the sacrifice of some sort of animal by a youth.

He almost asked his wife how she had come to pick out this pattern, but her growing fury checked him.

He saw her mouth and throat moving with unspoken words.

"Where is he now?" Mr. Zeller wondered.

"What does that matter where he is?" she said. "He has to be somewhere while he's home, but he can't go out with us."

"How idiotic," Mr. Zeller said, and he looked at his wife straight in the face for a second.

"Why did you say that?" She tried to quiet herself down.

"The way you go on about nothing, Fern." For a moment a kind of revolt announced itself in his manner, but then his eyes went back to the wallpaper, and she resumed her tone of victor.

"I've told him he must either cut it off or go back to New York."

"Why is it a beard upsets you so?" he wondered, almost to himself.

"It's not the beard so much. It's the way he is now too. And it disfigures him so. I don't recognize him at all now when he wears it."

"So, he's never done anything of his own before," Mr. Zeller protested suddenly.

"Never done anything!" He could feel her anger covering him and glancing off like hot sun onto the wallpaper.

"That's right," he repeated. "He's never done anything. I say let him keep the beard and I'm not going to talk to him about it." His gaze lifted toward her but rested finally only on her hands and skirt.

"This is still my house," she said, "and I have to live in this town."

"When they had the centennial in Collins, everybody wore beards."

"I have to live in this town," she repeated.

"I won't talk to him about it," Mr. Zeller said.

It was as though the voice of Ellen Whitelaw reached her saying, *So that was how you appealed to him.*

She sat on the deck chair on the porch and smoked five cigarettes. The two men were somewhere in the house and she had the feeling now that she only roomed here. She wished more than that the beard was gone that her son had never mentioned Ellen Whitelaw. She found herself thinking only about her. Then she thought that now twenty years later she could not have afforded a servant, not even her.

She supposed the girl was dead. She did not know why, but she was sure she was.

She thought also that she should have mentioned her name to Mr. Zeller. It might have broken him down about the beard, but she supposed not. He had been just as adamant and unfeeling with her about the girl as he was now about her son.

Her son came through the house in front of her without speaking, dressed only in his shorts and, when he had got safely beyond her in the garden, he took off those so that he was completely naked with his back to her, and lay down in the sun.

She held the cigarette in her hand until it began to burn her finger. She felt she should not move from the place where she was and yet she did not know where to go inside the house and she did not know what pretext to use for going inside.

In the brilliant sun his body, already tanned, matched his shining black beard.

She wanted to appeal to her husband again and she knew then she could never again. She wanted to call a friend and tell her but she had no friend to whom she could tell this.

The events of the day, like a curtain of extreme bulk, cut her off from her son and husband. She had always ruled the house and them even during the awful Ellen Whitelaw days and now as though they did not even recognize her, they had taken over. She was not even here. Her son could walk naked with a beard in front of her as though she did not exist. She had nothing to fight them with, nothing to make them see with. They ignored her as Mr. Zeller had when he looked at the wallpaper and refused to discuss their son.

"You can grow it back when you're in New York," Mr. Zeller told his son.

He did not say anything about his son lying naked before him in the garden but he felt insulted almost as much as his mother had, yet he needed his son's permission and consent now and perhaps that was why he did not mention the insult of his nakedness.

"I don't know why I have to act like a little boy all the time with you both."

"If you were here alone with me you could do anything you wanted. You know I never asked anything of you. . . ."

When his son did not answer, Mr. Zeller said, "Did I?"

"That was the trouble," the son said.

"What?" the father wondered.

"You never wanted anything from me and you never wanted to give me anything. I didn't matter to you."

"Well, I'm sorry," the father said doggedly.

"Those were the days of Ellen Whitelaw," the son said in tones like the mother.

"For God's sake," the father said and he put a piece of grass between his teeth.

He was a man who kept everything down inside of him, everything had been tied and fastened so long there was no part of him any more that could struggle against the stricture of his life.

There were no words between them for some time; then Mr. Zeller could hear himself bringing the question out: "Did she mention that girl?"

"Who?" The son pretended blankness.

"Our servant."

The son wanted to pretend again blankness but it was too much work. He answered: "No, I mentioned it. To her surprise."

"Don't you see how it is?" the father went on to the present. "She doesn't speak to either of us now and if you're still wearing the beard when you leave it's me she will be punishing six months from now."

"And you want me to save you from your wife."

"Bobby," the father said, using the childhood tone and inflection. "I wish you would put some clothes on too when you're in the garden. With me it doesn't matter, you could do anything. I never asked you anything. But with her . . ."

"God damn *her*," the boy said.

The father could not protest. He pleaded with his eyes at his son.

The son looked at his father and he could see suddenly also the youth hidden in his father's face. He was young like his mother. They were both young people who had learned nothing from life, were stopped and drifting where they were twenty years before with Ellen Whitelaw. Only *she*, the son thought, must have learned from life, must have gone on to some development in her character, while they had been tied to the shore where she had left them.

"Imagine living with someone for six months and not speaking," the father said as if to himself. "That happened once before, you know, when you were a little boy."

"I don't remember that," the son said, some concession in his voice.

"You were only four," the father told him.

"I believe this is the only thing I ever asked of you," the father said. "Isn't that odd, I can't remember ever asking you anything else. Can you?"

The son looked coldly away at the sky and then answered, contempt and pity struggling together, "No, I can't."

"Thank you, Bobby," the father said.

"Only don't *plead* any more, for Christ's sake." The son turned from him.

"You've only two more days with us, and if you shaved it off and put on just a few clothes, it would help me through the year with her."

He spoke as though it would be his last year.

"Why don't you beat some sense into her?" The son turned to him again.

The father's gaze fell for the first time complete on his son's nakedness.

Bobby had said he would be painting in the storeroom and she could send up a sandwich from time to time, and Mr. and Mrs. Zeller were left downstairs together. She refused to allow her husband to answer the phone.

In the evening Bobby came down dressed carefully and his beard combed immaculately and looking, they both thought, curled.

They talked about things like horse racing, in which they were all somehow passionately interested, but which they now discussed irritably as though it too were a menace to their lives. They talked about the uselessness of art and why people went into it with a detachment that would have made an outsider think that Bobby was as unconnected with it as a jockey or oil magnate. They condemned nearly everything and then the son went upstairs and they saw one another again briefly at bedtime.

The night before he was to leave they heard him up all hours, the water running, and the dropping of things made of metal.

Both parents were afraid to get up and ask him if he was all right. He was like a wealthy relative who had commanded them never to question him or interfere with his movements even if he was dying.

He was waiting for them at breakfast, dressed only in his shorts but he looked more naked than he ever had in the garden because his beard was gone. Over his chin lay savage and profound scratches as though he had removed the hair with a hunting knife and pincers.

Mrs. Zeller held her breast and turned to the coffee and Mr. Zeller said only his son's name and sat down with last night's newspaper.

"What time does your plane go?" Mrs. Zeller said in a dead, muffled voice.

The son began putting a white paste on the scratches of his face and did not answer.

"I believe your mother asked you a question," Mr. Zeller said, pale and shaking.

"Ten-forty," the son replied.

The son and the mother exchanged glances and he could see at once that his sacrifice had been in vain: she would also see the beard there again under the scratches and the gashes he had inflicted on himself, and he would never really be her son again. Even for his father it must be much the same. He had come home as a stranger who despised them and he had shown his nakedness to both of them. All three longed for separation and release.

But Bobby could not control the anger coming up in him, and his rage took an old form. He poured the coffee into his saucer because Mr. Zeller's mother had always done this and it had infuriated Mrs. Zeller because of its low-class implications.

He drank viciously from the saucer, blowing loudly.

Both parents watched him helplessly like insects suddenly swept against the screen.

"It's not too long till Christmas," Mr. Zeller brought out. "We hope you'll come back for the whole vacation."

"We do," Mrs. Zeller said in a voice completely unlike her own.

"So," Bobby began, but the torrent of anger would not let him say the thousand fierce things he had ready.

Instead, he blew savagely from the saucer and spilled some onto the chaste white summer rug below him. Mrs. Zeller did not move.

"I would invite you to New York," Bobby said quietly now, "but of course I will have the beard there and it wouldn't work for you."

"Yes," Mr. Zeller said, incoherent.

"I do hope you don't think I've been. . . ." Mrs. Zeller cried suddenly, and they both waited to hear whether she was going to weep or not, but she stopped herself perhaps by the realization that she had no tears and that the feelings which had come over her about Bobby were likewise spent.

"I can't think of any more I can do for you," Bobby said suddenly.

They both stared at each other as though he had actually left and they were alone at last.

"Is there anything more you want me to do?" he said, coldly vicious.

They did not answer.

"I hate and despise what both of you have done to yourselves, but the thought that you would be sitting here in your middle-class crap not speaking to one another is too much even for me. That's why I did it, I guess, and not out of any love. I didn't want you to think that."

He sloshed in the saucer.

"Bobby," Mr. Zeller said.

The son brought out his *What?* with such finished beauty of coolness that he paused to admire his own control and mastery.

"Please, Bobby," Mr. Zeller said.

They could all three of them hear a thousand speeches. The agony of awkwardness was made unendurable by the iciness of the son, and all three paused over this glacial control which had come to him out of art and New York, as though it was the fruit of their lives and the culmination of their twenty years.

"Do you ever think about Fenton Riddleway?" Parkhearst Cratty asked the greatwoman one afternoon when they were sitting in the summer garden of her "mansion."

Although the greatwoman had been drinking earlier in the day, she was almost sober at the time Parkhearst put this question to her.

It was a rhetorical and idle question, but Parkhearst's idle questions were always put to her as a plea that they should review their lives together, and she always accepted the plea by saying nearly the same thing: "Why don't you write down what Fenton did?" she would say. "Since you did write once," and her face much more than her voice darkened at him.

Actually the eyes of the greatwoman were blackened very little with mascara and yet such was their cavernous appearance they gaped at Parkhearst as though tonight they would yield him her real identity and why people called her great.

"Fenton Riddleway is vague as a dream to me," the greatwoman said.

"That means he is more real to you than anybody," Parkhearst said.

"How could it mean anything else?" she repeated her own eternal rejoinder. Then arranging her long dress so that it covered the floor before her shoes, she began to throw her head back as though suffering from a feeling of suffocation.

It was her signal to him that he was to leave, but he took no notice of her wishes today.

"I can't write down what Fenton did because I never found out who he was," Parkhearst explained again to her.

"You've said that ever since he was first with us. And since he went away, a million times."

She reached for the gin; it was the only drink she would have since the days of Fenton.

"Not that I'm criticizing you for saying it," she said. "How could *I* criticize you?" she added.

"Then don't scratch and tear at me, for Christ's sake," he told her.

Her mouth wet from the drink smiled faintly at him.

"What Fenton did was almost the only story I ever really wanted to write," Parkhearst said, and a shadow of old happiness came over his thin brown face.

Grainger's eyes brightened briefly, then went back into their unrelieved darkness.

"You can't feel as empty of recollection as I do," Grainger mumbled, sipping again.

Parkhearst watched the veins bulge in his hands.

"Why are we dead anyhow?" Parkhearst said, bored with the necessity of returning to this daily statement. "Is it because of our losing the people we loved or because the people we found were damned?" He laughed.

One never mentioned the "real" things like this at Grainger's, and here Parkhearst had done it, and nothing happened. Instead, Grainger listened as though hearing some two or three notes of an alto sax she recalled from the concerts she gave at her home.

"This is the first time you ever said you were, Parkhearst. Dead," she said in her clearest voice.

He sat looking like a small rock that has been worked on by a swift but careless hammer.

"Are you really without a memory?" she asked, speaking now like a child.

He did not say anything and she began to get up.

"Don't get up, or you'll fall," he said, almost not looking in her direction.

The greatwoman had gotten up and stood there like some more than human personage at the end of an opera.

Parkhearst closed his eyes. Then she advanced to a half-fall at the feet of her old friend.

"Are those tears?" she said looking up into his face.

"Don't be tiresome, Grainger. Go back and sit down," he said, with the petulance of a small boy.

Pushing her head towards his face, she kissed him several times.

"You're getting gray," she said, almost shocked. "I didn't know it had been such a long time."

"I try never to think about those things," he looked at her now. "Please get up."

"Do you think Fenton Riddleway would know you now, Parkhearst?" the greatwoman asked sullenly but without anything taunting in her voice.

"The real question is whether we would know Fenton Riddleway if we saw him."

"We'd know him," she said. "Above or beneath hell."

As evening came on in the "mansion" (*mansion* a word they both thought of and used all the time because Fenton had used it), they drank more and more of the neat Holland gin, but drunkenness did not take: was it after all, they kept on saying, merely the remembrance of a boy from West Virginia, that mover and shaker Fenton, that kept them talking and living.

"Tell me all about what he did again," Grainger said, seated now on her gold carved chair. The dark hid her age, so that she looked now only relatively old; it almost hid the fact that she was drunk, drunk going on to ten years, and her face was shapeless and sexless.

"Tell me what he did all over again, just this last time. If you won't write it down, Parkhearst, you'll have to come here and tell it to me once a month. I had always hoped you would write it down so I could have it to read on my bad nights. . . ."

"Your memory is so much better than mine," Parkhearst said.

"I have no memory," the greatwoman said. "Or only a grain of one."

She raised her glass threateningly, but it had got so dark in the room she could not see just where Parkhearst's tired voice was coming from. It was like the time she had called Russell long distance to his home town, the voice had wavered, then had grown, then had sunk into indistinguishable sounds. Parkhearst would take another drink of the gin, then his voice would rise a bit, only to die away again as he told her everything he could remember.

"Are you awake?" Parkhearst questioned her.

"Keep going," she said. "Don't stop to ask me a single thing. Just tell what he did, and then write it all down for me to read hereafter."

He nodded at her.

There was this park with a patriot's name near the lagoon. Parkhearst Cratty had been wandering there, not daring to go home to his wife Bella. He had done nothing in weeks, and her resentment against him would be too heavy to bear. Of course it was true, what he was later to tell Fenton himself, that he was looking for "material" for his book. Many times he had run across people in the park who had told him their stories while he pretended to listen to their voices while usually watching their persons.

In this section of the park there were no lights, and the only illumination came from the reflection of the traffic blocks away. Here the men who came to wander about as aimless and groping as he were obvious shades in hell. He always noticed this fact as he noticed there were no lights. Parkhearst paid little attention to the actual things that went on in the park and, although not a brave or strong young man, he had never felt fear in the park itself. It was its atmosphere alone that satisfied him and he remained forever innocent of its acts.

It was August, and cool, but he felt enervated as never before. His marriage pursued him like a never-ending nightmare, and he could not free himself from the obsession that "everything was over."

Just as children, he and the greatwoman Grainger longed,

and especially demanded even, that something should happen, or again Parkhearst would cry, "A reward, I must have a reward. A reward for life just as I have lived it."

It was just as he had uttered the words *a reward* that he first saw Fenton Riddleway go past, he remembered.

In the darkness and the rehearsed evil of the park it was odd, indeed, as Parkhearst now reflected on the event, that anyone should have stood out at all that night, one shadow from the other. Yet Fenton was remarkable at once, perhaps for no other reason than that he was actually lost and wandering about, for no other reason than this. Parkhearst did not need to watch him for more than a moment to see his desperation.

Parkhearst lit a cigarette so that his own whereabouts would be visible to the stranger.

"Looking for anybody?" Parkhearst then asked.

Fenton's face was momentarily lighted up by Parkhearst's cigarette: the face had, he noted with accustomed uneasiness, a kind of beauty but mixed with something unsteady, unusual.

"Where do you get out?" the boy asked.

He stood directly over Parkhearst in a position a less experienced man than the writer would have taken to be a threat.

Parkhearst recognized with a certain shock that this was the first question he had ever had addressed to him in the park which was asked with the wish to be answered: somebody really wanted out of the park.

"Where do you want to go?"

Fenton took from his pocket a tiny dimestore notebook and read from the first page an address.

"It's south," Parkhearst replied. "Away from the lagoon."

Fenton still looked too unsure to speak. He dropped the notebook and when he stooped to pick it up his head twitched while his eyes looked at the writer.

"Do you want me to show you?" Parkhearst asked, pretending indifference.

Fenton looked directly into his face now.

Those eyes looked dumb, Parkhearst saw them again, like maybe the eyes of the first murderer, dumb and innocent and getting to be mad.

"Show me, please," Fenton said, and Parkhearst heard the Southern accent.

"You're from far off," Parkhearst said as they began to walk in the opposite direction of the lagoon.

Fenton had been too frightened not to want to unburden himself. He told nearly everything, as though in a police court, that he was Fenton Riddleway and that he was nineteen, that he had come with his brother Claire from West Virginia, from a town near Ronceverte, that their mother had died two weeks before, and that a friend of his named Kincaid had given him an address in a rooming house on Sixty-*three* Street . . .

"You mean Sixty-*third*," Parkhearst corrected him, but Fenton did not hear the correction then or when it was made fifty times later: "A house on Sixty-three Street," he continued. "It turns out to be a not-right-kind of place at all. . . ."

"How is that?" Parkhearst wondered.

They moved out of the middle section of the park and into a place where the street light looked down on them. Fenton was gazing at him easily but Parkhearst's eyes kept to his coat pocket, which bulged obviously.

"Is that your gun there?" he said, weary.

Fenton watched him, moving his lips quickly.

"Don't let it go off on yourself," Parkhearst said ineffectively as the boy nodded.

"But what were you saying about that house?" the writer went back to his story.

"It's alive with something, I don't know what. . . ."

Fenton's thick accent, which seemed to become thicker now, all at once irritated Parkhearst, and as they drew near the part of the city that was more inhabited and better lighted, he felt himself surprised by Fenton's incredibly poor-fitting almost filthy clothes and by the fact that his hair had the look of not ever perhaps having been cut or combed.

He looked more or less like West Virginia, Parkhearst supposed, and then Parkhearst always remembered he had
thought this, he looked not only just West Virginia, he
looked himself, Fenton.

"What's it alive with, then?" Parkhearst came back to the
subject of the house.

"I don't mean it's got ghosts, though I think it maybe
does." He stopped, fishing for encouragement to go on and
when none came he said: "It's a not-right house. There ain't
nobody in it for one thing."

"I don't think I see," Parkhearst said, and he felt not so
much his interest waning as his feeling that there was something about this boy too excessive; everything about him was
too large for him, the speech, the terrible clothes, the ragged
hair, the possible gun, the outlandish accent.

"All the time we're alone in it, I keep thinking how empty
it is, and what are we waiting for after all, with so little
money to tide us over, if he don't show up. Claire cries all
the time on account of the change. The house don't do *him*
any good."

"Can you find your way back now, do you think?" Parkhearst asked, as they got to a street down which ordinary
people and traffic were moving.

A paralysis had struck the writer suddenly, as though all
the interest he might have had in Fenton had been killed.
He was beginning to be afraid also that he would be involved in more than a story.

Fenton stopped as if to remind Parkhearst that he had a
responsibility toward him. His having found the first person
in his life who would listen to him had made him within
ten minutes come to regard Parkhearst as a friend, and now
the realization came quickly that this was only a listener
who having heard the story would let him go back to the
"not-right house."

"Here's fifty cents for you," Parkhearst said.

He took it with a funny quick movement as though money
for the first time had meaning for him.

"You won't come with me to see Claire?"

Parkhearst stared. This odd boy, who was probably wanted by the police, who had come out of nothing to him, had asked him a question in the tone of one who had known him all his life.

"Tomorrow maybe," Parkhearst answered. He explained lamely about Bella waiting for him and being cross if he came any later.

The boy's face fell.

"You know where to find the house?" Fenton said, hoarse.

"Yes," Parkhearst replied dreamily, indifferent.

Fenton looked at Parkhearst, unbelieving. Then: "How can you find it?" he wondered. "I can't ever find it no matter how many times I go and come. How can you then?"

The sorrow on Fenton's face won him over to him again, and he felt Bella's eyes of reproach disappear from his mind for a moment.

"Tomorrow afternoon I'll visit you at the house," he promised. "Two o'clock."

A moment later when Fenton was gone, Parkhearst looking back could not help wait for the last sight of him in the street, and a new feeling so close to acute sickness swept over him. It was the wildness and freedom Fenton had, he began to try to explain to himself. The wildness and freedom held against his own shut-in locked life. He hurried on home to Bella.

Bella listened vaguely to the story of Fenton Riddleway. There had been, she recalled mechanically, scores, even hundreds, of these people Parkhearst met in order to study for his writing, but the stories themselves were never put in final shape or were never written, and Parkhearst himself forgot the old models in his search for new ones.

"Is Fenton to take the place of Grainger now?" Bella commented on his enthusiasm, almost his ecstasy.

There was no criticism in her remark. She was beyond that. Bella Cratty had resigned herself to her complete knowledge of her husband's character. There was, furthermore, no opposing Parkhearst; if he were opposed he would disintegrate slowly, vanish before her eyes. He was a child who must not be crossed in the full possession of his freedom, one who must be left to follow his own whims and visions.

She had married him without anyone knowing why, but everyone agreed she had done so with the full knowledge of what he was. If she had not known before, their married life had been a continuous daily rehearsal of Parkhearst's character; he was himself every minute, taking more and more away from what was *her* with each new sorrow he brought home to her. He became more and more incurable and it was his incurable quality which made him essential to her.

She was not happy a second. Had she seen the wandering men in the park after whom Parkhearst gazed, she might have seen herself like them, wandering without purpose away from the light. And though she tried to pretend that she wanted Parkhearst to have friends no matter what they were, no matter what they would do, she never gave up suffering, and each of the "new" people he met and "studied" cost her an impossible sacrifice.

There was something at once about the name Fenton Riddleway that made her feel there was danger here in his name as Grainger was in hers. Only there was something in the new name more frightening than in Grainger's.

As two o'clock approached the following day (an evil hour in astrology, Parkhearst had noticed covertly, for Bella objected to his interest in what she called "the moons"), both of them felt the importance of his departure. He had tried to get her "ready" from the evening before so that she would accept this as Fenton's day, when as a writer he must find out all there was to know about this strange boy. Parkhearst used the word *material* again, though he had promised himself to give up using the word.

"I suppose in the end you will let Grainger have Fenton," Bella remarked, a sudden hostility coming over her face as she sat at the kitchen table drinking her coffee.

Parkhearst stopped his task of sewing on a button on his old gray-green jacket.

It was only when his wife said that that he understood he did not wish to share Fenton with anyone, until, he lied to himself, he had found out everything Fenton had done. And then he corrected this lie in his own mind: he simply did not want to share Fenton with anybody. Grainger would spoil him, would take him over, if she were interested, and he knew of course that she was going to be.

"Grainger won't get him," he said finally.

Bella laughed a very high laugh, ridden with hysteria and shaky restraint. "You've never kept anybody from one another as long as you've been friends," she reviewed their lives. "What would happen," she went on bitterly, "if you couldn't show one another what you take in, what you accomplish. If there was no competition!"

"Fenton is different," Parkhearst said, pale with anger. Then suddenly, so shaken by fear of what she said, he told her a thing which he immediately realized was trivial and silly: "He has a gun, for one thing."

Bella Cratty did not go on drinking coffee immediately, but not due to anything Parkhearst had said except his pronouncing of Fenton's name. There had, of course, in their five years of marriage and in their five years of Grainger, been people with guns, and people whom he had found in streets, in parks, in holes, who had turned out to be all right, but now she suddenly felt the last outpost of safety had been reached. Their lives had stopped suddenly, and then were jerked ahead out of her control at last. She felt she was no longer *here*.

"Maybe Grainger *should* meet him," she said in a tone unlike herself, because there was no hysteria or pretending in it, just dull fear, and then she finished the coffee at the same moment her husband finished sewing the button on his coat.

Still holding his needle and thread, he advanced to her and kissed her on the forehead. "I know you hate all this," he said, like a doctor or soldier about to perform an heroic act. "I know you can't get used to all this. Maybe you aren't used to what is me."

Bella had not waited this time for the full effect of the kiss. She got up and quickly went into the front room and began looking out the window with the intensity of one who is about to fly out into space. He followed her there.

"Do you hate me completely?" Parkhearst asked, happy with the sense she had given him permission to go for Fenton.

It was nearly two o'clock, he noted, and she did not give him goodbye and the word to leave.

"Just go, dear," she said at last, and it was not the fact she had put on a martyr's expression in her voice, the voice was the only one that could come from her having chosen, as she had, the life five years before.

"I can't go when you sound like this," he complained. His voice told how much he wanted to go and that it was already past two o'clock.

Yet somehow the strength to give him up did not come to her. He had to find it in her for himself and take it from her.

"Go now, go," she said when he kissed the back of her neck.

"I will," he said, "because I know I'm only hurting you by staying."

Bella nodded.

When he was gone, she watched for him onto the street below. From above she could see him waving and throwing a kiss to her as he moved on down toward Sixty-third Street. He looked younger than Christ still, she said. A boy groom. . . . Sometimes people had half-wondered, she knew, if she was his very young mother. She stood there in that stiff height so far above him and yet felt crawling somewhere far down, like a bug in a desert, hot and sticking to ground, and possibly not even any more alive.

As necessary as Bella was to his every need for existence, his only feeling of life came when he left her, as today, for a free afternoon. And this afternoon was especially free. There was even the feeling of the happiness death might give. It was only later that life was to be so like death that the idea of dying was meaningless to him, but tonight, he remembered, he had thought of death and it was full of mysterious desirability.

It was one of those heavy days in the city when a late riser is not certain it is getting light or dark, an artificial twilight in which the sounds of the elevated trains and trucks weight darkness the more. Parkhearst hurried on down the interminable street, soon leaving the white section behind, and into the beginning of the colored district. People took no notice of him, he was no stranger to these streets, and besides he was dressed in clothes which without being too poor made him inconspicuous.

He was not looking at the street anyhow today, whose meanness and filth usually gave his soul such satisfaction. His whole mind was on Fenton. Fenton was a small-town boy, and yet all his expression and gestures and being made it right that he should live on this street, where no one really belonged or stayed very long.

It was difficult, though, to see Fenton living in a house, even in the kind of house that would be near Sixty-third Street. There must be some kind of mistake there, he thought.

He went on, pursued by the memory of Fenton's face. Was there more, he wondered out loud, in that face than poverty and a tendency to be tricky if not criminal? What were those eyes conveying, then, some meaning that was truthful and honest over and above his deceit and rottenness?

He was late. He hurried faster. The dark under the elevated made him confuse one street for another. He stopped and in his indecision looked back east toward the direction of the park where he had met Fenton: he feared Fenton had played a trick on him, for there was nothing which resembled a house on the street. He stood in front of a fallen-in building with the handwritten sign in chalk: THE COME AND SEE RESURRECTION PENTECOSTAL CHURCH. REVEREND HOSEA GULLEY, PASTOR.

Then walking on, he saw near a never-ending set of vacant

lots the house he knew must contain Fenton. It was one of those early twentieth-century houses that have survived by oversight but which look so rotten and devoured that you can't believe they were ever built but that they rotted and mushroomed into existence and that their rot was their first and last growth.

There was no number. It was a color like green and yellow. Around the premises was a fence of sharp iron, cut like spears.

He began knocking on the immense front door and then waiting as though he knew there would be no answer.

As nobody stirred, he began calling out the name of his new friend. Then he heard some faint moving around in the back and finally Fenton, looking both black and pale, appeared through the frosted glass of the inner door and stared out. His face greeted Parkhearst without either pleasure or recognition, and he advanced mechanically and irritably, as though the door had blown open and he was coming to close it.

"No wonder you had trouble finding it," Parkhearst said when Fenton unlocked the door and let him in.

"He's having a bad spell, that's why I'm in a hurry," Fenton explained.

"Who?" Parkhearst closed the door behind him.

"Claire, my brother Claire."

They went through a hallway as long as a half city block to a small room in which there was a dwarf-like cot with a large mattress clinging to it and a crippled immense chest of drawers supported by only three legs. The window was boarded up and there was almost no light coming from a dying electric bulb hung from the high ceiling.

On the bed lay a young boy dressed in overall pants and a green sweater. He looked very pale but did not act in pain.

"He says he can't walk now," Fenton observed. "Claire, can't you say *hello* to the visitor?" Fenton went over to the bed and touched Claire on the shoulder.

"He keeps asking me why we can't move on. To a real

house, I suppose," Fenton explained softly to Parkhearst. "And that worries him. There are several things that worry him," Fenton said in a bored voice.

"Look," Claire said cheerfully and with energy, pointing to the wall. There were a few bugs moving rather rapidly across the cracked calcimine. "Sit down in this chair," Fenton said and moved the chair over to Parkhearst.

"Do you really think," Fenton began on the subject that was closest to him too, "that we're *in* the right house maybe?"

Parkhearst did not speak, feeling unsure how to begin. For one thing, he was not positive that the small boy who was called Claire was not feebleminded, but the longer he looked the more he felt the boy was reasonably intelligent but probably upset by the kind of life he was leading with Fenton. He therefore did not reply to Fenton's question at once, and Fenton repeated it, almost shouting. He had gotten very much more excited since they had met in the park the evening before.

Parkhearst was noticing that Claire followed his brother with his eyes around the room with a look of both intense approval and abject dependence. It was plain that between him and nothing there was only Fenton.

"We've come to the end of our rope, I guess," Fenton said, almost forgetting that Parkhearst had not replied to his question.

"No," Parkhearst said, but Fenton hardly heard him now, talking so rapidly that his spit flew out on all sides of his mouth. He talked about their mother's funeral and how they had come to this house all because Kincaid had known them back in West Virginia and had promised them a job here. Then suddenly he picked up a book that Claire had under the bedclothes and showed it to Parkhearst as though it was both something uncommon and explanatory of their situation. The book, old and ripped, was titled *Under the Trees,* a story about logging.

"Doesn't anybody else live here?" Parkhearst inquired at last.

"We haven't heard nobody," Fenton replied. "There's so

many bugs it isn't surprising everybody left, if they was here," he went on. "But Claire says there is," he looked in the direction of his brother. "Claire feels there is people here."

"I hear them all the time," Claire said.

"No, there is nobody here," Parkhearst assured both of them. "This is a vacant house and you must have made a mistake when you came in here. Or your friend Kincaid played a joke on you," he finished, seeing at once by their expression he should not have added this last sentence.

"Anyhow," Parkhearst continued awkwardly while Fenton stared at him with his strange eyes, "it's no place for you, especially with Claire sick. I think I have a plan for you, though," Parkhearst said, as though thinking through a delicate problem.

Fenton walked over very close to him as though Parkhearst were about to hand him a written paper which would explain everything and tell him and Claire what to do in regard to the entire future.

"I think Grainger will give you the help you need," he explained. He had forgotten that Fenton knew nothing about her.

Fenton turned away and looked out the boarded window. Evidently he had expected some immediate help, and Parkhearst had only spoken of a name like a matchbox, Grainger, adding later that was the last name of a wealthy woman that nobody ever called by her first name. This was discouraging because of course Fenton knew he could never do anything to please anybody with such a name.

"Grainger will like you," Parkhearst went on doggedly, knowing he was not moving Fenton at all.

"You would be interested in going to her mansion at least," he said.

Claire, following Fenton's example, showed likewise no interest in the "great woman."

"If you promise me you will go with me to the house of the 'great woman,'" Parkhearst said (using that phrase preciously and purposely just as he had mentioned Grainger without explaining who she was or that she was a woman), "I assure you we'll be able to help you between us. Really help."

He had not finished this speech when he remembered what Bella had told him about his handing over Fenton to Grainger.

Fenton turned now from the boarded window and faced him. His whole appearance had grown surprisingly ominous as though Parkhearst had destroyed some great promise and hope.

"We don't have no choice," Fenton said, his words more gentle than his expression, and he looked at Claire, although he addressed his words to no one.

"I don't know what I'll do in the house of a greatwoman," Fenton went on. "Why do you call her *great?*"

"Oh I don't know," Parkhearst replied airily. "Of course she isn't, really. But is anybody? Was anybody ever?"

"I never did hear anybody called that," Fenton said. He looked at Claire as though he might have heard someone called that.

"Why is she great?" he wondered aloud again.

Parkhearst felt flustered despite his years of looking and collecting the "material" and talking with the most intractable of persons.

"If you come tomorrow, I feel you'll understand," Parkhearst told him, getting up. "I don't see why you act like this when you're in trouble." Then: "Where's your gun," he said irritably.

Fenton put his hand quickly to his pocket. "Fuck you," he said, feeling nothing there.

"Don't think I can get offended," Parkhearst said. "Neither your talk nor your acts. You just seemed a bit young to have any gun."

"Young?" Fenton asked, as though this had identified his age at last. His face flushed and for the first time Parkhearst noticed that there was a scar across his lip and chin.

"Please come, Fenton, when we want to help you," he said, almost as soft as some sort of prayer.

"I don't like to go in big houses. You said she was rich, too. Claire and me don't have the clothes for it. . . . Say, are you trying to make us a show for somebody?" Fenton asked, as though he had begun to understand Parkhearst. His face went no particular color as this new thought took hold of him. "Or use us? You're not trying to *use* us, are you?"

When he asked that last question, Parkhearst felt vaguely a kind of invisible knife cut through the air at him. He could not follow the sources of Fenton's knowledge. At times the boy talked dully, oafish, and again he showed complete and intuitive knowledge of the way things were and had to be.

"I want to help you," Parkhearst finally said in a womanish hurt voice.

"Why?" Fenton said in an impersonal anger. Then quickly the fight in him collapsed. He sat down on the cheap kitchen chair occupied a moment before by Parkhearst Cratty.

"All right, then, I'll come for your sake. But Claire has to stay here."

"All right, then, Fenton. I'll be here for you."

They argued a little about the hour.

Fenton did not look at Parkhearst as he said goodbye, but Claire waved to him as though seated in a moving vehicle, his head constantly turning to keep sight of the visitor.

"Who is that, Fenton?" Claire asked as soon as his brother had returned from closing the front door.

"He's a man who writes things about people," Fenton said. "He wants me to tell him things so he can write about me."

Fenton looked up at the high sick ceiling; the thought of the man writing or listening to him in order to write of him was too odd ever to be understood.

"Like you write in your little note papers?"

"No," Fenton answered, and turned to look at Claire. "I only put things down there to clear up in me what we are going to do next. Understand?"

"Why can't I see them, then, Fenton?"

"Because you can't, hear?"

"I want to read your little note papers!"

Fenton began to slap Claire, rather gently at first, and then with more force. "Don't mention it again," he said, hitting him again. "Hear?"

Claire's weeping both hurt Fenton deeply and gave him a kind of pleasure, as though in the hitting the intense burden of Claire was being lightened a little.

He had written once in the "note papers" a thought which had caused him great puzzlement. This thought was that just as he had wished Mama dead, so that he felt the agent of her death, so now he wanted Claire to be dead, and despite the fact that the only two people in the world he had loved were Mama and Claire.

Then he had to realize that the thing which stung him most about Claire when they were with strangers was his brother's not being quite right and that when he had been with the writer he had not felt this pain. There was this about the man who had turned up in the park, you did not feel any pain about telling him things, things almost as awful as those he had put down in the note papers.

"Why is it?" Fenton asked, raising his voice as though addressing a large group of people, "when I am so young I am so pissed-off feeble and low?"

Claire shook his head as he was accustomed to when Fenton put these questions to him. He had never answered any of them, and yet Fenton asked more and more of them when he knew that Claire did not know the answers.

Then Claire, seeing his chance, watching his brother narrowly, said, without any preparation: "I heard God again in the night."

Fenton tried to quiet himself in the tall room. It was always much easier to calm yourself outdoors or in a farmhouse, but in a small but high room like this when sorrow is heard it is hard to be quiet and calm. Fenton nevertheless made his voice cool as he said, "Claire, what did I tell you about talking like that?"

"I did." Claire began to cry a little.

"Are you going to quit talking like that or ain't you?"

Fenton said, the anger welling up in him stronger than any coolness he had put into his voice.

"Don't hit me when I tell you, Fenton," Claire cried on. "Don't you want to know I hear Him?"

Fenton's hands loosened slightly. He felt cramps in his insides.

"I told you those was dreams," Fenton said.

"They ain't! I hear it all day when I don't dream. . . ."

"Maybe somebody lives here, that's all." Fenton waited as though to convince himself. "I could forgive you if you dreamed about Mama and she come running to you to say comforting things to you. But you always talk about God. And I strongly doubt. . . ."

"Don't say it again, Fenton, don't say it again!" Claire sat up in bed.

". . . not only strongly doubt but know He's not real. . . ."

Claire let out a strange little cry when he heard the blasphemy and fell back on the bed. Claire fell so awkwardly it made Fenton laugh.

After this, Fenton felt the cramps again and he knew he must go out and get a drink. Yet because neither of them had had anything to eat since morning he feared that if he began drinking now he would not remember to get Claire anything to eat.

He began to rub Claire's temples gently. If only they were safe from trouble he would always be kind to Claire, but trouble always made him mean.

"It's so crappy late out!" he began again, moving away from Claire. "Why does it have to feel so late out everywhere?" This was one of the things which he had written on the note papers so he wouldn't feel so burned up and dizzy. "Even the writer says I am so young," Fenton muttered on, "yet why do I feel I only got two minutes more to do with?"

"It's late, all right," Claire said, still weeping some, but with a happy look on his face now. The small boy had gotten up out of the bed and was walking over to where Fenton now stood near the window.

"You heard me tell you to stay in bed, didn't you. . . . Didn't you hear, crapface?"

The boy paused there in the middle of the room, his mouth open disgustingly. But he had already turned his mind away from Claire. He whirled out of the room and was gone.

"He forgot his gun," Claire said looking out into the awful night of the hall. "He don't know how to use it anyhow," he finished and went back to the little bed.

Everything had changed so much since he had been Mama's son, nothing as little as forgetting a gun was remarkable.

"He's gone, he's gone," Claire kept repeating to himself. "Fenton's gone," he repeated on and on until he had fallen asleep again.

Fenton had soon found the taverns where his existence aroused no particular interest or comment. People occasionally noticed his accent or his haircut, but generally they ignored him. There was such an endless row of taverns and the street itself was so endless he could always choose a different tavern for each day and each drink. In the end he went to the places that served both colored and white. It would have been unreal of him to Mama had she known, but this kind of tavern made him feel the easiest, perhaps it was more like home.

He knew now (he began all over again) that Kincaid was not coming to find them in the house. And as he went on with his drink he knew that nobody was ever coming to the house because it was the "latest" time in his life and maybe the "latest" in the world.

"Then where will we end up?" he said quickly, aloud. He felt that some of the customers must have looked at him, but when he said nothing more nobody came over to him or said anything. He got out a pencil stub and wrote something on the note papers.

"Things don't go anywhere in our lives," he wrote. "Sometimes somebody like Mama dies and the whole world stops or begins to move backwards, but nothing happens to us, even her dying don't get us anywhere except maybe back. Yet you have to go on waiting, it's the one thing nobody lets up on you for. Like now we're doing for Kincaid and for what?"

Someone had left a newspaper on the bar, open to the want ad section. Fenton began reading these incomprehensible notifications of jobs. Someone once had told him, perhaps Kincaid, that nobody was ever hired this way, they were only put in there because the employers had to do it, and actually, this somebody had told him, they were really all hired to begin with, probably when you read about them.

Fenton remembered again that he did not know how to do anything. He had no skills, no knowledge. That was why the big old house with tall rooms was getting more ghosty for him, it was so much like the way he was inside himself, the house didn't work at all, and he was all stopped inside himself too just like the house. That was why it was like a trap, he said.

As he drank a little more he decided he must move on to another drinking place because the bartender had begun to watch him write in the note papers too much and it scared him.

He went on in search of the next place, but before he reached it he saw the ALL NIGHT THEATER, a movie house that never closed. Instead of choosing another drinking place, he decided to choose this, for the price of admission was nearly the same as that of a beer.

There was the same sad smell inside, a faint stink from old men and a few boys who had been out in the open, standing or lying on the pavement during part of the night. The seats did not act as though they were required to hold you off the floor. Faces twisted around to look at you, or somebody's hand sometimes came out of the dark and touched you as though to determine whether you were flesh or not.

Fenton did not notice or care about any of these things.

He scarcely looked at the picture, and half of the audience
must have been sleeping or looking at the floor, at nothing.

He did not know what time he woke up in the ALL NIGHT
THEATER. The audience had thinned out a little. The screen
showed a horse and a man crossing a desert, walking as
though they were not going to go much longer if they didn't
find some water or perhaps just a cool place to stop.

It was then that Fenton remembered Parkhearst Cratty
and the greatwoman. For the first time he began to think
about them as having some slight meaning, some relationship to himself. That is, they knew about him, and he existed
for them. He had gotten as far down in the dumps as possible and still be alive, and now he began to come up a little
out of where he was and to think about what Parkhearst
Cratty was jawing about.

The thought that anybody called the greatwoman should
want to see him struck him suddenly as so funny that he
laughed out loud. Then he stopped and looked around him,
but nobody was looking at him. The dead world of the
shadows on the screen seemed to look at him just then more
than the men around him.

Fenton sat a little while longer in the ALL NIGHT THEA-
TER, holding his notebook down to a little of the light at
the end of the aisle so that he might write down some more
of what he was thinking. Then having written a little more,
he gazed at the want ads again that he had carried along
with him and saw the words MEN MEN MEN under the difficult light.

Finally he got hungry and walked out into the gray street.
It was six o'clock in the morning and it would be a long day
until night came and brought Parkhearst Cratty and his
plans.

Fenton went into a cafe called CHECKER where some colored men were drinking orange pop. He ordered a cup of
black coffee, and then drinking that, he ordered another.
Then he ordered some rolls and ate part of those. After that

he ordered some coffee and rolls to take out, and started home to Claire.

Just before getting to the house, he went back to a small tavern he had missed before and had a whiskey.

It was funny, he reflected, that before coming here to the city with its parks and vacant houses he had almost never had a drink, and now he had it, quite a bit.

Claire stared at him, his face red and swollen from bites. Fenton had him get up and they began going through the mattress looking for the bugs.

"Where was you?" Claire wanted to know.

"*All Night Movie.*"

This answer perfectly satisfied Claire.

"Why don't you drink the coffee I brought you and eat those rolls?"

"I ain't hungry, Fenton."

"Drink the coffee like I tell you."

Fenton kept looking at the mattress. "I don't see any of the bastards," he said. "They must be inside the fucking mattress."

"Fenton," Claire soothed him. "I didn't dream last night at all or hear anything."

"So?" Fenton spoke crossly. He set the mattress down and then lazily began eating the rolls Claire had not touched.

"I didn't even feel the bugs biting," Claire said, pushing his face close to Fenton to show him, but his voice trailed off as he saw Fenton's heavy lack of interest in what he had done and thought.

Then all at once Fenton saw his brother's face, which was almost disfigured from the bites. Fenton's own fear and amazement communicated themselves frightfully to Claire.

"You look Christ awful," Fenton cried.

"Don't scare me now, Fenton," Claire began to whimper.

"I don't aim to scare you," Fenton said with growing irritability. "Have you been crying over Mama or is your face just swelled from bugs?"

"I don't know," Claire said, and he quit whimpering.

There was something terribly old and pinched now in Claire's small face.

Fenton took him by the hands and looked at his face closer.

"Ain't you well or what?" he said, the irritation coming and going in his voice, but finally yielding to a kind of sadness. "Why don't you tell me what is bothering you?" he went on.

He put his mouth on the top of Claire's head, and half-opened his lips noticing the funny little boy smell of his hair.

"You can tell me if you have been thinking about God now, if you want to, Claire."

"I ain't been thinking about Him," he said.

"Well," Fenton said, "you can if you want to. It don't matter anyhow."

"I don't think about Him," Claire said, as if from far off.

"I think I'll go to bed now," Fenton complained, looking at the cruelly narrow cot. "You slept some, didn't you, Claire."

"Yes," Claire said, a tired sad duty in his voice.

"Can I walk around outdoors now?" Claire asked, watching Fenton's oblivious brooding face.

"Yes," Fenton replied slowly. "I guess it's all right if the house is open when it's daylight. Nobody ain't coming in anyhow.

"Don't get lost, though," Fenton went on quietly as Claire began to go out.

"What's going on inside the little thing's mind?" Fenton said to himself. He loosened his heavy belt and lay down on the cot.

Fenton thought about how Claire thought about Mama. He himself thought a lot about her when actually he wasn't very aware even that he was thinking about her. Maybe he thought about her all the time and didn't even know it. But he never thought she was waiting for him on some distant star as Claire did.

"Claire," he said, beginning to sleep, "why is it one of us

is even weaker than the other. When West Virginia was tough why did we come clear over here? . . ."

Even though it was day it was night really, always, in this city and night like night in caves here in the house.

Fenton lay thinking of the long time before Parkhearst Cratty would come. He thought of Parkhearst as a kind of magicman who would show different magic tricks to him, but he knew not one would take on him.

"No damn one," he said, becoming asleep.

It was even darker somehow when he awoke, and he knew at once that Parkhearst Cratty was there, shaking him.

"Wake up, West Virginia," Parkhearst was saying.

Fenton's mouth moved as though to let out laughter but none came, as though there were no more sound at all in him now.

"She waiting for us," Parkhearst said.

Fenton said quiet obscene words and Parkhearst waited a little longer, situated as though nowhere in the dark.

"Where's Claire?" Parkhearst wondered vaguely.

"Ain't he here?" Fenton said.

"No," Parkhearst said, a kind of uneasiness growing in him again.

"Claire went out, but he'll be back," Fenton said, remembering.

Then when Parkhearst did not say anything in reply, Fenton said rather angrily: "I said he'd be back."

"Well, let's go, then," Parkhearst said lightly. "She gets cross when people are late," he explained.

Fenton held on to his belt as though that were what was to lift him out of bed, then got up, and turned on the light.

"You're dressed up!" He looked at Parkhearst and then down at himself.

They suddenly were both looking at Fenton's shoes, as though they couldn't help it, and as they both saw they were so miserable and ridiculous, they had to look at them objectively as horrors.

"I'm not really dressed up," Parkhearst said weakly, feel-

ing the weakness come over him again which he always felt
in Fenton's presence. "But come on, Fenton," he said, thinking of the boy's toes slightly coming through the shoes.
"She's sent a taxi for us, and it's waiting."

Fenton threw a look back at the room. "So long, house,"
he said, and he actually waved at the room, Parkhearst
noted.

They said almost nothing on the way to the greatwoman's
house. Fenton kept his head down as though he were pray-
ing or sick in his stomach. He did not look out even when
Parkhearst pointed out things that might have had a personal interest to him: the sight of the park where they had
met, or the police station.

At last the taxi came to the house. Fenton hesitated, as
though he might not get out after all. "Is this a mansion?"
he asked.

Parkhearst looked at him closely. Fenton's words always
had an ambiguousness about them, but there could be no
ambiguousness when you studied his face: he meant just
what he said, and perhaps that made the words odd.

They could hear the music from the outside.

"That is the new music the musicians are playing," Parkhearst explained. "Grainger doesn't really listen to it, but
she has the musicians come because there is nothing else
left to do, and it draws her circle of people to her."

Without knocking, they entered what was the most immense room Fenton had ever seen. It was almost as dark,
however, as the house where he and Claire had been waiting, and the ceiling was no taller. There were a number of
people sitting in corners except for one large corner of the
room where some colored musicians were playing.

At the far end of the room on a slightly raised little platform, in a mammoth chair, Grainger, the greatwoman, sat,
or rather hung over one side of the arm.

"My God, we're late after all," Parkhearst exclaimed.
"She's too drunk to know us, I'm afraid."

Fenton began to feel a little easier once he was inside the
mansion. No one had paid him the least attention. It was, in

fact, he saw with relief, not unlike the ALL NIGHT THEATER, for whatever the people were doing here in the mansion, they were paying absolutely no attention to him or Parkhearst or perhaps to anything. Yet they must have seen him, for he could see their heads move and hear their voices as they talked softly among themselves. And again like the ALL NIGHT THEATER, they were about half colored and half white.

Parkhearst was not doing anything as Fenton's attention returned slowly to him. They were in the middle of the great room, and his guide merely stood there watching Grainger. Finally, as though after a struggle with himself, he took Fenton's hand angrily and said, "Come over here, we have to go through with this."

They went up to the woman in the chair. She was possibly forty and her face was still beautiful although her mouth was slightly twisted and her throat was creased now and fat. Her eyes, although not focused on the two young men who were standing in front of her, were extremely beautiful and would have been intelligent had they not been so vacant. When Parkhearst would address her, she would immediately turn her head in the other direction.

"Grainger, I have brought Fenton Riddleway here to see you, just as you told me to do."

She did not say a word, although Parkhearst knew that she had heard him.

"She's angry," Parkhearst said, like a radio commentator assigned to a historical event which is hopelessly delayed. He sighed as though he could no longer breathe in this atmosphere.

"Everything is getting to be more difficult than anything is really worth," he pronounced.

"Please look at Fenton at least and we will leave then," he addressed Grainger.

Suddenly the greatwoman laughed and took Parkhearst's hands in her very small ones. Parkhearst gave a sound expressing relief, though his face did not lose the agonized look it had assumed the moment he recognized she was drunk.

"Are you going to be good now?" he inquired in a calmer voice.

She laughed cheerfully, like a young girl.

Fenton thought that she looked beautiful at that moment and he looked at her dress which was the kind he felt a princess in old books might have worn; it was so frighteningly white and soft and there was so much of it, it seemed to fill the little platform on which they were now all standing.

Then as Grainger's eyes moved away from Parkhearst they settled slowly and gloomily upon Fenton. They immediately expressed hostility or a kind of sullen anger. Then looking away from both of them, she picked up a drink she had placed on the floor by the chair and took a swallow so deep that she seemed to be talking to someone in the end of the glass.

"Haven't you had enough, tonight?" Parkhearst said gently. "It's that Holland stuff, too, and you promised me you wouldn't ever take that again."

"Cut that, Parkhearst, cut that," she said suddenly. "You've been boring me for a year now and I'm not listening to any more."

This was said in a tone that was tough and which was hard to connect with the soft long dress and the fine eyes.

"Well, give us something to drink then," Parkhearst retorted. "If you're sobered up enough now to be ugly, you can remember your duties as the hostess."

Grainger pointed contemptuously to a table where there were bottles and glasses. Then her gaze returned to Fenton, and the same hostility and suspicion crossed her face.

"Who is this?" she said, putting her hand on his face as one might touch what is perhaps a door in a dark house.

Fenton could only stand there, allowing her hand to be on him and looking down at her dress. He found that her gaze and touch were not unlike the soft glances that the characters on the screen of the ALL NIGHT THEATER had

given him last night, looking down while he wrote what he
had to write in the note papers.

His meekness and his quiet partially calmed the anger of
her expression.

"Don't you like Fenton, Grainger?" Parkhearst said, returning with drinks for himself and Fenton.

"Why didn't you fill mine up too?" she said, turning bitterly to Parkhearst.

"Because you've had enough. And I'm taking the drink
you now have away from you," he said, reaching for her
glass.

Grainger smiled at this and put the glass into his hand.

"Now, Grainger, wake up, clear awake, and look at this
boy I brought to meet you. You're always wanting to meet
new people and then when I bring them to you, you get
into a state like this and don't even know me when I come
in. This is Fenton Riddleway."

"I saw him," the greatwoman said. She kept eyeing her
drink, which Parkhearst had set on the table near her.

"How do you feel about the musicians tonight?" she inquired suddenly.

"I've heard them when they sounded more advanced,"
Parkhearst said. "But I wasn't listening to them at all. . . .
Anyhow, the new music sounds only like its name to me
now. It was only new that first night."

"So you brought Fenton to see me," she said, looking now
for the first time without hostility at the guest.

Fenton had finished half his drink and both he and Parkhearst had sat down on the floor at the feet of Grainger.

She began to grow quiet now that they were both with
her and both drinking. *If everything,* she had said once a
long time ago, *could be a garden with the ones you always
want and with drinking forever and ever.*

"Do you think you're going to like Fenton?" Parkhearst
began again.

"If you want me to, I guess I can," Grainger answered.
She looked at her drink on the table but then evidently gave
up the struggle to have it.

"He looks a little like Russell," Grainger said without any preparation for such a statement.

The remark made Parkhearst go a little white because Russell had been everything. Russell had been her first husband, the one who when he died, people said, made her go off the deep end and drink for ten years, to end up the way she was now.

"Only he's *not*," Grainger added. But she added this only because she saw Parkhearst change color. "Nobody could quite be Russell again," she said.

When Parkhearst did not reply, holding his face in a wounded quivering expression, the great woman flared up. "I said, could they, Parkhearst?"

"Just nobody could resemble Russell," Parkhearst said.

"Well, all right, then, why didn't you say that before?" she scolded.

She ignored his contemptuous silence and acted happy. "Russell was the last of any men that there were," she began, turning to Fenton. "He didn't love me, of course, but I couldn't live without him, every five minutes having to touch him or see him coming somewhere near me. . . ."

"That isn't true, Grainger, and you know it. Why do you lie to this boy, making out that Russell wasn't crazy about you? . . ." Then he stopped as he realized how deadly it was going to be ever to get started on Russell all over again.

"Upstairs," he wanted to tell Fenton, "there was that memorial room to him everybody has heard about somewhere but never seen, a shrine to his being, with hundreds of immense photographs, mementos, clothes, and everywhere fresh flowers every day. Grainger herself never went into the shrine, and Negro women kept the flowers fresh and the holy places dusted."

"Crazy . . . about *me?*" Grainger shot at him and a look of unparalleled meanness came over her face, so that she resembled at that moment a stuffed carnivore he had once seen in a museum. "Nobody was ever crazy about me. The only reason anybody's here now is I have more money than anybody else in town to slake them."

Parkhearst looked up at the word *slake;* he could not ever remember hearing her use it before.

"Look at them!" she shouted, pointing to the dim figures in the next room. "Nobody was ever crazy about me."

Both Fenton and Parkhearst gazed back at the people in the next room as though to see them, in the greatwoman's word, being *slaked.*

Then her anger subsided, and she gave Fenton a brief oversweet smile. Growing a bit more serious and commanding, she said: "Come over here, Fenton Riddleway."

Parkhearst gave a severe nod with his head for Fenton to go to her.

Fenton had hardly gotten to her chair when she reached out and took his hand in hers and held it for a moment. She laughed quietly, kissed his hand in so strange a manner that the action had no easy meaning, and then released it.

Parkhearst had risen meanwhile and poured himself and Fenton another shot of gin.

"You think I should have more?" Fenton said in a way that recalled Claire.

"Well naturally, yes," Parkhearst said, and trembled with nervousness. The comparison of Fenton with Russell did not augur too well. He felt a kind of throbbing jealousy as well as fear. It was the biggest compliment that Grainger had ever given to any of the men he had brought to her house. He felt suddenly that he had given Grainger too much in giving her Fenton and Fenton too much in giving him to her.

Parkhearst realized with a suddenness which resembled a break in his reason that he needed both Grainger and Fenton acutely, and that if he lost them to each other, he would not survive this time at all.

In the midst of his anguish, his eye fell upon both of them coolly, almost as though he had not seen either of them before. It was outrageous, rather sad, and frightening all at once; not so much because she had a dress that was too fine for royalty and Fenton looked somehow seedier than any living bum, but because something about the way they were themselves, both together and apart, made them seem more real and less real than anybody living he had ever known.

"He's Russell!" Grainger said finally, without any particular emphasis.

"No, he's not," Parkhearst replied firmly but with the anger beginning to come to make his words shake in his mouth.

"He is," she said, louder.

"No, Grainger, you know these things don't happen twice. Nothing does."

"Just for tonight he is," Grainger replied, staring at Fenton.

"Not even for tonight. He just isn't Russell, Grainger. Look again."

"I'm going to have a drink now," she threatened him. Half to her own surprise she saw Parkhearst make no attempt to prevent her. She walked rigidly, balancing herself with outstretched hands, over to the little table, filled her glass with a tremendous drain of the bottle, and drank half the draught at once.

"Grainger!" Parkhearst was frightened, forgetting he had permitted her to get up at all.

"All right, he isn't Russell, then. Or he is Russell. What difference! He can stay here, though. . . . Does he need anything?"

The drink, Parkhearst thought, perhaps has sobered her.

She sat down in the great chair and began staring at Fenton again. Then his clothes at last caught her attention.

"Would you accept a suit?" she began. "One of Russell's suits," the greatwoman said, turning her face away from Parkhearst as though to shield her words from him and give them only to Fenton.

Fenton in turn looked at Parkhearst for a clue, and Parkhearst could only look down, knowing that Fenton would never understand the generosity that was being offered, the giving away of the clothes of the dead young Christ.

"Why don't you go upstairs?" She turned in rage now on

Parkhearst. "Why don't you go upstairs with your jealous eyes and give him one of Russell's suits?"

As her face lay back in the chair, burning with rage, Parkhearst saw how mistaken he had been about her ever being sobered up by a drink. At that very moment the musicians stopped playing the new music for the evening, the hostess fell over, slightly, upsetting her drink, and then with almost no noise slipped to the floor and lay perfectly still, her drinking glass near her hand, without even a goodnight, lying there, as Parkhearst observed, looking a little too much like Hamlet's mother.

"We may as well go to my house now," Parkhearst said, after they had got one of Russell's suits on Fenton.

"What shall we do with my old clothes?" Fenton wondered, looking at them with almost as much wonder now as other people had.

Parkhearst hesitated. "We'll take them," he said. "This way."

They went downstairs away from the "shrine" and walked past the room where Grainger was lying on an immense silver bed with red coverings. She had her clothes still on. Parkhearst hesitated near the bed.

"I suppose we should say goodnight to her, in case she's conscious."

They both stood there in dead silence while Parkhearst tried to make up his mind.

"Grainger!" he called. Then he suddenly laughed as he saw the serious expression on Fenton's face.

"She's just out, she won't be up and around for God knows when," Parkhearst explained in his bored tone. "When she gets in these states she lies till she gets up or until they find her. I will have to come over here tomorrow and see how things are. . . ."

Then for the first time since they had been in the "shrine," Parkhearst gave Fenton a more critical look. Russell's suit had been a close enough fit all right; the greatwoman had not been too drunk to understand the relative sizes of the two men, although the trousers were a bit too short in the legs. The suit made a tremendous change, of course, and yet the boy who looked out from this absurdly rich cloth seemed to belong in it, despite the expression of pain mingled with rage imprinted on his mouth. He was a Russell of some kind in the clothes.

Parkhearst gave him a last look directly in the eye.

"My wife will be asleep," Parkhearst told him in a rather cross voice, "but if we speak low, she won't hear us. Anyhow we have to have coffee."

Parkhearst's home was an apartment on the fifth floor of a building that leaned forward slightly as if it would bend down to the street.

"I forgot you had a wife," Fenton remarked, looking at him vaguely. "I never thought of you as married."

"A lot of people can't," Parkhearst admitted. "I suppose it's because I never had a job, never worked."

Parkhearst observed with some satisfaction that this made no impression on Fenton. He believed that if he had said he had murdered someone, for instance, Fenton would have accepted this statement with the same indifferent air.

That, as Parkhearst was beginning to see more and more, was the main thing about Fenton, his being able to accept nearly anything. For one so young it was unusual. He accepted the immense dreariness of things as though there were no other possibility in the shape of things.

A cat came out of the door as they entered the apartment. They proceeded down a long hallway to a kitchen.

"I'll throw your old clothes on this bench," Parkhearst said. Then he began to fumble with the coffee can.

Before he began to measure out the coffee he stopped as though he thought somebody was calling to him from the front of the apartment. Then when he did not hear his wife's voice, he began to boil the water for the coffee.

Fenton put his head down on the tiny kitchen table before which he sat.

"Don't go to sleep, Fenton. You can't spend the night

here. My wife would die. . . . And Claire must be worrying about you."

"Not Claire," Fenton mumbled. "I thought I told you that we sleep at different times, on account of the bed being so small, and the bugs and all. There are hundreds of bugs." He began to think of the anguish they cause. "They crawl up and down, sometimes they go fast, and you can never find them when they bite. They stink like old woodsheds."

"Bugs are awful," Parkhearst agreed. "But," he went on, "about Claire. He may not miss you, but is he safe alone?"

"I'm too sick to care," Fenton said, his head on the table now.

"How are you sick?" Parkhearst wondered.

"Inside," Fenton replied, still not taking his head off the table and talking into the wood like a colored fortune teller Parkhearst had once known. "Where your soul's supposed to be," he spoke again.

Parkhearst stared at him.

"If there was a God," Fenton said quickly, raising his head from the table and giving Parkhearst an accusing look, "none of this would happen."

"Oh, it might, Fenton," Parkhearst answered. "You don't think He's all-powerful, do you?"

"Do you believe in Him?" Fenton wondered.

"I don't believe but I'm always thinking about it somehow."

"Do you believe Claire is dying?" Fenton said quickly.

"No," Parkhearst answered.

"I keep seeing him dead," Fenton said.

Parkhearst handed Fenton a cup of coffee. Then he sat down, facing Fenton. They both drank their coffee without continuing the discussion. Parkhearst from time to time would listen intently to see if Bella called to him, but there was no sound, no matter how many times he stopped to listen.

"I want to be dead like a bug," Fenton said and lay his head down on the table again.

"Drink all of that coffee and then I'll get you some more."

Parkhearst watched the thick hair come loose from the head and creep over the table's edge like a strange unfolding plant.

"Is this the first time you've ever been drunk?" Parkhearst's voice came from far away.

"I drink nearly all the time," Fenton said, and some coffee began to trickle down the side of his mouth. "When I go home," he went on, "Claire will be dead. I will be happy, like a great load has been taken off my neck, and then I will probably fly into a thousand pieces and disappear. I am sick of him just the same, dead or alive. He makes it too hard for me, just like Mama did. Both him and her talked too much about God and how we would all meet at His Throne on the Final Day. . . . Do you disbelieve in the Throne too?" he looked up at Parkhearst.

The writer watched him, silent.

Fenton was watching him also, almost as though from behind his thick disheveled hair.

"Keep drinking the coffee," Parkhearst said in a soft voice. He felt weak lest Bella should get up and see this. Then he began to feel irritated seeing Fenton in Russell's clothing.

"Grainger is an idiot," Parkhearst said.

"Are you in love with me too?" Fenton asked Parkhearst, but the writer merely sat there drinking, as though he had not heard.

Fenton did not say any more for a long time. Perhaps ten minutes passed this way in the silence of the city night; that is a silence in which although one cannot really say *this is a sound I am hearing now,* many little contractions and movements like the springs of a poorly constructed machine make one feel that something will break with a sudden crash and perhaps destroy everyone.

Fenton knocked his cup off the table and it broke evenly in two at Parkhearst's feet.

"What did you think of the *church* Grainger has for Russell?" Parkhearst said, getting up for another cup.

He poured coffee into the cup and handed it to his friend. "Drink this."

Fenton half sat up and gulped down some more of the coffee.

"Did you hear what I asked about her *church* for him?" Parkhearst began again.

"Why did she love Russell so?" Fenton asked, and the whites of his eyes suddenly extinguished his pupils so that he looked like a statue.

"He was nothing," Parkhearst said. "Rather beautiful. His mind worked all right, I guess. He was nothing. He had so little personality he looked all right in all kinds of clothes. I think he had millions of life insurance policies. He was a blank except for one thing. He loved Grainger. I think maybe he was the one started calling her by her last name, and now nobody calls her by her first. Grainger didn't love him, but he told her he loved her every ten minutes. It was funny, I could never figure it out, why he loved her. I used to stare at him to try to understand who he was. I think I know who Grainger is, but not Russell. Then he died in his car one night. Nobody knows what from. They said his heart. And he had all these life insurance policies. He was rich though before, owned factories and mines and patents and things. After that Grainger never had to think about work. But I think she's spent nearly all she has. When she has spent the last of it she will have to die too. . . ."

Parkhearst's voice ended with a little sound like an old phonograph record stopping but still running. He had not given the speech for any reason except the pleasure he took in telling it. "The way they find him in the car is so beautiful. He had been out drinking all night, and of course he and Grainger together. He said goodbye to her from that car he had from Italy, and she went dragging into her bedroom, not very much like Shakespeare but like the girl in Shakespeare they threw kisses into and out of the balcony, and then Grainger fell down dead drunk on her bed, and Russell still sat out there in the Italian car, trying to call somebody because he suddenly, I suppose, felt sick; the coroner said he had felt sick, Russell had opened his vest, and had blown the horn that only sounded like a small

chime (the neighbors told about that), and the next morning there he sat in the sun under her house, dead as time.
Grainger never mentioned how he died to anybody we
know. She doesn't even drink any more than she did then,
but there's something different about her, I guess, because
after he died she could never change but always had to go
on acting herself."

"The *church*," Parkhearst began again, getting up and
looking out into the black windows. "What do you think of
the *church?*"

"All those photographs of rich people?" Fenton said.

"Yes," Parkhearst nodded seriously. "And those fake poses
of her. She knows she is not the woman in those photos, of
course, because she wasn't the woman in her own mind
Russell said she was."

"Grainger knows the truth about herself," Parkhearst continued, "but it only makes things more impossible for her.
And it's really only money that keeps her alive, and it's
going, nearly gone."

"You make me sicker than I was," Fenton said suddenly.
"Why do you find out all these things about people when
they are so sad?"

"I don't know," Parkhearst said softly.

"How do you know all these things?" Fenton said almost
desperately. "Do you know about me like that too?" He lay
his head down on the table and didn't wait for Parkhearst's
answer.

Parkhearst said nothing.

Then Fenton got up. "I got to go back."

"Where?" Parkhearst was curious and anxious.

"The ALL NIGHT THEATER."

"Why don't you tell me about the ALL NIGHT THEATER
some time?" Parkhearst asked.

"There ain't nothing to tell. It's what it says, it goes on all
night."

"It's like the park then." Parkhearst had a very quiet voice.

Fenton did not say anything, drinking his coffee from the
saucer.

"It's morning," Parkhearst announced more cheerfully. "You can't tell when it's morning in a city place," Fenton said.

"You told me that before," Parkhearst said, "but that is only because you're Fenton that you think that."

The next day, Parkhearst woke up with a headache and the feeling of rags on his tongue. He knew without looking that Bella had gone to work.

He thought of the greatwoman almost at once and before he thought of Fenton. He would have to go to see her at once. She would still be unconscious, the wreck of her evening undisturbed yet by the maids.

His face looked old and thin and brown in the looking glass, old for twenty-nine. Yet how old did that look, except older than Fenton Riddleway?

Then all the part about Grainger and Russell and Russell's resembling Fenton or Fenton's resembling Russell came back.

"I suppose in Grainger's mind," he said aloud to himself, "she thinks she has already taken him over, away from me. Of course it's true, I've given her everybody she ever had."

He had forgotten Russell only because he had never counted him.

A not unusual thing was to smell flowers in front of Grainger's house. Today their perfume was stronger than usual. There was the silence of early day inside of the house, but there was evidence that the maids had come and gone, and noiselessly enough to have left her still sleeping in the front parlor.

The flowers, he noticed, were only roses. Grainger lay on the divan, a queer frayed silk coverlet over her. A tiny smile covered her mouth.

"Is the Queen of Hell conscious?" he said in a voice that struggled with both eagerness and contempt.

He began kissing her on the eyelids. "Open those big blue eyes."

Grainger opened her eyes, her smile vanished, and the accusing frown returned. "You cheap son of a bitch," she said groggily. "You never loved Russell. You never even would talk about him. You didn't understand his greatness. His going never even moved you."

"Shall I make you some breakfast now?" he wondered.

"You hated Russell."

He kissed her fingers.

"You make me sick. You cheap son of a bitch," she said, looking at him kiss her fingers. "I ought to hate you. Russell hated you. He said you were lacking in the fundamental. That boy you dragged here last night, what's his name? . . ."

Parkhearst told her.

". . . he hates you too. You know so damn much. You sit around seeing things so that you can write them down in a hundred years."

Parkhearst went on holding her fingers as though he were giving her the energy to go on.

He looked longingly at some hot coffee on a nearby table, then letting her hands fall slowly, he got up and went over to the table and poured himself a cup and began sipping.

"And why do we all love you, though, when you stink with cheapness, dishonor, not having probably one human hair on your body. Maybe I love you the most. . . ."

"Don't forget my wife," he said, and the expression *my wife* as he said it had a different quality than that of any other husband who had ever said the words.

"*Your wife!*" she said, getting up and staring at him. "She owns you, but I wouldn't call that loving. Anyhow, she's overpaid. . . ."

"Overpaid?" he said, his mouth dropping slightly.

They were both silent, as though even for them frankness had overstepped itself.

"What was I saying to you when we ran into this quiet period?" she began again.

"About my wife getting too much for her money," he said exhaustedly.

"Who is this Fenton?" she changed topics. "What did you bring him here for?"

"I thought he would be a change for you. You really ordered him anyhow, and have forgotten it."

"I never ordered *him*," she said carefully, drawing the silk coverlet up to her eyebrows. "Did you think he would remind me of Russell?" she put the question with coy crafty innocence, and he felt he would laugh.

"No, Grainger, it didn't occur to me at the time."

"Don't lie to me as though I were your wife!" she lashed at him. "If he hadn't looked a *little* like Russell would you have brought him here then?"

"Yes, I would, Grainger." He smarted now under her attack. "I brought him here because he was so much just himself. This boy is better than Russell," he took final courage to throw at her.

"I'm glad you said *boy*." Grainger was quiet under his blasphemy. "He's a child really. And I'm an old woman."

Parkhearst waited for her.

"How did you find him?" she went on, muttering now, less irritation in her voice.

"How do I find everybody?" he said, a kind of dull bitterness in his voice.

"I never find anybody at all," she said. "Are you jealous because I did something for him?" she wanted to know suddenly.

"Yes, I suppose," he said. "But after all I wanted to bring him here. I was willing to take the risk."

She saw the flowers for the first time.

"Do you know why I buy all these flowers?" she asked him.

"Of course," he said, impatient at her always changing the subject so abruptly.

"No, you don't," she said with a ridiculous emphasis. "Tell me why I have them then, if you know. . . ."

"Why do you have that church upstairs?" he said.

"Church?" she said, somewhat distracted and looking at him with her back to the window. He had forgotten that this was his private word and that he had not ever used it for her; and yet he had employed it with such force of habit, she knew it was his word and that he must say it all the time when out of her presence.

Recovering from her shock over the word, she began to talk about the flowers again: "I can see now you don't know everything after all."

"If there hadn't been any Russell, of course you wouldn't have flowers," he raised his voice as he would have had he lived an ordinary domestic life with ordinary people.

"Should I go to see him?" She changed to a new line of thought.

He stared at her with almost real anger.

"Should I return his call or not?" she roared. "Don't start being Christ with me again or something will happen."

"It's too silly even for you to say," he told her. "Returning a call to Fenton." His voice, though, softened a bit.

"He is very beautiful, isn't he?" she said. "More than Russell was."

"Grainger, you know we never agree with one another about who is beautiful or who is anything."

"He's more beautiful than Russell," she went on, both musing and commanding. "But there's something not right with him that Russell never had. There was nothing really wrong with Russell."

He looked up briefly at her as though something important had finally been said.

"When should I go visit him?" she asked him eagerly.

"We can't go today." Parkhearst acted bored. "Bella's coming home this afternoon from work."

"I wish you would quit mentioning Bella," she complained. "It's all you talk about . . . You get me involved with this new boy, and then you go off with your wife, and leave me without anything."

"Grainger, don't be a complete idiot all the time."

"*I'll* go," she said. "You'll stay home and entertain that Bella and *I'll* go. And every minute," she vituperated, "you'll be thinking of me and him together."

Parkhearst laughed a little, and then the pain of the scene which she had just presented to his imagination bore down with unaccustomed weight.

"You don't even know where he lives," he said. "I can just see you going in there in your finery."

He laughed such a nasty laugh that Grainger found herself listening to it as attentively as one of the "concerts."

The next thing Fenton remembered was standing in front of a wrestling arena known as Fair City. He was in front of a little wooden gate with his hands put through the partitions as though asking somebody for an admission ticket. It was still early morning, almost no one was on Sixty-third Street; and so removing his hands from the partitions at last, he began walking in the direction of the house.

Right in front of the house he stopped. He heard several voices singing something vaguely sacred. "It's niggers," he said peevishly, rubbing the back of his neck. He raised his eyes to the COME AND SEE RESURRECTION CHURCH. He leaned his head then gently over onto the pavement so that it was within a few inches of the curb and some of the coffee he had drunk came up easily. Then he got up and unlocked the door to the house and went inside.

He felt he must look creased and yellow as he opened Claire's door.

Claire was sitting on the kitchen chair but hardly glanced up at Fenton and only nodded in answer to his brother's greeting.

The sound of the colored spiritualists was just faintly audible here.

"How can they shout when it's morning?" Fenton asked, and then as Claire did not say any more, he asked, "I don't suppose anybody called?"

Claire merely stared at him.

"Ain't you all right?" Fenton said, going over to the chair and touching him.

"Dooon't," the boy cried, as though he had touched him on a raw nerve.

"Claire! Are you sick?" Fenton wanted to know.

"Don't touch my head," Claire told him, and Fenton took his hand away.

"Let me get you into bed, and I'll go for coffee and rolls," Fenton told him and he helped him into the cot.

"I don't want none," Claire said and he closed his eyes.

"You didn't notice my new clothes," Fenton complained.

"Yes, I did," Claire replied without opening his eyes.

"Do you like them?" Fenton said, looking around, as though to find some part of the room that would reflect his image.

"Kind of, yeah," Claire answered.

"I'll go for something for you now," Fenton encouraged him, but he didn't go. He kept staring at the deep pallor of Claire. He looked around the room as though there might be something there that would extend help to them.

Fenton looked at himself as he sat there on the chair in his new clothes. He wondered if he was changing; there was something about the wearing of those clothes that made him feel almost as if his body had begun to change, that his soul had begun to change into another soul. A new life was beginning for him, he dimly recognized. And with the new life, he knew, Claire would be less important. He knew that Claire would not like Grainger or Parkhearst and would not go to visit them or be with them. He knew that Claire actually never wanted to leave this room again. He had come to the last stages of his journey. Fenton tried not to think of this but it was too difficult to avoid: Claire had come as far now as he could. . . . There could be no more journeying around for him. And Fenton knew that as long as Claire was Claire he would not let him lead the "new life" he saw coming for him. There would be trouble, then, a great deal of trouble.

He wanted desperately to be rid of Claire and even as he had this feeling he felt more love and pity for him than ever before. As he sat there gazing at Claire, he knew he loved him more than any other being. He was almost sure that he would never feel such tenderness for any other person. And then this tenderness would be followed by fury and hatred and loathing, so that he was afraid he would do something violent, would strike the sick boy down and harm him.

"Claire," he said looking at him in anguish. "What are we going to do about this?"

Claire moved his closed eyes vaguely. "Don't know," Claire replied.

Fenton smiled to think that Claire did not ask what *this* was. Well, the boy was past caring, and it was plain enough what *this* was: *this* was everything that faced and surrounded them. It was plain, all right, what it was. Their trouble had made them both one.

"What do you want me to do?" Fenton said, his desperation growing. "Tell me what to do."

"We can't go away now, can we?" Claire said, and his voice was calmer but weaker.

Fenton considered this, taking out from his pantscuff a cigarette butt which he had begun in the greatwoman's house, lighting it swiftly with a kitchen match, and inhaling three powerful drags all at once.

Claire opened his eyes slowly and stared at his brother, waiting for the answer.

"No, we can't go away anywhere," Fenton said.

"Isn't there any place to go but here?" Claire asked.

"This is as far as we can get. Anyhow for the winter. . . . We have to stick in here now."

Claire closed his eyes again.

"Unless, of course, you want to go and live at Grainger's with me," Fenton said.

"What would I do there in her big house?" Claire said angrily, his eyes opening and closing.

"She would get a special room for you, where you could do anything you want. She could buy you anything you want, take you anywhere and show you anything. You would never know how happy you could be."

"What are *you* going to do there?" Claire wondered with surprise. . . .

"I'm going to marry her."

"Marry?" Claire sat up briefly in bed, but his strength could not hold him up, and falling back flat, he uttered: "You're not old enough."

"I'm more than old enough," Fenton laughed. "You've seen me enough times to know that. I got to make use of what I have, too. She thinks I look like her old husband."

"I ain't going to go there. . . . I ain't going to leave this house," Claire said.

"Well, suit yourself," Fenton said. "But I'm going over there. . . . The only thing is I don't believe any of it. It's a dream I keep having. Not one of those real pleasant dreams you have when you open a package and something beautiful falls out. In this dream even bigger more wonderful things seem like they're going to happen, getting married to a rich woman and living in a mansion and dressing up like a swell and all that, but at the same time it's all scary spooky and goddamned rotten. . . ."

"It's rotten, all right," Claire said. "You don't have to tell nobody that twice."

"Well, when there ain't nothing else you got to stoop down and pick up the *rotten*. You ought to know that."

"Not me. I don't have to pick it up if I don't want to."

"Well, then you can stick here till you choke to death on it," Fenton said passionately.

They both stopped as if listening to the words he had just said. They contained enough of some sort of truth and the truth was so terrible they had to listen to it as though it were being repeated on a phonograph for them.

"When do you aim on going?" Claire said suddenly, his voice older and calmer.

"In a day or so," Fenton warned him.

"Well it could be sooner. . . . You don't mind if I just stay here, do you?" Claire implored him.

"There's nothing to stop you staying here, of course," Fenton said irritably, twisting the hair around his ear. "This house don't have no owner, no tenants, nobody going to bother you but the spooks." He hurried on, talking past the pain that registered on Claire's face when he heard the words. "But I ain't coming dragging my ass over here every day just to see how you are when you could be living like a king."

"You don't need to come over and see me on account of I ain't asking you to," Claire said.

"Well, then don't be sorry if something happens to you. . . ."

"Nothing ain't going to happen and you know it," Claire shouted. "Why would anything happen to *me?*"

"Well, that's because you don't know nothing about cities is all," he said. "Do you know how many murders are done right in this one town?"

Claire did not answer for a moment and then said, "Those are rich people they murder. Like that old woman you're going to move in with. She's a likely murder person now. And you too if you get to be her husband."

"That's where you're wrong," Fenton said. "Most of the murders they do in this town are on bums, young boys and men that don't have no home and come from nowhere, these they find with their throats cut and their brains mashed out in alleys and behind billboards. Damned few rich people are ever found murdered in this town."

"You think you can scare me into moving into your old woman's house, don't you?" Claire said. "Well, you can do to her all you want to, but I ain't going to be there to watch you . . . fuck her."

"Now listen to that dirty-mouthed little bugger talk, would you. What would Mom think if she knew her religious little boy talked like a cocksucker?" He slapped Claire across the face . . . "after all I done for you," Fenton finished.

"Go be with that old woman, why don't you, and leave me alone," Claire warned him. "I don't need you nor her. I don't need nobody."

"You'll come bellyachin' around trying to get in touch with me, you'll come crawling like you always do some night when you get the shit scared out of you in this house, hearing the sounds that you can't explain, and maybe *seeing* something too. . . ."

Claire could not control the look of terror that appeared at Fenton's words.

"Claire," Fenton changed suddenly to a tone of imploring, "you got to listen to reason. You *can't* live in this old house alone. . . . Something *will* happen to you. Can't you see that. . . ."

"Why will it?" Claire said, his terror abating a little, searching in himself for some secret strength.

"Things happen here. Everybody knows that. Now listen, Claire," Fenton went on, "Grainger would be very good to you and you could be happy there with her, you don't know how happy you would be. You haven't ever been happy or comfortable before so you don't know what you're talking about. Anyhow, Claire, I can't leave you here. I can't leave you here. . . . I'd have to do something else first. . . ."

"I don't see why not," he said. "I would rather be dead than go there."

"You would not rather be dead. You're a tough little bastard and you would rather be alive and you know it. . . . I'm not going to leave you here, Claire. I'm going to take you with me and you may just as well make up your mind to it now. . . . Hear?"

"You won't even get to drag me because I'm not going. . . ."

Fenton's anguish grew. He knew he could not leave Claire and he knew Claire's determination would be hard to break. He felt suddenly an uncontrollable urge of violence against this puny, defiant, impossible little brother. If he had only not taken him from West Virginia in the first place. Or if he had only died as the doctor had said he would a long time ago. He knew that he *did* want to go on to the "new life" with Grainger and Parkhearst. He wanted to change, he wanted to wear Russell's clothes, he wanted the life that was just in sight and which Claire was now preventing. He knew that as long as there was Claire, whether he went with him or stayed in the house hardly mattered, because he knew that as long as there was Claire there was part of his old life with him, and he wanted to destroy all that behind him and begin all over again. Claire was a part of his old life, part of his disbelief in himself, the disbelief he could ever change and be something different. Claire did not even believe he could be married and love a woman. And though Claire was younger, he could exert this terrible triumph of failure over him.

Whether Claire stayed in the old house or followed him to Grainger's, he would exert a power of defeat over him.

Then suddenly Fenton realized that he did not want Claire to come with him. He preferred him to stay in the old house. And at the same time he knew that if he stayed he would never have a moment's peace. . . .

There was no way out that he could see. He could only stand there staring at Claire with impotence and rage.

"All right for you," Fenton said at the end. "All I can say is watch out, watch out something don't happen now to you."

A tent production of *Othello* was to take place that night near Sixty-third Street, the young man who had approached Fenton was telling him, and as somebody was following him he would welcome Fenton's company and protection.

"Who is Hayden Banks?" Fenton wondered, looking at the handbill which described the dramatic spectacle about to take place.

"Hayden Banks," replied the young man, "is one of the greatest living actors. You are probably seeing him just before he is to gain his international reputation. London is already asking for him. Few actors can touch him. He is playing, of course, Othello himself. The costumes are by a friend of mine, and I will introduce you to a good many of the cast, if you like."

"I don't know if I want that," Fenton said.

"You *will* go with me to the performance," the young man said.

Fenton did not say anything. He had to go somewhere, of course, there could be no doubt about that.

"I wish you would come with me because I'm afraid of

the man who is following me. Don't look back now. You
see, I'm in trouble," he explained. "You look like a good
kind of bodyguard for me and if you come with me I'm less
likely to get into . . . trouble. . . . And I can't disappoint
Hayden Banks. This is the last night of *Othello*, but I have
been afraid to go out all week because this Mexican is following me. I'm in awful trouble with him."

Fenton half turned around but he saw nobody in particular behind him, a crowd of people who all seemed to be
following them.

"I'll go with you," Fenton said. Then he looked at the
young man carefully. He was the most handsome young
man he had ever seen, almost as beautiful as a girl in boy's
clothes. He had never seen such beautiful eyelashes. And at
the same time the young man looked like Grainger. He
might have been Grainger's brother. He almost wanted to
ask him if he was Grainger's brother, but of course Grainger
could not have a brother. . . .

"You don't know what it is, being followed."

"What will he do if he catches you?"

The young man stared at him. Fenton could not tell
whether he was telling the truth or making this up, but there
was a look of fear on his face that must be genuine at least.

"I wish you wouldn't use the word *catch*," the young man
said.

"Are you afraid he will . . . hurt you," Fenton changed
kill to *hurt* before he spoke.

"I'm afraid of the worst," the young man replied. "And
you'll be an awfully good boy to come with me."

Fenton nodded.

The young man signalled a taxi and, waiting, said, "Those
are awfully interesting clothes you have on. I've never seen
clothes like that before. They remind me of some pictures
of my father, wedding pictures."

Fenton looked down at himself as though seeing the
clothes on himself for the first time. "These are clothes of a
friend of mine," he explained.

"Get in," the young man urged as the taxi pulled up beside them. "Get in and don't stare at the crowd like that."

"Was I staring?" Fenton said, like a man awakened from sleepwalking.

"Staring into the crowd like that might incite him. You have an awful look when you stare," the young man said, looking more carefully now at Fenton. "I hope I am going to be safe with *you* now. I don't usually pick up people on the street like this. And maybe you don't like Shakespeare." He began to examine Fenton now more carefully that he felt free of danger of being followed.

Fenton could see that his anxiety was genuine, but even so the way he said things seemed womanish and unreal, a little like Parkhearst. Both these men said things as though nothing was really important except the gestures and the words with which they said them. When he listened to either this young man or Parkhearst, Fenton felt that the whole of life must be merely a silly trifling thing to them, which bored them, and which they wanted to end, a movie they felt was too long and overacted.

"What is your name?" the young man said suddenly.

Fenton told him and the young man replied, "That is the most interesting name I have ever heard. Is it your own?"

Fenton looked down at his clothes and said it was.

"My name is Bruno Korsawski," he told Fenton.

They shook hands in the dark of the taxi and Bruno held Fenton's hand for many seconds.

"You may have saved my life," Bruno explained.

Soon they reached a vast lot deserted except for a giant circus tent before which fluttered, propelled by a giant cooling machine, banners reading HAYDEN BANKS THE GENIUS OF THE SPOKEN WORD IN OTHELLO. In addition to the angry puffing face of Hayden Banks on the posters was a picture of a rather old looking young man dressed, as Fenton thought, like a devil you might expect to see in an old Valentine, if Valentines had devils, but he lacked horns and a tail.

Fenton remembered vaguely of having read *The Mer-*

chant of Venice and he had heard from someplace that Othello had to do with a black man who tortured a white woman to death. He felt a vague curiosity to see Hayden Banks, however. There was nobody around the huge empty tent tonight, and the whole scene reminded him of the conclusion of a county fair which he had seen in West Virginia.

Bruno Korsawski was the kind of man who introduced all of his new friends to all of his old friends. His life was largely a series of introductions, as he was always meeting new people, and these new people had to be introduced to the old people. His idea of the world was a circle, a circle of friends, closed to the rest of men because of his world's fullness. He had thought that Fenton would be one of this circle. However, the introductions did not go off too well.

They went at once to the star's dressing room. A purple sign with strange heavy tulips drawn on it announced MR. HAYDEN BANKS.

"You dear!" Hayden cried on seeing Bruno. "You look absolutely imperial."

Mr. Hayden Banks did not really look human, Fenton thought, and it was not only the deformity of his makeup.

"This is my friend Fenton Riddleway."

Mr. Banks bowed, and Fenton could not think of anything to say to him. . . .

"Don't you love his name?" Bruno said to Mr. Hayden Banks.

"It's incomparably the best I've heard," Mr. Banks replied. "Uncommonly good. But you've got to forgive me now, I haven't put on my beard yet, and without my beard I'm afraid some of you may mistake me for Desdemona."

"It's been so charming seeing you." Hayden Banks held out his hand to Fenton, and then whispering in Fenton's ear, he said, "You charmer you."

Fenton again could not think of anything to say, and in the hall Bruno said angrily to him, "You didn't open your mouth."

"I guess I'm used to people who talk well and a lot,"

Bruno explained apologetically as they went to their seats, which were in the first row. "You see what influence can do for you." Bruno pointed. "The best seats: compliments of Hayden Banks."

A small string orchestra was playing, an orchestra which Bruno explained was absolutely without a peer for its interpretation of the Elizabethan epoch. "They stand untouched," he stated, still speaking of the orchestra.

Whether it was the nearness of the actors or the oppressive heat of the tent or the general unintelligibility of both what the actors said and what they did, Fenton became sleepy, and he could not control a weakness he had for breaking wind, which considerably upset Bruno, although nobody else in the small audience seemed to hear. Perhaps Fenton's slumber was due also to the influence of the ALL NIGHT THEATER, and drama for Fenton was a kind of sleeping powder.

When Hayden Banks made his appearance, there was a tremendous ovation from the first few rows of the tent, and for a while Fenton watched this tall bony man beat his chest with complete lack of restraint and such uncalled-for fury that Fenton was amazed at such enormous energy. He could think of nothing in his own life that would have allowed him to pace, strut and howl like this. He supposed it belonged to an entirely different world where such things were perhaps done. The more, however, the great Moor shouted and complained about his wife's whoring, the more sleepy Fenton became. It was, however, something of a surprise to hear him fret so much about a whore and have so many rich-looking people nodding and approving of the whole improbable situation.

"He kills Desdemona," Bruno explained, watching Fenton doze with increasing displeasure.

"Would you buy me a drink now?" Fenton asked Bruno during intermission.

At the bar, the bartender asked Fenton if he was old enough, and Bruno said, "I can vouch for him, Teddy," and exchanged a knowing look with the bartender.

"There is one thing," Bruno began to Fenton after he had nodded to literally scores of friends and acquaintances: "I wonder if you couldn't control yourself a little more during the soliloquies at least."

Fenton knew perfectly well to what Bruno referred but he chose to say, "What are those?"

"During the performance, dear," Bruno went on, "you're making noises which embarrass me since I am among friends who know me and know I brought you as a guest."

"My farts, then?" Fenton said without expression.

"Brute!" Bruno laughed gaily.

"Would you buy me another whiskey now?" Fenton asked him.

When they returned to their seats Fenton immediately dozed off and did not waken until the last act which, whether due to his refreshing sleep or to the fact the actors seemed to talk less and do more, was rather frighteningly good to him. Hayden Banks seemed to murder the woman named Desdemona (Aurelia Wilcox in real life) with such satisfaction and enjoyment that he felt it stood with some of the better murder shows he had seen at the ALL NIGHT THEATER. He applauded quite loudly, and Bruno, smiling, finally held his hand and said, "Don't overdo it."

After the performance, Bruno invited Fenton to meet the entire cast, and as drinks were being served now in the dressing room, Fenton drank four or five additional whiskies to the congratulations of nearly all present. At times Fenton would have sober moments and remember Aurelia Wilcox patting his hair or Hayden Banks giving him a hug and kiss, or the young man who played Iago and who looked even more like a Valentine devil off the stage whispering in his ear.

"Hayden says we're to go on to his apartment and wait for him there," Bruno explained finally to Fenton, showing him at the same time a tiny key to the great man's rooms.

"You were extremely rude to Hayden Banks. You act like a savage when you're with people. I've never met anybody like you. What on earth *is* West Virginia if you are typical?"

They were in Hayden Banks' apartment and Fenton, instead of replying to Bruno's remarks, was looking about, comparing it with Grainger's mansion. The walls had been painted so that they resembled the ocean, and so skillfully done that one actually thought he was about to go into water. Fenton stared at the painting for a long while, noticing in the distance some small craft, a dwarf moon and the suggestion of dawn in the far distance.

"Arden Carruthers did that painting," Bruno said. "Arden Carruthers is one of the most promising of the younger artists and this mural will be worth a small fortune some day."

Bruno was smoking something strange smelling which Fenton recognized as one of the persistent odors of the ALL NIGHT THEATER. As he smoked, he drew nearer to Fenton, and his expression of critical disapproval of the boy suddenly vanished.

"What are you clenching your fists for, as though you were going into the prize ring?" Bruno said.

Fenton sniffed at the cigarette and then suddenly knew what it must be. It was what had changed Bruno.

"You are very beautiful looking. The Italian Renaissance all over again in your face," Bruno said. He kept standing right over Fenton as though he were a bird that was going to come down on top of his head. He kept staring right into the crown of his head.

Fenton suddenly reached out and with violence seizing Bruno's wrist cried, "Give me some of that," so that the cigarette nearly fell from his fingers.

"Have you ever had any?" Bruno wanted to know.

"Give me some," Fenton said again, remembering now with terrifying insistence the smell in the ALL NIGHT THEATER. He felt that he could really dominate this man now as much as he could Claire. At the same time he was terribly afraid. He felt that something decisive and irrevocable was about to happen.

"Just smoke a little of it and don't inhale as deep as I did," Bruno said nervously. "I don't think you know how."

Fenton took the cigarette and began inhaling deeply.

"Now stop," Bruno said. "I don't have a warehouse of those."

"No wonder somebody was following you," Fenton laughed.

"I wonder which one of us is more scared of the other," Bruno said finally, and he sat down at Fenton's feet.

Fenton was about to say that he was not afraid of anybody, but Bruno began babbling about Fenton's shoes. "Where on earth did you get *those?* They're privately manufactured!" He stared at Fenton with renewed respect and interest. "You didn't get *those* in West Virginia."

Bruno stared at Fenton again.

"You haven't killed anybody, have you?" he said finally.

Fenton stared at him and he went on agitatedly, "Why, you've finished that entire cigarette. I hope you know what you've done and what it was. I'm not responsible for you, remember."

"Who the fuck is responsible?" Fenton said.

"Don't use that language," Bruno sniggered, and then got up swiftly and sat down beside Fenton. He began kissing his hair, and then slowly unbuttoning his shirt. He took off all his clothes, as from a doll, piece by piece, without resistance or aid, but left on at the last the privately manufactured shoes. . . .

The next thing Fenton remembered he was standing naked in the middle of the room, boxing; he was boxing the chandelier and had knocked down all the lamps, he had split open Bruno's face and Bruno was weeping and held ice packs to his mouth.

Then the next thing he remembered was Bruno standing before him with Hayden Banks who looked exactly like the murdered Desdemona. Bruno had a gun in his hand and was ordering him to leave.

"Don't you ever come back if you don't want to go to jail," Bruno said, as Fenton went out the door dressed in clothes that did not look like his own.

Morning is the most awful time. And this morning for Fenton was the one that shattered everything he had been or known; it marked the limits of a line, not ending his youth but making his youth superfluous, as age to a god.

He seemed to be awake and yet he had the feeling he had never been awake. He was not even sure it was morning. He was back in the old house, in Claire's room, and though he was staring at Claire he knew that his staring was of no avail, that he already knew what had happened and the staring was to prevent him from telling himself what he saw. He could not remember anything at that moment, he had even forgotten Bruno Korsawski and the production of *Othello* starring some immortal fruit.

Then the comfortable thought that it was breakfast time and that he would go out and get Claire his rolls and coffee. He was so happy he was here with Claire and he realized again how necessary Claire was to him, and how real he was compared to the Parkhearsts and the Brunos and the Graingers.

Claire, he said softly. He went over to the bed and began shaking him. The room seemed suddenly deadly cold and he thought of the winter that would come and how uninhabitable this deserted old wreck would be. . . . And Claire, he recognized, almost as with previous knowledge, was as cold as the room. And yet he was not surprised. . . .

He sat there suddenly wondering why he was not surprised that Claire was cold. And at the same time he was surprised that he could be so cold. He shook him again.

Claire, he said.

He began to be aware of a splitting headache.

He got up and turned on the sickly light. He was careful somehow not to get too close to Claire now that he had turned on the light, but stood at a safe distance, talking to him, telling him how he was going to get him some breakfast.

"Some good hot coffee will make you feel like a new boy, Claire," he said.

And then suddenly he began to weep, choking sobs, and

these were followed by laughter so unlike his own that he remained frozen with confusion.

"I'm going right now, hear?" he said to Claire. "I'll be right back with the coffee. . . ." Then he laughed again. The silence of the room was complete.

He hurried to the lunch stand and then ran all the way back with the steaming coffee and rolls.

He bent down over Claire but was somehow careful not to look at his face. His head ached as though the sockets of his eyes were to burst. He kept talking to Claire all the time, telling him how they were going back to West Virginia as soon as he got a little money saved up; they would buy a stock farm later and raise Black Angus cattle, and have a stable of horses. It was not impossible, Claire, he said.

He held Claire's head up but still without looking and tried to pour the coffee down his throat. "This coffee's strong enough to revive a stiff," he laughed, ignoring the coffee's running down the boy's neck, ignoring that none of the coffee had even got into his mouth.

"Eat this bread," he said and put some to Claire's mouth. He pressed the small piece of roll heavily against the blue lips, smashing it to the coffee-moistened cold lips.

"Eat this, drink this," Fenton kept saying, but now he no longer tried to administer the bread and coffee. "Eat and drink."

We have to go back, Claire. We want to go back to West Virginia, you know you do.

Then as though another person had entered the room and commanded him, Fenton stood up, and pulled the light down as far as he could to search mercilessly the face and body of Claire.

The light showed Claire's neck swollen and blue with marks, the neck broken softly like a small bird's, the hair around his neck like ruffled young feathers, the eyes had come open a little and seemed to be attempting to focus on something too far out of his reach. The brown liquid of the coffee like blood smeared the paste of the offering of bread around his mouth.

Fenton looked down at his hands.

After that he did not know what happened, or how long he stayed in the room, trying to feed Claire, trying to talk to him, trying to tell him about Black Angus in West Virginia.

Slowly the sound of Fenton's own voice worked him from the stupor he had been in, saying again and again, "You're dead, you little motherfucker. Dead as mud and I don't have no need sitting here staring you down."

For a good many days he walked all over the city, riding street cars when they were full so that he could shove his way in without paying, eating in cheap lunch stands when they were full and running out the back door without paying the bill. He found he could steal fruit and candy from grocery stands without much trouble. In the evening he would go to the Square in front of a large gray library and listen to the revivalists and the fanatics.

Older men sometimes invited him to a beer, men he met in the crowds in front of the speaker, but as he drank with them his mind would wander and he would say things which chilled further talk, so that after awhile absently he would look around and find himself alone looking down at his hands.

There was no respite for his misery during which time he slept in hallways, covering himself with newspapers he collected in alleys. By day he would go down to the docks and watch crews unload cargo, or he would go into a large museum where they kept the bones of prehistoric animals which he knew never existed. These big-boned monsters calmed some of his crushing grief.

But at last there came to him an idea which gave him some solace, if not any real hope or restoration. It was that Claire must be put in a sheltered place. He must have a service, a funeral. The thought did not occur to him that Claire was really dead until then; before he had only thought how he had killed him. And the thought that anybody *knew* he had killed Claire or was looking for him never occurred to him. What had happened to both him and Claire was much too terrible and closed in for the rest of the world to know or care about.

It was night when he returned to the house. He had vaguely remembered going upstairs weeks before and finding an old chest up there, an old cedar chest, perhaps, or merely an old box. He walked up the stairs now, using matches to guide his way. He heard small footsteps scamper about or it might have been only the echo of his own feet.

He stood in the immense vacant attic with its suffocating smell of rotting wood, its soft but ticklingly clammy caress of cobwebs, the feeling of small animal eyes upon him and the imperceptible sounds of disintegration and rot. How had he known there was a chest up here? As he thought of it now he could not remember having seen it. Yet he knew it was here.

He put himself on hands and knees and began groping for the presence of it. He came across a broken rocking chair. His kitchen matches lit up pictures on the wall, one of a girl in her wedding dress, another of a young man in hunting costume, one of Jesus among thieves. Another picture was a poem concerning Mother Love. At the extreme end of the attic and in a position which must have been directly above the room where he and Claire had lived and where Claire now lay dead was a chest; it was not a fragrant cedar chest, such as he had hoped, but an old white box with broken hinges and whose inside lid was covered with a filthy cloth.

But even more disappointing was that inside was a gauzy kind of veil, like a wedding veil and his eye turned wearily to the picture of the girl in her wedding costume as though this veil might be the relic of that scene. But whatever the veil was, it might serve this cause. It was not a fit resting place for Claire, but it would have to do.

He hurried now downstairs and into the room, with the sudden fear that Claire might have disappeared. He sat down beside him, and his agony was so great he scarcely noticed the overpowering stench, and at the same time he kept lighting the kitchen matches, but perhaps more to keep his mind aware of the fact of Claire's death than to scare off the stink of death.

It took him all night to get himself ready to carry Claire up, as though once he had put him in the chest, he was really at last dead forever. For part of the night he found that he had fallen asleep over Claire's body, and at the very end before he carried him upstairs and deposited him, he forced himself to kiss the dead stained lips he had stopped, and said, "Up we go then, motherfucker."

Malcolm

For
Vera
and
Jorma
and
to
Stewart Richardson
and
Carl Van Vechten,
heartfelt thanks

Contents

The Boy on the Bench

In front of one of the most palatial hotels in the world, a very young man was accustomed to sit on a bench which, when the light fell in a certain way, shone like gold.

The young man, who could not have been more than fifteen, seemed to belong nowhere and to nobody, and even his persistent waiting on the bench achieved evidently no purpose, for he seldom spoke to anybody, and there was something about his elegant and untouched appearance that discouraged even those who were moved by his solitariness. For one thing, he looked like a foreigner who would not be apt to speak English, and his *waiting* look itself was so pronounced that nobody felt like interrupting. He was obviously expecting somebody.

Mr. Cox, who was the most famous astrologer of his period, and also the greatest walker (it is said that he often covered forty miles in one day in fine weather) often passed the palatial hotel, and from his first sight of the young man seated on the gold bench felt a kind of exasperation, interest, and surprise all at once. For one thing, the boy's appearance, he felt, was an *augury*, and this was attested to further by the fact that his sitting there day after day on the bench could offer no earthly or practical purpose. Mr. Cox, furthermore, felt particularly responsible for this part of the city—in a spiritual sense, that is. He had lived here for his entire fifty odd years (though in appearance he could easily have passed for seventy or even eighty), and he felt obscurely that the young man on the bench offered a comment, even a threat, certainly a criticism of his own career and thought—not to say existence.

For one thing, nobody had ever sat on this particular bench that persistently before, and, in addition, no one had really ever sat on it at all before. A display piece, it had been placed there as a useless ornament, and even very old ladies waiting for cabs invariably spurned it, recognizing it by means of their worldliness and senility for the ornament it was. But the boy had taken it, had sat on it, had become part of it. Not recognizing his position with respect to the bench, it was therefore not surprising that he scarcely *saw* Mr. Cox, far from greeting that elder gentleman as the latter appeared each morning after his night's study of the stars and his "charts." Instead, the boy looked at Mr. Cox with empty and almost blind detachment.

Mr. Cox stared angrily, and the boy stared back, open-eyed and unimpressed. As Mr. Cox was at that period, in a sense, *the* city, the hotel, and, in his own mind, civilization, this stare on the part of so young a person could scarcely be brooked much longer. Either Mr. Cox must change the direction of his morning walks, which would be, if not a defeat, a total revolution in his way of life, or *he* must recognize the youth on the bench.

On an extremely fine morning in June, therefore, while on his way to advise a woman patron, Mr. Cox decided on the latter course: recognition.

"You seem to be *wedded* to this bench," Mr. Cox said to the young man.

The boy smiled, and looked at the bench, almost as if Mr. Cox had addressed it and not him.

"*You*," Mr. Cox said, fearing perhaps that the boy did not understand him, either through a defect of the brain, or through ignorance of the language.

"Oh, I'm here all the time," the boy began. "My name is Malcolm."

"Good morning then," Mr. Cox said, still a bit edgy. "My name is Cox."

Malcolm smiled again, but did not say any more. Mr. Cox, depressed perhaps by such an unpromising beginning, was about to move on again, but something about the boy's openness, benign acceptance of everything, and puzzling *expectancy,* made him linger.

"I suppose, of course, you are waiting for somebody. Your sister, perhaps," Mr. Cox began again.

"No," Malcolm replied, his attention meanwhile having wandered far afield, as Mr. Cox could plainly see.

Mr. Cox waited.

"I'm waiting for nobody at all," Malcolm explained.

"But you have such a *waiting* look!" Mr. Cox's exasperation got the better of him. "You've been waiting here—forever! For months and months!"

"You've seen me?" Malcolm was surprised.

"Of course I've seen you. I belong here, you know. This city—this—" and with so much explanation ready at hand for him to impart, he could only at last motion toward the strip of land which faced the sea.

Malcolm nodded. "In a way I suppose I am waiting," he said, a deep but dull look now on his face.

Mr. Cox wore an expression of helpfulness, and somewhat smug understanding.

"Yes?" the astrologer prompted, when Malcolm said no more.

"My father has disappeared," Malcolm said suddenly.

"Well, don't tell me you've been waiting for *him* all this time," Mr. Cox said, for the subjects of tragedy and death were most unwelcome to him, and he took it for granted that Malcolm's father was dead.

Malcolm was thinking over Mr. Cox's question. "Yes," he said at last, "perhaps I may be waiting for him." And he laughed an agreeable strong laugh.

"Waiting for your father!" Mr. Cox expressed impatience and even derision, which, together with helpfulness and smugness, were characteristic of him.

"I'm afraid I have nothing better to do," Malcolm said.

"Ridiculous!" Mr. Cox was quite put out now. "You see, I took special notice of you," he went on, by way of general explanation, "because nobody has ever sat on this bench before. I don't think anybody should sit on it!"

"Poppycock," Malcolm said with a firmness which rather surprised Mr. Cox.

"I am speaking of the hotel regulations, you know."

"Well, I am a guest here, and I sit where I please," Malcolm ended this part of the discussion.

Rebuffed by this, Mr. Cox was again about to move on and even forget that he had ever entered into a conversation with the boy, when Malcolm said: "Don't tell me you are on your way."

"I've a great deal on my mind," Mr. Cox said lamely.

"Could you tell me what that might be?" Malcolm said at once.

"I see, of course, that you have not heard of me," Mr. Cox cleared his throat and looked down at his unpolished walking shoes. "I am an astrologer," Mr. Cox now looked Malcolm full in the face.

"People still study the . . . *stars!*" Malcolm welcomed this idea with surprise.

"People!" Mr. Cox drew back in anger. He was about to reply to Malcolm's astonishment when his eye fell on the boy's clothes, which were, it was not difficult to see, of the most expensive stuff—too expensive for the depleted epoch they were in, and of a taste whose exact character eluded him.

"Did I hear you say, then, you had no one?" Mr. Cox began his inquiry again.

"No one?" Malcolm thought for a moment, and then, shaking off this question, continued, as it were, with his own line of conversation: "I would invite you to sit down, sir, but I don't think you want to, and I would not want to ask you if you didn't want to comply."

"Your way of refusing to give information?" Mr. Cox inquired in a bored tone.

"I can give you all the information I have," Malcolm said. "I am, then," he began, "as they say, an orphan, and I have had more than enough to live on, but I have, right now, nothing at all to do. And things are, well, a bit too much for me, you see. So I sit here all the time, I suppose."

"Suppose?" Mr. Cox commented. "You *know!*"

"Well, sir," Malcolm nodded. "Yes, I know."

Mr. Cox was suddenly alone with his thoughts—had he left Malcolm he could not have been more so. He could go on asking questions of the boy, of course, but asking questions was not precisely his forte: it was giving answers which was his life work. At the same time, he did not feel he could leave, with so many things still up in the air. And he was sure, too, that Malcolm did not want him to leave, at least not until they had really *begun.*

Almost reading Mr. Cox's thought, Malcolm said: "I suppose if somebody would tell me what to do, I would do it."

"Would that be wise, though, for one so young?" Mr. Cox asked Malcolm to consider this.

"If I could leave the bench," Malcolm said, and he touched it now with his hands, "I would risk it!

"But my training, you see, sir," he continued, "is very limited—almost to my study of French. My father, you know, knew French very well, and continuously read Verlaine."

"Continuously . . . *Verlaine?*" Mr. Cox asked.

But the boy had gone ahead: "I don't have a head for languages, though, and I'm afraid I have gotten almost nowhere in any other line."

"Then it's a good thing you have plenty of money." Mr. Cox gazed from the bench to the hotel.

"But that's what I'm beginning . . . not to have!" Malcolm cried. "You see, it's running out."

"Then we'll have to hit on something at once," Mr. Cox said, relieved perhaps now that he had got somewhere, at least. Nodding perfunctorily, he took out a small notebook from his breastpocket, on which were stamped the signs of the Zodiac, and said: "When were you born, Malcolm?"

Malcolm was silent.

"Don't tell me you don't know," Mr. Cox scolded.

"I'm afraid you're right: I don't," he admitted.

"Then I don't see how you expect me to help you," Mr. Cox was very much put out, and he closed his small notebook with a bang. "I don't think I ever met anybody who didn't know when he was born!"

"But since *he* disappeared, I've had nobody to remind me of dates," Malcolm appealed to the older man.

"You mean to tell me your father never talked with you about plans?" Mr. Cox hammered away now. "Plans for when you were grown up."

"Grown up?" Malcolm hesitated on that phrase, for it was the first time he had ever thought it would be applied to him.

"Grown up," Mr. Cox repeated, severely gloomy.

"No," Malcolm slowly shook his head, and a faint shadow, perhaps of age, crossed his face for just a moment, "My father," he began—and there was something in the way he said this word which hinted more at ignorance than at knowledge—"my father seemed to feel I was always going to stay just the way I was, and that he and I would always be doing just about what we were doing *then*. That is, sir, going to the fine restaurants, horseback riding and sailing, and sitting in big hotel rooms with him looking at me so proud and happy. He was glad I was just the way I was, and I was glad he was just the way he was. We were both satisfied. You have no idea, Mr. Cox, sir."

"I may have no idea, but I am somehow not surprised."

"We were very happy together, my father and I," and Malcolm sighed faintly.

"Well, I believe that part of your story, but for God's sake, Malcolm, you're not happy now, and you've got to do something about it!"

"Do?" Malcolm exclaimed, and he half got up from the bench.

"Yes, *do*," Mr. Cox hammered again.

"But what is there to do?" Malcolm appealed to him now. Mr. Cox folded his thin arms over his chest.

"There's only one thing for you to do now," the astrologer exclaimed. "Give yourself up to things!"

"Give myself up to . . . things?" and he got clear up this time from the bench and one could see that Malcolm was neither tall nor short for his age, but looked as if he had always been this height and would continue to be.

Mr. Cox was also rather surprised to see how strong Malcolm looked physically in comparison with the somewhat weaker development of his mental powers.

"Please be seated at once," Mr. Cox commanded.

Malcolm sat down.

"The whole crux of the matter," Mr. Cox continued, "is your father gave you all he had, including his undying affection, I gather, and what have you done with such *largesse?*"

"*Largesse?*" Malcolm wondered.

"I thought you knew French," Mr. Cox assailed him. "*Largesse* is the horn of plenty: it's *everything.*"

"Perhaps if I came home with you, sir—" Malcolm suggested, beginning to feel now how really bad off he was and, probably, had always been.

"Out of the question!" Mr. Cox was firm. "I can only see you, so to speak, on the bench."

"So that we will be passing acquaintances?" Malcolm wondered, briefly.

"I can give you people, though, if it's people you think you are looking for," Mr. Cox softened his refusal. "But I'd rather begin with . . . well, *addresses,*" he said.

"Addresses, sir?"

Mr. Cox nodded.

"That is," the astrologer added, "if you want to give yourself to things—to life, as an older era said . . ."

"I've got no choice," Malcolm cried. "But *addresses?*"

"Addresses," Mr. Cox repeated.

"Here is the first," and the astrologer handed Malcolm what was a calling card. "I want you to take this card," Mr. Cox used his lecturing-voice now, although this tone only succeeded in plunging Malcolm more and more into dullness and inattention, "and you are to call on the person whose name is written on it, *today,* at five o'clock."

"I will do no such thing," Malcolm replied, after a long

pause, folding his arms, but then suddenly he put out one hand and took the card, and studied it for a moment.

"Why this . . . this . . . is an . . . undertaker's card!" Malcolm drew back in consternation.

"What has his profession got to do with your meeting him," Mr. Cox exclaimed. "You wanted to begin, I thought you said. And Estel Blanc," the astrologer now named the person on the card, "is after all not going to embalm you!"

"Estel Blanc indeed!" Malcolm's displeasure was intense. Suddenly he threw the card on the ground. "I will have nothing at all to do with such an absurd introduction. And you, Mr. Cox, sir, must have taken leave of your senses."

"Pick that card up at once," Mr. Cox commanded icily. "What on earth would your father think of you if he saw you acting in this manner. You are going to leave the bench and you are going to call on Estel Blanc. Or you can sit here till Doomsday!"

"Addresses," the boy scoffed. "Estel Blanc."

"If you do not obey me," Mr. Cox warned, "there is no reason for our ever meeting again. You were a wealthy boy, I say *were*, mind you, and you have no character and no friends. Sitting here all day long moping over your father, who probably died a long time ago—"

"*Disappeared*, sir," Malcolm interrupted.

"Yet," Mr. Cox continued, ignoring Malcolm's interpolation, "when help in the shape of an address arrives, you wish to do nothing. You wish to remain on the bench. You prefer that to *beginning* . . ."

Malcolm considered this.

"Very well, then," the boy acknowledged his hastiness, and he picked up the card which he had thrown on the flagstone. "I will do as you say in this one case, and because my money is beginning to go"—speaking this last phrase to himself.

"You will do as you are told since you don't know what to do at all," Mr. Cox told him. "And remember the exact hour with Estel Blanc," Mr. Cox warned. "I will call him, and he will be expecting you."

Having covered so much in so short a time, both Mr. Cox and Malcolm felt that they had known one another a great while, and their goodbyes were therefore perfunctory as in the case of friends of long-standing.

"I will see you tomorrow, then, on the bench," Mr. Cox said in parting. "We will discuss your meeting with Estel at that time."

"Understood, sir," Malcolm replied, nodding twice to the elder man, who hastened off now in the direction of the shoreline.

Malcolm looked at the card.

Estel Blanc

Estel Blanc lived in an unremodeled Victorian house with over-size shutters, twenty-five foot ceilings, and marble-topped tables everywhere. He wore a somewhat long puce jacket with real diamond buttons, so that Malcolm was very much at home at once, for he thought that he and his father were travelling again, and that they had met Estel in their travels.

Furthermore, Estel had had the thoughtfulness to prepare some Spanish chocolate for them to refresh themselves with.

They sat there at five o'clock, therefore, spooning out the chocolate and eating toast along with it, when Malcolm's eyes fell on some unusual paintings which were hanging loosely on all the white walls of the room.

"Did you paint these, sir?" Malcolm wondered.

"No, no." Estel put down his chocolate cup. "*I* paint? I hire them done."

"They are quite out of the way," Malcolm told him.

"Thank you," Estel said. "They were out of the way, it is true, once, and although they are out of the period now, they can somehow always be relied upon to fetch compliments. That is why, in the main, I have them: compliment-fetchers."

Estel toyed for just a split second with the highest and largest of his diamond buttons—and then brought out very quickly: "Where did you say you met Mr. Cox?"

Estel Blanc's question was so sudden and so loud and the Spanish chocolate so thick that Malcolm choked and had to be patted, finally, on the back by his host.

"I'm afraid I have been a little impolite," Estel apologized for his question, but Malcolm could only signal to him that he was not yet ready to go on conversing with him, and in the rest between conversations, observing Estel more closely, Malcolm saw, once his eye had been coaxed away from the puce jacket and the diamonds, that Estel Blanc had the darkest skin of any person he had ever seen.

Left to himself in conversation, Estel could only ask questions now to which Malcolm could reply by nodding or shaking his head:

"Could you have met Mr. Cox at the Raphaelsons, by chance?" Estel wondered. "No, don't try to answer! Let me guess."

Malcolm, however, to be helpful shook his head now, meaning he had not met Mr. Cox at the Raphaelsons, and as he did so his coughing became more acute.

"Mineral water?" Estel wondered, and when Malcolm nodded, Estel brought him a tall Venetian glass which he had had all ready, perhaps, for just such a contingency.

"I met Mr. Cox on the bench," Malcolm unexpectedly brought out after he had consumed only a small volume of the water.

"The bench? . . . Of course," Estel said. Then suddenly reflecting that he had said *of course* to something he had not understood in the least, the host cleared his throat, shifted his legs on the chair on which he was seated, and said in a loud, almost menacing, voice:

"*What* bench?"

"The bench . . . he is going to get me off of," Malcolm cried.

"Go on, go on," Estel said, concentrating intensely.

"The bench I sit on in front of my hotel," Malcolm brought out.

Estel Blanc nodded faintly, and touched his nostrils with a heavy handkerchief which he took out of his breastpocket, and his host was too polite, Malcolm decided, to continue this part of the conversation with further questions. Estel was, however, about to say "*You met him, then, by chance*" when Malcolm, trying to assist the conversation along, said: "You are, I believe, Mr. Blanc, in the profession of undertaking."

Estel lowered his chocolate cup which he had been about to place to his lips, and said, after a rather patient pause: "Just call me *Estel* when we are conversing like this *tête à tête.*"

"But as to your question in regard to my profession, that of *mortician,*" Estel Blanc looked deep and thoughtful, "I have retired as of this spring. I'm forty, you know, and I was losing my art—frankly. People hadn't quite begun to notice that my powers were going, but *I* had. And *I* was what was important to my profession: later the world will know that. And, young man,"—here he looked at Malcolm with as firm a scrutiny as if he had held a monocle, or even a telescope to his eyes—"I was proud of my profession, inordinately proud, no matter by what name it was called!"

"I didn't mean to imply, sir, that it wasn't a fine profession."

"Say no more," Estel warned. "We've concluded the topic! More chocolate?"

"No thank you, sir, it was very rich."

Estel had set his mouth to say something which, by his expression, should have been important, when a peremptory rap was heard from behind a large Chinese screen which closed off the furthest section of the room in which they were sitting.

"We're not ready, Cora," Estel shouted to the screen. "Not ready at all!"

"What on earth was that?" Malcolm wondered.

"Cora always wants to begin before I've half-talked to people," Estel reminded himself that Malcolm was not the usual kind of guest. "We always offer entertainment to visitors," Estel made an attempt at explanation, brushing off a few crumbs of the toast which clung to his jacket and buttons. "I have so many entertainers around still from the old funeral-parlor days, you know . . . And I feel I owe them something, frankly."

"You must be extremely . . . well-fixed," Malcolm said, feeling some sort of compliment should be in order.

Estel Blanc smiled restrainedly. "Well, Malcolm, I like to feel, to quote my white friends, *comfortable*. But *rich*—that is another matter," and he tapped Malcolm's knee with one of the unused chocolate spoons.

"I understand," Estel Blanc continued, "from Mr. Cox, that you have lost a very dear father? Am I right?" and at that moment Malcolm thought he could detect for the first time this evening the exact manner and bearing of the *undertaker* in Mr. Blanc's voice and gesture, especially with regard to his eyes and hands.

"Yes," Malcolm replied slowly, "my father's death or disappearance—no one knows which it really is—has left me with very little to fall back upon."

"It is nice, however," Estel said, in a rather nasal tone now, "that speaking of *comfortable,* he left you in such pleasant circumstances, shall we say."

Malcolm shifted in his seat, and was about to reply to this statement when a loud clapping was heard from behind the same screen.

"Excuse me," Estel Blanc said in a cold but dignified tone, "but it seems we *are* about to begin."

Estel walked over to the high mantel over the fireplace, picked up a small box, extracted from it an oblong tiny disk, lit it, put it on a burner, sniffed it, and quickly resumed his seat near Malcolm.

"Cora Naldi always insists on incense for her number," Estel said. "As I think I said, she used to be in my funeral choir, you see."

Malcolm nodded.

Estel Blanc's hand fell to a light-switch, which he touched gingerly, and the lights in the room dimmed considerably. A gong sounded from an indeterminate part of the room.

A white hand removed the screen which had separated this section of the room from Malcolm and Estel, and from behind this a pair of heavy curtains was exposed, these then

suddenly parted, and the two conversationalists were
brought face to face with Cora Naldi.

Malcolm was never able to tell anybody later what or
who Cora Naldi was. He was not even sure at times she was
a woman, for she had a very deep voice, and he could never
tell whether her hair was white, or merely platinum, or
whether she was colored like Estel or white like himself.
She both sang and danced in loose shawls, and gave a kind
of recitatif when her throat got tired from her singing
numbers.

One song, which she sang two or three times, went:

> And is it so that you were there?
> And is it so you were?
> And is it so that while you were
> Cherries were your ware?
> Pale cherries were your ware?

But Malcolm's attention to her was, in any case, continuously disrupted by the fact that Estel Blanc talked to him
during the entire performance, explaining how he had written all the music which Cora Naldi was singing.

The strong perfume of the incense, the over-rich quality
of the Spanish chocolate, and the bombarding of his ears
with both Cora Naldi's songs and Estel Blanc's comments,
made Malcolm, as Estel Blanc later told everybody, not a
receptive audience.

Indeed, Malcolm must have dozed off from time to time,
for, after a while, he was awakened by Estel Blanc's rich
baritone voice talking to him alone—the little Chinese screen
was up again, the curtain was in no way in evidence, and
with those were gone likewise the smell of incense and the
sound and presence of Cora Naldi.

"I am puzzled," Malcolm heard the baritone voice of
Estel Blanc saying, "by your coolness, detachment, and
lack of receptivity." And Estel went on to wonder, perhaps
to himself, although he spoke out loud, if this coolness on

Malcolm's part did not have something to do with Estel's
"racial strain," as he put it, or indeed to Malcolm's possible
prejudice against Estel's having been in a profession which
is seldom looked upon as aesthetic, though, as he immediately pointed out, undertaking is perhaps the most aesthetic
of all professions, and indeed the most universal.

"But I am not sure what you mean by receptive!" Malcolm
cried, seizing on this one word out of Estel's discourse. "And
I do like you, Estel, and I am willing to just forget you were
an undertaker or a mortician or a . . . a . . . *Abyssinian,* or
anything!"

"Oh, dear God," Estel implored, and he immediately got
up from the chair he had been conversing in, and began
hurriedly pacing up and down the room, repeating somewhat religious exclamations of displeasure.

"Overlook anything I may have said, sir," Malcolm
begged him—"especially if it has offended you!"

Estel only shook his head, meaning Malcolm had again
said the wrong thing, and continued his pacing and his religious exclamations.

Then, perhaps relenting, the older man said, "But, of
course, Malcolm,—your age. That is what it all comes to,
naturally."

The storm had lifted, and Estel laughed.

Going up to Malcolm, he opened the boy's jaw, looked
in at his teeth, then pushing back his head, he looked carefully at his eyes.

"You're not more than 14!" Estel told him. "Mr. Cox said
you were all of 15!"

Pacing again about the parlor, Estel went on: "But what
does it matter, actually: 15 or 14, or 12. I have, since childhood, always lived among the mature, and indeed, if I may
say so, the over-ripe." The dark man laughed with somewhat histrionic bitterness. "I am afraid I have forgotten there
was youth—in your case, dear Malcolm, almost infancy . . ."

And he suddenly went over to Malcolm and shook the
boy's hand.

"Come back in twenty years, and we shall understand one

another," Estel said, and he ushered Malcolm rather hurriedly in the direction of the door.

"But I would ever so much like to come back again," Malcolm said. "I . . . enjoyed it all, sir. It was . . . *travel* to me."

"Travel?" Estel Blanc considered this, dubiously. "No, I am afraid I cannot see you again soon, or indeed at all," and he pulled at the sleeves of his jacket.

"I am flattered, of course," Estel went on, "that Mr. Cox should have thought of me as a kind of introduction for you to a greater world. But I am not in my element with the immature. I must be firm about this. I am not in my element . . . But come back, like I say, in twenty years!"

Having entered a slightly greater environment from the one the bench and the hotel had for such a long time given him, Malcolm was somewhat loath to allow the door of Estel Blanc's house to close on him. He stood as long as decency would allow him on the threshold, then, seeing that there was no way to prolong his visit, he stepped out onto the pavement, and in doing so—as he was to tell Mr. Cox the next day—walked right into the open arms of a policeman.

Coming out of the police station two or three hours later, whom should Malcolm see waiting for him but Estel Blanc himself, muffled up in a light coat which he wore in the manner of a cape.

"You said twenty years," Malcolm cried, and the thought actually did cross his mind that perhaps after all he had been imprisoned in the police station for that length of time.

"An auspicious beginning to your career," Estel said, somewhat pleasantly, somewhat acidly, for that was his permanent manner. "I saw the police sergeant make the arrest," the dark man said, "and although our *soirée* together was a total failure, I did feel some small sort of responsibility for you. I'm so relieved they let you off, of course . . ."

"The police captain and the sergeant both were very kind

to me," Malcolm reflected, "once they found out I was not the person they were looking for."

Estel nodded, waiting for more

"They said it was a confidence man they were after, and my good clothes, for a moment, led them to think I was he. But when they saw that I was not. . . ."

"When they saw you were not a grown man." Estel bobbed his head up and down. "Yes, everything is permitted to youth!"

"But how did you know?" Malcolm seemed thunderstruck.

"I know the police," Estel remarked.

"The police sergeant, who was the one who had arrested me," Malcolm went on pointedly, "even invited me back."

"Invited you back. That is real success!" Estel told him.

"I don't suppose *you* have changed your mind, by chance, about me," Malcolm ventured.

"No, no," Estel replied, "*I* am not here to invite you back. Really, Malcolm, you are terribly backward mentally. No, my decision rests just where it did when you left . . . We are not meant for one another's company, and until you are more mature, conversation itself, let alone friendship, is impossible."

The boy looked down disconsolately.

"The main reason why I have been waiting outside for you, in such an undignified position for me—is quite a simple one."

Malcolm smiled, his eagerness returning.

"You see," Estel fingered a piece of cardboard on which some words had been scribbled, "I am usually No. 1 on Mr. Cox's list of addresses, and so it was quite natural that he should have entrusted Address No. 2 with me—to give to you, of course, when the time came . . . But when the time came tonight, well, I forgot is all!"

"Address No. 2!" Malcolm cried.

"Oh, what enthusiasm," Estel commented. "I sometimes almost regret my decision with regard to you when I hear your freshness of tone. But to business . . . As I said, Cox has entrusted me with giving you Address No. 2. Here, take it, it's yours."

"Address No. 2," the boy read, holding the cardboard reverently, and reading what he saw there: "Kermit and Laureen Raphaelson. Why, what beautiful names . . . Are they also . . ." Malcolm hesitated.

"No, they are not Abyssinians, if that's what you mean," Estel said pointedly, placing the ends of his handkerchief, which seemed to have been dipped in some strong liquid, to his nostrils. "You will, I hope, find them to your taste!"

"Please, please, sir, tell me how it was that I have offended you," Malcolm began again, but a violent movement from Estel's cloak-and-coat stopped the boy.

"And you have stood out here . . . in the cold air waiting for me," Malcolm went on deeply apologetic.

"Yes, the cold June *cold* air," Estel replied, and he took the boy's hands and shook them with ceremonious restraint.

"Now this is goodbye," the dark man told him. "As I say, your career has begun auspiciously. The police sergeant episode alone is proof you have a charmed life. Keep close to your bench and Mr. Cox's addresses, and nothing can go amiss. And remember, dear boy, when you are mature, come back to see me. I will be here."

Estel bowed, and retreated slowly walking backwards directly to his house, which was only a short half-block from the police station. An old sign

THE BLANC EMPIRE MORTUARY

now unlighted looked down upon them.

"I do wish you wouldn't be so final," Malcolm said, but too low for Estel to hear him.

When the undertaker had disappeared into his house, Malcolm felt very lonely and tired. The events of the evening had been much too exciting and stimulating, and had he not just then looked down and seen the new address, he believed he would have burst into tears. Yes, there could be no doubt, he was beginning life, and with his usual silent evening prayer addressed to his father, wherever he might be, dead or alive, lost or found, he hastened back to his hotel suite.

Kermit and Laureen

Malcolm found himself the next evening in a long hall waiting for the buzzer to admit him to the apartment of Kermit and Laureen Raphaelson.

But as the buzzer had not worked for many weeks, perhaps even years, Laureen herself appeared to open the door, a stout young blonde woman whose face was covered with white moles.

She wore a look of extreme suspicion, together with mechanical expectation and boredom.

"You're from Professor Cox?" she said.

Malcolm nodded.

"The little man is not in his parlor yet," Laureen said, ushering him into her home.

"He is not?" Malcolm replied, wondering to whom she was referring.

"As a matter of fact," Laureen continued, and they now entered the front room of the apartment, "he is in the pantry finishing his supper. He often eats in there alone now just to spite me. He refused to eat even his cabinet pudding with me tonight. I am afraid Professor Cox may be right, and we are headed for the divorce courts."

Laureen pointed out a large over-stuffed chair for Malcolm to sit down in.

"Divorce courts are entirely out of my range of experience," Malcolm told Laureen. "But I am sorry you are headed for them."

"I haven't said a divorce is actually imminent, mind you," Laureen thought better of the subject.

But Malcolm was not listening, for he was experiencing the depth of the over-stuffed chair, most of whose stuffing had come off through age onto the floor beneath it.

Malcolm was about to exclaim "But what a deep chair, Laureen," when the latter cried out: "The little man!" in such a loud voice that Malcolm was startled, and leaped out of the chair, though it cost him great agility and effort to do so.

"You have a caller," Laureen addressed the person who had entered the room.

Malcolm at first mistook the latter for a child, but then realized that, limited though his experience in such matters was, the person was a man, and a midget.

"Why, who are you?" Malcolm could not prevent himself from exclaiming.

"*Her* husband," Kermit Raphaelson, the "little man," pointed with malice and glee in the direction of Laureen.

Malcolm was not only astonished to see that Kermit Raphaelson was a midget but that he looked quite handsome and clever, and differed from any other young man only in the matter of size: one merely felt one was looking at him with the wrong end of the eye-piece.

"I'm so glad to see somebody fresh and young!" Kermit cried. "And don't look so surprised, Malcolm," he continued. "Ignore Laureen, if you like, and pay your best attention to me. *I'm* the lonely one!"

"Good God alive," Laureen cried, raising her eyes to the ceiling. "It's beginning already."

"Yes, we are married," Kermit laughed, sitting down in a small chair specially designed, it was clear, for him. "Married, and married, and *married.*"

"I beg of you not to bring on a scene in front of this child," Laureen turned to her husband.

Kermit ignored her although he shot an oblique black look from beneath his lowered eyelashes.

"So you," he turned again to Malcolm, "are the boy who is infatuated with his father."

"I?" Malcolm pointed a finger at himself. "Infatuated?"

"Professor Cox has already told us all about you," the midget explained.

"But there's nothing yet to tell," Malcolm protested

against the *all*, which sounded to him both complete and frightening.

"There is a great deal to tell, *always*, Malcolm," Kermit spoke somewhat gravely now.

"And you really are married," Malcolm said staring closely at Kermit.

Kermit lowered his eyes. "*She* proposed," he explained, pointing to Laureen.

"I warn you," Laureen cried. "I will not tolerate your telling secrets about our marriage to a third party again!" Laureen continued to stand, perhaps because she had not yet made up her mind whether to leave or to stay, and because also she was in an extremely bad humor, which Malcolm's arrival had only worsened.

"Why did you choose to come to see us, Malcolm," Kermit said, edging his tiny chair closer to his guest.

Malcolm remembered his disastrous evening with Estel Blanc and did not reply immediately.

"Well, why did you come?" Laureen was severe. Both Kermit and she now stared at the boy fixedly.

"*Why* did I come to see you?" Malcolm swallowed, looking from one to the other, for the contrast between the two was stupefying to him—Kermit so small, Laureen so large and plump and commanding.

"Why, Mr. Cox ordered me to," Malcolm admitted under all the scrutiny and severity.

"You had no interest then, in us, for ourselves?" Laureen interrogated.

"None whatever," Malcolm replied without expression or regret or belligerence in his tone.

"We see," Laureen told him, and she smiled quietly triumphant.

"I suppose you know about my evening with Estel Blanc," Malcolm went on.

"Of course we know about it!" Kermit said. "Professor Cox keeps us pretty well informed, you know, as to what all his friends are doing and thinking."

"Professor Cox! That awful old . . ." Laureen began, but

instead of finishing what she was to say, she sat down in a tall straight-backed chair, and began rolling herself a cigarette, a process which took a long time owing to her hands trembling so much.

"Professor Cox," Laureen began again when her cigarette was rolled, "Professor Cox has ruined Kermit here with his ideas. We were *so* happy before we met him."

Kermit laughed sardonically at this point.

"Laugh all you wish," Laureen turned her back now on her husband and sat facing Malcolm. "Kermit and I were happy. But that old . . . Malcolm," she said suddenly, "you must give up Professor Cox if you want to grow into a fine and trustworthy man."

"Laureen, my dear," Kermit addressed his wife, "if you are going to sermonize, I will have to ask you to leave the front room, and go out and sit with the cats in the back parlor."

"You should tell Malcolm how many cats you have," Laureen said, "so that he can have a picture of where you are ordering me to go."

Kermit, however, said nothing, but made ironic little faces at Malcolm, who broke out into stifled guffaws.

"We have fifteen cats!" Laureen said in a tragic voice, but then hurrying on, in her telegraphic impulsive style: "Malcolm, am I getting across to you? . . . Professor Cox is not a man whom you should know at your age. I am trying to help you!"

"On what grounds should I not know Mr. Cox?" Malcolm inquired.

"A brilliant rejoinder to her stupid command," Kermit cried.

"Kermit, for pity's sake," Laureen begged her husband. "My husband," she explained, "is scarcely any better than Professor Cox, I am ashamed to admit. But I can see that you, Malcolm, are not yet corrupt . . . Not completely, at any rate," she studied the boy a little more closely.

"Thank you, Laureen," Malcolm told her, and again Kermit exploded into laughter, and Malcolm receiving this laughter as a compliment nodded briefly to the midget, and then directed his full attention back to Laureen.

"Professor Cox commands people to be their worst!" Laureen said.

"Nonsense," Kermit interrupted. "He tells them to do what they must do in any case, and they are merely free to be what they have to."

"All of Kermit's metaphysical ideas are taken lock, stock and barrel from Professor Cox," Laureen said patiently, looking at the bare wood of the floor.

"Professor Cox has a rather low opinion of Laureen at the moment," Kermit informed Malcolm.

"Low?" Laureen said. "Well, not just of me, Kermit," she went on. "He has a low opinion of everybody. Malcolm," Laureen said, moving her chair closer to that of the young boy and as she did so she touched him gently on his empty *boutonnière*, "do you know what Professor Cox suggested only last week to me—this is to show you the danger and the risk you run with him . . ."

Malcolm shook his head.

"But you're so young to hear it!" Laureen reflected. "So terribly young and unaware." She shaded her eyes with her hand, perhaps overcome by the thought of Malcolm's ignorance.

"No one's too young to hear anything about people!" Kermit cried disgusted. "And where is my hot tea, by the way? I asked you for my tea nearly an hour ago, and all you have been doing all evening is walking up and down complaining over your lot as a woman. If you kept up your womanly duties about the house, brought me my supper on time, and prepared my tea like a decent housewife, you wouldn't have time to be unhappy, wouldn't have time to worry about Professor Cox's commands."

"My dear, didn't I bring you your tea?" Laureen cried. "I won't have it said I have neglected my duties by you, no matter what may happen later on . . ."

Laureen immediately hastened to a small table, where the tea was already prepared, and brought Kermit his cup.

"Will you join Kermit in a cup of tea?" Laureen asked Malcolm, and when the latter nodded, she brought him the same kind of cup which she had given her husband except that this one had a crack in it, which Malcolm stared at some time before finally putting his lips to it to drink.

After sipping his tea with a critical expression for a few moments, Malcolm said in a rather stentorian voice:

"What did Mr. Cox command you, Laureen?"

"My precious," Laureen said, and going up to Malcolm she kissed him on the cheek.

"What a ridiculous display of pretended emotion," Kermit cried, addressing his wife. "I will tell you what Mr. Cox commanded her," he turned immediately to Malcolm.

"Let me tell it, Kermit," Laureen begged him. "I want the boy to hear it without your embellishments."

"Will you allow me to entertain *my* guest in *my* fashion, or shall I ask you again to step into the back room?" Kermit thundered at her.

Laureen bowed her head.

"We are poor people," Kermit began in a trembling voice, while Laureen held her head in her hands, like a woman in a court trial scene. "I make very little as an artist—" and here he pointed in the general direction of the many easels, oil paintings, empty frames, and sculpture which filled the large room. "Laureen, although a brilliant stenographer, can seldom keep a position, owing to her wish to meddle in the higher business of the offices where she is employed. Quiet!" Kermit roared when he saw Laureen make a motion that she wished to speak. "Knowing my wife's *propensities,*" Kermit said vindictively, "Professor Cox merely and sensibly proposed that Laureen go out with certain gentlemen who would pay her for her compliance with their wishes, since she was not entirely unknown for her favors before her sudden proposal of marriage to me."

The midget took out a cowboy handkerchief and wiped his mouth, and examined one of the inexpensive rings on his index finger.

"Laureen had promised me when she proposed marriage

to me," the midget continued, "that once I had agreed to be her husband and our visit to city hall was concluded, my days of struggle and difficulty would be over, that I could devote myself solely to my art, and at last achieve the full development and flowering of my talents. The exact opposite has been true. Since the prolonged week-end of our honeymoon in Pittsburgh, there has not been a day or night when we have not worried about food or necessities—I do not mention luxuries—and the little money I had inherited she, incompetent thing, has squandered in her mismanagement! I had to sell my finest oils for a song!"

"Exaggerations, dolly," Laureen cried.

"But, Malcolm," Kermit suddenly recovered his self-possession, "I did not agree to have you come to our house merely to let you hear about us."

"But it is so interesting and different," Malcolm exclaimed. "You see there is nothing to hear about in my case. I am, well, as they say, a cypher and a blank."

However, Kermit and Malcolm soon found their attention turned to Laureen, for she was giving what seemed to be a speech:

"When one's husband no longer respects one, when he can tell the most intimate secrets of marriage in front of a third party," Laureen was saying, "there is indeed nothing for one but the *streets.* Malcolm." Laureen said to the young man in particular. "I want you to know what Professor Cox proposed to me."

"What boredom! What repetition!" Kermit said.

"Do I look like a street-walker?" Laureen demanded going directly up to Malcolm. "Answer me, dear boy, for you are not yet corrupt . . ."

When Malcolm did not reply, Laureen drew even closer to him: "Do I, or don't I?"

"But aren't you . . . already one, dear Laureen?" Malcolm cried in consternation. "I thought your husband . . ."

Kermit laughed uproariously, while at the same time he pointed to the back room as a signal for Laureen to leave.

"Go back there and talk to the cats," Kermit ordered her.

"I want to have a *quiet* talk with Malcolm. I certainly deserve to see somebody else in the evening beside your own horrible blonde self."

"A true pupil of Professor Cox," Laureen exclaimed. Then turning benevolently to Malcolm, Laureen kissed him briefly on the forehead, and with a dramatic gesture of laying her hand across her mouth, she retired into the back room.

After a luxuriant silence, Malcolm asked: "Are there really cats back there?"

"As Laureen said," Kermit nodded, "there are fifteen."

"How sleepy I am suddenly," Malcolm said.

"Sleepy—at this hour?" Kermit expressed shock.

"Conversation makes me quite sleepy," Malcolm explained. "You see, usually all I have to do with people is have them wait on me. A maid will bring me a cup of chocolate, or the man from the tonsorial parlor will cut my hair and nails, and I exchange a few words with the leader of the string orchestra in the hotel, but no more than that. But since I have met Mr. Cox, I have been having rather long conversations with people, and it has made me quite sleepy."

"Lie down on the sofa and I will talk to you, then, while you rest," Kermit told him.

"I'd rather you didn't talk while I lie down," Malcolm said, and he went over to the sofa and stretched out. "In a little while," he told his host, "you must summon a cab, and I will go to my hotel."

"No, no, you can't leave in such a peremptory manner, not after you just got here, and after Laureen has left so that we can have our private talk!" Kermit complained.

"But what more is there to talk about? We've covered everything here, haven't we?" Malcolm cried, lifting his head a little to see Kermit more closely.

Kermit laughed and finished his tea.

"How odd though that Laureen should be a . . . a . . ." Malcolm mused.

"Odd she's a whore?" Kermit yawned. "Well, it's the only thing she ever wanted to be, and why she thought marriage would straighten her out, God only knows, especially marriage with me," and he picked up one of his paint brushes and inspected it briefly. "I never thought marriage would *straighten* me out," Kermit went on. "But I did think it might be a kind of long rest for me. But it's been a real workout, let me tell you, and as I say, never a day passes we don't worry about money."

The midget sighed and shook his head.

"I do not seem to recognize women like that when I meet them," Malcolm remarked.

"You do have beautiful clothes," Kermit said looking at Malcolm.

"Do I?" Malcolm looked down at himself. "They're all suits my father picked out years in advance of my being this size," Malcolm explained. "He has picked out suits for me all the way up to the age of eighteen. I think he had a presentiment he would be called away, and he left me plenty of clothes."

"Your father *was* quite extraordinary," Kermit asserted.

"That's what I tried to tell Mr. Cox," Malcolm cried, "but he wouldn't believe me."

"Oh, he probably believed you," Kermit said. "He only wanted to test your belief. To make you talk."

Malcolm nodded. "But I'm glad *you* think my father was extraordinary," the boy said. "You see, he's all I've got. And now I don't have him." And a short sob came out from Malcolm's throat.

Kermit looked at his wrists, and then at his empty tea cup.

Malcolm sat up just then, though, laughed, and then immediately lay down again, exclaiming: "I am too sleepy to sit up."

"I hope you won't command me to stop talking," Kermit said winsomely.

"I would rather you didn't," Malcolm replied, "but if you don't mind me never answering or not really listening, perhaps it's all right if you do go right on talking."

"Very well, then," Kermit said, "I will do just that, because I am awfully fond of talking."

"There is one thing, though, I must get straight before you begin your talking," Malcolm informed Kermit. "Are you a dwarf or a midget?" And Malcolm sat up briefly on the sofa.

"Oh, goodness," Kermit said after a short pause. "I'm neither."

"Neither?" Malcolm was so surprised he sat all the way up and put his feet down on the floor. "Why, you certainly must be one or the other!"

"No, no, *no!*" Kermit said, becoming very red in the face. "How stupid can one be?"

"But you're so small," Malcolm cried. "You *must* be a midget!"

"I'm not big," Kermit was patient now but sternly emphatic, "but I am no different from other men—fundamentally." He stood on this statement.

"You're just short, then?" Malcolm inquired.

"That's one way of putting it," Kermit agreed.

"But I've seen you in circuses—that is, I've seen short little men like you."

"Not like me!" Kermit shook his head, and he wiped his mustache with his cowboy handkerchief. "You've seen nobody like me," he repeated, and suddenly he stuck his tongue out at Malcolm, and opened his eyes very wide like a movie actor.

"Golly, how awful you look when you do that," Malcolm observed.

"I am awful sometimes," Kermit laughed a bit tunelessly.

"I think I like you, though," Malcolm said. "You're not *usual.*"

"Well, I could say the same thing of you, Malcolm, though I won't," Kermit replied. "You are not too bright, I gather, but you have your own charm, and an air of . . . innocuous fellowship."

"You don't do anything disgusting like embalm people here, do you?" Malcolm wanted to know.

"Oh, back to Estel Blanc again," Kermit scolded. "No, as

I told you, I am an oil painter, though nobody ever buys
anything that I paint."

"You are the first painter I have ever known," Malcolm
informed him. "Of course, I had never known an undertaker either until the other day."

Suddenly they both heard loud outcries in the back room,
and soon Laureen rushed out, her hair down, and her dress
torn, holding her arm, which had blood on it.

"Peter bit me and scratched me," she cried. She seemed
near hysterics.

"Fetch that pitcher over there," Kermit ordered Malcolm.

Malcolm brought the pitcher to Kermit and the latter
quickly threw the contents on Laureen.

The water, or whatever it was in the pitcher, was a sooty
color and when it had covered her head completely, Malcolm thought that Laureen resembled ever so noticeably
Cora Naldi, but of course the two ladies were not at all
alike, and Laureen wore no wig, and probably could not
sing a note.

Laureen continued to cry even after the water had been
thrown on her, but she was less vociferous.

"Now come over here and sit down on the footstool beside me, and I will talk to you," Kermit told his wife.

Laureen obeyed him, and once seated on the stool, she
complained softly: "Why can't we get rid of those beasts!
They invariably bite and take their spite out on me."

"You must learn to live with them, and love them, dolly,"
Kermit said, using the same pet name which she had awhile
before employed for him. He kissed Laureen gently on the
hair.

"Live and love, dolly," Kermit told his wife.

They had both almost completely forgotten Malcolm, who
was kept standing up waiting to be recognized, and who
finally after several minutes walked slowly over to the front
door.

"Good night then," Malcolm cried after several minutes
more of waiting, during which the married couple cooed
and embraced.

"Oh, Malcolm," Kermit cried. "You're not *going!*"

"I see a cab outside," the boy cried, "and I don't like to be away from my hotel suite much longer, you see."

Kermit expostulated.

"I'll be back, though," Malcolm said. "That is, if you will *let* me."

"But the evening is still young," Kermit explained. Then, resigned to Malcolm's going: "You don't know what marriage is," Kermit called helplessly from his position with Laureen. "But do come again, dear boy. You're awfully different, and it's been more than enjoyable."

"Yes, do come again, dear Malcolm," Laureen cried to him. "And forgive our not getting up. You'll understand when you're married, though."

"Do call us, dear Malcolm," Kermit shouted from beneath the heavy embrace of his wife.

"Thank you for the evening. Thank you for everything," Malcolm cried, going out. "Good night to both of you."

A Second Visit

Now that Malcolm was going out into the great world, so to speak, he felt compelled to write down some of the things, at least, which happened to him, for he was sure they were very important, and would be even still more so in the future. But as he had never been to school regularly owing to his having always been travelling with his father, or waiting for his father to return, he had very little command of language, and could seldom do more than copy down some of the things which his new friends, especially Professor Cox, said.

However, after his meeting with Kermit Raphaelson, Malcolm wrote down a statement original to him, which was found later among his effects: "Married love is the strangest thing of all."

Meanwhile, a small envelope had arrived from Professor Cox, containing Address No. 3. but Malcolm did not open this immediately, but put it in his breast pocket for later study.

The next day, on the bench, Mr. Cox questioned Malcolm concerning his visit to the Raphaelsons.

Pleased that Malcolm had been successful there, Mr. Cox sighed with relief: "If you hadn't got on with the Raphaelsons, well, I will tell you, dear boy," and he shook his finger at Malcolm, "I would, I am afraid, have had to give you up."

"Entirely?" Malcolm cried.

"Entirely," Mr. Cox said. "I was talking it over with my wife only last night. If he fails again, I said . . ."

"You mean there is a Mrs. Cox!" Malcolm was thunderstruck, for it never occurred to him that an astrologer would have a wife.

"Of course," Mr. Cox replied. "Everybody is married, Malcolm. Everybody that counts. And you will have to begin thinking about it, too."

"But what would I have done . . . if you had given me up?" Malcolm wondered almost to himself. "I mean, what would I have done about *addresses!*"

Mr. Cox smiled.

"Well," the astrologer mused, "you've got to remember, sir, that you have been off the bench twice . . . And I suppose that in the end,—sink or swim, as the old saw has it,— you would have *swum.*"

"Thank you," Malcolm said.

Then turning his attention to what puzzled him very much, Malcolm went on: "I don't understand why Kermit will not admit he is a midget."

Mr. Cox whistled shrilly. "He has a certain personal right to deny it, if he wishes to," he said, an air of dubiety about him.

"I asked him if he was one, and he was firm about not being one at all," Malcolm expostulated.

"That is so like Kermit," Mr. Cox agreed. "He has never told anybody that he is a midget. His mother evidently never told him he was one, and never referred to it, so that when finally he grew up,—well, he didn't actually know it, his life had been that sheltered. Laureen proposed to him when he was only 17, and they were married at once. He has really never known the world, much less, in fact, than you, for at least you have travelled with your father."

"Yes," Malcolm agreed. "I have seen things around me to a greater extent than the little man."

Mr. Cox looked away toward the sky-line in the manner of one who has a matter of persistent concern there.

"You're not leaving so soon, sir!" Malcolm exclaimed, for he had a hundred questions to ask of Mr. Cox.

"The day will come," Mr. Cox went on, just as though he had not heard Malcolm's question at all, "the day will come when he will have to admit he is a midget, and go on from there."

"He can't just go on acting like a little man, you mean?" Malcolm put the question to him.

"Not if he is the only one who believes it!" the astrologer answered immediately.

Mr. Cox took out his small notebook with the zodiacal signs on the cover, and wrote down something hurriedly on one of the pages inside.

Then turning his attention briefly to Malcolm, he said:

"Now that you have Kermit to visit, I won't be spending quite so much time with you here on the bench . . ."

"And I cannot visit you, and *your* wife?" Malcolm tested Mr. Cox again.

"Quite out of the question *now*," Mr. Cox said. "Our relationship must remain on a certain *professional* level."

"I see," Malcolm said.

"But I think you are beginning to win *through*," Mr. Cox told him enthusiastically, and shaking hands he took leave of his young friend.

"Don't forget Address No. 3: they're quite ready for you, you know!" he said in parting.

"I knew you would not fail me," Kermit exclaimed when he saw Malcolm entering the door of his studio. "Come in at once."

The little man dropped his paint brush, pushed back the easel on which there was a half-completed oil painting, and advanced toward his friend.

"But what's happened to everything?" Malcolm wondered, for nearly everything in the studio had been broken, or thrown about: the plaster casts of gods, masks of celebrities, canvasses, articles of furniture—all lay strewn and dismembered as in a junk shop.

Kermit did not say anything for a moment, then as Malcolm continued to gaze wonderingly at him, the little man explained: "Laureen has left me."

"Left *you?*" Malcolm considered this with astonishment.

"Oh, what's so surprising about that," Kermit added, a

new kind of bitter quality in his manner. He ushered the boy to a seat.

Kermit sat down now also, on his specially designed chair, but a different one from the fancy carved chair he had sat on at his first meeting with Malcolm.

"What beautiful chairs you always sit in," Malcolm said.

"I make them myself," Kermit explained, without enthusiasm.

Malcolm shook his head in incredulity and admiration.

"Yes," Kermit went on, indifferently, "I have a whole carpentry shop in the back where I make things such as you see around you. It's closed just now. That is, the cats are living out there . . . Before I married Laureen, the cats lived wherever I was, that is, throughout the whole studio, but when she came things had to change. She demanded affection at first of all the cats, and then she was partial to Peter and cruel to the others. Then she tired of Peter and was cruel to him and kind to the others. Finally, she was cruel to all of them. They wearied her. The same treatment was accorded to me."

"I can't get over that you are married at all," Malcolm exclaimed.

A flicker of displeasure crossed Kermit's face.

"I mean," Malcolm saw the look, "you could have perhaps . . . *waited.*"

"I think that is about all one can say about my marriage, perhaps," Kermit said, somewhat enigmatically. "But then who should I have married?" he added as an afterthought, perhaps to himself.

Kermit clapped his hands, and a young man without a shirt on appeared.

"Ginger beer for two people," Kermit commanded.

"Who on earth is that?" Malcolm wondered.

"He is my morning servant," Kermit explained absent-mindedly.

"He has such a powerful build," Malcolm noted.

"He is planning to open a gymnasium in the fall," Kermit explained, "and of course he has to look the part if he is to get pupils. But you do like ginger beer, don't you?" Kermit said, a bit more affable again.

"I don't know that my father and I ever drank ginger beer," Malcolm studied Kermit's question perhaps a bit too pedantically to suit his small host.

Kermit merely said, "Your *father*, I see," and then added quickly: "You have had a long life in hotels, haven't you?"

"Yes, we—that is *I*, now, have always lived in hotels. Big ones and little ones. But now that my father is no longer here, my money is beginning to go, and—" Malcolm said no more, a look of surprise and horror on his face at the thought that his money would, one day, all go.

Kermit was about to say something comforting when the half-naked young man came in with a tray containing the ginger beer. But as Malcolm looked again he was almost certain that the young man had nothing on at all, the way the light now fell on him.

In this morning light, too, Kermit looked a good deal older, and crosser: he looked about twenty-two.

The young undressed man did not seem to know how to talk, but he poured and filled with ice the ginger beer in a professional and efficient manner.

Kermit kept looking irritably from Malcolm to the young servant, and from the young servant to Malcolm, and finally the midget said:

"Your *father* probably would not approve of my introducing you to a morning servant, but I feel your education could be extended, as does Professor Cox, so therefore I introduce you to O'Reilly Morgan. O'Reilly—Malcolm."

O'Reilly Morgan, the morning servant, nodded politely and said *pleased* and *great morning* and Malcolm began to get up to shake hands, but Kermit shook his head at him, meaning that would not be necessary and pray keep his seat.

"Wouldn't O'Reilly Morgan care to have some ginger beer with us?" Malcolm inquired when the servant had gone out of the room.

Kermit swallowed some of the beer very fast and choked a little. Then frowning severely, he said quickly: "Another time, perhaps. Just now I have to explain the very bad news to you about Laureen. And I don't want *him* to hear," and Kermit gestured in the direction of the kitchen and O'Reilly.

Kermit rapped vigorously on his chair arm, for Malcolm's attention had begun to wander a little.

"I *say*, I want you to give me your undivided attention," Kermit said. "I have a very important thing to communicate, and I don't want to shout."

"But what is it?" Malcolm leaned forward, and he felt again that he was beginning life.

"I must tell you how Laureen left me," Kermit cried, and he was very pale, as pale as if he had said he had killed her.

"You saw her last time just before the act, so to speak, and just when I thought she loved me the most. She's betrayed me, you see, from the first, and at last, she has betrayed me completely by leaving."

"She discovered who you were then?" Malcolm asked, eager to understand.

"Who I *was*?" Kermit's voice shook.

"I mean . . . I . . . ," Malcolm faltered.

"Say exactly *what* you mean," Kermit cried, and he stood up, and in doing so, Malcolm saw to his further confusion that Kermit was scarcely any taller standing up than when he had been sitting down. Malcolm's look of surprise only increased, if anything, Kermit's ill-temper.

"Say exactly what you are thinking. I command it!" Kermit said.

"I only meant," Malcolm winced, "she discovered at last —well, as Mr. Cox says, that you are a . . ."

"A midget! A midget!" Kermit roared. "Is that what the old pederast calls me behind my back?"

"Old *what*?" Malcolm cried, but his question was drowned in a loud crash, that of Kermit's throwing to the floor the entire tray containing the ginger beer bottles.

O'Reilly quickly entered the room, but as quickly retreated.

Kermit had, however, sat down again and was weeping quietly, but with a modicum of control.

Malcolm came over to where the little man sat, but the latter vociferated at him:

"Don't touch me! I don't want pity from my *calumniators!*"

"You use such difficult words this morning," Malcolm complained, almost weeping himself.

Suddenly Kermit seized Malcolm's hand, and said in an imploring voice: "Why did she do it, Malcolm, when she was all I had?"

Malcolm wished to say something consoling, but he was afraid that he would again bring out the wrong word at such a dramatic moment.

O'Reilly again entered the room, this time wearing a kimono, and carrying a small tray with a medicine bottle. He handed Kermit a tiny pill, which the little man took perfunctorily, and swallowed, refusing the water the servant proffered him. O'Reilly immediately withdrew again.

"Oh, I hadn't loved Laureen in months," Kermit went on, steadier now. "She had lost her sparkle, and she almost disgusted me at times. But I had got so used to her and her waiting on me. I will not pretend about myself. I had come to expect her help, Malcolm. Her going away has meaning in the economic realm!"

Malcolm nodded soberly. Then wanting to say something encouraging, the boy said: "Kermit, you don't have the *voice* of a midget: you have the voice of a very young man."

Kermit's mouth opened slowly and closed, but he did not appear to have heard the compliment. He continued: "When Laureen left me last night, I seemed suddenly to have reached my majority in age. I realized that I was beginning life at last. Alone, as everybody is."

"And it's pretty scary," Malcolm volunteered.

Kermit scrutinized the boy slowly in the manner of one who is seeing him for the first time.

"We are both alone," Kermit mused. "How fortunate, after all, that Professor Cox exists and that he brought us together. We are both in an impossible situation."

"Certainly *I* am," Malcolm affirmed.

"But why you more than I?" Kermit was put out with the boy.

"You have something," Malcolm told him. "Talents. Look at your art, and your chair-making. And your marriage, which means you know women. I have nothing. I can do nothing. All I have is the memory of my father. My father—"

"Shit on your father!" Kermit cried at him.

Malcolm stood up mechanically, white with terror, and trembling all over.

There was a total silence in the room.

Kermit got up slowly and came over to Malcolm. His head reached only to the boy's waist and prevented him, humiliatingly enough, from speaking directly to Malcolm's face: his words, in fact, addressed themselves to his navel. Kermit could only tug at the tall boy's trouser legs.

"Malcolm," he cried, "you must forget I ever said it!"

Malcolm moved away from him, and sat down in a straight-back chair some feet away from where the midget was now left standing alone.

"You must listen to me, and you must forgive me," the voice of the midget came hollow and distant like something heard in a deserted subway station.

Malcolm tapped on the wood of the chair with his index finger.

"You must listen to my apology, dear Malcolm," Kermit pleaded, and he had quit crying.

"How can I ever listen to you again?" Malcolm finally spoke. "And how can I forgive you? To have said *that* about my father. This is the last straw of what can happen to me. I must pack and leave the city today. Why I have stayed this long here I don't know. And on a bench to boot."

"Listen to my apology at least," Kermit begged, and he

actually raced over to where Malcolm was sitting so stiffly, and pulled savagely on Malcolm's jacket.

"You have no right to desert me," Kermit protested. "We're under the same star!"

"Is this some of Mr. Cox's astrology now?" Malcolm wondered bitterly.

"Malcolm, try to put yourself in my place. I have just given up my entire world by admitting who I really am. And I'm depending on you so. I have nobody else to depend on!"

"A likely story coming from a man who insults the dead," Malcolm said.

"I *apologize.* I apologize from the heart. Don't I know that your father was a princely type, judging by the son. Don't I see breeding and culture in every line of your face."

Malcolm nodded slightly.

"Then don't torture me any further, and forgive me."

"I don't know whether I can forgive you or not, Kermit. I don't know what my father would have done under the circumstances. If you had just said *damn his hide* or *to hell with him* that would have been terrible enough!" And Malcolm again shivered with horror.

"I meant really nothing but irritation, not irritation against you and certainly not against your father."

"Very well, then, Kermit, you are forgiven for this once," Malcolm said.

Kermit pressed the boy's shoulder in a token of gratitude.

"Laureen! Laureen!" Kermit began muttering now, walking about the studio, and tapping his forehead from time to time. "Did I tell you who she ran away with?" Kermit inquired suddenly.

"She ran off with somebody?" Malcolm inquired.

"How else would she go!" Kermit thundered, some of his old anger coming back. "She ran off with a Japanese wrestler . . ."

Malcolm lowered his head, too tired now to take in any more of the complex events of the world. But after a moment he found the strength to inquire:

"Was he—the Japanese wrestler—also a *small* man?"

Kermit gazed at Malcolm for an interminable length of time, before replying: "He was the usual size for a man," and he spoke with great dryness and restraint.

"But Laureen will *eventually* return to you," Malcolm offered this weak consolation.

"Not Laureen," Kermit said. "No, I was only her pre-husband, her breaking-in man. Now she has gone on to the real thing, as she said when she left. She's gone on to the—well, why not say it in front of children—" he spoke almost to himself. "She's gone on to the real equipment!"

And Kermit became plunged into the deepest gloom.

Address No. 3

The third address from Professor Cox had been written with a flourish of the pen which swooped down on the margin of the pale green paper like a finger of warning. It said merely:

MADAME GIRARD
THE CHATEAU

"But it doesn't tell where," Malcolm had exclaimed in his hotel suite.

Going out into the street, he had summoned a cab, and consulted with the driver concerning the address. The driver had immediately recognized it, to Malcolm's relief, and told the boy that it was the *best address*, perhaps the only *real* address in the city, and certainly the only one for high-livers, he told Malcolm, with a slight note of gravity in his voice.

A footman at the Chateau opened a white door on the boy, and Malcolm was taken immediately upwards in a green and gold elevator which smelled strongly of patchouli and rose water.

The footman directed Malcolm, when he had alighted from the elevator, to a very narrow but very tall door, which looked more like a linen chute than an entrance. On the door, showing unmistakably it was the right one, was a message written on thick letter paper:

MALCOLM: YOU ARE EXPECTED: MADAME GIRARD.

The footman said goodnight, and disappeared into the elevator.

Malcolm opened the door, and as he did so pushed his face into that of a young man in a Texas hat.

"You're *Malcolm!*" the young man, who had a very flushed face, and who was carrying a tall iced drink, said.

"How did you know me?" Malcolm wondered, but the young man began pulling him up an additional staircase, without replying to his question.

"Madame Girard is demanding a settlement from her husband," the young man informed him, tinkling the ice in his drink. "You're just in time for the evening performance."

Malcolm and the young man now entered a room almost as large as a cathedral.

Madame Girard herself faced them. She was dressed in a riding outfit, and her riding whip lay at her feet, together with several bottles, some empty, some half full. Her face was scratched, so that one would have suspected she had ridden through brambles, and her makeup was smeared so unevenly across her face and mouth that she resembled a clown more than a woman. Malcolm wished immediately that the beautiful riding habit which Madame Girard was wearing could have been bestowed on Kermit, for he was sure the midget would have looked better in it than Madame Girard.

"Who admitted this child?" Madame Girard demanded, picking up a glass of plain vodka.

Mr. Girard, her husband, a short man of middle years, with a distinguished brow, now came forward to explain to his wife:

"Professor Cox called up and asked if this young man could not be received."

Mr. Girard bowed to Malcolm and went to take his hand, but Malcolm had got both his own hands so tightly enmeshed in his trouser pockets—for the suit he was wearing was an old one which his father had picked out for him some time back, and it was becoming too small—that he was unable to return Mr. Girard's greeting and handclasp.

"And who gave *you* leave, sir, to accept invitations by proxy for me?" Madame Girard demanded of her husband.

"I have a great mind to take proceedings against you, with reference to the matter which we discussed earlier in the evening!"

"Please try to be more hospitable, Doddy," Mr. Girard addressed his wife.

"Don't use pet names for me in front of strangers," Madame Girard cautioned her husband.

"Sit down please a moment," Madame Girard commanded Malcolm, and she went up close to him to get a better look.

As Malcolm looked hastily about the great glass room beyond which one could catch glimpses of the ocean and the lights of cities—he caught sight of at least ten young men who were all seated on identical straight-back chairs—all facing Madame Girard, the sole member of her sex in the room—and all silent, like a mute chorus.

"Are all these gentlemen friends of Mr. Cox?" Malcolm said in a loud voice, for he did not feel at all comfortable in such a charged atmosphere. Everybody laughed at his remark—the ten young men laughing together very much like a chorus—all except Mr. Girard, who looked down at the carpet.

"Why is it you are not entering into the spirit of the party?" Madame Girard asked her husband. "Do you want me to begin proceedings against you at once?"

Mr. Girard put his pipe into his mouth without looking away from the carpet.

Malcolm said in his same loud voice: "I had no idea it was going to be like this."

"What is *it?*" Madame Girard demanded.

"Your gathering or party or whatever you call it," Malcolm replied. He was not impressed with Madame Girard or her friends, the young men, and he showed it.

"We are here for the sole purpose of considering taking proceedings against my husband," Madame Girard spoke gravely, "and I think I can do this quite properly without comments from the newly-arrived."

"Perhaps Mr. Girard may want a divorce first," Malcolm

said, and again there was a chorus of laughter from the young men seated on the chairs, and Mr. Girard himself this time smiled from behind his pipe.

"As you may not know," Malcolm began, addressing himself to everyone present, and still employing his loud voice, "Mr. Cox, the well-known astrologer, is introducing me to all of his friends this year in the hopes that I may be a little less inclined to be lonely."

"That follows," Madame Girard tasted her vodka loudly.

"You must drink a *great* deal, Madame Girard," Malcolm said, a note of genuine worry in his voice, and there were again cries of laughter, but greatly muffled this time, while Mr. Girard bit his pipe and looked away toward a row of vases all filled with fresh garnet roses.

"What was it you said?" Madame Girard inquired, a kind of stunned craftiness in her voice, like one who must discover the precise detail which will convict her enemy.

"I think you are intoxicated, madame," Malcolm said.

The laughter from the young men now became unrestrained.

"Do you realize in whose home you are?" Madame Girard said in a breathless voice.

And in still lower tones: "And do you realize who *I* am?"

Malcolm nodded, and said: "This is the third place I've visited at Mr. Cox's request"—and he turned to face everybody in the room—"but I can't say it is the most pleasant or comfortable of the three."

"Hear him?" Madame Girard cried, standing up now. "He's a critic, not a guest. And not only a critic, but a spy! A spy of Mr. Cox's, that's it . . . Throw him out! *Throw him out!*"

"Doddy, *dear*," Mr. Girard begged her, walking over to his wife and putting his hand on her arm gently.

Madame Girard sat down quickly perhaps because she was beginning to lose her balance rather than because she wished to obey her husband.

"I believe I have heard mention of your *father*," Mr.

Girard changed the topic of conversation, addressing Malcolm directly.

"He's a spy from old Mr. Cox!" Madame Girard began again, for she did not like the topic of conversation to be changed without her giving the cue.

A faint tittering from the young men came and went.

"You really knew my father!" Malcolm was all ears, but he did not say this with quite the enthusiasm he might have shown a few days earlier. Malcolm suddenly felt—even as he spoke to Mr. Girard—that the image of his father was slightly blurred in his own memory, and so he sipped the drink of vodka which a servant had just handed him.

"I do not think your father exists," Madame Girard cried, lifting her glass again. "I have *never* thought he did."

Malcolm swallowed hard, then opened his mouth to say something.

"And what is more," Madame Girard continued to hold the floor, "*nobody* thinks he exists, or ever did exist."

"That's . . . that's . . . blasphemy . . . or a thing above it!" Malcolm cried, standing up, while Mr. Girard went up to him and attempted to say something quietly in his ear. "And this is the first time where I have ever attended a . . . a . . . *meeting*," Malcolm chose this word after looking at all the young men on chairs—"a meeting where the person in charge was . . . drunk."

And Malcolm again turned his attention to Madame Girard as if begging her to explain the situation to him.

"As I said earlier in the evening," Madame Girard turned her full attention now to the young men on the chairs, "I have no choice. I must take proceedings against Mr. Girard."

"Doddy, dear," Mr. Girard implored. "You do not need to take proceedings tonight . . ."

He took her glass of vodka from her and handed it to a servant who was passing by at that second.

"An enemy! A husband!" Madame Girard commented, narrowing her eyes.

Suddenly she began to weep, and all the young men except Malcolm looked very uncomfortable, while the latter, on the contrary, moved his chair a bit closer now to be able to study Madame Girard's features better.

"All my young *beauties* on their uncomfortable straight chairs—see how I am suffering!" Madame Girard implored them. "Come and comfort me, beauties," she cried, stretching out her arms to the young men.

"What a pretty face she must have under all that melted makeup," Malcolm pointed out to Mr. Girard.

Madame Girard stopped crying for a minute, and then asked her husband if he had a handkerchief, which he immediately produced from his breast pocket and handed to her.

"Wipe my face free of any blemishes," she commanded him.

"Oh, I've been through so much," Madame Girard told the room, as Mr. Girard wiped her face free of the mascara and the rouge. "Nobody knows what I have suffered! That is why I feel so often I *must* start proceedings. There ought to be a reckoning for such suffering."

"Doddy," Mr. Girard said softly to his wife.

"And with this *spy* here from Mr. Cox," she began whimpering again. "He will go directly again to that old fraud and tell him *everything* about this evening, and then Cox, blast him, will call all of his clients and tell them how I was not at the top of my form this evening."

"But why," Malcolm cried, suddenly standing up, and coming over to Madame Girard, who seemed surprised and perhaps frightened that he drew so close to her, "why *did* Mr. Cox send me here?"

"Why?" Madame Girard thundered at him. "You mean you are actually as stupid as everybody says you are! *Why?* Have I not given you the reason a score of times this evening. Yes, it is true, what everybody says about you, you have no mind. But you are Mr. Cox's spy, whether you know it or not. For he must have information at any cost . . . And to think I am not in top form!"

She now wept uncontrolledly.

Mr. Girard was so upset that as a special concession to

Madame Girard he now brought her a small glass of French champagne, which she sipped, while he assiduously dried her tears with his handkerchief.

Mr. Girard at the same time motioned for Madame Girard's young "beauties" to leave their straight-backed chairs and gather round her to cheer her.

Madame Girard smiled faintly when she saw the young men surrounding her in a circle, in the center of which now stood Malcolm.

"Why? why?" Madame Girard turned to her husband, "did you spoil this beautiful evening by introducing a spy in our midst," and she pointed again at Malcolm.

"You are not going to order me out then like Estel Blanc?" Malcolm asked, despondency and gloominess in his voice.

"Estel Blanc," Madame Girard cried, stung to the quick. "Oh merciful God!" and she burst again into weeping.

"You should have *never* mentioned his name to her," Mr. Girard was both reproving and apologetic. "She fears him more than anybody else."

"You see," Madame Girard explained, when she had recovered from her new fit of tears, "this child knows only the worst people, and knows, indeed, only my enemies. Oh, make him leave, Girard, for pity's sake, make him leave."

"Doddy, remember your long years of position," Mr. Girard begged her. "Remember *society,* if you will not remember your position."

"Oh, it's so hard to bear one's burdens some times," she said, drinking more of her champagne. "And we don't need him," she pointed to Malcolm. "Don't I have my beauties already?"—here she recognized with a peremptory nod the young men—"Why aren't *they* enough. Why must we have a paid informer in the shape of this brainless, mindless, but—" and here Madame Girard paused as if seeing Malcolm for the very first time—"this very *beautiful* young boy?"

"Perhaps we should all drink to Madame Girard!" Malcolm cried, astonished at her lightning change of attitude toward him, and he raised his glass, and even as he did so, everybody could see that he was quite drunk himself.

"My dear, dear young friend," Madame Girard cried. "Oh, thank you."

All the young men and Mr. Girard now raised their glasses, and Malcolm, too, with some difficulty raised his again, got his glass to his lips, drained it, while a servant immediately replenished his glass for him, at a sign from Madame Girard.

"Leave Mr. Cox," Madame Girard addressed Malcolm. "Be my own, and not his."

"Let us all drink again to Madame Girard," Mr. Girard cried nervously, and the young men all gathered round him, and some patted him on the back, relieved at the breaking of the tension in the room.

"Do you know, my young, my very young dear friend, the company you are keeping?" Madame Girard stood up now, seized one of the garnet roses from a vase, and in a twinkling had pushed it into Malcolm's hitherto unused lapel.

Malcolm kissed Madame Girard lightly on her cheek, reeling toward her.

"Answer my question, wonderful young man," Madame Girard demanded, and she seemed almost sober. "Do you know the company you keep? Do you know, dear boy, what Mr. Cox himself is?" she cried.

"Why, a pederast, of course," Malcolm reeled, his piercing loud voice a bit shaky and thick.

"What!" everybody cried at once, and the young men stared at one another in open-mouthed astonishment and disbelief.

"What word did I hear?" Madame Girard exclaimed, a bemused smile lifting her cheeks.

"I don't intend to repeat myself!" Malcolm cried, draining his glass. "My father never did! . . . Hurrah!" he shouted, and suddenly he fell to the floor in a sitting posture.

Madame Girard rose from her chair, pushing aside the ten "beauties" and her husband, went swiftly over to where Malcolm lay slowly sinking into her thick carpet, and like a woman who has decided at last to come to terms with her own fresh decision, she bent low over the boy, a complete change of will and soul in her face. She stopped again, as if seeing him for the first time, she held her hands to her breast, the change in her mind registering itself now in her heart:

"You are a real prince, Malcolm," she cried. "Oh, forgive me. An authentic—"

And Madame Girard muffled the word she was saying by kissing him vociferously on his hair as he lay staring at her from his sitting posture.

"Royalty!" she cried pointing out Malcolm to the other guests staring anxiously at them both. "Royalty."

A Visit from the Magnate

Malcolm passed the next few days talking from time to time with Mr. Cox, who stood as usual before the boy, while the latter was seated on his bench, and in writing down his "conversations" with the personages of the addresses.

Mr. Cox agreed that Address No. 4 should not be given to Malcolm until he had completely digested the scenes and significance of the first three addresses.

Then, shortly after this, one late evening, Malcolm was surprised when, as he lay in his large canopied bed listening to the different sea-shells which his father had bought him when they had been on their travels, he heard through the incrustaceans of the shells, the uncommon sound of the telephone ringing.

Answering it, he was still more surprised to hear the voice of Mr. Girard, who was, he said, telephoning him from the lobby of the hotel.

"Can I see you, Malcolm?"

Mr. Girard was sober and prepossessed, as always, for although he may have been accustomed to consume as much alcohol as Madame Girard, his strong will resisted all stimulants.

It was Malcolm who was not at ease, for it was the first time anybody had ever telephoned to see him since the days his father often dropped in unexpectedly from Denver or San Francisco from a business deal. Helplessly listening to Mr. Girard on the phone, Malcolm was not able to reply at once, owing to his confusion.

Mr. Girard, hearing only Malcolm's breathing on the other end of the wire, and no response to his inquiry, apolo-

gized again for the lateness of his call, but repeated his wish
to see the boy.

"I don't see why you can't see me, if you don't mind seeing me just dressed in my bathrobe," Malcolm finally said.

"I will be right up then," Mr. Girard told him.

In Malcolm's suite, Mr. Girard looked much younger and
more handsome, but also, oddly enough, more careworn and
worried than he had in the Chateau.

He seemed at home in the large faded elegance of Malcolm's hotel suite, and Malcolm immediately offered him a
tumbler of ice water.

"I felt somehow we were of the same station in life," Mr.
Girard began, and he took a seat on the divan "—even
though I am so much older than you. How old are you, Malcolm?" he wondered.

Malcolm swallowed, and moved his fingers, like one who
is counting.

"Fifteen, sir," the boy replied.

Mr. Girard looked at him hesitatingly.

"That is, sir, I will be in December, I think," Malcolm
added.

"I see," Mr. Girard said. "And it is now June, isn't it? . . .
Well, you see, I am thirty-seven, so that I am easily old
enough to be your father."

"Yes, you are, I see," Malcolm answered. "My father, however, looked older, though perhaps stronger, than you. He
looked nearly forty."

"I hope I have not disturbed you," Mr. Girard continued.
"But my coming is dictated by an emergency."

"Nothing serious?" Malcolm expressed concern. "Madame Girard has not taken ill or died?"

"Madame Girard is home sleeping in her private wing of
the Chateau," Mr. Girard replied. "I simply came here to
make a very unusual suggestion to you, and I hope you will
hear me out. I have come, though—I must make clear—on
my own volition, despite the fact that Madame Girard herself ordered me to come."

Mr. Girard wiped his forehead with his pocket handkerchief.

"You seem, Malcolm, so close to me in general background and point of view, and Madame Girard has taken
such an immediate and violent fancy to you, also, that we
wondered—" and here Mr. Girard took out a small silver
box which contained some pastilles and popped one hurriedly into his mouth—"we wondered if you would care to
come with us to our country house for the summer. Everything would be taken care of, of course, and you would not
have to give up your hotel suite, as I would be glad to take
all responsibility with regard to that . . ."

"Why, I am speechless with surprise at your generosity,"
Malcolm exclaimed, and he got up and walked about the
room for a minute or two.

"Would you care to listen to one of my sea-shells for a
moment?" Malcolm offered one of the larger shells.

"Are you paying close attention to what I have proposed
to you, Malcolm?" Mr. Girard was a bit grave at that moment, and he did not accept the proffered sea-shell.

"Oh, yes, sir, very close attention," Malcolm replied. "Nobody has ever invited me anywhere, you see, except my
father. I have not been out of this hotel, mind you, except
to go occasionally to other hotels—that is, until I met Mr.
Cox."

Mr. Girard tapped somewhat impatiently on the wooden
end of the divan.

"You will make both me and my wife very happy if you
will come," Mr. Girard said in the manner of a man con-
cluding an agreement. "And we may expect you then?"

"But I would have to leave all of my new friends!" Malcolm cried out.

"Your new friends?" Mr. Girard said with the surprise of
a man who hears something totally unforeseen and something uncalled for, to boot.

"Kermit Raphaelson and Mr. Cox, especially," Malcolm
informed him. "I don't count Estel Blanc really—not as a

friend—though perhaps in twenty years, as he said himself, that might be a possibility."

"I don't recognize these people except by name," Mr. Girard was somewhat withdrawn now. "You see, Malcolm, I am often gone, and don't always get to know my wife's friends. Often, in fact, I've never heard their names and then returning late to the Chateau from a long trip, I meet them face to face for the first time. And often I never see them again after our first meeting."

"You don't seem to care, then, for the friends of others," Malcolm observed.

"Well, dear Malcolm, I won't deny that I have never liked any of my wife's friends. You are the first."

"You mean, you really are in earnest about me?" Malcolm was surprised.

"Why, of course I am in earnest!" Mr. Girard replied a bit hotly. "I am always in earnest."

"But you see, Mr. Girard, sir, you do not understand," Malcolm assured him. "Until I met Mr. Cox on the bench my whole life was just this hotel suite. There was nothing much to it. And now suddenly, invitations from everywhere, people ringing me up at midnight. There is almost *too* much of it."

And Malcolm went up and shook Mr. Girard's hand, who, not being exactly ready for such a display of etiquette, stood up, and his sudden raising of his knees pushed the boy away from him, so that the latter came close to losing his balance.

Mr. Girard remained standing in this awkward posture.

"I feel, Mr. Girard, sir," Malcolm said, recovering his composure, "that life is actually *beginning*."

"I feel very much the same as you, Malcolm," Mr. Girard replied, "and although my life is over in the sense of a beginning, I seem to see it starting all over again in you. Perhaps it is because you are like a son to me. But as I said earlier in the evening, I believe that you are in my own general situation and in my part of the world."

"Thanks to my father," Malcolm said.

"No, not thanks to your father," Mr. Girard assured him.

"Thanks to you. It is to you we all look, and not your father."

"That is very hard for me to believe, Mr. Girard," Malcolm said.

"What is hard?" Mr. Girard questioned, concern written all over his face.

"That you place such a high estimate on me, sir. You see, my difficulty is I can hardly place any estimate on myself. I hardly feel I exist."

"You feel you don't exist?" Mr. Girard weighed the boy's words.

"That's right. And when other people pay so much attention to me all at once, I feel something has gone wrong somewhere . . ."

"Everybody is fond of you," Mr. Girard said. "At least we are, and I am certain everybody else must be likewise."

"Thank you, Mr. Girard, sir," and Malcolm looked down at the gold embroidery on his dressing gown.

"Then you will accept the invitation, Malcolm?"

"I will be happy to *accept* it, Mr. Girard."

"Please call me by my first name, although I am more than twenty years older than you."

"What is your first name?" Malcolm wondered somewhat bashfully, hesitating to ask such a question of so great a man.

"Girard," Mr. Girard said.

"But that is your last name, sir?"

"My last name and my first name are the same."

"You mean you are—"

"Girard *Girard*, that is right. When I was a young man, it was very hard to bear, but now that I'm old, I like it."

"You are a very likeable old man," Malcolm affirmed.

"I felt perhaps that you admired me, and that is one of the reasons I wanted you to come with us. My wife, however, is very much the partisan of you."

"She is?" Malcolm swallowed, hesitating on the word *partisan*. "Thank her, please."

"Now when do you think you can make your little visit?" Girard said.

"Oh, I can't come," Malcolm replied firmly.

"What?" Girard said, a note of imperious anger in his voice, so that he assumed his full character as billionaire and magnate in one change of expression.

"It has nothing to do with you," Malcolm said calmly walking up and down the room.

Mr. Girard drank all of the ice water in his glass, opened his *pastille* box with a snap, looked into it, took nothing out this time, and closed it with another snap.

Malcolm was somewhat taken aback at how fierce Girard looked at that moment.

"I can't leave the bench," Malcolm told him. "And I don't think I can just walk out on Kermit and Mr. Cox."

"Well, bring them along with you," Mr. Girard expressed some relief—"if that's all!"

"I don't even know whether I can call you Girard, sir," Malcolm went on.

"Because of my extreme age?" Girard wondered.

"I don't know what it is, sir," Malcolm said. "Maybe because to address you so sounds . . . *insubordinate*, I believe they say."

Girard Girard stopped, then said: "Well, who the devil cares what you call me. Call me anything or nothing, but come!"

Mr. Girard tried to smile and look pleasant.

"You see," Malcolm continued, "I'm terribly afraid of leaving here where I'm always alone, and waiting, and going to where people may demand me at all hours . . ."

"No one will demand anything of you that you don't want to give," Mr. Girard said patiently, and Malcolm felt that the great man's patience was rapidly diminishing.

"I must turn down your kind invitation," Malcolm summoned all his bravery.

"There must be some other reason which you are not giving."

"No, *Girard*," Malcolm made the effort with his name—"there is none. I can't explain the reason except that it has something to do with the bench, Mr. Cox's instructions, and

also my new friend, Kermit, who, by the way, must be very
hurt that he has never been invited to the Chateau to meet
Madame Girard, and of course, sir, you . . ."

"I see," Girard said, ignoring nearly everything Malcolm
had said. However, he made no motion to leave.

"I want to please you very much," Malcolm said after a
long silence. "And Madame Girard, too, though I don't
know why I want to please her, except I do."

"Then you'll reconsider?" Mr. Girard cried in a loud voice.

"I *want* to come," Malcolm told him. "But I'm afraid I
can't."

"What then are you afraid of?" Girard now thundered.

"I believe, sir, as I said, it has something to do with leaving the bench."

"Don't call me *sir!*" Girard commanded with icy severity.
"And what in hell is this bench . . ."

"The bench . . . from where I get all the addresses.
Where, in fact, I got yours, Girard Girard!"

Girard knitted his brow.

"My head is still spinning from all the addresses, those
past and to come . . . And there are dozens more yet. Perhaps hundreds. You must give me time, Girard Girard."

"But what in thunderation is this bench," Girard was less
angry now.

"It's below the hotel where I always waited for my father
to come home."

Mr. Girard's mouth opened and shut.

"I had hardly spoken to anybody since my father's disappearance and/or death when Mr. Cox tried to introduce
me to life and people."

"Mr. Cox!" Girard threw up his hands.

"My father's death has left me—"

"Exactly!" Girard interrupted. "Going to the country with
us is precisely what you need."

But there was now no conviction or feeling in the billionaire's voice. Instead there was hesitancy, and sadness.

"We will be your father and your friends," Girard said
finally. He went up to Malcolm and was about to put his

hand on the boy's shoulder, when, changing his mind, he allowed his hand merely to fall downward like a benediction.

"At least consider it," Girard said.

"I will," Malcolm replied.

"And don't look so sad," Girard admonished him. "I never knew, of course, about the bench or I would have been more careful about what I said."

"No apology is needed, Girard Girard, sir."

"Thank you," the elder man replied.

"And I am so grateful for your visit," Malcolm went on. "Please don't tell anybody what I have said here to you. You see, Mr. Cox knows everything about me, though I have not told him a thing. He just knows it. As an astrologer, you see . . ."

Girard did not reply to this, but instead went on to talk about Malcolm's possible visit. "You must inform Madame Girard as soon as possible. We hope to leave any day now, and we must have you in the bargain."

"I will give it my undivided attention," Malcolm said.

"That's right, that is what you should do," Girard said. "Sleep on it, as they say."

Malcolm yawned.

"Good night," Girard said. "And remember, you are ours."

Malcolm said goodnight and opened the door for Girard onto the long gray-carpeted hall. "Thank you, sir, and a very good night."

"There Is No More for Me to Do"

Malcolm had slept until past two o'clock in the afternoon because of the lateness of Girard Girard's visit, so that any meeting with Mr. Cox on the bench did not seem feasible. Malcolm did not reach the bench, in fact, until nearly four o'clock, and by then he sensed that the astrologer had come and gone.

Malcolm walked resolutely therefore to Kermit's, rehearsing as he went the exact words he would use to tell the midget of his last night's visitor.

It was no real surprise for Malcolm, however, on entering the studio to find both Kermit and Mr. Cox engaged in what appeared to be a very close *tête-à-tête*. They both looked somewhat guilty on seeing Malcolm, perhaps because they were then talking about him.

"Where were *you* at the appointed hour?" Mr. Cox assailed Malcolm. "I waited for you for nearly ten minutes!"

"Are you speaking of my not being at the bench?" Malcolm brought out somewhat indifferently, because he felt so much stronger owing to Girard Girard's call.

"And who else around here has a bench?" Mr. Cox cried.

"I can't ever remember having kept regular hours or appointments with *anybody*," Malcolm said, and he recalled at that moment that Madame Girard had used the word "royalty" with reference to him only a few nights ago. He therefore fancied that his speech and manner at this moment must seem royal also to Kermit and Mr. Cox.

But both Mr. Cox and Kermit were looking at him with cold and even critical eyes.

"I had such a late visitor last night," Malcolm addressed

his words now to Kermit. "And I made certain arrangements at that time also for you, Kermit," he added for the midget.

"A busy boy," Kermit said, somewhat cool, though with no real irony.

"Are you attempting to tell us by gesture and word that you no longer need us?" Mr. Cox said, ignoring the news of Malcolm's late visitor, and going to the bottom of Malcolm's psychology of the moment.

Malcolm was surprised at Mr. Cox's unpleasant tone. He had known Mr. Cox was not very kind or warm-hearted, but he had not known until now that his tone could be so nasty.

"Who have you been recommending me to?" Kermit ignored Mr. Cox's question, and went back to Malcolm's visitor. "I can't wait to know."

"I had, as I said, an unusual visitor," Malcolm began again. "In fact, I should say that I had a visitor for the first time since my father disappeared and/or died. My father was my only visitor before, not counting bootblacks and hotel managers."

"How you do repeat yourself, dear Malcolm," Mr. Cox raised his eyes to the ceiling, and Kermit cleared his throat delicately.

"What a cold contemptuous person you can be at times, Mr. Cox," Malcolm remarked.

"Hear! hear!" Mr. Cox cried, and Kermit smiled broadly, for Mr. Cox was almost never criticized to his face, though he received nothing but criticism behind his back.

"Mr. Cox was also denounced at the Chateau the other night by Madame Girard," Malcolm informed them.

"My being denounced by Madame Girard is hardly news to me," Mr. Cox took this up. "A woman who owes all her success to me naturally must defame me frequently in order for her to feel that she exists in her own right at all."

"She doesn't exist . . . in her own right then?" Malcolm was concerned.

"Well, how did she strike *you*, dear Malcolm?" Mr. Cox interrogated.

"But I don't want to tell you about my evening with Madame Girard this afternoon," Malcolm interrupted. "That might have been all right for a morning on the bench, but—"

"Then what do you want to tell about?" the astrologer inquired.

"Why, his visitor, of course, you old—" but Kermit checked himself before he said the word, laughing at the same time, perhaps because he saw that he had at last a supporter in Malcolm against Mr. Cox's long tyranny.

"Perhaps I should save my story until Kermit and I are alone," Malcolm ventured.

"You will tell what it is you have to tell here and now, and we'll have no more of this young-person coyness and drooling about," Mr. Cox commanded.

"I am not at all frightened of your manner," Malcolm told Mr. Cox bravely.

"Everything you have—everything you've ever been discussing for days now," Mr. Cox began, "you owe to me. Try to remember that when you feel proud and free!"

"Are we to hear Malcolm's adventure, or are we to discuss our indebtedness to you, sir?" Kermit addressed Mr. Cox.

"What happened," Malcolm said without any further delay, "is that Girard Girard came to see me in person last night, at midnight."

Both Mr. Cox and Kermit were too thunderstruck to reply immediately.

When not even Mr. Cox could bring himself to comment on this intelligence, Kermit, after some struggle, brought out: "Do you fully realize the honor which has been paid you, Malcolm?"

"Honor?" Malcolm replied, seriously trying to understand now.

"How could he realize, *fully* or *at all!*" Mr. Cox said, flushed and irritable.

"Malcolm," Kermit exclaimed, going over to where the boy was seated, and taking his hand vigorously into his, like one who is to communicate with the deaf and dumb. "Girard Girard is a billionaire, a maker of presidents, a friend of royalty—a MAGNATE!"

"A friend of royalty?" Malcolm caught at this one phrase.

"Wined and dined by crowned heads, an African explorer, and a poet!"

"A poet?" Malcolm was puzzled and not very much interested.

"*The* man of his period," Kermit concluded.

Then turning to the astrologer, the midget said hopelessly: "Professor Cox, he is not impressed."

"Well, how could you expect him to be?" Mr. Cox was very put out. "He's had only three addresses, and this was a plunge I had not expected him to take at all. Perhaps never . . . Girard Girard! . . . Oh, it's quite premature . . ."

"You're angry Girard came," Malcolm cried, standing up, for he felt suddenly he had been betrayed.

"Why he calls Girard by his first name," Kermit noted with stupefaction.

"Don't be ridiculous, Malcolm," Mr. Cox scolded Malcolm's having suggested they were angry. "Angry at *you!* Be seated at once," and the astrologer made a snorting kind of sound.

"For God's sake, tell us what happened," Kermit said, disbelief still struggling with amazement.

"Why . . . nothing happened," Malcolm said, feeling now almost that perhaps Mr. Cox was right, and that he understood nothing, and that if Girard's coming had not been exactly a dream, it had not added up to anything more than his arrival and departure.

"You mean Girard Girard simply looked in on you for no purpose," Mr. Cox exclaimed.

"It was midnight," Malcolm began, "and I was listening to my South-sea shells in my bathrobe."

"Ahem," Mr. Cox said.

"And Girard Girard was all of a sudden on the phone wanting to see me."

"I would give ten years of my life to be so honored," Kermit said.

"I told Girard Girard all about you," Malcolm addressed Kermit now, "though, of course, I didn't describe you in *detail*, but merely said you were a young unattached man, and my best friend."

Kermit clapped his hands. "You will receive an award for that," the midget told Malcolm.

"You imbecile," Mr. Cox now turned his attention to the midget. "You sound—the both of you—like a couple of schoolgirls,—all excited over the visit of a—common manipulator of the stock market."

Kermit stuck out his tongue at Mr. Cox, and turned back to Malcolm.

"It seems that both Madame Girard and Girard Girard feel they have to have me for their very own," Malcolm said, and he felt that with this sentence he had told the whole interesting story, and so he rested his hands in his lap, and was silent, expecting that his auditors would take up the conversation from there.

But when neither Mr. Cox nor Kermit added anything, but sat waiting expectantly for more, Malcolm added, by way of elucidation: "They love me, I guess, the Girards."

"Completely incredible—the whole shebang!" Mr. Cox shifted on his chair.

"You know Malcolm does not lie," Kermit told the astrologer. "But you can't stand to hear of success, of course, especially with regard to one of your own friends. Success in others is for you what hell is to a pious believer, and success is the defeat of any plans you may have for your friends."

"I don't believe the Girards could love anybody but themselves," Mr. Cox ignored Kermit. "Madame Girard can't think about anything but herself, in any case, for more than five minutes, without becoming panicky."

"They—" Malcolm continued, musing, "or rather Madame Girard through Girard Girard invited me to spend my vacation in the country with them."

"At their country estate?" Kermit cried.

"That's the place," Malcolm replied.

Even Mr. Cox was convinced by this statement, and he sat back slowly, collapsing downward until his hands touched the floor. It was all over, he knew. He had done it, he had set the ball rolling, and it had rolled further than he had ever dreamed or contemplated. Malcolm was definitely "in"—long long before he was ready, and long before Mr. Cox had seen any indication—astrologically—that Malcolm was anywhere near his goal. Malcolm had arrived, without ever having put his foot on the first rung of the ladder. He was the protegé, after an evening's talk, of the country's most powerful man.

"But do you know what has happened to you?" Kermit questioned the boy.

"Of course he does not," Mr. Cox was still acid. "But as you say, Kermit, he could not lie about it. Nobody could invent a thing this large. No, Malcolm has simply done it."

"But what have I done?" Malcolm cried.

"You've captured *them*," Kermit shouted. "Isn't that enough for one lifetime?"

Then remembering his conversation with Girard Girard, Malcolm said in his slow loud voice:

"But I turned the invitation down."

"What?" Kermit leaped to his feet from the chair in which he had been sitting. Malcolm shielded his face, for the little man's expression was so threatening the boy feared he was about to be attacked. But Kermit only remained frozen in his tracks with vicarious chagrin.

Mr. Cox put his hands over his eyes and bowed slightly, and then shook his head.

"But Girard Girard persuaded me at the last that one day I *must* accept," Malcolm added weakly, and Kermit and Mr. Cox gave out sighs of partial relief in the thought that all had not been won, then, only to be thrown so wantonly away.

"Malcolm should have a keeper," Mr. Cox said to Kermit. "How he has kept alive this long is a mystery, of course."

"I'm not going to their country estate without you, Kermit." It was Malcolm's turn now to stand up and tell his questioners. "I told Girard Girard that, in so many words."
Kermit did not answer, but he turned very pale, and looked away from Mr. Cox, who was observing him closely.
"I believe there is no more for me to do here," Mr. Cox said suddenly, getting up, for he could no longer conceal that he had not been prepared for Malcolm's surprise, and nothing in his own science had warned him of the event.
"Sit down, Professor Cox," Kermit fulminated. "You've played God long enough. You'll act now like other mortals . . ."
And Kermit beat on a small gong for his morning servant, forgetting that it was not morning, and that O'Reilly Morgan had gone.
"There is so much to think about," Kermit said, referring, all knew, to Malcolm's visitor. "And so much to plan."
But Mr. Cox had already gone toward the door. He had, after all, perhaps done enough for both of the young men. He hesitated with his back to them, and then taking hold of the knob, opened the door, and went out without another word.

The Girards Call on Kermit

One afternoon, following a vague warning of their arrival, a Rolls drew up in front of Kermit's studio, and Madame Girard, Girard Girard, and Malcolm all got out and stood before the door.

The small figure of Kermit waited, his eyes fixed on the bolt and chain of his door: he feared these might give under the combined pressure of the three visitors outside.

They had come, of course, he knew, to take him to the country mansion. He had agreed to go—in some indefinite future—but now that he saw the sudden splendor of Madame Girard, the princely calm and command of Girard Girard, and the unbelievable youth of Malcolm, he acknowledged to himself that he could not open the door to them. He could not, he knew, be happy. The sight of such wealth and effulgence blinded him. He had intended, of course, to open the door, to receive them. O'Reilly Morgan had already made the tea, a special blend he had purchased only that morning. The entire studio had been washed down in ammonia, followed by patchouli oil and rose water (Madame Girard's *sina qua non* for habitations), and was in immaculate order. And Kermit had planned to receive Madame Girard in the style she was led to expect everywhere. Then, at the very last of the reception, Kermit had been going to tell Madame Girard calmly, even a little majestically, that other commitments would prevent him from accepting her kind invitation. She would protest, of course, but in the end would give in, regretful, and leave, while caring more for the little man than if he had accepted and gone with her.

The spectacle of the three persons outside his shabby ramshackle studio pierced his breast with such force that he felt he might fall insensible if they did not depart at once. At the same time, even if he had now desired it, he would never have had the strength to be able to lift the bolt and latch and admit them.

After a few moments, a humiliating realization crossed Kermit's brain. He saw, gradually, that Malcolm had from the first recognized his "outline" against the glass door: Malcolm had recognized him but was not letting the others know. Of course, it would have been too great an insult for Madame Girard had she known he was hiding there behind the door, and so the boy had kept silent.

Kermit could not move now, he could not even show to Malcolm that he knew the latter had recognized him. He stood there like a prisoner in stocks, helpless to run even and hide from his shame. He had deceived them, and here he stood, the shadow of his perfidy and deceit falling upon them: he had said he would go with them to the country, and now he had bolted the door against them, and had, in effect, insulted them with his contempt.

Kermit saw Malcolm's feverish and concentrated frown. Then, suddenly, he heard Malcolm's voice saying to Madame Girard: "I'm certain he *has* to be in there!"

"He has *chosen* not to see us," Madame Girard said with her haunting fear that those she really wished to know feared and avoided her.

"Perhaps something has happened to him," Girard Girard suggested, and he went up to the door and beat loudly on the old frail glass.

Kermit drew back briefly. The sound of so much power being exerted on his door by one of the most influential living men was too upsetting to his already frayed sensibilities. The little man began slowly retreating backwards into the room reserved for the cats.

He knew now that he could never go with them. He was too used to poverty, to the routine of deprivation, to his little empty life of complaint and irritations, and the final inanity when he tucked himself in his small bed. To be suddenly translated into a car with a monogram that looked like a vehicle from another civilization, to be surrounded by what was, in effect, royalty, and to see Malcolm enthroned as the favorite,—he could never do this. He retreated still further back, and as he did so, the movement of his back pushed open the door, and all the cats, seeing their prison open, rushed out with cries of wildness and relief into the front room and began scratching and meowing on the pane of the tall glass door before which Madame Girard now stood.

Madame Girard gave out cries of delight when she was aware of the presence of the cats.

Malcolm pushed his face against the glass of the door, and as he did so, the lock sprang open, and they were all admitted into the studio.

Kermit, though himself invisible in the dark back part of his studio, was able to see his visitors clearly, and observed that Malcolm was near tears, calling out: "I can't go alone, Kermit, you don't know what will happen! I can't go alone! Come out, and don't be a coward."

Madame Girard now raised her voice: "Come here this instant, Kermit. I am issuing a command, do you hear me? A *command*."

At this imperious order, Kermit felt that he could no longer stand the suspense and the pressure, and calling out to them, he said: "Go away! I can't bear the splendor of your being here!"

"What is it you can't bear?" Madame Girard cried, trying to see into the inky blackness of the studio's interior so that she could catch some short glimpse of the little man.

"I can't stand the splendor of your presence!" Kermit repeated.

"The splendor of our *presence!*" Madame Girard cried, for she feared her ears deceived her.

"Open the door to your closet, and come out at once, when I command!" she exclaimed.

"I could never, *never,*" Kermit now groaned, his head pressed against the narrow door of the back room.

"The little creature is moaning!" Madame Girard commented, at which words Kermit's weeping became more audible.

"Open your door, and come out," Malcolm cried to Kermit.

Girard Girard now added his voice to that of the others, but with the calm and dignity which Kermit would have expected from so famous a man.

Worn out from his emotion, Kermit let himself slowly slip to his knees where he genuflected before the thin wooden door, which separated him from his visitors.

Madame Girard continued to knock with her soft gloved hands on the glass pane of the door, Mr. Girard offered counsel, and Malcolm urged Kermit to come *for his sake,* if for no other.

Kermit attempted several times to answer one or another of these eloquent appeals, but his voice always choked up, and no words came out.

After a wait, the three visitors went slowly away and sat in the Rolls waiting for the little man to change, perhaps, his mind.

They seemed, the three of them, to Kermit, to wait there for hours, while he never moved from his position of kneeling. Dusk fell. Then, as the night was beginning to show itself in all its black city completeness, the engine of the Rolls started and his splendid visitors motored off into the void.

"Kermit has rejected me," Madame Girard said, as they drove off.

"I'm afraid it's me he's rejected," Malcolm replied. He looked now almost as small as Kermit from his position alone in the back seat of the Rolls. In the heavy rich-smelling leather and severe uprightness of the car, he felt that he was going to his own funeral. He was impatient to jump out and rejoin Kermit in the studio. He knew that he did not belong with "royalty" any more than Kermit had believed himself to belong with them.

Soon Malcolm began sobbing in earnest.

"Oh, no, no," Madame Girard cried, turning about and looking at him from the front seat where she sat stiffly at a distance from Girard himself, who was driving.

"I am not very manly, I suppose you are thinking," Malcolm blew his nose on his sleeve.

"I cannot *stand* emotional crises in others," Madame Girard explained her position. "This must be attended to, Girard," she turned to her husband. "Do something at once."

"We will drive and think," her husband made the rejoinder.

"There is nothing to think," Madame Girard took this up. "Kermit has rejected all of us. He stood back there, probably staring at us as if we were odd-plumaged birds in a sanctuary."

"That was the worst thing about it," Malcolm agreed. "To see his little shadow in the glass door watching us. Too afraid to make his presence known."

"How could he be afraid—when it was only love I wanted to bring him?" Madame Girard said.

"We could telephone him, perhaps, and tell him what it is that we actually wish of him," Girard proposed. "People often cannot refuse a request when it is telephoned."

"I must also have a drink," Madame Girard said in her deepest voice.

"What of?" Malcolm asked, rather severely and loudly.

Madame Girard thought for a long time, while humming, and then said, very quickly, so that everybody jumped a bit: "Dark rum."

"Completely out of the question," Girard assured her.

"Explain the meaning of that last remark," Madame Girard addressed her husband.

"Your drinking days are over. At any rate, with me present. I know that at night you sometimes run off and get it, or perhaps when young men come they *secret* it into you but, on the whole, your drinking days are over."

"He pronounces my sentence of doom with the *sang-froid* of an ape," Madame Girard said. "You are an ape. It was your malign presence which frightened the midget!"

"Never use that word!" Malcolm exclaimed.

"Sir?" Madame Girard cried, turning about again to look at Malcolm.

"Kermit doesn't think he *is* a midget," Malcolm told her. "He was about to strike me one afternoon for almost *thinking* it."

"How perfectly remarkable," Madame Girard said, her mind temporarily lifted for a moment from her desire for drink. "How intensely significant."

Thinking still more, Madame Girard asked: "What *does* he think he is?"

"I feared you were going to ask that," Malcolm confessed.

Madame Girard nodded, understanding.

"I don't suppose he has quite decided what he thinks he is," Malcolm suggested.

"Perhaps, however," Girard spoke up, "if we knew what he thought he was, we would be able to persuade him to come with us."

"You could persuade nobody—*nothing!*" Madame Girard exploded, and her husband bent slightly under the vigor of her attack.

"You hen-peck Girard, I observe," Malcolm commented.

Madame Girard turned her blazing mascaraed eyes with the purple puffs under them directly into the line of Malcolm's flashing teeth.

"How do I do that?" she wondered, more curious than belligerent.

"You reduce him to a smaller size than he should be," Malcolm ventured.

"I am quite a strong man, reduced or not," Girard laughed.

"He is very strong," Madame Girard agreed looking at her husband. "But we're off the subject," she reminded them. "We have to have Kermit or we have to go home, because Malcolm would cry himself into the hospital, should we set off for the country now."

"We *must* go to the country," Girard said. "My lungs require that air."

"You will do as you're told," Madame Girard affirmed. "Drive to the Avenue of the Temples."

"But that's far far out of our way!" Girard protested.

"Did you hear what I said?" Madame Girard demanded. "I said The Temples!"

"And with me not having been near the bench for what seems days," Malcolm sighed, almost to himself.

"I insist a phone call to Kermit is in order," Mr. Girard returned to his original idea.

"Well, there are phones in the Temples," Madame Girard gave in a bit, grudgingly.

"What *is* to become of Kermit?" Malcolm said, realizing all in a flash what the life of the little man must be.

"Beautiful small men like that go on living," Madame Girard assured him.

"How did you know he was beautiful?" Malcolm wondered.

"Silhouettes tell all," she replied.

"I thought his voice was distinguished," Girard said.

"Everything about him was distinguished," Madame Girard summarized their afternoon. "And that wonderful studio. I wish to buy it as soon as possible."

"*Buy?*" Girard said.

"You heard me," Madame Girard was cold now. "I must own the studio."

"I don't think it's for sale," Malcolm informed her.

"Oh, it's too beautiful, of course, but it's for sale, naturally —if I want it—it *has* to be!"

"Here are your Temples," Girard said, pointing out to them with a wave of his gloved hand the ruins of an old Japanese-style building.

The ruins struck a kind of autumnal chill in each of them.

"Where are the telephones?" it was Malcolm who spoke up at last.

"Near by," Girard assured him. "And I *will* call him."

"The Temples bring back so many memories for me," Madame Girard said in an altered voice, and she put her gloved hand over her eyes. Malcolm studied her very closely.

"Do you want your veil?" Girard asked her, looking down, unaccountably, at the floor of the car.

"Madame Girard wears a . . . *riding* veil?" Malcolm wondered, too much surprise for politeness in his voice.

"Here it is, my dear," Girard said, ignoring Malcolm's remark, and he handed Madame Girard a bluish purple cloth, which he had taken quickly from a compartment in the car. She placed the cloth over her face immediately.

"A riding veil should prove very attention-bringing to any possible walkers at this time," Malcolm told Madame Girard.

"This veil, of course, would bring attention wherever it was displayed," she replied.

She touched it at that moment, gingerly, with her hand.

"You could be the headless huntsman," Malcolm told her.

"Texture is all," Madame Girard said, "substance nothing."

"Shall I now telephone Kermit?" Girard brought them back to the afternoon and their failure.

"But all means, use every way of persuading him," Madame Girard consented.

"You will excuse me, then, while I do so," Girard said.

Both Malcolm and Madame Girard bowed to him, and he went off in the direction of the Japanese Temples.

Girard Girard was gone such a short time that Madame Girard had scarcely spoken ten words to Malcolm through the blue veil which now cut her off from the world. Malcolm, however, had decided that her veiled appearance went very well with the Temples and the melancholy of the light, and was about to tell her this when Girard Girard returned, looking, Malcolm thought, somewhat happier than when he had left. He looked assuaged.

"It's good news I bring," Girard said.

"Let *us* decide its quality," Madame Girard told him. "Come into the car and tell *only* what happened. If comments or adjectives are to be supplied, we shall do so."

"I see," Girard said, and smiling, he took his position at the wheel.

"Was I gone long?" Girard wondered suddenly.

"You were gone the normal length of time," Madame Girard replied.

"I seemed to be gone a long time," he explained.

"It was not long," Malcolm told him.

"I think the reason for the seeming length of my stay was that I had to talk with a man named Professor Cox."

"No!" broke from both Malcolm and Madame Girard.

"Mr. Cox is everywhere," Madame Girard said, shaking her head, and she lifted her veil momentarily. Malcolm decided that he liked Madame Girard better with her veil on than off, and was about to tell her so, when Girard went on: "Professor Cox was very evasive."

"How could he be straightforward?" Madame Girard inquired.

"He was, in any case, very firm," Girard admitted.

"Well, he is firmly evasive, we might say," Madame Girard commented.

"I asked him naturally for Kermit, since I was not able to recognize the voice which answered the phone."

"Continue," Madame Girard commanded her husband.

"'This is Mr. Cox,' the voice then identified itself. And I asked, 'Would you please call Kermit to the phone, then, Mr. Cox, for it is to him I wish to speak.' Mr. Cox replied, however, that he had no intention of doing so, for Kermit was in the throes of nearly complete collapse. 'The throes of collapse?' I inquired, acting surprised, though, of course, I was not . . ."

"Of course you were not!" Madame Girard nodded.

"Throes?" Malcolm wondered, frowning.

"'The little man cannot under any circumstances speak to you Girard Girard,' Mr. Cox then said."

"'But I am asking you,' I said to Mr. Cox, 'humbly. We are ready to go to our country house, and it is imperative that he go with us, or Malcolm cannot accompany us either. Three people are waiting for his answer.'"

"'The answer,' Mr. Cox then told me, 'is NO.'"

"No!" Malcolm cried, pounding his head with his fist.

"'No for how long, Mr. Cox,' I then asked him," Girard Girard said.

"'No forever,' Mr. Cox replied."

"Forever," Malcolm said.

"And he refused to allow a man of your caliber to talk with Kermit," Madame Girard was pale with indignation.

"Mr. Cox told me that Kermit would never be able to say yes again to anything," Girard Girard finally brought out the statement.

"No!" Malcolm cried, but Madame Girard raised her hand for silence.

"'And do not call Kermit again,' Mr. Cox commanded me," Girard Girard went on. "'I will call *you* should he ever say *Yes* in the interim.'"

"Then why in hell did you look so merry when you came back here to the car?" Madame Girard demanded to know of her husband.

"I was only laughing at Mr. Cox's tyranny," Girard Girard said. "He is a prig, too, as well as a tyrant."

"A prig?" Malcolm paused over the word.

"Oh, that always goes with tyranny!" Madame Girard tossed aside Malcolm's confusion.

"To think I had almost entrusted my life to Mr. Cox," Malcolm said, almost whispering.

"So you had," Girard Girard was firm about this.

"And now he has such power over Kermit!" Malcolm remarked.

"He can't do anything to Kermit," Madame Girard was positive.

"Because he is a prig or a tyrant?" Malcolm wondered.

"What has his prig-hood to do with his power?" Madame Girard inquired. "His prig-hood is only his manner. Mr. Cox's power emanates from another source. But on Kermit it is wasted."

"I see," Malcolm said.

"He will never win," Girard Girard said.

"Never," Madame Girard agreed.

They all three sat there thinking of how Mr. Cox, however, did have Kermit, and the wires were, so to speak, down, or at least in the hands only of Mr. Cox.

Then Girard started the motor.

"Where are you taking us?" Madame Girard exclaimed.

"For a drive about the water."

"But not to the country estate!" Malcolm warned.

"Oh, do you think we could go after this shattering experience?" Madame Girard scoffed. "Not even if I had a whole cave of dark rum waiting for me!"

"We will go to the country tomorrow," Girard said. "My lungs must have that air!"

"We will go when I give the command, and not until," Madame Girard said, suddenly removing her veil, and as she did so, Malcolm gasped to see her beautiful, though haggard, eyes, again.

"You talk of your lungs!" Madame Girard scoffed. "But you never consider my *thirst!*"

Girard Girard opened his mouth to say something.

"Silence!" Madame Girard anticipated him.

"Do you ever consider my thirst?" she vociferated again.

But again when Girard Girard attempted to reply, Madame Girard cried out first: "Do not open your mouth. Silence!"

Malcolm held his head in his hands.

"Girard Girard," Madame Girard said, shaking the veil at him, "have you ever given my thirst at any time the serious attention, say, Professor Cox has given it—the very few times he has given it? You may answer this question."

"I have," Girard Girard replied, somewhat bashfully, as Malcolm thought.

"You lie!" she screamed. "You lie in front of this innocent boy witness."

They drove on for a moment of silence.

"It's so infernal to be thirsty, and to have your thirst interdicted," she said in a whisper. She wept a little, then bracing herself, she cried: "Your lungs can rot! Do you hear? Rot!"

"Yes, it's *you*," Mr. Cox said, without any real surprise, but with a sourer tone than Malcolm had ever heard in the astrologer's voice before. "While everybody thinks you are living in Madame Girard's country house, here you are on the bench—as if nothing had happened to you since your father's death."

"I couldn't go to the country without Kermit," Malcolm said, no conviction in his expression. "The Girards were too . . . *imposing*" (here Malcolm borrowed a word),—"too imposing to be alone with."

"Subterfuges! Dodges! Oh, how I know you," Mr. Cox shook his head. Today he carried a fancy toothpick in his mouth, and his tone seemed even more cutting and insolent than usual.

"Everyone in and out of the Girards spoke slightingly of you," Malcolm told Mr. Cox, with the expression of one merely vacantly reporting the facts.

"Those in the possession of the truth are hardly ever thought well of," Mr. Cox said coolly enough.

"You are in the . . . possession . . . of . . . ?" and Malcolm stood up briefly, but sat down just as quickly at a gesture from his mentor.

"I thought you knew I had it," Mr. Cox said calmly, a little pleasant humor coming into his face.

"I don't believe I would *care* to have it," Malcolm said finally, a bit disconsolate again.

"Well, dear boy," Mr. Cox considered this. "I think you have accomplished a great deal without it. That sometimes happens, you know. But in your case, too, you don't need

to worry about it—because you're not going to be bothered
with having it!"

"I suppose when you say I've accomplished a great deal
—you mean my conquest of Madame and Mr. Girard," Malcolm said.

"Who else?" the astrologer nodded.

"Madame Girard relies on you an awful lot, too," Malcolm
thought aloud. "Yet she continually condemns you, as does
Girard Girard."

Mr. Cox removed his toothpick from his mouth, but did
not reply.

"You are a magician, as they say—as well as an astrologer,"
and Malcolm shook his head at the complexity of things.

Mr. Cox did not bother to reply to this statement, but
hurried on:

"All the people whom I stir to action—and there are an
awful lot of them, let me tell you—they *somehow* fail . . ."

"But what are the actions you stir them to?" Malcolm
complained because he did not, as usual, understand.

"Mind you," he went on, "I don't care how much they
talk against me, or how much they talk with one another—
though the only real talking *I* will do. But I want them to act
out the parts they are meant to act out with one another!"

"And what parts would those ever be?" Malcolm wondered, not able at that moment to smother a wide yawn.

Mr. Cox waited for Malcolm to close his mouth.

"I have arranged all the situations," Mr. Cox spoke without
his usual optimism. "Why can't *they* act? I have brought
the right people together, and the right situations. I'm not
such a fool as not to know *right people* and *right situations*
when they're together. But nothing happens. Nothing at all."

"You *may* have made a mistake!" Malcolm boldly suggested.

"No, no, Malcolm," and the astrologer was quite gentle
now. "It's the stars," Mr. Cox spoke with resignation in his
voice. "What else can you call it? There's just no help for
it. Everything is played out."

"You mean I've left the bench, then, for no reason at all?"

"No, Malcolm, we won't give up, stars or no, though I may have to pay for this remark later," and Mr. Cox whistled in a simulation of high spirits. "For if the Girards didn't win over the forces"—here the astrologer looked furtively to the horizon—"perhaps this might do the trick, as a desperate remedy"—and he pulled out a small card and thrust it into the hand of his young friend.

"Another address!" Malcolm crowed.

"Do your rejoicing later," Mr. Cox was again severe. "And as to enthusiasm, child, get rid of it. It can only lead you to commitments, and not just *some*, but a legion. Fear it . . . Now, go to it, and we may meet again, and if not, well, then not, and may success be yours."

Taking out his toothpick from his mouth, and giving Malcolm a vigorous farewell nod, Mr. Cox left just as unceremoniously and quickly as ever.

"You're the new boy?" Eloisa Brace said, looking out at Malcolm from the basement door of her three-story house, but not opening the door to him.

Malcolm was listening to the sound of the alto sax which was coming from upstairs, but his glimpse of the strong chin and fierce blue eyes of Eloisa Brace stopped him a little. He had never seen such a strong-looking woman. He couldn't tell her age because she looked so imposing. Her blonde hair was long and thick and hid her forehead.

"Malcolm?" Eloisa Brace inquired. "Is it you?"

He nodded.

"O.K., then, either come in or go out. You can't just stand there, O.K., you know. I'm giving a concert."

Eloisa Brace said a few more O.K.'s, for she put this expression after every few words she uttered.

"Mr. Cox . . ." Malcolm began.

"Yes, yes, O.K.," Eloisa Brace told him, irritability and impatience rising anew in her.

"You're awfully *cross* tonight, aren't you?" Malcolm asked her.

Eloisa opened the basement door at last, and Malcolm went partially inside the room.

"Is that the new boy?" a man's voice demanded, and a young man with a beard and thick glasses hurried down the back staircase which led from the concert room above to the basement where Malcolm and Eloisa were now standing.

"Will you please take over from here, O.K.," Eloisa Brace turned to the young man. "You know I can't stand kids. And the musicians are waiting."

Eloisa let out a great sigh of relief and disappeared up the stairs from which the young bearded man had just descended.

"My wife is a bit nervous when we have the concerts," he told Malcolm.

"Eloisa Brace is *your* wife?" Malcolm asked.

The young man nodded. "But do come clear into the room, why don't you? Don't stand against the door," he asked Malcolm.

Malcolm came further into the room, and became immediately absorbed in looking at the furnishings about him: it was not unlike Estel Blanc's—only, if anything, gloomier, but as at Estel's, paintings adorned all the walls, but here there was a great display of stuffed birds, especially owls sitting on varnished perches, and the furniture was all very old and worn, like what one would expect on a farm.

"Yes," the young man told Malcolm, "you are just as Mr. Cox described you," and he held his spectacles against his eyes to see the boy more clearly.

The man was very friendly, though rather in the manner of a doctor, and Malcolm smiled under this attention. He thought that this man was perhaps the most friendly person he had ever met.

"Some wine, Malcolm?" the man handed him a cracked jelly-glass filled with red liquor.

"I usually don't drink," Malcolm replied.

"Do have some," his new friend urged him.

"You're so . . . very polite," the boy noted.

"You're much nicer than I even thought you would be for a boy of your class," the man said. "My name, by the way, is Jerome."

Malcolm accepted Jerome's hand, and smiled.

"I don't suppose you have heard of me," Jerome inquired, a vague hopeful emotion coming into his voice.

"Just as the husband of Eloisa Brace," Malcolm told him.

"Well, of course, Eloisa is at present a bit more famous than me," Jerome admitted. "As a painter, you understand." He pointed to the paintings on the wall, which were by Eloisa.

Malcolm looked at the paintings now again. They were portrayals of a woman wandering at night, a woman with long hair and a strong chin, but with a soft, kind, even moony, expression, garbed in a long flowing robe. The different women depicted in the paintings, Malcolm decided, both were, and were not, Eloisa. The real Eloisa was so much crosser and older in everyday life.

"Didn't Mr. Cox tell you what I was famous for?" Jerome brought Malcolm's attention back from the paintings to himself.

"No," Malcolm replied. "He just mentioned you as Eloisa's husband."

"How typical of Mr. Cox," Jerome said.

Then: "You see," Jerome went on, "I was in prison."

"I see," Malcolm tasted his wine, and nodded.

"For burglary," Jerome informed him.

"How did you ever come to get here then?" Malcolm wondered, and he pointed to the room in which they were now sitting.

"You charming fellow," Jerome laughed. He poured Malcolm some more wine. "I've heard all about you and your *bench!*"

"But—" Malcolm began by way of explanation, and surprise.

"No more need be said, sir," Jerome cried, raising the palm of his hand. "It's all all right here. Everything is all right here."

"But you said you were a burglar," Malcolm managed to get out.

Jerome tasted his wine with loud deliberative smacks. "That's right," he finally said. "I got ten years for it. The state pen."

"You must have . . . stolen an awful lot," Malcolm decided.

Jerome laughed. "Somehow *you* can say that," he told Malcolm. "Yes, Malcolm, I stole one hell of a lot."

At that moment Jerome seemed to have forgotten all about Malcolm, and he merely looked out past where they were sitting into the inner darkness of the next room. Then coming back to his guest, Jerome said, "Yes, Malcolm, you are looking at nothing less than an ex-con."

"I'm very proud to know you," Malcolm said, and he finished his second glass.

"Do you know what I am talking about, Malcolm?" Jerome said more gravely, but still with great friendliness.

"Yes," Malcolm said thoughtfully. "I was just wondering though, if Estel Blanc may perhaps have at one time—maybe not for ten years, you know—*been* one."

"Estel Blanc!" Jerome's smile faded into an offended and shocked look. "Why, he's not in our class at all! For one thing, he's a total snob. Whatever made you think he would be an ex-con."

But Malcolm's sunny calm restored Jerome's good humor.

Malcolm, however, continued: "You see," he said, "I don't really know what an ex-con should look like on account of you seem just like anybody nice to me."

"Like anybody nice?" Jerome smiled.

"Well, maybe not so awfully impressively nice as Girard Girard, say," Malcolm reconsidered. "But in so many ways you are so much sweeter than he is."

"*Sweet*—O.K., thank you, Malcolm," Jerome said, and he was at that moment, anybody could see, very sweet, and he smiled, perhaps thinking of his own sweetness.

"You and I, Malcolm, are quite different in all things—

in every way—and yet we like one another, and we are alike," Jerome told him. "Here," he pointed out, "you're not drinking up."

He poured Malcolm some more wine.

"But you see—I don't drink," Malcolm reminded him.

Jerome made the tasting sounds again from his own replenished glass.

"Jerome—what *is* an ex-con?" Malcolm said suddenly.

Jerome stopped tasting. He paused. "A man who's been in prison. An ex-convict, you know," he replied without looking at the boy.

"And you really *were* in prison," Malcolm considered this.

"Here," Jerome pointed out to him. "I wrote a book about it."

"How difficult *that* must have been," Malcolm observed.

"Would you like to read my book?" Jerome inquired, eagerness and anticipation in his expression.

Malcolm was about to tell Jerome that he could not say, for he had never read a *complete* book, when Jerome, without waiting for an answer, hastened to a little closet nearby where there was piled a stack of books, all with the same title, and brought one copy back to Malcolm.

The book's title was *They Could Have Me Back.*

"What a nice title," Malcolm said. "Is that you naked on the cover?"

Jerome smiled and touched Malcolm lightly on the ear.

From upstairs came the thick rich tones of the sax and the bass.

"Do you dig that music, Malcolm?" Jerome kept his mouth very close to Malcolm as he said this.

Malcolm half-smiled.

"I don't read very much," Malcolm explained, handing the book back to Jerome.

Malcolm put his hand slowly to the place on his ear where Jerome had touched him.

"What was that for?" Malcolm said.

"Look, Malcolm," Jerome said, "I know you make a point of being dumb, but you're not that dumb."

Just then the music upstairs stopped, and Jerome hastened away from Malcolm and sat down on the floor and began talking very fast about how he was a writer and was now finishing a study of delinquency among minors.

Footsteps sounded on the staircase.

"Jerome, are you coming up here or not?" Eloisa Brace's voice sounded severe, but shaky.

"In a minute, darling," Jerome said.

"Look," she continued, "the musicians want to see you about the arrangement for the new number. Please consider others for once in your life. Is that boy still down there?"

When there was no answer either from Jerome or Malcolm, Eloisa cried: "Don't keep me waiting now, after all my trouble to bring Grig and Goody together here tonight," and they heard her footsteps retreating upstairs.

"My wife," Jerome smiled both sweetly and sadly, and he winked at Malcolm.

Malcolm looked down at his empty glass.

"More?" Jerome said.

Malcolm made no effort to refuse, and Jerome poured another brimming glass.

"I do want you to read my book," Jerome said, sitting on the floor by Malcolm's chair now, and grasping the boy's foot lightly. "I want you to because, well, because I guess you don't seem to have any pre-judgments about anything. Your eyes are completely open."

Jerome pulled on Malcolm's pant cuff.

"Look, Malcolm," he said suddenly. "I'm not a queer or anything, so don't jump like that when I touch you. You do something to me because I guess you just seem like the spirit of . . . life, or something, and I wouldn't have said anything so corny before in all my life. But hell, you do."

"I see," Malcolm said, and he looked down at Jerome's hand which rested on his leg.

"Will you be a good friend, then?" Jerome asked Malcolm.

"Of course, Jerome," Malcolm cried, like one startled from sleep.

"Thank you, Malcolm."

They sat now close together, while upstairs the music had begun again.

"It's going to be a wonderful friendship," Jerome said thickly, his mouth pressed against Malcolm's trouser legs. "But you must give up Mr. Cox and Girard Girard. They won't do for you at all. They don't believe in what you and I believe in . . ."

"But what do we believe in?" Malcolm said, and he made a motion to stand up.

"Sit still," Jerome put his hand on the boy's knee with force. "Just sit still, please."

Jerome cocked his head, swallowing the wine in his glass. "What do we believe in, Malcolm? What a pleasant, pleasant question. I'm so awfully glad you said *we*. I will appreciate that a long time. A hell of a long time from now I will think of that question of yours, Malcolm: what do WE believe in. You carry me right back to something, Malc . . ."

"You see I don't know what I be——"

"Don't spoil it, Malc. Don't say another word."

"Jerome," Malcolm's voice came shaky and tiny now.

"Don't spoil anything now!" Jerome commanded again, his eyes soft and half-closed. "Don't speak."

At that moment, the glass fell out of Malcolm's hand, and without another syllable, the boy toppled unconscious out of his chair and onto Jerome's lap, head first.

"Jesus Christ," Jerome said, opening his eyes.

A Portrait Is Begun

Malcolm woke up in a very small bed unlike his own, without a canopy, and found himself with a wall against him on one side and on the other a dark-skinned man who was snoring.

Malcolm had never, he thought, since the probable death of his father, seen such a distinguished looking man.

Still somewhat asleep, the boy said, "Are you by chance, then, royalty, sir?" It was a kind of rhetorical question, an echo from Madame Girard's rather than anything that Malcolm meant to address to his bed-fellow. But the dark-skinned man frowned, and quit snoring.

"Sir," Malcolm pushed the man, addressing him now directly, "who are you?"

When there was no answer, Malcolm looked about him. There was no way to get out of bed without practically pushing the dark man out of bed at the same time, for the bed was much too small for two persons—it was too small for the majestic type of person who was sleeping next to him, and Malcolm, already pinioned against the wall-side of the bed, could not move without pushing the stranger.

At that moment, the man opened one eye, then the other, and then yawned widely.

"Sir," Malcolm began again, "this is the first time I have not slept in my own bed, and I am quite surprised."

The dark man nodded, still yawning from time to time, and then scratched slowly and deeply under his arm pits.

"Who are you, sir?" Malcolm inquired again.

"I know who you are," the man replied, and he looked pleasant and calm, though grave.

"You have an even richer voice than Estel Blanc," Malcolm noted, but was about to correct himself at once for having mentioned the unpopular undertaker, and there was, furthermore, no connection between the two, he realized, except that, of course, they were both of the Abyssinian race.

The man reached behind their common pillow and brought out a handsome small comb with which he began tidying his hair and beard, while excusing himself for doing so.

"I don't suppose you *are* . . . royalty, though please forgive me if you are," Malcolm said.

"Well, forgive *me*—for forgetting to introduce myself, Malcolm. George Leeds, sir, the piano player with the quartet."

Malcolm shook hands with George Leeds and told him how pleased he was to meet him.

"Everybody who is a friend of mine calls me Grig," George Leeds then added.

"May I see your hands, then, Grig?" Malcolm asked.

"Oh, I'm not lying to you about my profession," George Leeds smiled, stretching out his hands for Malcolm's inspection.

"Those are piano player hands," Malcolm commented.

"Well, I'm not royalty, kiddo," George told him. "Not the royalty you're talking about."

"May I borrow your comb now, sir?" Malcolm inquired, and George passed it to him with a short bow.

"So you passed out in the basement last night," George Leeds commented.

"Passed out?" Malcolm frowned, wondering, and putting down the comb briefly.

George Leeds stared at him, and then speaking slow, pronouncing each syllable as to a foreigner: "DRUNK. FELL UN-CON-SCIOUS. At feet of your host."

"Jerome the burglar!" Malcolm remembered, with a short snort of recognition.

George Leeds smiled, and stretching out hugely, cracked the bones in his spine.

"That seems a hundred years ago," Malcolm said, passing the comb back to George.

"Jerome a hundred years ago!" George inquired.

"My father seems a thousand years ago," Malcolm told him.

"By the way what's the slant on this father of yours? Seems that's all people talk about in this part of town: is he or ain't he, et cetera."

"Oh, he's been dead or disappeared for nearly a year now," Malcolm said. "Mr. Cox has been introducing me to all of his address people, you see, and that is how I got in with Jerome."

"Got in with him?" George turned about painfully in the narrow space of the bed, and took a better look at the boy.

"Nearly every day, you see, Mr. Leeds, I get a different address. I'm beginning life, I guess you might call it. You would never believe all the people I get to meet," Malcolm explained, but so close was the confines of their sleeping quarters, he found himself speaking direct into the piano player's ear, as one would to a stone deaf person.

"I think maybe I do believe it," George Leeds replied, and then he put his hand on Malcolm's forehead. "No," he said, after a pause, "you don't have no fever."

"Thank you," Malcolm said, immediately putting his hand to where George Leeds had placed his.

Malcolm was just about to tell George Leeds about Kermit and the Girards when Eloisa Brace entered the room bearing a tray of steaming coffee.

"O.K., how are all of my *fellows* this morning," Eloisa said. There was no trace of her irritability of the night before.

She kissed both of them briefly on the forehead, and handed each of them his cup of coffee.

"Cramped quarters," Eloisa commented on the bed.

"This is his first night in a strange bed," George Leeds pointed out to Eloisa Brace, cocking his head at Malcolm.

"I slept very well," Malcolm replied ceremoniously.

"Fine, fine," Eloisa said.

"And I think I know the reason why," Malcolm continued.

Eloisa and George stared at him.

"It's because the piano player smells like coconuts," Malcolm said with a kind of slow triumph.

"Coconuts!" George Leeds exclaimed. "I accept that as a compliment, Malcolm."

Malcolm was about to continue speaking when Eloisa Brace said that she wanted a word with him alone as soon as possible.

"I hope it's not about anything personal and serious," Malcolm was disturbed.

"It is and it isn't," Eloisa told him. "The fact is," she said, and she began tidying up the bottom of the bedclothes a bit, "I would like to paint you, Malcolm."

Malcolm smiled insipidly.

"Eloisa wants to draw your *portrait,*" the piano player further explained to the boy.

Malcolm nodded.

"Good," Eloisa Brace said. "It's a commissioned portrait, practically, you see," she went on. "I have an idea Madame Girard may want it, once it is completed. So we must begin immediately after you've had your coffee . . ."

"But I have to go to the bench some time this morning," Malcolm explained.

"Bench?" Eloisa said, for she had only vaguely heard of this aspect of Malcolm's life. "No, no, we've made all the arrangements with your hotel manager. You're to move in here while you're having your portrait done."

"With the piano player?" Malcolm stared at George Leeds.

"Well, not exactly. You will, I mean, have a room *somewhere,* though my house is just full up at the moment. O.K.? Well, hurry, Malcolm," Eloisa Brace commanded. "We don't have too much time to lose."

"Is all this correct?" Malcolm turned to the piano player.

Yawning, George Leeds replied: "You see, Malcolm, I just stick to the piano. And the rest of the world and the people, too, even nice people like you, well, I just kind of tend to let them go, if you don't mind me saying so."

Eloisa Brace watched Malcolm, waiting.

"Eloisa has already begun his portrait!" Mr. Cox was speaking to Kermit, who was lying on the sofa in his own studio, covered in quilts, sick with a bad cold.

"Everywhere Malcolm goes, flowers spring up," Kermit commented hoarsely.

Mr. Cox paused lengthily, then said: "He was simply lucky enough to have found us."

"You mean, of course," Kermit sat bolt upright in the sofa, "lucky enough to have met you." His nostrils palpitated from his exertion.

"Let's not quarrel when you're ill," Mr. Cox said.

"Quarrelling is something nobody can forbid me," Kermit reminded him. "When I cease to quarrel, I will cease to be."

Mr. Cox was about to make some comment, perhaps metaphysical, on this remark, when Kermit hurried ahead of him:

"I can hardly wait, nonetheless, to see Eloisa Brace's portrait of Malcolm."

"But your sharp little eyes can surely visualize it already," Mr. Cox rejoined.

"No, my sharp *little* eyes cannot!" Kermit sat up all the way now on the divan, and put his feet on the floor, and with a loud bang put on his derby hat, which he usually wore only when he was painting.

"All of Eloisa's portraits, whether they are of her or others, look just like Eloisa," Mr. Cox reminded him.

"This one will be different," Kermit was emphatic.

"You seem to be praising another artist," Mr. Cox cautioned, "—which, I must say, is a new tack for you to take."

"Did I say anything in praise of Eloisa Brace? I wouldn't dream of doing that. She can't paint, and she can't draw, and she can't even see. But—" and here Kermit threw off the covers of his bed onto the floor, and stood up solidly—

"she does have a definite feeling for young men like Malcolm, and that feeling will triumph in this case and produce a good painting, perhaps a masterpiece. That often happens to painters without talent—they do one fine thing."

"All you're saying is you're a bit partial to Malcolm," Mr. Cox shook his head.

"All I can say is I live only to see that finished portrait," Kermit replied.

"The thought that Malcolm is living there is more interesting to me than that he is being painted," Mr. Cox pointed out.

"It must be a good deal more strenuous than living in a whorehouse," Kermit observed. "I suppose the poor boy has already been taken to bed by a score of people there."

"Eloisa did speak to me a bit—almost on that very subject," Mr. Cox began. "She is sorry, she told me, that Malcolm cannot have a room of his own as he did in his hotel. And she runs such a busy house, you know—all those travelling musicians coming and going at all hours, that Malcolm has to sleep with a different person each night, and sometimes—when there is real crowding, Eloisa has to move him in the middle of the night to a different bed. Often it's more apt to be three in a bed than two . . . Malcolm told Eloisa that it was like travelling in Czechoslovakia during a war."

"I'm glad for his own sake that Malcolm's father is dead," Kermit said, and he pulled his derby hat low over his eyes.

"There you go again, with your lower middle-class prejudices coming out," Mr. Cox exploded. "Everybody has to begin some time, and Malcolm is beginning."

Kermit shook his head. Then: "What will Eloisa Brace do with the portrait?" Kermit asked.

"But I thought you knew," Mr. Cox pooh-poohed his pretension of ignorance.

"What could I know, lying here in my widower-hood?" Kermit demanded to know, and he walked over to his easel, where an empty canvas stared at him. He put a few strokes on it with a pencil, and then put the pencil down.

"Everybody knows Eloisa will sell the portrait to Madame Girard," Mr. Cox said.

Kermit nodded, a slow strange smile on his mouth.

"Oh, to be wanted, adored, sought after," Kermit began, and he went back to his bed, took up a small bottle of camphor, and smelled of it. "A boy comes in off a summer bench," the midget continued, "and is immediately wined, dined, courted, carried off in private limousines, *painted*, while I, with all my talents and training and charm—well, Mr. Cox, it's the ash can for me, that's about all anyone can honestly say."

Mr. Cox got up to leave, humming. "You had your chance, I'm afraid," the astrologer said gravely.

"Before you go," Kermit said in a low voice, his eyes looking away from Mr. Cox, "answer me one simple question: Does Malcolm have any mind at all?"

"I will answer your question with another one: Do you think he needs one?" Mr. Cox said, and he was already at the door which led to the street, which he opened, without another word of parting to the midget.

"I can't help being interested in jazz musicians any more than a fish can keep out of water," Eloisa Brace confessed, as she was painting Malcolm's portrait. "Jazz musicians are my fare, and almost always have been."

"Doesn't Jerome interfere?" Malcolm wondered.

"Move your chin just a little more to the right, hon," Eloisa told him.

Returning to his question, she smiled, then said: "Jerome knew everything about me when he married me. We both knew the chances we were taking."

Malcolm nodded, but kept his chin in place.

"I gave up a rich husband for Jerome," she stopped painting, perhaps remembering briefly that earlier marriage and husband. "But I've never regretted it. Not that we're happy, Jerome and I. We've never known a day of rest. While with my first husband, I was *outwardly* happy, you see—had nothing but rest. But with Jerome, well, I don't have a thing,

and not really a happy moment. Get poorer every day—he
can't find work because of what he is, and we do nothing
but quarrel. But, Malcolm, it's *life* with Jerome . . . Here
I am, telling you everything," she said, squinting at the portrait, for she was more than a little near-sighted.

"But when do you find time to be married?" Malcolm
asked, and added, at the look he got from Eloisa: "I mean
with so many jazz concerts going on and all."

"Marriage is something that just goes on and on inside
of you, Malcolm," Eloisa said. "Concerts begin and end, and
musicians come and go, but a real marriage just keeps going."

She painted slowly and rhythmically now, a soft look on
her mouth.

Malcolm cleared his throat vociferously.

"It was Jerome, you see, I was worried about," the boy
finally said.

"Jerome?" Eloisa wondered, putting her brush down, and
taking up a second, smaller one in its place. "Why on earth
should anybody worry about Jerome?" she frowned. "For
the first time in his whole life he's *safe*."

"Well, it's so sad he has to remember he's an ex-con all
the time," Malcolm noted.

"Oh, everybody's entitled to a few memories when he's
potted," Eloisa shrugged this off. "And marriage has taken
the place of all that old prison trouble. He just likes to
remember when he's potted is all. Grown-up people, you
see, Malcolm, have long memories: you remember that."

"Poor, poor Jerome," Malcolm exclaimed softly.

Just then the telephone rang. Eloisa sat still, looking
gloomy and thoughtful, and then turning to Malcolm, she
inquired: "Would you have the heart to answer that, and
then come and tell me who it is? But don't tell whoever
it is that I am in."

Malcolm nodded, and going over to the little stand where
the telephone rested, took off its receiver.

He paused, listening to the cascade of sounds at the other
end of the wire, then looking up at Eloisa with wide eyes,
he whispered: "Just guess. It's Madame Girard!"

Eloisa raised her eyes to the ceiling.

"Will you talk?" Malcolm asked Eloisa.

"I don't suppose I have any choice in the matter," the painter said. And she took the receiver from Malcolm's hands.

"I know you are lonely, my dear," Eloisa said to Madame Girard on the phone. "But you can't *can't* come here. No, no, no, my dear, you cannot!"

"But you have a young man there named Malcolm," Madame Girard's voice boomed. "And I wish to bring him to my home to stay. No, I haven't as yet considered adoption. It's not quite that kind of relationship, but of course it may come to that."

"But, Madame Girard," Eloisa implored. "You know I am painting his portrait." Eloisa regretted she had given this piece of information at once.

"Then I must purchase it at once," Madame Girard exclaimed. "Do you hear . . . I have not been so taken with a young person in years."

Eloisa motioned to Malcolm to fetch her the tray with the brandy decanter and glass, which he brought to her in a trice.

"What are those oral sounds I am now hearing?" Madame Girard asked a moment later.

"I'm sipping brandy," Eloisa explained to her.

"At nine thirty in the morning?" Madame Girard interrogated suspiciously.

"Telephones always upset me so, Madame Girard, you know that, and when it's a long phone conversation, often a finger of brandy gets me through."

"I know *nothing* of your habits," Madame Girard replied. "All I know is Malcolm is there, when he should be here, and I must come for him. I discovered him, and I claim him."

"Madame Girard, listen to reason!"

"Why should you people who have no money or background be entrusted with him?" Madame Girard said. "Let those who can, take him."

"But the portrait," Eloisa cried. "You forget that I am doing his portrait—which you say you one day will purchase."

"You can come to the Chateau and finish it," Madame Girard told her.

"I cannot, and I will not, Madame Girard," Eloisa stood firm.

"I am claiming my own is all," Madame Girard said, more calm now. "I am simply asking you to hand over Malcolm. He's no longer on his bench, and I have as good a claim as anyone. We want him to go to the country, and I need his special kind of companionship. Girard Girard, as you know, is no comfort to me any more. I need youth and freshness around me. I am imploring you, Eloisa."

"Think of the brandy I am having to consume, Madame Girard, to sustain me in this telephone conversation," Eloisa appealed.

"Eloisa, I will have Girard Girard send a whole case up to you for your unpleasant task. What brand did you say you use?"

"Oh, please, you know we buy only a cheap domestic."

"You shall be sent *Napoleon* today," Madame Girard assured her.

"No favors, please," Eloisa rejected her. "You know what Jerome thinks of favors. And Malcolm must absolutely stay until the portrait is done."

"No, no, you shall come here to paint him. Meanwhile, I am getting ready to make my visit to you at once."

"We will bar the door, Madame Girard. Your wealth and position cannot force open the entry to a private house."

"You are rejecting my friendship and my generosity," Madame Girard cried. "You are rejecting *me*. When all I wish to do is *give*. Why, why cannot *you* see reason?"

"Malcolm is not going to be handed over to you. When his portrait is finished, we will call you up—not until."

"You wish, I see, then, for me to employ force," Madame Girard said with regret.

"Consider me. Consider Malcolm," Eloisa now implored her.

"Consider you. Consider him," Madame Girard harumphed. "You poor innocent thing. What do you know of real suffering? What if your husband was in a different woman's bed each evening, and then upon his arriving home at last had time only for a business talk on the transatlantic cables. Contemplate that for suffering."

"I know, Madame Girard, your marriage is a difficult one, but consider—"

"Consider you! You have your jazz musicians. You have a loving, though idiotic, husband. You have your art. Now you have Malcolm. I have nothing."

"Madame Girard, this phone is simply weighting me down, and as a result I am drinking too much. I am not a heavy drinker like you, and as you know my brands are not imported. I won't be able to paint unless you hang up, and then you will have no portrait."

"Unless you give me permission to at least come to your home, I vow I will kill myself," Madame Girard informed her.

"Madame Girard," Eloisa said, "suicide is your own decision. I will not respond to your customary threats."

"Eloisa," Madame Girard cried. "Be generous, if you cannot be reasonable. I will pay you . . . anything."

Eloisa suddenly hung up, without replying.

"She may kill herself this time," Eloisa said, taking a drink of brandy. "But I rather fear we will see her instead as a visitor here."

Malcolm nodded gravely.

"But whatever happens in these next few days or hours, or even weeks," Eloisa said, going over to Malcolm, and straightening his necktie, "don't leave, do you hear. No matter what happens. Don't go away with anybody. Your portrait must be finished, do you hear?"

Madame Girard Confronts Eloisa

At that moment, George Leeds, the piano player, appeared in the room in evening dress and announced to Eloisa that the concert was about to begin on the third floor and that her presence was seriously "in request."

Malcolm was about to say something to George—how different he looked from the man who had combed his hair in their common bed!—who nodded affably at the boy, but Eloisa began giving Malcolm instructions before regretfully excusing herself, and warning him not to leave the room under any circumstances, and that she would return just as soon as the concert ended.

Eloisa and the piano player then went out together, and a few minutes later, the sad persistent notes of bass and sax, piano and vibraphone and drums drifted down to him.

Malcolm felt himself then entirely alone, more alone than had he remained on the bench. In the lonely emptiness of the house, with its castle-like high ceilings, the feel of the gray thick carpets beneath his feet, and the self-portraits of Eloisa, the drawings of Negroes looking out from their pale eyes, of strange perhaps non-existent animals gazing at him from canvases everywhere, Malcolm remembered his early travels with his father in countries whose names he could no longer recall. But this time, he was more hopelessly alone, in addition to not understanding anything around him. And at the same time he rather felt that perhaps he belonged here as much as anywhere, with the colored musicians, the paintings, and the different bed each night.

A cat came up from the basement and examined him with a look, and then went on to the floor above. The three

floors in the house were all of them furnished with identical furniture and with Eloisa's paintings, and all of them
punctuated hour by hour with the notes from the bass and
sax and piano.

Everywhere in the house, no matter at what hour, one
felt that it was afternoon, late afternoon breaking into twilight, with a coolness, too, like perpetual autumn, an autumn
that will not pass into winter owing to some damage perhaps to the machinery of the cosmos. It will go on being
autumn, go on being cool, but slowly, slowly everything
will begin to fall piece by piece, the walls will slip down
ever so little, the strange pictures will warp, the mythological animals will move their eyes slightly for the last time as
they fade into indistinction, the strings of the bass will
loosen and fall, the piano keys wrinkle and disappear into
the wood of the instrument, and the beautiful alto sax
shrivel into foil.

How long Malcolm slept he did not know, but waking up
suddenly he first saw the cat looking at him again, and
then—Kermit.

"The little man," Malcolm exclaimed. "You've escaped!"

Kermit laughed, a mischievous curl of pleasure on his
lips. "I was about to turn you into a cat," he told Malcolm.

"Be seated at once," Malcolm commanded, like a man in
his own house. "How did you come to get in here?"

"The door was open, and I walked in from my morning
stroll," Kermit informed him.

"I didn't know you ever took . . . strolls," Malcolm said
with some surprise. "You're not *afraid?*"

"Afraid a dog will swallow me?" Kermit laughed, an edge
of bitterness in his expression.

"I'm afraid for you . . . is all," Malcolm was serious.

"And so the great woman painter and jazz queen has succeeded in making you a prisoner," Kermit began.

"She may have," Malcolm acknowledged, "but then perhaps I was one before."

"I see you as one, yes," Kermit agreed. "But, from the

bench . . . to the cat-house, which I suppose one could call it. Well . . ."

Kermit laughed somewhat too heartily, while Malcolm merely sat with his hands in his lap.

"I am, you see, *persona non grata* here," Kermit said when he had finished laughing, "—or in plain words, Eloisa hates me. It took not a little courage to come in here."

"Why does such a successful woman hate *you?*" Malcolm wondered, his chin loose, and his eyes full of puzzlement.

"It's an old feud," the little man replied, in evident relishment of what he was about to tell. "Years ago—two years, in fact, I called her on the telephone—her instrument of torture—and well, with four or five drinks to fortify me, I simply said to her, 'Eloisa, my dear, why is it I'm not good enough to ever be invited to one of your *soirées?*' She was struck speechless with whatever emotion an old retired whore like her is struck speechless with. Then while she was pinioned in her own silence, I went on: 'Is it the quality of my painting which critics find so infinitely superior to yours which keeps me off your list, or is it the fact that my good looks and graceful presence make your unappetizing grossness and overblown charms so especially *detestable?*'"

"You said *that?*" Malcolm leaned closer.

"I said I was drunk," Kermit replied acidly—and then going on, with all his former delight: "She actually apologized then and there, said my not having been invited was an oversight, et cetera, and was *never* intentional, but I was not so easily appeased . . . 'There is one reason, dear Eloisa,' I went on, 'why my name was perhaps never on your list.' . . . 'What on earth reason would that be?' she cried, her voice shaking and thin . . . 'Your husband, dear Eloisa,' I told her, 'is so fond of my kisses!'"

Malcolm jumped up and walked over to a corner of the room, standing there motionless and silent like a schoolboy sent to punishment, while Kermit laughing at his own anecdote with closed eyes at first did not perceive his friend had walked off from him.

"What on earth are you doing in that corner?" Kermit

cried, when he had recovered from his mirth. "Come out
from there at once . . ."

When Malcolm did not move, Kermit went over to him,
and took his hand in his.

"Has the little midget failed to entertain his royal high-
ness?" Kermit said somewhat soberly, and he led Malcolm
out from the corner.

"Sit down," the little man now commanded Malcolm,
and the boy obeyed, a sober look on his face.

"Tell me, dear child," the midget said. "Are you by chance
a virgin?"

Malcolm's throat moved, his vocal organs appeared to
be repeating Kermit's question.

"Do I have to draw a picture for you?" the little man shot
an angry glance.

"Not exactly," Malcolm replied.

"Not exactly what?" Kermit said irritably.

"Not exactly . . . a virgin, I guess," Malcolm said, and a
helpless grin came over his mouth.

"Well, speak up then. God knows I'm not old enough to be
your *father* . . . But if you're missing in the basic information of life, I can always take a minute out for you in the
name of friendship."

Malcolm nodded.

"How many girls have you been to bed with?" the midget
interrogated.

"Girls?" Malcolm swallowed.

"It's girls we are talking about," the midget proceeded.

"Well, you see, my father—" Malcolm began.

"I thought we would come to that," the midget said.

Then going up to Malcolm, and shaking the boy, the little
man said: "Now see here, see here—" when the sound of
heavy footsteps made both of them look up.

"*Petit monstre!*" Eloisa Brace cried, entering the room,
and addressing Kermit. "Take your hands off Malcolm at
once."

MALCOLM

"I am caressing him, you plain fool," Kermit addressed the painter.

"Forgive me," Eloisa said quickly and contritely, perhaps recognizing the real danger of Kermit's enmity toward her. "I didn't mean to speak so sharply . . . There's been so much excitement here today."

She broke into a short sob, which she immediately controlled.

"I don't mean to not be your friend, Kermit," Eloisa continued. "Though I fear you are not mine."

"I could discuss this all so much better," Kermit explained to her, "if we had something refreshing and at the same time alcoholic to drink. Something destined perhaps for one of the many parties which I seem always to have missed here."

"Kermit, please," Eloisa's temper flashed for a minute. Then looking briefly at Malcolm, she got up, explaining that she would bring Kermit a drink at once.

"I've always heard from those who have had invitations to your parties," Kermit detained her, "that you have excellent Spanish brandy. Do you have any today, dear Eloisa?"

Eloisa Brace covered her face with her painting hand, and sighed: "It's always this way with me. I don't have any, as a matter of fact, Kermit—not at the moment. Will you please *please* believe me, and have something else in its stead?"

"What is in its stead?" the little man wondered, holding his index finger over his temple in the manner of one who wishes to hear an important reply.

"I have some wonderful California red wine," Eloisa cried enthusiastically, a bit too loud. "Jerome and I have just discovered it, and we can't get enough of it."

"But you did manage to keep some modicum for little visitors like me?" Kermit inquired, narrowing his eyes.

"Allow me all the hospitality I can offer you," Eloisa implored him.

"I know, dear Eloisa, that you have finer wines in your house than your California substitute—satisfying though it

may be to old Jerome, who went for so many years without
wine at all—"

Here Eloisa attempted to interrupt the midget with a
word, but the little man clapped his hands imperiously, and
continued:

"*BUT*, as *I* too am a reasonable person, and since this is
my first visit to a house whose entrance has always hitherto
been denied to me—I will accept, shall we say, what in
serious houses is proffered to the domestics?"

"Kermit," Eloisa began, and it was only at that moment
that Malcolm noticed that she was wearing an evening dress
which had a rather bad tear in the behind—"Kermit, let us
not spoil this afternoon. For Malcolm's sake alone. We
should not let him see us as only adults should see one
another!"

Kermit was preparing a reply, but Eloisa vociferated in
her glad voice:

"And now to your wine," and went out of the room.

"She never asked me what I wanted!" Malcolm said vacantly, like one who has only come awake.

"The idea of crashing in on us like that, without knocking
or a how-do-you-do or anything. And in that ridiculous cast-
off torn dress." Kermit scoffed. "And just as you were about
to tell me something important, Malcolm, about yourself."

"I?" Malcolm pointed in an expression of surprise to his
chest.

"Tell me at once what it was you were going to say?" Kermit demanded.

Malcolm stammered, for so much, so very much had
occurred, it was becoming more and more difficult to remember what had happened and when, not to mention an
unimportant thing like what he was about to say a few minutes ago.

But while he was still stammering, Eloisa entered with a
tray on which stood three glasses and a bottle of unlabelled
red wine.

"Pardon me, Kermit, if my hands shake too much to pour
you each your drink," Eloisa said. "Malcolm," she turned

to him, "Would you pour each of us a drink from that bottle. O.K.?"

"First, do you have an apron for me to put on?" Malcolm inquired, looking anxiously at his suit.

Eloisa and Kermit exchanged looks.

"*I* will pour each of us whatever it is in the bottle," Kermit stepped in, a lordly contempt in his voice for both Malcolm and Eloisa.

"No, no, I will pour now," Eloisa said. "My hands have quit trembling . . ."

"But, dear Eloisa," Malcolm assured her. "I would gladly pour, but all *bartenders* wear aprons, and I was only asking—"

"Silence," Eloisa shouted. "I can't endure another thing from anyone. I will pour, do you hear?" she thundered at both of them.

And trembling, she poured in great haste three glasses full of red wine.

"To all of us!" she cried with great vigor, raising her glass.

"To Girard Girard!" Malcolm exclaimed loudly, to which he got no response from either Kermit or Eloisa Brace.

"All the time I was on the third floor attending the jazz rehearsal," Eloisa said, "I could not control my nerves. I felt —perhaps because Malcolm is here—something terrible was going to happen. I could hardly wait to get back here to see if everything was all right."

"Be happy you can lead such a full life," Kermit told Eloisa. "Accept danger as part of the risk."

"Please," Eloisa said, and she looked happy for the first time that afternoon.

"I will not *please,*" Kermit told her. "You have experienced nearly everything, except perhaps being under fire in battle: marriages, musicians, art, love, all the dazzle and excitement that can only come to a figure of the arts—"

"You're rubbing it in now," Eloisa became ill-tempered again.

"No, I am speaking from the heart," Kermit assured her. "You deserve your coterie, such as it is, and you deserve your position. You have conquered where perhaps no other woman ever set foot."

"I knew it!" Eloisa cried helplessly. "You're ribbing me."

"You invented modern jazz, don't deny it," the little man went over to Eloisa's chair.

"Stop him," Eloisa implored Malcolm with a look of futility.

"And your marriage to Jerome!" Kermit went on. "Is it not the marriage of the century?"

"Kermit, stop right there with my marriage. If you go further—" and she made a frantic gesture. "I can't hear—no, not even a compliment concerning my marriage. My marriage is too close, somehow, to—"

"Too *close* to what?" a deep feminine voice cried from the entrance to the room.

All eyes looked up to see Madame Girard coming into the center of the room, a sun parasol in her hand.

Closing her eyes, and raising her parasol gently into the air, she said: "Let no one converse until I have given the sign."

Madame Girard cleared her throat, but she did not need to wait for silence: she had created the deepest kind possible.

Addressing again now her auditors, she said: "I have only come here to claim what is my own. A reasonable request. I am, of course, a reasonable woman. Let there be no interruptions, please!" Madame Girard turned to Malcolm, who had stood up only, as a matter of fact, to hear her better, but she had construed his movement as an attempt to interpolate.

"Sit down," Madame Girard commanded Malcolm *sotto voce*.

She continued, closing her eyes again:

"Why should the rest of the world know plenty, happiness, domestic satisfaction, love—while I am shut out from all these things, deprived of a woman's *human* station in life, turned in upon my own devices, and saddled—" here she

opened her eyes directly and immediately upon the tray
with the wine bottle, then closed them again—"*saddled* with
a husband who knows not whether I am alive or dead, and
cares, yes, cares—*dear* Eloisa, I can feel you are shaking
your head, so stop!—cares LESS."

"Madame Girard," Eloisa managed to get out.

"Silence, I say," Madame Girard addressed herself briefly
to Eloisa. "I know you are a woman of talent, perhaps genius,
but your words, your advice, whatever you have to offer
here this afternoon is worth no more to me than yesterday's
bath water . . ."

Kermit shrank into his chair, his bravado of a moment
ago completely vanished, while gazing glassily at the
woman he had feared so long to meet, but since she kept her
eyes closed, allowed him for the time being to stare at her
with impunity.

Malcolm began to look sleepy, and Eloisa Brace, overcome
by the day's fare of brandy, wine, fear, and confusion began
whimpering softly.

"I have been called *unreasonable* by fools," Madame Girard went on, her eyelids still tightly closed and fluttering
like a medium who sees the ghost she had never thought to
catch. "I, who am the most reasonable of women, the kind-
est, the most generous, the one who wants to give all her
love. Yes, all!"

Here, Madame Girard opened her eyes wide, and, when
they fell on Eloisa, the latter cried out: "Stop her, oh, stop
her, somebody!"

Madame Girard closed her eyes again, but then, changing
her mind, she opened them suddenly and said, "Will you
be quiet, lady, while I am delivering my speech? Why do
you think I am here, but to get you to see reason! hear reason! follow reason!"

"Reason!" Eloisa cried. "For good God's sake, why does
this house not fall upon us when such words are spoken."

Kermit brought Eloisa her wine glass, which, in the confusion of Madame Girard's entrance, she had put down and
left forgotten.

"I have been wronged," Madame Girard continued, and raising her parasol a bit too carelessly, the point of it caught one of the stuffed owls which rested on the mantel, and brought it flying to the carpet, where it suddenly disintegrated into a heap of dust and feathers.

"Don't touch it," Madame Girard warned, at the signs of motion on Eloisa's part. "You shall be repaid—triple—for this damage.

"But to get back!" she went on. "*Wronged* not only by that satyr Girard Girard who has divided his lifetime into passion for money and lust with servant girls—"

"No, no, Madame Girard, you wrong him," Malcolm exclaimed, standing up.

"Will you keep these immature ephebes seated and silent, or shall I summon someone who can?" Madame Girard turned her anger against Eloisa Brace. She was about to continue when her attention was distracted by the extreme awe written on the face of the midget.

Strolling with her parasol quickly over to where the little man sat cringing—looking, as Madame Girard later described him, like a kinkajou at noon—Madame Girard studied him closely for a moment, and then delivered a resounding kiss, as stooping, she bent over his mouth.

She immediately returned to the center of the room to resume speaking.

But Kermit, touching himself on his mouth, had exclaimed: "I have been anointed then."

"Merely recognized, not anointed," Madame Girard informed him, aside.

"Madame Girard, my dear friend," Eloisa said, making a last effort, and rising she took the older woman by the hand. "You must go upstairs and lie down, and I will call your husband. You are going to be very sick, if you do not listen to me now."

"Go away, my dear," Madame Girard recommended to Eloisa. "You are eternally *de trop*. I am speaking primarily to *them*—" and she pointed to the two men. "You, on the other hand, should be at work painting, supplying the world with your genius, but not appearing in public. You are too ugly to appear in public, even a public as small as this room. Let the world feast its eyes on young beauties like theirs—," and she swept her arms in the direction of Malcolm and Kermit— "but let work-a-day geniuses like you keep to themselves in work-rooms. To your work-room, genius! To your work-room!"

"Don't you see, my dear," Eloisa continued to hold Madame Girard by the hand, "you are bringing about a *crise.*"

"Then, do *you* go to bed, my dear. I myself am fresh as a daisy. Who could not be in such company?"

"You have given me a splitting headache," Eloisa complained.

"To your work-room, then. Work is the sovereign cure for headaches. You know that. Ah, how beautiful you *were*," Madame Girard reflected softly, looking directly into Eloisa's face. "How beautiful you were before your *second* marriage. Your hair was like ripe wheat—no, don't deny that it was. A delight to the eye, and hand. And now look at it. Look at you. You have allowed that burglar to defile you, to *common* you, that's what. Even your speech is no longer dignified, harumphing O.K.'s in a stream. And you've gotten a pot on you from drinking with him. Oh, how my heart has ached for you, Eloisa. I will not deny it. But my feelings for you must not interfere with my own words of advice, which are wise and true for you: Leave this room! Go to your work! You are fit now for nothing but labor. Leave me to these beautiful young men. Did you think I came to see you? Never! Go! Leave! We have no further need of you, do we, my handsomes?"

Malcolm and Kermit both gaped at Madame Girard, too engrossed by what they heard to answer her by so much as a nod.

Eloisa began walking about the room, weeping and drinking from time to time now direct from the wine bottle.

"A woman who calls herself my friend," Eloisa said weakly.

"There is no friendship here, my dear," Madame Girard

replied. "You sullied my friendship for you by marrying
that jail-bird. Had you cared for me you would never have
gone through with such a marriage. I am here today to pay
tribute to these two young men, and I implore you for the last
time to leave the room. I beg, and I demand it."

"You are leaving me no choice," Eloisa Brace said with
great steadiness, putting down the wine bottle.

"No choice for what?" Madame Girard asked, a hint of
apprehension in her tone.

"I am going to call Girard Girard," Eloisa warned her.

"He is in Iowa making four million dollars."

"Then I shall call the authorities," Eloisa said, her voice
and manner completely unlike her own.

"Authorities, your foot!" Madame Girard sneered, and she
moved over to the table on which sat Malcolm's wine glass,
which was more than half full, and which she now drained
at a swallow. "They have called the authorities a thousand
times for me," she regaled them. "But do you think they
dare take me? When they know who I am? Never. And do
you know, even if they did not *know* who I was, why they
would never dare take me?" she stared at everyone in the
room, all of whom, she saw, hung on each word that now
came from her. "Of course you don't know why! How could
you? They don't take me because I *know* everything! And
they can see that knowledge on my face! For that reason,
even if they should be called, they would never disturb
me . . ."

Going immediately over to Malcolm after she had said
this, she began kissing his sideburns, moving from one to
the other in rapid succession.

"It is for you alone," Madame Girard said, "that I made
this difficult trip, that I came to see your beautiful face . . .
living, *and* portrayed in oil . . ."

Madame Girard stopped suddenly, like one who is listening for a sound which will be a signal and cue.

"Where is that portrait, you swindler?" she addressed
Eloisa.

"Malcolm! Kermit!" Eloisa said fiercely. "We must tie her. We must tie her or she will begin to destroy things."

"*They* won't help you," Madame Girard hurled at Eloisa.

"Hold her," Eloisa commanded the boys.

Neither of the young men budged.

"You see," Madame Girard laughed. "You can do nothing. Go call your authorities."

Madame Girard had, however, forgotten one thing about Eloisa Brace: the latter's athletic prowess.

Eloisa closed her eyes, bracing herself for the supreme effort, while Madame Girard, already swaying on her feet, laughed deliriously at her imagined victory.

"I will never leave," she was crying when Eloisa Brace looking remarkably like a boxer who has re-entered the ring, advanced toward the great woman, and delivered two blows, a powerful left, and then a right to the chin, and Madame Girard tottered and then fell silently, a sad smile on her mouth, to the floor, and lay there in an attitude like that of the stone queen, asleep through all the ages.

"Pick her up and carry her to the east guest room," Eloisa commanded the two men quietly, and Malcolm and Kermit hastened to obey her.

The Oration of Madame Girard

"But why should I leave your house, if you love me?" Madame Girard was speaking to Jerome Brace, late the next day, lying back in the largest bed in the house, to which Malcolm and Kermit had, with great difficulty—they had dropped her twice on the staircase—carried her.

Madame Girard held her hand to her "mouse," inflicted on her by Eloisa, and, as Jerome noted admiringly, one of the blackest eyes which he himself, in his own specialized career, had ever seen.

Madame Girard was proud of Jerome's acknowledgment of her "mouse," but soon she began to complain again of her treatment—not so much of Eloisa's "brutality,"—she had admired the painter's daring attack on her—but of Jerome's insistent order that she leave the premises.

Madame Girard denied that Jerome loved her any more.

"We do love you, Madame Girard, more than you will ever know."

"My mother used to employ that same phrase to me, and yet it was she who ruined my life with her undiscriminating affection."

"*I* love you, Madame Girard," Jerome said, taking her small hand in his.

"Yet you ask me to leave the premises," she shook her head.

"Only because we love you."

"Don't you realize that you are asking me to give up the one thing I now wish more than anything in the world," Madame Girard expostulated.

Jerome watched her.

"Because I am with the ones I love now," she went on. "The little Kermit—" she suddenly spoke in "baby-talk" over this phrase. "Malcolm, Eloisa, George Leeds, and the musicians, and *you*, wonderful you." She held out her arms to him, and Jerome kissed her quietly again, this time on the hair.

"It's not," Jerome began sitting down on the bed beside her, "it's not as if you could never come to see us again."

"Oh, but it is," she replied. "It is, and you know it is."

"Madame Girard, a *little* reason, please."

"I must stay because love is here," she told him.

"You will diminish a good deal of that love if you stay!" he warned.

Her eyes darted about in her head, and then, whispering into his ear, she told him: "But I will be good—for you."

"You were never good in your life, Madame Girard. Your whole life has been devoted to not being good for your friends. And it is this quality in you that makes us love you: you cannot be good."

"I cannot?" she asked, craftiness and sweetness in her voice.

"You can NOT," Jerome repeated for her.

"But this time, I *will*. I will command myself."

"Madame Girard, consider the man you are talking to."

"Jerome, the burglar," she said, hopelessly considering her situation.

"How people of privilege always put things so coarsely," Jerome said. "It is really only the downtrodden who have all the sensitivity."

"I have suffered too much to be fine any more," she said, speaking now into the wall.

"What I was trying to tell you," Jerome continued, "is I know men and women from prison, and I know that you don't reform by saying you mean to. Besides, you have no intention of reforming. You want to be naughty."

"I want to be?" she considered this.

"It's the only part you can play now."

"You mean I have limited myself," Madame Girard

reached for one of the *brioches* which they had brought to her at her insistence.

"Consider," Jerome said, "you have acted this one part for as many years as you have been married to Girard Girard, who worships, or at least, worshipped the ground you walk on."

"Don't go into my years of marriage and my age," she warned him. "I know how old I am, and you need not give a chronicle of my life."

"I had no intention of referring to your age. But you have played your naughty role for a great long time."

"Jerome," she said, chewing the *brioche* critically, "your trouble is you have left life and gone on to religion."

He laughed, superior to this comment.

"The worst kind of change," she went on, "has happened to you. You're a reformer. A do-gooder. You think because you were a burglar and did time that you have a blueprint for everybody outside. You're every confounded preacher and evangelist I have ever known."

"Tell me what they're like."

"Like they know the answers before they even heard the question. Yes, you're one of the truth boys, and though you have a lot more honey on your tongue than most of them, *no thank you*, Jerome, *no thank you*. You've ruined Eloisa, but keep your hands off my soul."

"Madame Girard, you're being pretty hard on me."

"And don't keep addressing me with my full title," she reminded him.

"What should I call you then?"

"Just address me with your eyes, and I'll judge you from there."

Jerome smiled, and his gaze fell down to one of Madame Girard's exposed feet, whose nails were freshly painted.

"Then there is nothing for Eloisa and me to do but what we have always done in this situation?" he said, standing up.

"Do you mean to call Girard Girard again, or only the police this time?" she wondered.

"Girard first, of course, and then, if necessary, the police."

"And to think I am talking to an ex-con," Madame Girard said. "You're as dumb and mean as any damned arm of the law you could turn to."

"We have to lead our own lives, Madame Girard," Jerome said.

"And yet you talk about love," she mused, wiping off her fingers of the crumbs from the pastry.

"By the way," she added. "That *brioche* was stale."

He bowed.

"Do you think I care, Jerome, if your *brioche* is stale. Not at all."

"Then why mention it?"

"We should mention everything. Otherwise no friendship, or love is possible. You yourself have taught me that, and you are 'cured'."

Jerome cleared his throat.

"We are not asking anything impossible of you," Jerome continued in his (as he himself could not help noticing now) *pastoral* manner. "We are merely asking you to go to your beautiful home and to your husband."

"Do you know what is happening in my beautiful home at this very moment?" Madame Girard demanded, raising her hand upwards.

Jerome waited for her answer.

"Girard Girard is in bed with the laundress."

"And are you clear of any responsibility in this?"

"I suppose I am responsible for everything," she replied. "But why go home to see what my irresponsibility has produced. I ask you this, Jerome, and this time reply as your old burglar self, and not as my pastor."

"Madame Girard," Jerome began hesitatingly, and with the unmistakable note of loss of patience.

"Don't tell me you love me again, either," she warned, "or I may lose that stale *brioche*." She held her hand to her breast.

"I'm afraid we have no choice but to take measures with you," he said lamely, perhaps quoting something somebody had once said to him.

"Is that all?"

"Why can't you believe in us?"

"Why can't you love me enough to let me stay and enjoy my 'beauties,' Malcolm and Kermit, and my admiration for Eloisa."

"For one thing, Malcolm is having his portrait painted, and you would upset all order and calm around here."

"I would be still as a tomb," Madame Girard begged.

"You would want to watch, you know you would. And then watching, you would begin to criticize, or you would ruffle up Malcolm's hair, or you would begin teasing the cat."

"I have never teased a cat in my life, and I was raising cats long before you even thought of being a criminal!" she said hotly.

"Madame Girard."

She began weeping softly.

"If only *one* person cared," she said. "But nobody does. Except perhaps old Mr. Cox. He *does* listen to what I have to say, and he does *not* tell me he loves me when he commands me to do something ridiculous."

"Do you think Mr. Cox would allow you to eat *brioche* in his bed?" Jerome wondered.

"Mr. Cox has never ordered me out of his house," she defended the astrologer.

"Only because you have never been in it," Jerome said acidly.

"Mr. Cox gives me all he can, but he does not pretend he has very much for me. You, like all evangelists, pretend you do."

"You are accusing us of bad faith."

"I am only saying you speak more than you feel."

"We are, then, hypocrites."

"You talk about love a good deal more than you do anything about it, especially you. Or perhaps especially Eloisa," Madame Girard hesitated. "No, especially both of you. You are professional 'lovers' like the Christians used to be."

"Don't use those terms with regard to us."

"I had forgotten all about how old-fashioned Christians

acted until I met you," Madame Girard was firm. "I knew
there was some fly in your ointment, but I thought you were
a bit soft-brained from prison. But now I know what it is!"
she cried in triumph.

"Madame Girard, I'm asking you—" he cried.

"You are an old-fashioned Christian looking for your
flock."

"Please," Jerome said, red-faced. "Don't be indecent as
well as obnoxious."

Madame Girard rose high in her bed, and slapped him
vigorously across the mouth.

"Sit down," she commanded. "I won't have you trying to
pretend I am uncontrollable so that you can beat me. Don't
I see the sadist in you? Sit down at once."

Jerome sat down, the same deep red on his face.

"I saw through you the day Eloisa married you," Madame
Girard told him. "Your honied words, your honied love.
Under all your honey runs a conduit of venom."

"I will not listen to your raving."

"You people who talk and talk about love all the time,"
Madame Girard ignored his interpolation. "You're the least
of the lot. If you did anything about it, you wouldn't have
to tell it. I'll bet if I offered you a million dollars right now
you would walk out of this room and leave Eloisa on her
can. And don't I know why you want Malcolm and Kermit
to yourself, too."

Jerome gave her at that moment such a smile of patient
condescension and untouchable superiority that Madame
Girard's face fell, and she began to weep again.

"You don't love anybody," she sobbed. "You don't love
Eloisa, you don't love me, you don't love Malcolm. And you
say you're 'cured.' Of what? Cured of everything but talk,
that's all, that's the cure, cured to go on your selfish evan-
gelical way acting superior to other human beings and being proud you were a goddam burglar and can now sit
around with your less fortunate straight middle-class fellows,
and act superior to them because they are dumb enough to
say they don't know to all your pious questions. Yes, you

know everything, but wait, just one moment—," and here
Madame Girard stood up in the bed and pointed a finger at
him with such sternness that the smile on his face slowly
disappeared.

"I issue a prognostication on you: your 'cure' is over! Do
you hear? You are no longer 'cured.' A long set-back is about
to overtake you, and you are to go back and learn the lesson
you have forgotten from your burglar days, that love is deeds
and not honied talk."

"And now, Madame Girard," Jerome told her, "will you
please get up and get ready to leave like a good girl?" And
he gave her a chaste kiss on her brow.

"Condescension! condescension!" Madame Girard cried.
"The last weapon!"

Girard Girard had come, summoned by an intoxicated
and distraught Eloisa Brace, and he was waiting, frowning
and gray in his handsome raincoat, when Madame Girard
came painfully down the long two flights of stairs from the
guest room where she had just finished her long interview
with Jerome.

Madame Girard stopped at the landing of the second
flight of stairs in order to stare at her husband.

"I suppose I have interrupted some *amour* of yours with
the kitchen help?" she levelled her attack.

Girard Girard barely looked up from his stance in the
middle of the lower room.

"My husband does not speak to me," Madame Girard said
to Eloisa Brace, who standing at the entrance to the room,
was weeping and hiccuping.

"Ignored by my own husband, ordered out of the house
by a burglar, pommelled by my dearest woman friend—ignored by my beauties," and she waved a gloved hand at
each of these persons in succession. "Can any one deny that
my empire is in ruins?"

"Madame Girard," Eloisa cried, going part way up to her.

"Halt!" Madame Girard whispered, and she seized a
sprig of greenery which was trailing from a heavy vase.

"I will *not* hear anybody speak of love again," Madame Girard announced. "You are all, yes all of you, professional love-speakers. Girard Girard, Eloisa, Jerome, the burglar, all of you speak of your great beating love-full hearts. Yet you will not endure my presence here for more than a few hours. You tear me away from the only pleasure that now remains to me in my mature years"—here she threw the sprig of greenery at Girard Girard on whom it fell as air.

"You call men to come for me whenever you tire of my repetitions, whenever my presence ruffles your comfort, whenever your boredom spouts out of its foundationless depths . . ."

"She is giving the oration," Girard Girard cried in a hopeless voice.

"Yet you," Madame Girard went on, motioning to Girard and Eloisa Brace, "spare yourselves no pleasure. And what would you do if you did not have *me* to talk about, to feel superior to? What pleasure *that* would take away from you! What pleasure indeed!"

She began to weep a little, but then becoming dry-eyed and mildly savage:

"Without me, your life would have no imagination. For though you cannot stand me in the flesh, my spirit and will are all that keep you going. You are all of you dependent on me for life."

"Christ in heaven!" Girard exclaimed.

"Who has stolen my parasol?" Madame Girard suddenly said in a low voice, like an old actress breaking off at rehearsal.

"Your parasol is here, my dear," Eloisa said, producing it with a swiftness that seemed obscene.

"Ah," Madame Girard cooed. "So you were ready for me . . . You have spared no time at all in having the final preparations for my eviction . . ."

Madame Girard went up closely to Eloisa now as if to study a rare stone. Slowly, while Eloisa exchanged looks of fear and doubt with Girard Girard, Madame Girard pressed her lips against Eloisa's forehead, kissing her several times.

Then looking carefully and critically at Eloisa, Madame Girard said: "You have no beauty left. Your skin, which was never handsome, is now that of a woman without either age or youth. You belong to the nameless waves of the middle-aged."

Eloisa sobbed softly.

"Can any husband looking on that skin feel love?" Madame Girard appealed to the entire room.

There was a long silence.

"Answer my question," Madame Girard commanded Eloisa. "As an artist you are obliged to answer."

Eloisa sat down on the sofa near Girard Girard, and picked up a glass of brandy, which had been left there from the day before.

"Can any man looking at your face see love or even a woman. The answer, my dear Eloisa, is no. You are no longer a woman. Are you an artist indeed? That remains to be seen when the portrait of Malcolm is finished. Are your powers as an artist allied to your powers as a woman? If they are, you are done, finished, through forever."

"Madame Girard," Eloisa cried in great anguish, "you must leave at once."

Girard Girard now advanced toward his wife, galvanized into action by Eloisa's cry.

"Don't touch me, either of you," Madame Girard warned. "I will go out to the car alone, and I will get into it unassisted by anybody. I am leaving this house, of course, forever."

"No, no," Eloisa said. "You will not leave until you promise me you will return in a happier time."

"Eloisa suddenly remembers how very wealthy the both of us are," Madame Girard addressed herself to her husband. She adjusted her scarf about her throat.

"I want, however," Madame Girard added, "I want the portrait of Malcolm, and Girard Girard will pay you for it now."

Eloisa attempted to say something, but her throat had not been sufficiently moistened by the brandy.

"How much is the portrait?" Madame Girard demanded.

"But it is not finished! And you have not seen what is finished!" Eloisa exclaimed.

"How much will it be when finished?" Girard Girard inquired.

Eloisa stood thinking.

"Is five thousand too much to ask?" Eloisa ventured at last.

"Five thousand?" Madame Girard said, beating her parasol into the rug. "Five thousand is not my price for anything."

Girard Girard and Eloisa waited, tense, for her further deliberation.

"Is that price not satisfactory to you then?" Girard Girard addressed his wife.

"*Five* thousand is not my kind of price for anything, I repeat," Madame Girard expostulated. "Give her ten thousand or nothing."

"Is ten thousand a satisfactory price, Eloisa, my dear?" Girard questioned, looking at the painter warmly and sympathetically.

"Ten thousand," Eloisa gasped, surprised, genuinely surprised.

Girard Girard, however, was already taking out his checkbook.

"But you have not seen the portrait," Eloisa cried weakly. "What if you should not like it?"

Girard Girard meanwhile had written with great rapidity and flourish a check for the amount agreed upon, and handed it now to the painter.

"I have *never* paid five thousand for anything I wanted," Madame Girard warned everybody in the room.

Clapping her hands swiftly, Madame Girard announced, perhaps to cut off the warm looks being exchanged by Girard Girard and Eloisa Brace: "We are leaving."

Going up to Eloisa quickly, Madame Girard kissed her wetly on the mouth and said, "Despite all, you will always be dear to me, Eloisa," and both Madame Girard and Girard Girard left the house at once without another word.

"I have been *enriched!*" cried Eloisa Brace. "I am no longer what you can exactly call a pauper, let us say."

Jerome, Malcolm, and Kermit (the latter having, in the confusion, stayed on and *on*)—all three came up to her at that moment like a delegation of congratulation, although her statement had been as private as a soliloquy, and the sight of the check appeared to have removed her from all other human contact.

"Ten thousand smackers!" she moaned.

Singling out Kermit, then, Eloisa Brace bent very low and kissed him on the head.

"You are at the pinnacle of your career," Kermit said calmly.

"Thank you, dear," Eloisa replied, all her bitterness against the little man for the present vanished.

"I am the husband of a rich woman," Jerome said, and he was very pale. He sat down on the small wooden chair which Girard Girard had briefly occupied while waiting for Madame Girard to descend.

"Why are you so white?" Eloisa asked her husband, and she turned also to look at the faces of Malcolm and Kermit, perhaps seeking an explanation of her husband's pallor from them. The two young men, however, both showed pink poker-faces, and of the two, Malcolm showed the lesser emotion. Money, after all, had never been anything special to him, although of late what he had was rapidly dwindling, and had Eloisa said she had just got one million dollars, Malcolm would have probably been just as impressed or unimpressed.

But Jerome knew what money meant, and so Eloisa turned her full attention to him.

"Jerome, dear, you must explain your attitude, and your paleness."

"Must I?" he said, and there was a strange ominous bitterness in his tone.

"What change has come over you?" Eloisa begged to know, and Malcolm saw that her former character of dominance—which he had experienced the night of his arrival, changed now to dependence, almost panic.

When no one spoke, Malcolm began eating a Delicious apple, and his chewing filled the silence.

Eloisa studied Girard Girard's check, meanwhile, admiring the signature, as well as the denomination, and then advancing to the bureau, she took down a purple velvet box, and laid the check inside.

"I wish you would speak, then," Eloisa told Jerome suddenly, her back to him.

"What would you have me speak?" Jerome replied distantly, more distantly than she had ever heard him.

Malcolm's chewing continued.

"It has been a completely full two days," Eloisa remarked after a long silence.

"Ending in wealth for one of us," Jerome commented, with dogged unpleasantness.

"For one of us," Eloisa cried, distracted, and wheeling around at her husband. "What is the meaning of *one?*"

"You heard me say *one,* very well, *one* it is," Jerome raised his voice, and then leaped up and turning unexpectedly in the direction of Malcolm, he seized the apple almost from out of the boy's mouth and threw it into the fireplace.

"I hate both those goddam capitalists, the Girards," Jerome cried.

Eloisa Brace began wringing her hands, and Malcolm stared open-mouthed, pieces of apple still unchewed showing on his half-protruding tongue.

Kermit was looking blackly angry in his own corner.

"But you yourself were always wishing for money," Eloisa expostulated. "And they paid it for a *painting*."

"They did not, and you know they did not," roared Jerome.

"Oh, my darling," Eloisa Brace said, and she went up to her husband and put her head on his shoulder.

Jerome roughly shook her off, saying, "Stand over there with the boys, and don't act a role which you don't feel."

Eloisa went obediently to the part of the room where the boys were stationed. Malcolm had picked up his apple, dusted it off, and was again chewing, and Eloisa could not help but place a warning finger against his mouth.

"I wish you would explain it all to me, dear Jerome," Eloisa attempted to soothe him from her new position in the room.

"Why should I explain what is crystal clear?" Jerome said tensely. "Madame Girard has no high opinion of you as an artist."

"But the tribute of the money," Eloisa gasped, struggling not to hear more.

"Must I tell you in *primer* terms?" Jerome cried.

"I am afraid primer terms are required," she said, after thinking a moment.

"You wish brutality, I guess," Jerome emphasized to her.

"I want things said, yes I do," Eloisa said with more vigor than she had employed up to now.

"Madame Girard, like many in our circle, is infatuated with Malcolm," and here Jerome pointed to the boy in question, and Malcolm half-rose, bowed slightly, and swallowed the remains of his apple.

"Oh, but Jerome," Eloisa begged him. "There had to be a picture, after all, whoever the subject: it is the picture that matters!"

"Of course there had to be a picture," Jerome said with menacing sweetness.

"Then all is settled: all is settled, and well," Eloisa urged on him.

"All is not settled, and nothing will ever be well between us again," Jerome called out to her, livid with anger.

"How familiar and complete this all is," Kermit said, suddenly coming out from his corner.

"Be silent at once, and don't play any role in this, *Kermit*," Eloisa turned on him.

Kermit showed his teeth in his well-known sardonic silent laugh.

"Why is *nothing* settled?" Eloisa turned to the argument with her husband.

"That money is a bribe and nothing more. By accepting the money," Jerome cried, and in his excitement his spittle sprinkled itself upon his wife's face—"by accepting the money, you not only proclaim to the world that you have ceased to be a serious artist (which Madame Girard believes anyhow), you have given her, to quote one of her phrases, *carte blanche* to enter this house at any time she escapes from her husband's surveillance. And she probably thinks she owns Malcolm, too—although he may be as disgustingly wealthy as she and her crooked financier husband, for all I know."

Malcolm now stepped forward to say something, but Eloisa pushed him rudely (he thought) back into the corner with Kermit.

"Then, as usual, all I have done, and all I have attempted is a mistake," Eloisa summarized their discussion.

"I am speaking of the situation, I have not come to you as yet," Jerome replied.

"But I have created this situation. Where is your honesty if you pretend now I am innocent of anything?"

"You have accepted money on false premises."

"Then what is your wish and decision in the case?"

Eloisa held out her arms to him in a token of resignation.

"There can be only one decision," Jerome told her.

Eloisa stood watching him, pale as he was now, and when he did not say any more immediately, she turned her back on him, and went to the sideboard, took down the brandy bottle, and poured herself a generous draught.

"Don't drink . . . quite yet," he asked her.

"I must have a drink to hear what it is you are going to say."

"You do not know what I am going to say," Jerome was savage again.

"There is nobody in this room so feebleminded he does not know what you are going to say," she cried.

"What I was about to say, Eloisa, is—you drink as much as Madame Girard," her husband said to her.

"And you have come to the point of moralizing more than Mr. Cox," Eloisa retorted.

"Mr. Cox was mentioned," Malcolm cried to Kermit.

"Silence," Eloisa turned on the boy again. "Be silent or leave the room!"

"Will you control yourself?" Jerome sang out to her, and he went over to his wife and took the brandy glass out of her hand.

"You will allow me then no deadening of the pain to come," Eloisa said.

"You have not only betrayed yourself," Jerome said, "you have cheapened our marriage."

"Yes, it is always I, *I*, who am low, and you, *you* with your years of suffering who are noble."

Kermit laughed aloud at that moment from his corner, but nobody thought to correct him.

"Tell me, then, what your impossible wishes are," Eloisa said in a stifled voice to her husband. "Tell me or be silent."

"Eloisa," Jerome said in his quiet firm voice, the voice he had used to convince Madame Girard that she must leave the house—"you know perfectly well it is you who must tell me."

"I knew you would say that," and Eloisa folded her arms across her breast.

"I shall sit down, now," Jerome was calm, "and wait for your statement."

"I will break under the pressure some day, and then you will regret some things," Eloisa warned him, but without conviction, and she went to the brandy bottle again, and drank directly out of it this time.

"An Amazon out of her period," Kermit exclaimed in a loud voice to Malcolm, who seemed to have fallen into one of his sleepy attitudes, and did not appear too attentive to what was transpiring.

"I am to tell you, then, what it is I am to do," Eloisa began again.

"I will not open my mouth until the right decision has been made," Jerome was unshakable.

"Must my life *always* be heroic?" Eloisa said with routine bitterness. "Is there to be no rest anywhere, no oasis in the . . ."

She opened her arms again to Jerome, but he turned away gloomily.

"How can I say what you want me to say?" she appealed again to him.

"You must choose between me and the rich. The decision is simple," he broke his own silence.

"My nature is more complicated than your decision, I fear," Eloisa said.

"A choice, however, must be made," he warned her again.

"Why did it have to happen? Why did I have to *see* the money, then—to know its pleasure—only to give it up."

"You're actually going to give up money then?" Malcolm said, opening his eyes from the half-slumber into which he had been plunged.

Eloisa let out cries of pain on this remark, and Jerome admonished Malcolm to silence.

But Malcolm whispered with Kermit, and Kermit nodded, and laughed softly.

"Were there ever two such days of pain for me in a row?" Eloisa cried. She looked momentarily and savagely in the direction of the boys, and then going up directly to the little velvet box, she took out the check which Girard Girard had signed with such a flourish only an hour before.

She held the paper before her an instant, like one who sees more written on it now than she had at first discovered, and then suddenly tearing it all up before them, she tossed the pieces into her mouth, and began chewing them.

"Eloisa!" Malcolm cried, going up to her.

Jerome stood up now, and commanded, a benign expression coming over his recent scowl—"Let her alone. Let her do what she must."

She ate a bit more of the check, and then seeing Jerome so close to her, she struck him soundly over the jaw. He was silent, like a man perfunctorily measuring the precise force of the blow.

Kermit broke loose now in uncontrolled laughter.

"You're all of a pack!" Eloisa cried out suddenly, looking at all of them. "You're all fairies, that's what. All a pack of fairies. And you let women carry the burden, while all you do is talk. Damn all of you! Fairies! Fairies!" she cried, weeping, and seizing the brandy bottle, she ran out of the room.

"*Leave Me* Madame Girard"

During his courtship of her, many years before, Girard Girard and Madame Girard had often sat in a dark wood on the other side of the lagoon from the Japanese Temples, but still within earshot of the bench on which Malcolm was later to sit. Girard Girard had here asked her to marry him, and she had, of course, refused.

Another few days had passed, and Fall shaking down the last leaves, he had asked her again. This time, silently weeping over her passing youth, she could not speak but nodded rather vigorously for a woman of her temperament. Girard Girard, like the magician he was, already holding the ring in the palm of his hand, pushed it with painful vigor onto her finger, and kissed her heavily on her mouth. (The trap opened and closed, as she told Mr. Cox later, and all old and dear things were forever replaced by marriage.)

"You are then victorious," Madame Girard had said to her husband-to-be.

"We are both victorious," he told her with what she knew was excessive pride.

"What kind of victory can that be?" she cried, amazed. "What kind of victory is it in which we are *both* winners?"

It was then that Girard Girard knew, if he had not known before, that marriage with her would be a continuous contest.

"There must be victories for both," he told her, "if there is to be victory for one."

"But victory has always been only *my own*," she countered, "unshared with another. A victory shared would be somebody else's, not my own."

She looked at her ring with surprise now.

He waited for a reply to occur to him, shuffling his feet on the oak leaves that formed a carpet for their interview.

"I am always alone in victory," she exclaimed, frightened at the changes that now suddenly appeared about her on all sides, like cracks in an ice floe.

"You are no longer unprotected, no longer alone, is all," Girard Girard kissed her again on the mouth.

"My real victories cannot be shared," she insisted to him. "No one understands my victories."

"You cannot forbid me to rejoice in your success," Girard said, and he touched the finger on which he had placed the ring.

"I can forbid you to feign you are rejoicing over my success, but I will not," she explained. "I will be generous."

"Thank you," he replied, nodding.

They both stood up, and he embraced her. She gave no sign of acquiescence or happiness.

"Now we are together," he said, more pleading than asserting.

She was silent.

"May I not now call you Madame Girard, which you always said you would forbid me to call you until you had said *yes.*"

She forced down his arms from where they had held her, and looking past him to where the trees stood nearly naked over the lagoon, she said, "I will now be Madame Girard to the entire world. I will be no one else."

No one had ever addressed her again by anything except that name.

Madame Girard recalled these things to herself, almost aloud, from that long yesterday afternoon, while she listened intermittently to Girard Girard entertain her at the piano. He played Scarlatti tolerably well, and he was playing him now to quiet her.

"In a little while you will go out to commit your routine adulteries," she said to him above his playing.

"And," she continued, unsure whether he had heard her or not, "while you embrace laundresses and chambermaids, I am deprived of the sight of Malcolm, before whom I only wished to light candles. My loves have always been of that type. The candle-lighting type."

Madame Girard, who had never loved and perhaps never respected Girard Girard, now suddenly whetted her own interest in him as a result of his incessant unfaithfulness to her. She sometimes followed him now in a taxi to simulate attention and desire, and as she watched him meet a woman and drive off with her speedily to some second-class hotel, she felt a kind of slow distant imitation of love that should have come to her full-force the afternoon long past when he had put the ring on her hand.

She observed his animal vigor as it descended into his hands on the piano keys.

"The music, like all else he touches," she said aloud, but inaudible to his ears, "is but the overture to his sexual perfection with women."

But a thought that had come to her even before the afternoon of the lagoon had been recurring to her now with a kind of feathered swiftness, like that of a poisoned arrow which, she knew, would this time leave its fatal mark.

She had never loved Girard, and Girard, of course, had never precisely loved her as a woman. He had worshipped her, satisfying his appetite with the blossoming bodies of common women, but (and here the feathered arrow whizzed horribly about her ears) his worship had grown with the years. As she lighted candles to handsome young men like Malcolm, he had never ceased keeping a whole altar of lights burning to her. Now suddenly (and here she felt the poison of the arrow strike her) he would no longer light candles to her. The last match had been put to the last wick.

Girard Girard no longer loved Madame Girard.

And within a few days, or hours, or months, she knew, he would take the title from her. She would have no name. Another Madame Girard would replace her.

"Stop!" she cried suddenly, and she threw a candelabrum at him as he still sat at the piano.

He waited there, flushed with some new emotion, the candelabrum having missed him by inches.

"You hit a wrong note," she explained, and they both knew she said this as a lie, even though he *had* hit a wrong note.

He got up without a word, and this was the first time her shaken mind recognized that *it* had finally occurred.

He put on his great coat which he wore only for the most crucial of business deals.

"No, Girard," she expostulated, and at that moment, they both recognized victory passed forever from her to him.

"Girard Girard!" she cried, going up to him.

Now he took *her* arms and put them down away from him.

"Do not look to me," he said, and immediately he had said these words, he trembled, shaken with the power of his own excommunication of her.

"I will kill myself this time," she said.

"That, dear child, is your choice," he stood like stone before her, and the depth of his gaze never left him. He was granite, she saw, with his new character, his new and complete victory.

"You will have to look at me as I lie crushed and bleeding," she said, but almost to herself now, because she knew he was going out of her life altogether.

"Madame Girard, you must for this one time listen to reason," he said finally, and for a moment, and a moment only, he threw back his heavy coat with the colored silk lining on which his name blazoned like a shield.

Her eyes fell on the intense gold letters of his identification, seeing perhaps then her own identity melting away into the letters of his name.

"Girard Girard," she pleaded. "I mean to kill myself."

"You remember, your victories were all to be your own," he recalled the lagoon for her.

"That was *then*," she insisted, like a woman he had never known.

"This is now," Girard commanded by his tone.

"I will not, of course, kill myself merely to please you," she began. "You are free to do what you can and what you must. When I walk out of here tonight, I will walk out forever."

"But victory is always mine," she now echoed him, hollowly. "Do you not recognize me?" she inquired, a new kind of wildness in her face. "I am Madame Girard."

He advanced now like an actor in an over-lengthy unsuccessful play who is about to make a speech after which the curtain must fall precipitously upon his last syllable.

"You are no longer Madame Girard," he said.

She faced him now without defence, wordless, with the expression of almost any woman, his laundress, his charwoman.

"You have ceased to exist," he told her.

"I am not . . . Madame Girard?" she whispered.

"When I go out of this house, I will not return. I go out this time to *be* married."

"You cannot know marriage," she cried. "I forbid you, and you cannot know it anyhow."

She laughed unsteadily, and going over to a closed cabinet, she opened the door, and looking back in mild defiance, she drew out a small pistol.

He made no motion to stop her.

"I will always be Madame Girard. A command from you cannot destroy my identity."

"I am issuing no command in this case, as you yourself must see," he told her.

She stared at the pistol.

"You are the one, my dear, who has ceased to be Madame Girard. I have not touched you," he said finally.

"How could I cease to be she! Was I not she last night when you wrote the ten thousand dollar check for Eloisa Brace?"

"It was your last night of existence," he explained.

She half-levelled the pistol at him.

"I am divorcing you in order to marry Laureen Raphaelson."

Madame Girard raised the hand with the pistol like one who may command an entire army to extinguish itself, and then letting her hand drop before she gave the omnipotent gesture, she exclaimed weak and without humor: "The wife of the midget."

"We have found one another," he said, picking up the pistol which she had let fall to the floor, and placing it on top of a reading desk.

"I will not allow you to degrade yourself," she began. "You can marry *anybody* else. I will urge you, in fact, to marry a woman of your class. But I will not allow you . . . her."

Suddenly the idea came to her: "And *she* will be Madame Girard?"

"She will indeed," he replied.

"But you could so much easier change *your* names than I mine," she begged.

"You forget who bestowed his name on you. And you have never realized that *all the time*"—and here he advanced almost threateningly upon her—"that victory was always mine. I *am* victory."

She bent under the words.

"You are victory now," she admitted. "But I will destroy you . . ."

"And through what?" he cried.

"Through a beautiful young man."

He laughed.

"I am Madame Girard," she went on. "The whole world has always known me as she, the whole world will not so quickly lose its memory."

"The world remembers only what power and money tell it," he spoke to her like one who merely reads from a document. "And my power and money now decree that you no longer exist."

"Victory has always been mine," she repeated incoherently.

"That was in the lagoon, in the days when I had this strange love for you. And strange it was," he laughed.

"Girard Girard," she cried. "Patience, pity. I can change!"

"There is a limit to time and fortune," he said. "You are now—history."

"But without my name, without your fortune," she cried.

"My dear," he made a gesture of writing, "you will continue to be wealthy."

A cool pity came into his voice. "You will be comfortable, richly entertained. You will be able to see your 'beauties.'"

"But my name!" she cried. "I am known everywhere as Madame Girard."

"Your name must be taken from you. Has already *been* taken."

"You mean to destroy my identity, then?"

"Your friends, your young men, will come to see what is you. Your pure victory, as you have always called it, is now. You are completely free—can't you see?"

"But I need the name. The name is mine."

"It is too late," he said. "Laureen is waiting for me. We have so much to discuss. And there is so little time for the kind of happiness I know I can have with her."

"My name! You cannot take it. Take the money, the victory, but leave me as I was: Madame Girard."

"Fate has already moved. You speak as the melancholy young woman should have spoken on the lagoon so long long ago."

"Girard Girard," she pleaded and she went down on her knees to him.

"It has been a week of melodrama," he said, fatigued. "A lifetime of melodrama."

He buttoned his great coat.

"Your shoes are so beautifully shined," she wept.

Suddenly she kissed his shoes.

"Leave me with what I was," she begged. "Leave me *Madame Girard.*"

She saw the shoes withdraw from her embrace, and a moment later she heard the closing of the massive outside door.

At the Horticultural Gardens

Very early in the morning, while still sleeping heavily in a large bed, on the third floor, which he shared with three musicians, Malcolm was awakened by Eloisa Brace.

"Girard Girard has asked that you come at once to see him at the horticultural gardens," she cried.

Malcolm opened his eyes slowly and gaped at her.

She repeated her question to the grumbling and complaint of the three musicians, one of whom wore a silk stocking over his head as a night cap, and all of whom had actually only just turned in a few minutes before and just gotten nicely to sleep.

"It is very important for your future, Malcolm," Eloisa Brace went on. "You MUST go to see him."

Malcolm looked at her, uncomprehending.

"Remember, your money is going, you have given up your hotel suite, and your father will not return from the dead."

"But my portrait!" Malcolm cried.

"There is no portrait now, kiddy," Eloisa said solemnly. "Remember?"

"You are turning me out bag and baggage?" the boy cried.

"For Christ almighty's sake!" the musician with the silk stocking on his head raised up, enraged at the disturbance.

"Shh, come immediately, Malcolm," Eloisa said. "You have no choice. O.K.? No choice at all in the matter."

She hurried him to the bathroom, where he put on his clothes, and downstairs in her basement kitchen she hurriedly gave him a cup of coffee with milk, and then took him to the curb, where she hailed a taxi.

She kissed him goodbye.

"I am not turning you out, Malcolm—I am turning you over to stronger hands. Please remember that we love you, Jerome and I. But when all is said and done, Malcolm, kiddy, you are not in our class. O.K.? I hope I do not offend. And I really feel that Girard Girard has the key to your future."

"But the bench and all," Malcolm expostulated, as he was put into the cab. "Kermit . . . And Mr. Cox . . . And yes, even Estel Blanc . . ."

"You will see them again, Malcolm, when better days come to us all," Eloisa said to him from behind the pane of glass of the taxi.

"Goodbye and good luck, for you will need it," she cried. "We are just not of your class," she repeated, as the taxi drove off.

As it began to disappear with the boy, she sighed, relief and hope coming into her eyes.

"Destination?" the chauffeur inquired, but Malcolm was groaning in the back seat with sleep, confusion and despair, and did not reply.

"You said something?" Malcolm finally addressed himself to the driver.

The chauffeur repeated his question.

"Why," Malcolm thought for a while, "the horticultural gardens, I believe she said. Did you not hear the lady say that?" he inquired.

"I believe I did, sir," the driver responded.

"I'm leaving everything behind!" Malcolm told the driver. "And I don't know any other part of the city at all . . . My hotel, my bench, Mr. Cox, Kermit, Jerome, the piano player —everything behind!" he cried out, inconsolable.

Girard Girard came out from the entrance of the horticultural gardens when he heard the approach of the taxi, paid the driver, and helped Malcolm down from the cavernous back seat.

He ushered the boy into the first room of the greenhouse, which was devoted to tropical plants.

"I called you here, Malcolm," Girard Girard said, "only because you are, I know, my friend. I hope that you consider yourself my friend also, despite the fantastic difference in our ages and our respective positions in life."

Girard Girard motioned to the boy to sit down on a stone chair, which appeared to be the only article of furniture in the tropical garden.

"I am therefore appealing to you, Malcolm," Girard Girard said to the boy.

Perhaps owing to the heavy sultry heat of the horticultural gardens, or to the shock at his break with his life, Malcolm was slow to extend his sympathy to the older man, or respond to his speech of welcome, for the boy said nothing at all, and finally, in an attempt to suppress his yawning, he hiccuped loudly in the mossy silence of the gardens.

"Are you going to reject me, too, Malcolm?"

Malcolm stared at the cavernous circles which surrounded Girard's eyes, adding ten years to his age. He looked like a handsome but demolished angel.

"Reject you, sir?"

"Malcolm," the older man said at once, "I have left Madame Girard."

"Left her?" the boy hiccuped again.

"Shall I call an attendant for some water?" Girard inquired, somewhat irritably.

Malcolm shook his head.

"Our twenty years of life together—Madame Girard's and mine—are at an end," Girard impressed upon the boy's mind.

Malcolm nodded, holding his hand tightly against his throat to prevent another hiccup.

"But I have left her—only because—*only because* I am to be married."

"My congratulations, sir," Malcolm bowed slightly.

"Malcolm," the older man said, looking searchingly into the boy's face, "do you understand what I am saying to you?"

The boy nodded, then smiled.

"You are so winning," the older man almost complained. "But do you *know*, do you *hear*, do you *comprehend*? Oh, how I need you at this moment. Need somebody. I am entirely, entirely alone," he cried.

"Sir," Malcolm began again.

"No, don't speak," the older man said. "I don't say this in anger, but in despair. Malcolm, you do NOT understand . . ."

"I do, sir, I do . . . And I try!"

"You don't understand, Malcolm, and perhaps that is why, well, I need you more than anybody else. For though I am to be married—almost indeed at once—I need you and I mean to have you . . . Madame Girard shall not have you to herself!"

Malcolm opened his mouth to reply to this, but Girard was already speaking again:

"I am going to marry Laureen Raphaelson, Malcolm."

"Laureen . . . The little man's *woman?*"

Malcolm hiccuped.

"*Woman?*" Girard Girard flushed.

"Forgive me, sir," Malcolm said. "I only met Laureen once, you see, and that was the evening before she went off with the . . . Japanese wrestler."

"Oh, that old story. An invention of Mr. Cox."

"I only know, of course, what people tell me," Malcolm explained.

"Malcolm, you *are* of my class, and you must understand a man's principles: one does not marry a woman because she is a virgin."

The boy agreed gravely.

"You see, Malcolm, with Laureen I will be the father of children: sons will come after me who will bear my name. While with Madame Girard: our future was only our present, our future was only . . . well, Madame Girard!"

"But you prefer Madame Girard to me, is that not it?" Girard asked, looking intently at the boy's eyes.

"No," Malcolm said in a choked and rather old voice. "I

prefer you, Girard Girard. You were my favorite address. Only, I think of you and Madame Girard as together, and when you will be apart . . . I don't know yet what to say."

"You see, Malcolm—and you must already know this— Madame Girard has expressed the wish ahead of everybody else, to have you. My desires in this matter were, I admit, second. But what I have brought you here for is to ask you as humbly as possible, if you will not . . . choose *me* instead of her."

"Choose you for what, sir?"

"For my own—for Laureen's and my own."

"Oh, sir!"

"I will be your *father* if necessary, though I know that is something that would be difficult . . ."

"No, no," the boy stood up. "There was only one father," Malcolm said sternly, his eyes flashing. "You may be great, but you will not take the place that he occupied alone and first."

"Malcolm, I have no desire to offend your father's memory."

"Your desire was not asked, sir," Malcolm said. "You replace nobody."

"I have put it awkwardly, Malcolm. Kindly reconsider . . ."

Suddenly a violent hiccup came from Mr. Girard's interlocutor.

"Please be seated again, Malcolm, and let us be calm."

The boy sat down.

"We will begin again, if necessary, all over," Girard Girard paced up and down in front of the stone chair.

Malcolm muttered something between his teeth, but the look of intensity on his face was so incredible at that moment, that Girard Girard took out a handkerchief from his breast pocket and wiped his face carefully.

"In all humbleness, Malcolm," the older man began again, "consider my offer."

"But what is your offer, sir?" the boy was severe.

"Come live with me and my new wife, accept all we have

to offer, feel secure and loved with us. Ask whatever you wish of us."

"But I had everything until just a few days ago," the boy cried. "And suddenly, having left the bench entirely . . . for reasons I do not recall—I have *nothing*."

"But you have me. You have us."

"I have lost everything!" the boy said, and then his violence disintegrated into a sudden calm and even sweetness.

"You will not come with me, then," Girard Girard said.

Malcolm shook his head.

"You wish to go to Madame Girard?" the older man wondered, somewhat stupefied.

"No, no," the boy responded.

"But then what are you going to do? You cannot go back to your hotel suite. It is rented . . . And no longer being a pensioner there, so to speak, I fear the bench is barred to you likewise . . ."

The boy shifted in his hard seat. Perhaps at last the realization of his position became clear, for turning to his would-be protector, he demanded:

"Would you repeat what you just said, please, Girard Girard?"

"I will repeat anything you may wish," the older man said. "However, I have forgotten my exact words . . ."

"You said, I believe, sir, that I had nothing to go back to!"

"Ah, yes, of course. You see, I have this wedding on my mind—not to mention the tiresome affair of the divorce. Of course, I remember . . . It was simply that the hotel can never take you back, as I said."

"I am barred to it?"

"Well, not barred, but that expensive period of your life is simply over, dear boy. As over and done with as those days when your father came home from a long business trip and tucked you in at night. You're nearly grown up!"

"Grown up? Why, then, whatever will I do?"

"You can go ahead alone, of course," and here Girard Girard gave the boy a look of pity mixed with horror, "or you can come with me, and allow me to open all doors for you."

"All doors," Malcolm repeated.

Going up to Malcolm now in a manner uncommon for the financier, he seized the boy by the shoulders vigorously and shaking him, said:

"You can't go on by yourself!"

"But what if Mr. Cox should give me more addresses!" the boy got out while still being shaken.

"More addresses!" Girard exclaimed, letting loose of the boy. "Do you know what you are talking about? Obviously not. Then listen: Mr. Cox *has* no more addresses . . ."

"No more at all?"

"Not a single one. No, that old dodge is out. And besides, how could he give them to you when you're so friendly to me? And besides!" but here Girard stopped, owing to the look of panic on the boy's face.

But he continued anyhow, despite Malcolm's expression: "And besides," he finished, "Mr. Cox would hardly give you another address since *you are off the bench.*"

"Off the bench!" the boy cried, realization pouring into his eyes.

"Choose me, dear Malcolm. Choose us."

"A wedding," the boy mused. "And so many things, so many ways!"

"Tell me your answer is yes."

Malcolm nodded, gravely smiling.

"I knew you would give in," Girard cried, happy. "I will make things up for you, let me tell you. And I will try never to replace anybody either. I have learned my lesson there, too."

Malcolm sat back now on the stone chair.

"But I have not a minute," Girard Girard told him. "A most important engagement. I must leave at once. But you stay here, Malcolm, for I will be back in an hour at the most to pick you up. Don't go away, do you hear? Now that I've found you, I don't want to lose you for anything, you see."

"Please do not go away without me," Malcolm stood up,

and Girard Girard had never heard the boy speak with such strength, though his voice cracked a little, for it was changing. "Take me with you."

"Quite out of the question," Girard told him. "My engagement is of the utmost importance, and you would only be in the way. Stay here, as I say, and within the hour I will be back again. And we will both begin life together!"

Malcolm smiled.

The two friends shook hands, and in another moment, Girard Girard had left Malcolm to thoughts and expectancy.

Malcolm Meets a Contemporary

Malcolm waited in the horticultural gardens.

An hour passed, then two. He grew hungry, but he saw no place where he could get anything to eat.

For a while he strolled about the grounds, always being careful to be within earshot of the stone chair on which Girard Girard expected to find him on his return.

But after a while, the shadows of evening began to fall, and still no sign of his great and powerful friend.

At five o'clock, an attendant appeared, informing the boy that the horticultural gardens were about to close.

Malcolm waited therefore outside the building on the greensward, but in a short while another attendant informed him that this was not allowed, as the entire grounds were about to be closed, and that he should go out through the gate and stand on the sidewalk near the arterial, if he was waiting for somebody.

"But Girard Girard is expecting me *here!*" Malcolm told the attendant.

The attendant, who recognized immediately the name pronounced by the boy, thought for a moment, then said:

"But he would never return now! It is not his way. You had better go at once to his house."

"He has no house now that he has left Madame Girard," the boy replied.

The attendant clicked his tongue.

Malcolm was already walking in the direction of the sidewalk and the arterial. As he reached the walk, he heard from behind the closing of the tall gates of the horticultural gardens, and the snap as they locked themselves against him.

Standing waiting there, Malcolm was surprised at how quickly night came, and a cool breeze from the west reminded him that summer was over.

"Girard Girard," he muttered bitterly.

Malcolm leaned against a telephone pole which was covered with posters announcing the appearance in the neighborhood of a popular singing star. He perhaps dozed a little, then was awakened by the sound of a motorcycle whizzing past. When the motorcycle had gone past him, it stopped suddenly, wheeled about dizzily on its own tracks, and returned dead level to Malcolm. The driver, who was even darker than Estel Blanc or George Leeds, stopped, removed his goggles, and opened his mouth to say something to Malcolm, but at the very last second, did not speak at all, merely showing his even ivory teeth.

Malcolm took, therefore, the initiative, and wished the motorcyclist a good evening.

"You one of the contemporaries?" the motorcyclist said, not replying to Malcolm's greeting.

Malcolm said he begged his pardon.

"If you one of the contemporaries, get on behind me, and we'll go right over to Melba's, and if you ain't, it don't matter too awful much anyhow, on account of you is the type."

Malcolm was about to tell the motorcyclist that he was waiting for Girard Girard, but with the command "Stow it!" the boy next found himself behind the motorcyclist headed away from the city, in a whirlpool of rushing air.

Occasionally he would hear the name *Melba* come from the driver's mouth, blown to him by a torrent of air, but the rest of the man's words were carried away by other currents, and never reached him. And Malcolm was too downcast and even embittered by Girard Girard's failure to show up to feel any wrongdoing in leaving the horticultural gardens. Apparently Girard Girard was more interested in his coming wedding and his present divorce than he was in Malcolm, and with Mr. Cox and the addresses and the bench and Kermit, all swallowed up in the past, he was more than pleased that he could be driving off with someone like this who showed every friendly intention and interest in him personally. And the new driver had a most pleasing perfume of nasturtiums about him, together with a voice which, while not perhaps as rich as the baritone depth of Estel Blanc, was much more warm and friendly.

After driving very fast for a good many miles, during which the entire landscape flashed past them a soft dissolving mass, the motorcyclist brought the vehicle to a dizzying halt at a gasoline pump, which had no attendant, and which was not illuminated clearly.

Taking out a small flashlight from his hip pocket, the motorcyclist with his other hand held a key to the gasoline pump, and having opened the pump, proceeded to fill his tank, and then seeing the quizzical look on Malcolm's face, said:

"This here tank belongs to Melba and the contemporaries."

Before Malcolm again had time to inquire about Melba and the contemporaries, they were again flashing through the landscape.

After another hour or more of travel, they drew up to a roadhouse, which bore no sign of life of any kind, and appeared without the faintest illumination.

"If you need to fresh yourself up, you can go back there," the driver pointed in the direction of a clump of trees behind the roadhouse.

Malcolm shook his head.

"You *is* a contemporary?" the motorcyclist asked with a sudden desire for confirmation.

Malcolm was about to answer, but the driver had already turned away from him, headed for the door of the roadhouse, and said:

"Melba will know anyhow if you is or isn't."

They now opened the heavy front door and walked into a small room, where ten or twelve men and women were seated drinking, while a very young woman, standing on a platform, was singing to them.

"That one singing there is Melba," the motorcyclist pointed out to Malcolm.

Melba stopped singing briefly to examine the two new arrivals, her eye resting a long time on Malcolm, then questioningly to the motorcyclist, and finally she nodded to the latter, and made a quick gesture with her hand.

"You made it!" the motorcyclist slapped Malcolm on the cheek with vigor, and then shook hands with him.

"Another contemporary!" the driver announced to the people who were seated listening to Melba, who had again begun to sing, some of the words drifting over to where Malcolm and the motorcyclist stood:

> *When you said goodbye, dark daddy,*
> *Did you know I had not yet said hello?*

Malcolm and the driver sat down at a table to wait for Melba to finish her number, after which, Malcolm was informed, she would join them, and give them some pointers about what they could do next.

A young man wearing a tight sash about his middle came up just then and asked them what drink they wished to choose.

"Do you have a preferential?" the driver asked Malcolm, and when the latter said that at the moment he did not, the driver told the man with the sash to bring the usual.

"I'm so glad I didn't make a mistake when I done drew you," the driver told Malcolm. "What if you hadn't been the right one waiting there?" he laughed.

He seemed so much happier and relaxed now that he told Malcolm his name, Gus.

"Who are you?" Gus wanted to know next.

"Malcolm," the boy replied.

"What a non-usual name," Gus commented.

Their drinks arrived, and Gus said that they should toast

the contemporaries, and they both raised their glasses briefly.

When you said goodbye—

—the final notes now poured forth from Melba's throat, and in a sea of applause she trod directly through the audience to the table at which Gus and Malcolm were waiting for her.

"Meet a contemporary," Gus told Melba with some excitement.

"Of course, Brownie, of course," Melba said impatiently. "I recognized him im-med-i-ate-ly. He's just about my age category."

Malcolm looked at Melba more closely, and he was surprised and pleased to notice that actually she was *not* much older than he.

While Melba ordered a drink from the boy in the sash, Gus whispered in Malcolm's ear: "She worth her weight in cash. She *terribly* rich."

"Quit whispering, Brownie," Melba told Gus. She took Malcolm's hand in hers.

"What if he hadn't been a contemporary, huh?" Gus laughed nervously now, exchanging a look with Melba.

Malcolm was about to ask them what a contemporary was, but suddenly his old desire to ask questions deserted him. He found that he did not care now what anything was. Too much had happened, too many people had come and gone in his life, and feeling a sudden warmth and pressure from Melba's hand, he mechanically brought this hand to his lips and kissed it.

"I have had such a short long life," Malcolm said, meaning this remark to be silent and for himself, but by accident the words came out loud and strong, and Melba, extremely pleased by what he had said, immediately drank a toast to him.

"I could marry you," she told Malcolm.

Malcolm pressed her hand again.

"You can't get married again, Melba," Gus told her. "Think of—"

"That will do, Brownie," Melba said. And when Gus began to speak again, she cried, "I SAY!"

Gus looked down at his drink, and Melba explained more softly, "Brownie was my first husband. Old No. 1, as we sometimes call him."

"I'm not ashamed of it, Melba," Gus said.

"I'm so glad he found you," Melba turned again to Malcolm, and she kissed him warmly on his mouth. "Do you think you could find happiness with me?" Melba said.

Malcolm was suddenly sure. "Yes," he said, "Melba, I do."

"Isn't it all wonderful?" Melba turned briefly to Gus. "Are you sulking again?" she criticized the driver.

When he did not answer, she posed her question:

"Would you marry me, Malcolm?"

"It's too sudden," Gus told Melba. "Wait till Tuesday."

"What in God's name is Tuesday to me," she was highly critical of Gus again. "I gave up the days of the week after Freddie's time, and after you did all those dirty legal things to me . . . Why should Tuesday matter?" she complained, angry tears in her eyes.

Melba pressed Malcolm's hand again.

"You're the first real find Gus has ever made," Melba explained to Malcolm, her lip quivering still a bit. "Do you really care for me?" she inquired now of Malcolm after a pause in which they had all finished their drinks.

"I do, Melba," Malcolm replied, and he did. Having lost Girard Girard and Mr. Cox, Kermit, and the bench, he held more tightly to Melba than he had ever held to any other human being, with the exception, of course, of his father.

"Melba, I DO!" Malcolm cried suddenly, and he kissed the girl on her throat.

"I've never been so quickly surprised, or so quickly happy!" Melba began, but at a look from Gus she began complaining again: "You begrudge me this happiness, don't you? Answer me, don't you? You begrudge me this tiny tiny bit of happiness in my life of pettiness and struggle . . ."

"Melba, honey, happiness is the last thing I *be*-grudge you," Gus told her. "But I don't want you to rush into matrimony this here time. Think of how many other old times you done got stung. Think of the courts, Melba, honey."

"He begrudges me," Melba explained to Malcolm.

"How did you know he was a contemporary?" Melba inquired suspiciously of Gus now, cocking her head in the direction of Malcolm.

"I have *some* tendencies!" Gus became somewhat riled.

"I think it was all just a . . . a beautiful accident . . . for which you don't have no thanks or credit coming!" Melba cried, and her false eyelashes waved in the tempest of her breath.

Gus put his fists in his eyes and said goddamn it all to hell, she would try to take away his credit.

"All right, all right," Melba said apologetically to Gus. "I will give you this credit. I won't harp needlessly on things that can't be proved. You found this baby, and I will be eternally grateful to you. Eternally."

She patted Malcolm's hand.

"God, we will be happy," she whispered. "Everything will be taken care of," she winked, omniscient.

Malcolm made a sound, which resembled a coo, and which he had never heard come from himself before, so that he sat up straight, startled.

"Isn't he *beautiful*, Brownie?" Melba called Gus's attention to the boy now. "Have you noticed his three dimples when he smiles?"

Gus made the strange little groaning sounds again, and began to put his fists in his eyes, then put them down manfully on the table with a bang.

"But *you're* beautiful, Melba," Malcolm was telling her. "You're . . . the beautiful one!"

"Nobody has said that to me since I was twelve," Melba dabbed at her cheek briefly with her napkin.

Gus covered his eyes with his palm now.

"If you feel you want to marry me, dearest," Melba told

Malcolm, "we can have Gus here announce it. Everybody here, almost, is a contemporary."

"Melba, sweet Jesus!" Gus cried in a voice which had broken to falsetto.

"Resume your normal baritone when you wish to communicate with me," Melba spoke to Gus.

"Malcolm," Melba turned her full attention to him again, "I don't even care if you are a contemporary or not. Of course, I knew Gus lied to me about you. But I'm willing to marry you if you are willing to marry me. I've simply got it is all, it's come like lightning, and . . . well, I've been got."

"He ain't OLD ENOUGH!" Gus cried, in his regular voice now.

"Don't listen to him," Melba said, tapping on the marble of the table. "Besides, everything is always arranged. Brownie feels he has to be a little more careful than I do, though he's the most daring man in the world. Six weeks of marriage teaches you an awful lot about a man. But our marriage, Malcolm, will just last on and on, precious . . ."

Leaning over the table, she kissed him a long time now on the lips. "Breath like a hay-mow!" she pointed out.

She shook her head, tears standing in her eyes again.

"I think Brownie should announce the engagement and/ or marriage," she said *sotto voce* to Malcolm. "I have some more numbers to sing tonight, you know."

A trio had taken the place of Melba as she was talking to Malcolm and Gus, but a signal had been just given that she was to resume her part of the program.

"I think just a short announcement of our engagement is in order," Melba said to Gus.

"Darling, you do love me, and you want to marry me— before they announce our betrothal over the loudspeaker?" Melba said anxiously to Malcolm.

"Melba, *yes!*" the boy said.

"Oh, Brownie," Melba turned to Gus, "I'll never forget you for having brought Malcolm to me, dearest. Don't ever let me forget this great favor you have committed for me . . ."

When Gus, however, did not get up from the table to announce the engagement, Melba became very upset again. "Did you not hear me tell you?" she commanded the motorcyclist. "You are to announce our engagement and/ or marriage. Kindly do so at once. The trio has played its last number minutes ago. . . . I'm nearly ready to go on!" Gus got up slowly, opened his leather riding jacket, from under which a handsome watch chain of the last century was suspended, and clearing his throat, his immense rich voice informed the entire room of contemporaries of the coming marriage of Malcolm and Melba.

"On Tuesday next!" Melba, standing up, informed the room.

Owing to his having drunk perhaps more than was his custom, or perhaps because he had stood so long on his feet in the horticultural gardens, Malcolm had some special difficulty in getting up, but with Melba and Gus's assistance, he finally did rise and acknowledge the applause and recognition of the audience. After which he and Melba kissed one another in front of everybody.

"This is to be a serious and life-long affair," Melba informed people, tears again in her eyes.

Malcolm then sat down again at the table with Gus, while Melba went up to the stage microphone and sang again her three numbers, including the one which, Gus explained, had made her internationally famous:

> Hot in the rocker,
> But so cool on the grain—!

At the end of her last number, Melba hastened, after only a perfunctory acknowledgement of applause (so rare to her) to Malcolm and Gus's table, where she kissed the boy passionately, but with perhaps a slight bit more restraint.

"My only one," she explained to Malcolm, and she handed him a roll of bills, "now that our marriage is a fact which only time will make final, I want things to be all up and above board. We could so easily consummate everything there is to consummate here and now, as Brownie and I once did so long ago, and Freddie, too, but as I told the contemporaries a few minutes ago, I want this marriage to last. It's to be the real thing, Malcolm, precious," and here she placed a napkin to her eyes. "I've got the real thing is all, Brownie," she turned weeping to the motorcyclist. "Lightning, that's all you can say about it."

When she had got control of her voice, she went on:

"Brownie will take care of you. He'll be like a father to you . . . Don't interrupt me!" she warned Malcolm when the latter made vociferous sounds of interpolation. "I have to sing another number in a minute owing to that mammoth applause I am getting, and I just wanted to say that I want Gus here to take awful good care of you. Tuesday will be here before we know it, but we mustn't meet again till then . . ."

Kissing Malcolm again on the mouth for the last time, Melba turned briefly to Gus, to whom she handed a small fat package of something, and whispered:

"Mature him up just a little while you're gone," and without another word or nod to either of them, she made her way to a small door marked AUTHORITY, and opening it, disappeared.

The Tattoo Palace

"How the A-all am I goin' to mature you up by Tuesday," Gus inquired of Malcolm, as the two rode off again together on the motorcycle, this time in the direction back to the city. "You motherless bastard," Gus complained, turning his head around.

"My father is the one who is missing!" Malcolm shouted to Gus through the wind, but Gus did not let on he had heard a thing from him.

"Do you know the honor you have all just received?" Gus inquired, turning his head back to Malcolm. "Marriage with *her*."

"I think I do," Malcolm shouted into Gus's ear.

"She's the greatest now, and will be the greatest then," Gus said.

In their heated conversation Gus had forgotten to stop at the private contemporary gas pump to refill his tank and, as a result of this oversight, near the edge of the city his motorcycle stopped, out of fuel.

"That's what distraction will do for you," Gus complained peevishly. "Hop down, and let's go hunt for a pump."

They walked slowly together toward the pink glow of the city.

"We got only till Tuesday, mind," Gus kept repeating. "Only till Tuesday."

"Will it be a big wedding, sir?" Malcolm inquired.

Gus paused, staring at him.

"What you call me *sir* for if you a contemporary? Is that a *code* word you picked up in some other society?"

Gus stopped dead in his tracks. "What you call me that for, Malcolm?" He relented a little when he had studied the boy's face.

"Just for the usual," Malcolm explained, fancying his speech now did sound like that of a contemporary.

"Then *don't!*" Gus warned him. "Don't *sir* me."

And then without another word Gus sat down on the curb and began making sounds which resembled sobbing a great deal.

"I can't give up that damned bitch!" he said.

"Who?" Malcolm comforted him, putting his hand on Gus's sleeve.

"Who, he asks me who?" and Gus's voice broke again into falsetto.

"He asks me who," Gus shook his head, seeming to be talking to his shoes. "Melba's in my blood," he sighed. "It's like that awful kind of malaria they can't do nothing for you with . . ."

Gus began to quiet down then a little. Then, getting up slowly, he said:

"Come on, Malco, we got to go through with this. I would cut off my right arm right up to here for her, but I will make you her husband or bust in the attempt . . . You keep full confidence in me now."

Malcolm nodded.

After they had walked a few more blocks, Gus said he had to rest again, as he was not a walker, and they sat down on the curb.

"Look at all this money Melba give me to mature you up with," Gus said, pulling out a roll of bills from his pocket. "That one bill curlin' around my thumb there is a thousand dollar one."

Malcolm glanced briefly at the bill.

"You not impressed," the motorcyclist said. "I hope this wedding ain't goin' to waste on you."

Down the street a little way, its many-colored lights moving and gesticulating like a brightly lit kaleidoscope shone a sign with the words

ROBINOLTE'S TATTOO
PALACE

Malcolm read off the words.

"That's the place now to be matured," Gus said, ironical. Malcolm exclaimed: "My father had a tattoo, and he often said to me,–" and in his excitement the boy spit on Gus's face, for which he immediately apologized, "my father said to me, 'One day you must be tattooed, son.'"

Gus looked off, disgust and weariness on his face.

"Are you tattooed, by any chance?" Malcolm inquired, more to punctuate the depressing silence than to have his question answered.

Gus looked at him with pity.

"I been admired by women all my life for my chest and arms, and my body in general," Gus began. "Why have them chopped up by needles, or *dis*-jointed by designs?"

"But one or two tattoos for a wedding is surely . . . well, *usual*," Malcolm brought out, swallowing hard, and wondering at the same time where he had ever heard what he had just said.

Gus replied immediately: "But I BEEN married! Three times!"

"Get tattooed with me," Malcolm said, unaware again what prompted him to say these words.

"Do you know what you are?" Gus inquired, a strange equanimity and warmth coming over him. "Persuasive, that's what."

"You agree then?" Malcolm cried, his enthusiasm mounting.

"If we should get tattoos," Gus began, opening his jacket and taking out his nineteenth-century watch for a look at the hour, "if we have the tattoos, we must have the real ones, you know: the spread-eagle one on the chest, especially. The rest don't really count. Real men have to have the chest tattoos or nothing."

"My father–" Malcolm began, but Gus put his hand over the boy's mouth.

"I got the floor, kiddy," Gus went on. "Now you don't need the peter tattoo, say," he explained in his deepest voice, "on account of Tuesday, but we could easy get fixed up for all the rest."

"Hurray!" Malcolm clapped his hands together.

"You a *brave* boy?" Gus asked him, and he smiled for the first time at Malcolm, and his ivory teeth flashed in the dark between them.

"As I say," Gus went on, "I done been there before, and I know Professor Robinolte, the tattoo king, but before, you com-*pre*-hend, I only was to *watch*."

"I suppose it is bloody," the boy ventured.

Gus thought for a moment. "I didn't see much *blood* . . . More the sight of white lips and occasional screams." He laughed. "A few fainted that day. Mostly sailors."

"Well, I should be more scared, but somehow I'm not," Malcolm told Gus.

He yawned. "For one thing," the boy said, "I'm too sleepy to be scared."

Gus studied Malcolm. "I wish *I* could be sleepy," he said. "I been *wide*-awake all my life, and I need some rest. I could take a long long rest."

"Should we have a drink before we go?" Malcolm wondered.

"No," Gus answered. "I think a man has got to simply surrender to them needles and the pain."

"I always thought that . . . Abyssinians were braver than other people," Malcolm said, bringing his face closer to that of the motorcyclist's.

"A-byss—!!" and here Gus broke off into a snort and a laugh. "You do me up," he said after a moment.

"But why fear a little needle?" Malcolm wondered, perhaps to himself.

"You wait and see," Gus told him. "I been everywhere. One war and then Korea . . . But when it comes to lie still and be dotted on by the old tattoo man, that's a kind of bravery I do not got. But we got to mature you, like she say, that's the thing . . . And you know what I think of Melba, not to mention what I owe her . . ."

Gus stood up and pushed out his chest, perhaps already feeling the beginning of the tattoo professor's art upon him.

"Say, how about you," Gus finally said. "You TERRIBLE young it seems to me to be *de*-corated."

"I'm not so young now anymore," Malcolm told him, still sitting on the curb. "And it will be a change, you see. I like a certain amount of change. The only thing about a tattoo is, once it's done, I don't suppose you can undo it away again."

"That's so," Gus said. "But you was the one asked now, hear?"

The Tattoo Palace was both severe and cosy—severe because it bore every witness to the painful operations enacted within—the electrical tattooing needles, the bloody rags, the bottles of disinfectant and smelling salts, and the bloodstains on the floor; cosy because Professor Robinolte himself, the tattoo artist, was a pleasant blond young man who exhibited four front gold teeth, and cared for all his customers like members of his family, sending them annual birthday and Christmas greetings, and often advising them on their domestic and professional careers, while somewhere behind him soft music poured forth, and the air itself was sprayed with moderately expensive *eau de cologne*.

However, an air of terrible expectancy weighted the atmosphere.

The password to allow anyone to enter Professor Robinolte's *boutique* was a secret one, which Gus now whispered in the professor's ear.

"Meet Melba's husband-to-be," Gus next pointed Malcolm out to Professor Robinolte.

"Not again so soon," Professor Robinolte cried, but nevertheless congratulated Malcolm. "I used to think that Melba was young," the professor said taking a better look at Malcolm. "But this one—!!"

"How about decorating the bridegroom up a bit," Gus got down to brass tacks. "Melba would like him a few months older anyhow."

"You know the law, Brownie," Professor Robinolte was a bit coy.

"Don't give me no law talk now," Gus said wearily, and he sat down on an ice-cream chair.

"I'll tell you what, Brownie," Professor Robinolte toyed with the largest of his electrical needles, and blew something off the tip of it. "I'll tattoo the kid if I can tattoo you in the bargain."

"There we go again!" Gus shook his head. "What I ain't done for Melba."

"I've never got a real good tattoo on anybody with your special color skin," Professor Robinolte complimented the motorcyclist in strictly professional tones. "I'm so tired of pink and tan skins."

Gus spat on the floor.

"All right," the motorcyclist began, "I won't chicken on either Melba or her here-bridegroom." And he peeled off his leather jacket and would have taken off the shirt beneath it, had Professor Robinolte not halted him with a gesture.

"Grooms first, please," the professor said. Then: "Remember when *you* were Melba's husband, Brownie?"

Gus made a significant sound with his lips at the professor, and moved his ice-cream chair back out of the main arena.

"As far as I'm concerned—did you say your name was Malcolm?" the professor began, "as far as I'm concerned—in case we should both of us ever be before the police and the courts—you are all of eighteen years old tonight . . . Is that clear?"

The thought of being eighteen years old was pleasing to Malcolm, and he agreed now that he was. Eighteen, unlike fifteen, was full of promise and adventure.

At a signal from the professor, Gus assisted the latter, and in the twinkling of an eye, lifted Malcolm up and put him in a kind of reclining chair, and removed all of his clothes, depositing these in a basket behind them.

The professor quickly traced on Malcolm's chest the outlines of a black leopard which was the design Gus had, after a moment's study, chosen for the boy.

Malcolm laughed a good deal while the tracing was done,

so close to his nipples, and Gus turned a peculiar shade of indeterminate color while watching.

When the actual work with the needle began, with its accompanying bouncing ominous sound, Malcolm looked more grave, but at the same time amused.

"Don't you feel anything?" Gus asked Malcolm several times, when the professor would stop momentarily to sponge off the blood from where it had obscured the design.

Malcolm shook his head. The professor exchanged looks with Gus.

After the long but highly successful session of putting the black panther on Malcolm's chest, during which Malcolm seemed to have dozed off, Professor Robinolte shook the boy and asked him if he was prepared to have the carnations placed above his right biceps, and the daggers on his forearms.

Malcolm said he was, and these designs were perpetrated, too.

The entire difficulty came with Gus who, of course, later felt very small and ashamed.

While stretched out on the same chair, submitting to the black panther tattoo on his chest, Gus fainted three times, but always insisted on the tattooing being resumed again —over Professor Robinolte's protests. However, only one carnation was given the motorcyclist, and the professor was pleased, at the end of the operation, at the triumph of color on Brownie's chest, despite the countless difficulties which beset them.

Gus blamed his faintheartedness on his concern for Malcolm, and for his having first watched the savage needles at work on so young a man.

But Professor Robinolte told him brutally and often that Gus was simply not the type who could be tattooed, his two war-records notwithstanding.

Bandaged and dressed again, the two men stood taking their leave of Professor Robinolte who—after promising to send them birthday greetings and Christmas cards for the rest of their lives—warned them not to use water on their fresh tattoos, not to expose the tattoos to the unprotected sun, and above all, take it easy and not touch or scratch the wounds.

Professor Robinolte then complimented Malcolm on his amazing bravery which, he said, he had never quite encountered before, and congratulated him on his coming marriage to Melba.

"You could hardly be in more competent hands," Professor Robinolte told him, though a certain air of dubiety and concern crossed and re-crossed his face.

"You will be the pride of all women and some men, to half-quote somebody," the professor called to them, as they left his *boutique*, and Gus and Malcolm walked off toward the center of town.

"And good luck!" Professor Robinolte shouted. "Christ knows you need it," he said in lower tones to himself.

At Madame Rosita's

They walked slower and slower toward the city, owing to the fact, as Gus explained again, he had been a motorcyclist too long to know how to walk, and he didn't actually like to be seen walking any more, it kind of hurt his self-respect, and another reason, he would not deny it, he was a bit knocked off by those electric needles of Professor Robinolte.

Clearing his throat and putting his arm around Malcolm, then, in tones of fatherly intimacy, Gus said, "Kiddy, I didn't bring you out here for you just to have your hide embroidered. I got to ask you a plain question now on account of there is Tuesday."

Malcolm nodded, smiling.

"To put it delicate-like, Malco," Gus stopped now in his tracks, "have you ever been completely and solidly joined to a woman?"

"Well," Malcolm remembered, "in a brief kind of way."

"Brief, huh?" Gus said, snorting. "Now see here," but just then a twinge of pain in his chest made him stop for a moment. "See here now . . . On account of who you are marrying, kiddy, you got to be ready . . . An old tattoo ain't any number-one preparation. If anything it may make you too sore to *be* a good groom. No, Malco, what I am talking about is good old solid Nature. Have you been joined to a woman the way Nature meant? Yes or no."

Malcolm opened his mouth, but it closed immediately again.

"I can see you ain't," Gus said. "Well, that's what Melba sent us out for, to mature you up."

Gus then pointed with his arm to a large house in the near distance.

"Do you see that house over there," he asked. "That's where I'm going to take you. Rosita's. Madame Rosita's, they used to call her. You heard of her?"

Malcolm shook his head.

"You ain't heard of *any*-thing," Gus complained, and then he said well, that was what he was for, et cetera.

They went up to the house before which was a sign that read

PRIVATE AND TURKISH BATHS

CABINETS AND OVER-NIGHT COTTAGES

$2.00

They went down a flight of stairs, and Gus rapped lightly on a small wooden partition, which immediately opened, and a man with a green visor looked out.

"Gus, is that really you!" the man said. Then, looking at Malcolm, he exclaimed: "Where did you find *him?*"

"A Turkish bath for me, and a room upstairs for the boy here," Gus explained.

The man was about to say something, perhaps in protest, when Gus handed him part of the roll of bills which Melba had given him.

"I was just wondering, Gus," the attendant said obsequiously, "if you had observed that that boy has blood stains on him."

"They just tattooed him," Gus retorted.

"This way," the man replied, coughing nervously, ushering them into a waiting room down which tall coat-hangers were lined like trees, and off each coat-hanger was the door to a room.

Gus, turning to Malcolm, said, "Now downstairs here, kiddy, is the Turkish bath department, and upstairs is where you are going to go. When you through, come down here and wake me. Which is my room, Miles?" he addressed the attendant.

"You pick one out. Nobody here tonight at all," Miles replied.

"All right now," Gus fumbled about, almost as if he had lost his sense of balance, and then looking straight ahead of him, almost blindly, he said: "What number is this now . . ."

"Twenty-two," Miles said.

"That will be me, then," Gus told Malcolm. "I'm twenty-two."

Just then a woman of indeterminate age, with purple markings beneath and on her eyelids, entered, bringing with her the mixed perfumes of, say, bay rum (domestic), and lily-of-the-valley.

"Brownie, darling, it's been *years!*" the woman cried, and she hit him playfully with her fist on his chest.

Gus bent double under the blow, coughing loudly.

"It's Professor Robinolte's needles," Malcolm explained to the woman, who was staring at Gus with a puzzled twist of a smile on her lips.

"Fine shape you're in to come to see me," she said, after a pause of uncomprehension.

Gus resumed his normal standing position again, and whispered, "It's the boy this time . . . I'm just going to take a brief shower and a snooze. . . . Ain't had no sleep in a week, you know . . ."

"Let me get this all down," the woman said. "You're sending *him*" (she pointed to Malcolm) "upstairs for *you.*"

"Break him in, for Christ's sakes will you?" Gus said, coughing wearily, and he sat down on a chair near his coat-hanger, and began taking off his shoes.

"You do like I told you now, back in the street," Gus admonished the boy. "I want you to go through it all just like I told you Nature meant."

The woman made a contemptuous sound with her lips at Gus.

"Come on with me, honey," the woman then told Malcolm, and giving Gus a last severe look, she and Malcolm started off together without another word.

"And don't come back without you had it," Gus managed

to shout at Malcolm. He coughed very loud, and then he tried to say something else, but the words could not be heard.

Four or five hours had passed when Malcolm tiptoed back to Room Number 22 of the Turkish Bath sections, rapped, then when there was no answer, opened the door softly, and peeked in.

Gus lay on a small cot, unclothed now except for his tattoo bandages, which were, however, nearly coming off.

Malcolm sat down on a small white chair which was next to the cot.

"I did just like you said, Gus," he told the motorcyclist. "All the way through three times! So it looks like I'll be a bridegroom after all."

Malcolm thought that Gus smiled, and he was pleased.

"Don't you think we should be getting back to our motorcycle now?" Malcolm inquired.

The rays of the morning sun were pouring in from a tiny window above Gus's cot.

"Time to get up," Malcolm yawned enormously, and he tapped Gus gently, being careful to choose a place that was not tattooed.

Malcolm went on talking, meanwhile, about how Madame Rosita herself had complimented him, and given him tea, and presented him with a little keepsake, namely an old-fashioned shaving mug with a picture of George Washington and the first American flag, which he now showed to Gus.

But Gus slept on.

Blood had hardened and caked through the bandages over his chest. Looking a little more closely at his abdomen, Malcolm started a bit, for he thought he could observe no rise and fall of that part of his friend. Malcolm looked at his mouth, too, which was strangely drawn and silent.

"Gus," he said rather loudly. "Brownie! *Morning!*"

Malcolm drew out a small piece of paper from his pocket, and put it in front of Gus's mouth and nose, for his father had always told him that this was the sure way of determining whether a person was alive or dead. But nothing came out from the motorcyclist to stir the paper.

"Gus," he shouted now, and he put his hand on the dark man's forehead and on the tight black curls of his head.

"Gus," he said, feeling the cold of the man's body, "—you're dead!"

Hurrying to tell the attendant, Malcolm dropped his new gift of the shaving mug, which fell into twenty or thirty small colored pieces to the floor.

He had some difficulty in arousing the attendant, and when the attendant did come out from his small cubicle, he was not the one who had been called Miles at all, of the night before.

"Gus is dead in Room Number 22!" Malcolm cried.

"Who ain't at this hour?" the man replied gruffly and suspiciously.

Malcolm took hold of the attendant's arm, urging him to come.

"Look, Lord Fauntleroy," the man said. "Get out of here before there's any trouble. You're too goddam young to be in here in the first place. Who let you in?"

"Gus . . . the dead man!" Malcolm cried.

Coming clear out from his cubicle, the man took hold of Malcolm and ushered him to the front door.

"Now get out," he ordered, kicking the boy, and he slammed the door on him, after giving him a further kick.

"Get out and stay out!"

Malcolm stood, however, outside the door, knocking and gesticulating in the direction of Room Number 22.

"It's Gus," he cried to the attendant, who had already disappeared back into his cubicle. "Gus, the motorcyclist! Can't you understand?"

For the first time since his father's disappearance, Malcolm shed not just a few, but a torrent of tears. He cried all the way back to the edge of the town, a flood of weeping which he had never thought could possibly come from a human being. He no longer felt he was a man at all, as he had at Madame Rosita's, and at times he whimpered like a five-year-old child.

He stopped near a telephone pole, on which there was a picture of Melba before a microphone, and a caption under the picture, AMERICA'S NUMBER ONE CHANTEUSE, and vomited for a few minutes.

Then wiping his mouth and his eyes, with a handkerchief which he believed Gus himself must have given him, he carefully kissed the picture of Melba on the telephone pole. "So long, lovely," he said.

It never occurred to him then, in his despair, that he would ever find Melba again, and the thought of marriage was as remote as any other thing in his past, his father's voice, or the bench.

All he knew he could do was keep walking.

Melba's Marriage

Malcolm's adventures might have been continued indefinitely had it not so happened by chance, days later, that Melba, driving in her second ex-husband's Daimler, stopped at a roadside drugstore for cigarettes and mascara, when she caught sight of her husband-to-be at the soda fountain spooning up the last of a strawberry soda, while telling the clerk, who seemed to hang helplessly on his words, what was an involved story.

"Precious!" Melba cried in stentorian tones.

Everyone in the drugstore recognized that voice. Before Melba could take another step toward Malcolm, she was surrounded by admirers and autograph-seekers, who demanded her signature on matchboxes, hot-dog wrappers, and soda-fountain straws, while a gasoline attendant asked her to write her name with lipstick on his forehead, which she immediately did.

"Gus is dead, Brownie is dead!" Malcolm cried, having got off the stool to the soda fountain, but unable to advance toward Melba owing to her crowd of admirers.

Melba nodded, meaning, it seemed, she knew all about Gus.

When the crowd had once dispersed a little, Melba went up to Malcolm and kissed him quietly. Someone flashed a bulb from a camera.

Back in the front seat of her car, the leather being so badly torn it was difficult to sit still in comfort, Melba explained to Malcolm the trouble she was having with her Hollywood manager.

Melba knew all about Brownie or Gus's death, and would

not talk about it for a good stretch. Then turning her attention to Gus briefly, she said: "But haven't you seen the newspapers, for crying out loud? I had to attend the damned inquest . . ."

Before Malcolm could say more, Melba had kissed him fifteen or sixteen successive times on the mouth.

"Oh, angel, is it ever good to see you," she said. "Another five minutes, and I would have *never* found you. I would have ended up marrying someone else . . . sure as fate."

Pulling open a compartment in the car, Melba then brought out a packet of letters.

"From your friend Madame Girard," Melba said. "She's trying to prevent us getting married."

"You know Madame Girard!" Malcolm exclaimed.

"I know everybody," Melba said, rather severely, and Malcolm suddenly felt the gulf which separated him from fame. After all, of course, everybody knew Melba, even if she didn't know everybody, and she was as famous in Japan and India as she was in Paris and Chicago.

"Now how about that wedding," Melba said, starting the motor. "Tuesday, you know, came and went in a *big* hurry. But I got the license, with a little bomb or two at city hall, and I got the justice of the peace under wraps. All we have to do is appear. How about this PM?"

Malcolm cried yes, and bent over to kiss Melba, but she said not while she was driving, and that she had spent one year in a California hospital for kissing a marine while driving.

Malcolm then mentioned Gus again, and Melba was again severe.

"Don't give Brownie another thought, if you value my time and my love. For one thing, he was jealous of you, anyhow. But for Christ's sake, it was his time to go and all, good grief. He'd had it, and it was his time."

"His tattoos didn't kill him?"

"Tattoos, your mother. Why, Brownie had been half-dead for years. Most of his guts were blown out in Korea. Still, he kept on going. And on what? God knows. Don't give him a thought, precious. He was sweet, and of course I married him at one time, but it was his *time* to go," she said, narrowly missing a curve, "and there just isn't anything to be sorry about. When it's your time, well, it is.

"We'll be terribly happy together," Melba went on. "But you'll have to give up this Madame Girard woman, though Christ knows why she's called that, and whatever she may have meant to you. She's *dangerous!*"

"But what about Girard Girard?" Malcolm exclaimed.

"Oh, why ever even *think* about him," Melba was firm.

Both Madame Girard and Girard Girard made several attempts to communicate with Malcolm. Girard Girard himself wrote a letter on embossed stationery so thick that it had burst through the envelope, and part of it was lost, in which he explained the reason for his having failed to keep his appointment with Malcolm in the horticultural gardens. Melba did not show this communication to Malcolm.

Malcolm and Melba were married in Chicago, after a good deal of difficulty owing to Malcolm's lack of a birth certificate, and his general appearance. After the ceremony had taken place, they flew to the Caribbean, as Melba said she loved to be in countries where everything was blowing up, and the USA was much too quiet for her in any case. Also, she wanted to meet some of the new Cuban musicians, who put us all so to shame.

After a week in Cuba, however, Melba grew homesick for her country house, which, as yet, Malcolm had never even seen, and as Malcolm, too, was nostalgic for the environs of those places where he had had his bench, and had met Mr. Cox, Kermit, Estel Blanc, and the Girards—although all of these persons Melba had forbidden Malcolm ever to see or communicate with again—the couple returned to begin their matrimonial career.

Madame Girard telephoned four or five times daily, and as Melba was nearly always gone, Malcolm welcomed these communications from his old life, although Madame Girard was drinking so heavily, she seldom told him much, or actually said much herself.

Malcolm told Madame Girard that he liked marriage very much, though it took a great deal out of him. He hoped that Madame Girard would come soon, to visit, and he told her about his new tattoos.

Melba had brought back a young Cuban man to be Malcolm's personal valet, but as the latter spoke very little English, Malcolm's only verbal communication with the outside world was largely on the telephone with the weather-report operator and, when she was sober enough to know that she was talking with him, Madame Girard.

Madame Girard finally broke the news to Malcolm that Girard Girard had secured a divorce from her and finally married Laureen Raphaelson, and that Laureen was already pregnant.

"Marriage for him," Madame Girard explained, "was not emotion, but to produce an heir to his fortune."

About the fourth month of Malcolm's marriage, the Cuban valet pointed out to Melba that her young husband was losing weight, but the singer was quick to assure the Cuban that he must remember American men did not weigh so much as the easier going Latin peoples, and the subject was not brought up again.

Melba was extremely busy that fall and winter, and seldom came home except to sleep when, as she said later, every joy of marriage was tasted, though rapidly, to the full.

A strange thing did happen, she remembered later, long long after Malcolm's time. It was on one of her few free evenings, and she and her young husband had gone to a well-known night club.

As usual now, Malcolm drank a great deal too much, and talked a good deal more about his father, Mr. Cox, and Kermit, and Melba complained, as she now did more frequently, that the more she heard Malcolm talk the less she realized they had in common, except, as she was hasty to add, *that one thing, dear,* and after all, she added, what is marriage based on but that.

"I didn't marry you for your mind," Melba always said, "and you do get better looking every day. I like you thin, but I suppose I would like you fat, too. And though you're not exactly the type I would spot on the street, once I've come to be with you, you're the only one out of a large assortment."

She kissed Malcolm several times. She had had her hair tinted a different shade for this evening and was wearing special immense dark glasses designed specially for her, so that she could pretend nobody recognized her, and could let herself go a little bit more.

Malcolm kept excusing himself to go to the men's room, which always annoyed her, and yet these little breaks from his talk were not unwelcome.

"You're annoying, kiddy," Melba said, "but you make up for the whole crumby thing back at the house."

Their drinks that evening were the usual rum sours, with a dash of something special Melba always carried with her, she didn't tell Malcolm what.

It was after their tenth or twelfth rum sour with Melba's own little special recipe thrown in that Malcolm cried out in the loudest voice she had ever heard him use—the voice almost of a man now:

"That's HE—my FATHER!"

Melba tried to restrain him, but he got up quickly from his table and went in the direction of a middle-aged unemphatically distinguished man, who might have posed for sparkling water advertisements.

The man went into the lavatory, and Malcolm followed.

"Father!" Malcolm cried, stretching out his arms to the man, who was washing his hands gingerly in a deep bowl of water. "Where did you *go* all this time?"

The man looked up briefly, unflustered and calm. Having washed his hands, he examined his mustache closely in the mirror.

"Don't you recognize me?" Malcolm cried to him. "I would recognize *you* anywhere!"

The man now opened his mouth and examined his teeth carefully, touching the front two teeth to remove, perhaps, a particle therefrom.

Going up close to the man, Malcolm touched him gently on his shoulder.

"If you will only allow me, sir, I can identify you . . . By the small bullet hole you carry beneath your collar bone."

"Would you allow me to pass," the man told Malcolm, and he made an effort, aiming at equanimity, to go out.

"You are pretending not to recognize me, sir!" Malcolm cried. "Is it because I married Melba, or because I left the bench?"

"Allow me to pass," the man said, greatly disturbed.

"If you will not allow me to recognize you, let me show you your own identification mark. Remember, father, you always told me that if any questions were ever asked in a fatal emergency, you could be identified by this small gunshot wound which you suffered in the armed forces."

Grasping the man, then, by his collar, Malcolm attempted to undo his shirt in the hope that the exposure of the bullet wound would prove beyond cavil that he was his father and that Malcolm was his son.

Becoming now seriously alarmed, the man cried for assistance, which only led to Malcolm's seizing his "father" more securely, while the latter, now panic-stricken and feeling Malcolm seize him not only about his chest, but also securely about his leg, in a sudden paroxysm of anger and terror, knocked the boy heavily to the marble floor, just as a policeman entered the room.

"Arrest that pederast!" the man said to the officer. "He attacked me!"

"Sir," Malcolm cried, addressing perhaps his "father" and the police officer together, "oh, sir, I am NOT Mr. Cox . . . I am MALCOLM!"

The "father" seeing perhaps now that Malcolm was indeed too young to be anything, snorted, wheeled, and walk-

ing out of the lavatory, disappeared into the inner recesses
of the night club.

But what was Malcolm's relief and joy when looking
more closely at the policeman from his position on the floor,
he saw that the officer was the very same man into whose
arms he had rushed that evening long ago on the occasion
of his visit to Estel Blanc's.

The police officer, who had recognized Malcolm even
more promptly than the boy had recognized him, helped
him up from the floor.

"Again I find you in suspicious surroundings, although
older," the officer said, and he examined the bump on the
boy's scalp.

The officer shook his head seriously, ignoring the babble
of *thankyou sirs*, et cetera which came from Malcolm's lips.

"What did that gentleman call you?" the officer wondered.

"My father?"

The policeman gazed wonderingly at Malcolm.

"Why, a pederast," Malcolm answered the policeman's
question.

"Are you one, sir?" the officer asked in a thin grave voice.

"Why, I don't believe I'm old enough, am I?" Malcolm
replied.

The officer folded his arms, thinking.

"You have to study the stars a good deal to be one, you
know," Malcolm added for the policeman's information.
"Mr. Cox, the astrologer, would be able to tell you."

The policeman's jaw moved slightly up and out, but as
he did not say anything, Malcolm continued:

"Would you care to meet my wife, sir?"

"You've gone and got married, in the bargain?" the officer
exclaimed.

"Yes," Malcolm admitted, a bit shame-faced, "though I
had to tell the marriage bureau I was 18. But do please come
and meet Melba. She's awfully famous."

The policeman pinched off some lint which had become
attached to his handsome uniform, and then told Malcolm

that he would not be able to accept his invitation but how
pleasant, actually, it had been running into him again after
all this passage of time. He then shook hands with the boy,
and as a last gesture, patted Malcolm rather soberly on the
shoulder:

"Always behave like a man, Malcolm, and you'll have
nothing to regret."

Just as the boy was about to leave, the officer, struggling
and reluctant, but earnest, called him back again, and clearing his throat loudly, said:

"If I were you, Malcolm, I believe I would look up that
word the man you called your 'father' used about you in
this lavatory. I don't think you know what a good many
words mean, as I recall our interview of some time past, in
the station—probably all owing to you not having gone to
school enough."

"I see," Malcolm considered this advice. "But I don't
know, sir, whether I will have the time to look the word up
or not, you see. I'm awfully busy now that I'm married."

"You *take* the time, Malco," the policeman said. "And
now run on back to your *wife.*"

"Thank you, sir, and good luck, sir!"

When Malcolm had gone, the police officer went over to
the same wash basin which the "father" had employed,
removed his smart hat, and then quickly lowering his head,
allowed water to trickle over his scalp and forehead.

"My father refused to recognize me," Malcolm told Melba
when he had returned to her table.

Melba looked glassy at him. She had drunk a good many
of her special concoctions while he had been gone.

"Look, kiddy," Melba said. "I've been meaning to give
you this speech, but the long and the short of it is: grow up
a little. That wasn't your father. I've known that old pot
since I was ten. He's nobody's father. And what's this *idée*
unfix about your father. Who wants a father? It's been old
hat for years. That old pot, I repeat, was nobody's father."

"But he looked like him to a T," Malcolm insisted, rubbing the bump on his scalp.

"Millions of men look like millions of men, especially Americans," Melba said, beginning on a new drink the waiter had just brought her. "In fact, most men look like most men. That's why I go for you, kiddy. You're unique all over."

She kissed Malcolm wetly on both his eyes, and he flushed with excitement.

"He wasn't my father?" Malcolm inquired from her after a while, and he shifted in his seat several times.

"With my fame and money," Melba told him, "and your special gift, blow your father," and she motioned for him to sip her drink.

"Blow my father!" Malcolm echoed, and then hearing his own voice, his jaw dropped loosely.

"Say, kiddy, are you all right?" Melba said, somewhat concerned.

"Blow my father!" Malcolm said.

"Don't say that again," Melba adjured him, and her mouth set.

Malcolm stared in the direction of, but not focussing on, Melba.

Looking at her bridegroom a bit more closely, she asked: "Say, kiddy, who gave you that knock on the head? And you got a real shiner coming!"

"Blow my fath—" Malcolm began, and then put his hand to his mouth to show he should not say that.

Melba put her fingers to the boy's scalp, and bringing her hand down saw it smeared with the well-known fluid, as she called it, which at her touch had begun trickling down his forehead and face, like a rivulet in spring.

Melba quickly staunched the flow with a napkin she took from the empty table next to them.

"Have a drink, kiddy," she said. "It's wonderful for cuts and bruises and abrasions of all kinds."

"Maybe my father never existed," Malcolm said, and his tones were now like those of Melba's.

"Who the hell knows if anybody ever existed?" she said, but her old gay manner was missing. "You relax now, kiddy. Forget what happened in that lavatory, and drink up. Last call for alcohol, like they say. Drink up."

"It's Not *Twenty Years!*"

When Malcolm woke up the next afternoon, his hair, except for where the blood had dyed it a startling crimson, was snow white, *whiter* indeed, as he remarked to Melba, in bed, than he had ever remembered his father's being. "You look simply grand," Melba said, "not to mention it's a miracle of some dumb kind. Jesus, are you beautiful. I want to just stay in bed and look at you. Jesus, white hair, kiddy."

"I am O.K., then, Melba, girl?" Malcolm wondered, and his voice again did not quite sound like his own.

"You ain't never been better, kiddy," Melba assured him. "Let Mama kiss her white-haired angel boy."

Melba kissed him on his new hair.

Then loosening Malcolm's pajama tops, she began kissing him on the chest.

He tried to return the compliment by kissing her hair, but his head hurt too much when he moved it.

"Your white hair goes so good with your pink skin," Melba remarked. "It makes you look both dark and light."

"Melba, honey, ring for the coffee. I'm awful excited over you like always, but I seem too dizzy to make love."

"I'll ring for the coffee," Melba said, still entranced. "And I'll make all the love today. Don't talk about making love. What did I buy you for, kiddy?"

She kissed his chest again.

"Answer me that," she said. "What did I buy you for?"

"You bought me?" Malcolm groaned a bit, under her caresses.

"Down-payment, lock, stock, and barrel," Melba replied,

leaving a watery kiss behind. "Mmm. Talk about plums for texture. And with white hair!"

Drinking her coffee later, she walked up and down the room, occasionally darting a glance at Malcolm, who remained quiet and still in bed. Practising her new repertoire, she sang one of her favorite songs, especially now for Malcolm:

> *I'm a little bit of this and that,*
> *But I'm all one solid piece for you!*

Malcolm smiled weak but appreciative from the bed.

If there is one thing that is fatal to most men, Mr. Cox always told his followers, it is marriage. Malcolm was not precisely a full-grown man, but he was a man, and marriage in his case may have proved fatal.

Not one of the circle surrounding Madame Girard and Mr. Cox had ever thought that Malcolm, who had been with them such a short time, would go from them in the particular way he did. But after it was all over, everybody agreed that it was almost the only way he could have gone from them.

Too young for the army, too unprepared to continue his schooling and become a scientist, too untrained for ordinary work—what was left for him but marriage? And in his case, marriage supplied him with everything that he had up to now lacked, and also gave him his unique way of leaving the world, in which he had perhaps never belonged (as some people said) in the first place.

Marriage which ushers most people into life, in Malcolm's case, therefore, ushered him into happiness—and death.

Whether Melba sensed that Malcolm was dying, no one ever knew. She was too busy ever to talk with anybody, and besides, she did not know Madame Girard and Mr. Cox and their circle, and they were the only ones who would have been able to tell her what state Malcolm was in.

Melba's chief source of interest during this period was

that after so many weeks of incessant marriage, she found she was still not pregnant, and could therefore continue both her professional career and her marriage duties to Malcolm without fear or constraint, and what is more, they could, husband and wife, go their separate ways quite freely, as before marriage.

Since the night he had recognized his "father" and cut open his head, Malcolm found himself too weak ever to be out of bed, and in this state the happy thought hit him to write down all his conversations with Mr. Cox, Girard Girard, Kermit, and others in English, but shortly after he began this, he caught an extremely bad cold, which his Cuban valet said was really pneumonia, and after that, Malcolm wrote down everything in French, as this seemed the easier language in his increased weakness.

Melba knew French very well, but, as she explained, since she had begun to read his "conversations" in English, she lost all the little interest she had had in them once he switched to another language, and so nobody ever saw them again until Malcolm himself was no longer counted among the living.

As Malcolm felt his strength ebbing rather than returning, a fixed melancholy stole over him, and the sight of the falling leaves and November skies fixed this feeling in him still more deeply.

Melba advised him to drink more and have more frequent conjugal duties with her. He tried both of these, and actually became even more addicted to them, but his melancholy, far from disappearing, grew more pronounced and virulent.

He continued to lose weight, although his mental vigor, such as it was, remained unimpaired, and he spent all his time now recording his "conversations" with his former friends, who were still unable to see him owing to his marriage.

A few evenings before he died, he called Melba to his room and informed her that he had been bitten by a small buff-colored dog.

Melba greeted Malcolm vaguely, as she was nursing a hangover, and was still also a bit puzzled at having wakened up that morning to find herself in bed with Heliodoro, the Cuban valet, whose extreme handsomeness must have won her over to him in her cups.

Leaving the sick room almost immediately, and a bit fed up being married to someone who would be sick, Melba decided on a longish drive with the Cuban as the best simple way of quieting her nerves, and it was already morning when she remembered Malcolm's remark about the dog bite.

To be on the safe side, she summoned a physician.

But it was, of course, as she remarked later to Heliodoro, just her luck, and a bit of a bit too late for medicine.

The physician, a man, who, as Melba noted immediately, looked fatally ill himself, gave this diagnosis: Malcolm was dying, he claimed, from acute alcoholism and sexual hyperaesthesia, and all that could be done for him now was give him every comfort and a quiet bed to himself.

Melba was going to tell the physician that nobody today died of the things he was accusing Malcolm of, but she felt there was no use having an argument if bereavement should come to the house.

"He is not dying, then, from a dog bite?" Melba inquired, taking the physician to the car which, she saw, was what must have at one time been a fairly decent Cadillac.

"There isn't a single bite on his body," the physician said, after a lengthy pause.

"He insists a dog bit him," Melba said, and she looked at her drink, which she had carried out with her to the car.

The physician, excusing his near forgetfulness, then hastily wrote out a prescription which he handed to her.

Melba still waited on, her glass in hand, why she never understood later, until the doctor got into his broken-down car and drove off. She even waved to him from the drive with her glass.

Melba went into Malcolm's room and sat down quietly on the bed by him.

When she looked into his face, she felt the physician might be wrong in the diagnosis, but right about his taking a trip.

"Am I going to lose my little Number 3?" she inquired softly so as not to disturb the boy too much.

Malcolm opened his eyes briefly and smiled.

"Do you know what is happening?" Melba asked.

"Call Madame Girard to come here," Malcolm said drily. "I can't remember all of my conversations with her, and can't get it written down, you see. Mr. Cox, I know, wouldn't come, because he is so happily married, or I might call him."

"You are going to die, kiddy," Melba said, taking his hand, which bore her ring on it. She kissed the ring.

"Call Madame Girard and tell her to come," Malcolm repeated.

"All right, kiddy. Can do," Melba said vaguely.

On being informed of Malcolm's grave condition, Madame Girard left the party which she was giving, and which she had planned to last for three days, and drove to Melba's country house.

Going in without announcing herself, Madame Girard walked past Melba without so much as a greeting, and sat down on the bed beside Malcolm.

Melba herself had taken a drug which would not allow her to feel extreme grief or unpleasantness of any kind, and she was content to leave Madame Girard and her husband together while she went into the front room to practice her repertoire for an evening performance.

Madame Girard wished, above all, to have Malcolm recognize her, not only because she now saw that it was Malcolm who was the idea of her life—despite their short term of friendship—but because she had so many things yet to tell him, including Girard Girard's message of friendship to him, and his plea for forgiveness for not having returned to the boy in the horticultural gardens last summer.

Madame Girard kept placing cold compresses on his forehead to relieve him of some of his fever.

As a reward for her patient care, there came a moment when he opened his eyes, and looked at her, but almost immediately closed them again.

A few minutes later, he said in his usual loud voice: "Estel Blanc on a white mare!"

Sometimes also he shouted "Hurrah!" but he never gave any evidence again that he had seen Madame Girard.

Several times during the evening, Madame Girard heard Melba singing her internationally famous number:

I'm a little bit of this and that
But I'm all one solid—

so that finally Madame Girard got up and closed the heavy inner door between the sick room and Melba.

Madame Girard had come to stay, until everything was over.

Once, near the end, she thought that all of her patient waiting and care was indeed to be rewarded with "recognition," with a word to her, from Malcolm, for the boy started up in bed, opened his eyes, and stared at her.

"Malcolm," she whispered.

"It's NOT twenty years!" he cried, and fell back again, without even seeing her.

Toward morning, Madame Girard heard Melba go out the front door, and a moment later the sound of the Daimler's motor.

Madame Girard had gone to the window to see if the Cuban valet was in the car with Melba, but in the dark she could not tell.

Returning to Malcolm's bed, she put her hand to his cheek.

"Prince!" she called out, feeling the iciness of his flesh.

She had missed, she saw immediately, his last single minute: Malcolm's short long life was at an end.

As Melba did not return that day, nor the next, nor did Madame Girard ever see her again, she herself took charge of the funeral ceremonies.

The florists of the town discussed Madame Girard's funeral expenditure for years to come. She had, for instance, ordered—even if she perhaps did not quite get—a quarter ton of roses, and an equal amount of violets, so that Malcolm's last hours above earth were passed in a green house of sweetness and foliage.

One anonymous spray also arrived in what was perhaps meant to be the simulacrum of a bench.

Madame Girard, however, informed no one of the funeral. It was completely private so far as she was concerned and, so to speak, a command performance, with herself as the only audience.

She was greatly displeased, almost annihilated, however, that there was a ketchup factory in the nearby vicinity, and since the ketchup season was at its peak at the time of Malcolm's funeral, the burned saccharine smell of tomatoes struggled desperately with the evanescent perfume of violets and roses.

Horses with black plumes in the European tradition carried the corpse to a small private burial ground purchased for the occasion by Madame Girard herself. A trumpeter-voluntary—a young military person who happened by chance to be in the neighborhood—was asked to perform, which he did creditably.

The only flaw in the ceremony was the repeated insistence of the local coroner and the undertaker—later they were both silenced, it is said, by money—that there had been no corpse at all, and that nobody was buried in the ceremony.

Thus, the only proof that Malcolm had died and was buried, rested with Madame Girard herself, and in time her story became full of evasions.

But nobody could deny that there had been a ceremony, and that a casket had been lowered into a special plot, and that Madame Girard herself had been present at all of the aforementioned.

When the ceremony was over, Madame Girard saw, com-

ing down the dusty country road on foot, none other than
Girard Girard.

They exchanged looks, but did not speak, and then with
a short glance at the freshly-dug grave, Girard Girard ac-
companied his former wife back to an inn, where after a
long silence, punctuated only by the sounds of their spoons
moving in their coffee, Girard Girard excused himself and
returned to the city.

Madame Girard, in any case, had long ago forgiven Girard Girard, since she never gave up her title or name, and
continued to be the most effective individual force of her
society.

She remained in the country until the following morning,
looking over Malcolm's papers, and taking as many as she
could find into her custody.

Since that day, Malcolm's grave, which has no marker
beyond a stone bearing his name, has been poorly cared
for, and fallen into complete neglect, though since it was
purchased in perpetuity one can believe that his remains, if
they are there, will be allowed to rest on for whatever por-
tion of time may be reserved for the earth and the world.

A few years after the preceding events, Mr. Cox, through
one of those rare second strokes of fortune, found another
young man—a bit older, it is true than Malcolm—who became his pupil and went through over 25 addresses with
the elder gentleman—and finally, much to Mr. Cox's surprise
and even jealousy, took up an independent life-study of
astrology, and entirely eclipsed his master.

Kermit, about two weeks after Malcolm's death, met a
young, though retired, and very wealthy motion picture
star, who was immediately taken with the little man, and
they were married in a somewhat ostentatious ceremony in
a suburb of San Francisco.

Eloisa Brace was awarded a life-pension by an anonymous donor (who almost surely was Girard Girard) and
was thus able to devote her entire waking life to painting,
but her sudden security, many believed, destroyed her last

vestiges of talent, and both she and her husband occupied themselves more and more to a program of social betterment for the community.

Estel Blanc became the successful entrepreneur of a small opera company, giving selections from the best modern operas, with Cora Naldi as permanent guest star.

Girard Girard, after a time, became the father of six male children—and this was for him the realization of a vague ambition and yearning which he had had, unconsciously, all along: the founding of a dynasty perpetuating his name.

Madame Girard was the constant companion of a young Italian biochemist, who shared the Chateau with her, and wished to marry her, but she refused to give up her "title," as she continued to call her name. The closeness of her association with the Italian, which became permanent, led (many believe) to her giving up the bottle entirely.

Melba was married in Yucatan to Heliodoro, the Cuban valet, with whom she had disappeared shortly before Malcolm's death. To everyone's surprise, she found herself reasonably contented and happy with him, remaining his wife for over five years. Her voice, however, has failed and she no longer sings publicly.

A year or so after Malcolm's supposed death, there was a somewhat convincing rumor that he was alive again, and the "favorite" of a circle much more advanced than the Cox-Girard-Brace consistory, but the rumor proved to be, finally, without foundation.

Everybody was surprised, nevertheless, after the talk about his being alive again had died down, to realize that Malcolm, in the interim, had been almost entirely forgotten, and was no longer a subject of conversation anywhere.

Madame Girard, however, though she never mentioned Malcolm—indeed she had no one to mention him to, since her new friends, such as the Italian biochemist, had never heard of him—Madame Girard continued to read with interest and surprise the 300 pages of manuscript which Malcolm had left behind him, in French and English, his "conversations" with his friends, and although they had been written at times in delirium, and always in high fever, they continually held her attention, and she regretted he had not lived to record all the conversations he had ever had with all whom he had ever met.